Alice

Sophie M Berlin

ISBN 580-0-0988-3456-4

To my wonderful children,
Joshua, Lewis Katrina and Savannah.
Also to my band of merry classmates
led by Hil Slavid,
who have given me so much encouragement and support
to actually make this book happen.

Chapter 1

The trees swung, their heavy boughs resisting the harsh winds
pulling them like angry dancers back and forth. It had only just
turned April but April showers had already been thundering down
on the slate roof tiles for nearly a month. I gazed out of my little
window with only enough energy to raise my head from my
pillows. I was well propped up with a mountain of pillows on
account of my ailing lungs that had fallen prey to almost every
infection that they could. I had assumed I was dying and so quite
rightly had made sure that I said my prayers every day so that my
soul would be pure to enter heaven. However the village doctor
had visited, examined me and assured me that I would recover
and soon be able to go out and once again be active once the
weather was warm enough. That was last year. Sure enough he
hadn't actually forecast a year for my recovery but after eighteen
months in bed I was feeling frail and weary, afraid that I would
shrivel up like an old lady and my next venture outside would be
encased in a box ready to be buried under a tree in the graveyard.
I had no friends. Nobody was allowed to come near me for fear of
consumption or TB or all kinds of contagious illnesses that their
parents feared I may have. Sometimes I would watch people
outside my little window, laughing or more recently scurrying out
of the rain their hoods pulled tightly around their ears. The wind
sighed. The pain in my chest seemed to tighten like a vice around
my ribcage. It was no fun being so ill and feeling like a prisoner
to my unrelenting condition. A tap on the door, which then swung
open. Mrs Dunn the nurse sailed in. She was a bright cheery lady
with dark brown hair and big blue eyes. Her voice was sweet and
kind. Her manner considerate and caring. If circumstances would

have been different, I would have wanted my mother to be just like her.

"Hello sweetie" She chirped as she pulled the curtains apart and the room began to fill with sunlight.

"Had a good night?"

"Same as usual" I replied despondently, noticing that the rain had suddenly stopped and a warm stream of orange light was bathing the room

"Coughed my heart out and brought up tons of spit"

"Poor love" She came and draped her arm around me. Her body warm. Her arms soft.

"Look at your hair! Needs a good brush and let's do something pretty with it."

I smiled at her. She was amazing and I was in awe of her, and imagined that this was the way that my mother would have been. But I was alone. My mother had died in childbirth and my father was now away with his regiment serving in some remote part of Africa. The staff at home did their jobs well enough but that was all it was to them, just employment and then they went off to their homes, their families and laughter. I wanted laughter. I wanted smiles. I wanted that feeling of complete happy satisfaction that only a mother could give her daughter. Only I had no mother and I missed so terribly that feeling that in my imagination I craved. Mrs Dunn was so perfect. She had two boys much younger than me, they were perhaps ten and eight, she always spoke of them as her little men. When I first became ill the housekeeper brought me trays of food, which she left on my side table, then without fuss left me to eat alone. I hated that. I wanted some caring woman to spoon feed me soup and wipe my chin with a muslin cloth but I was no different to the cat in the parlour that had her food scooped into a bowl and was left to fend for herself. When I became completely bedridden it was decided I needed a nurse. First I objected to the intrusion of yet another stranger but when Mrs Dunn came in on that first day her face beaming, her chubby arms tenderly bathing me and arranging my pillows I knew that somehow she had been sent to me. At first I thought that my mother up in heaven, seeing my loneliness had sent to her poor child so desperately needing love. The more Mrs Dunn came and cared for me the more I imagined that she was my mother or even a reincarnation of her returned to fulfil the job which she had been cruelly taken from.

"Look you've hardly touched your food. Open wide here comes a big train into the tunnel!"
I chewed the mouthful of food smiling at being treated like a three year old even though I was seventeen. When my plate was empty she smiled at me stroked my shoulder and kissed my forehead. A wonderful reward for just finishing a plate of food. Mrs Knight the housekeeper was an older lady although I had no idea whether she was fifty or ninety. She was rounded probably on account of all those pies cakes pastries and sweetmeats that she endlessly churned out in the kitchen. She had a greying wisp of hair above her lip that always drew your eye when speaking with her. It was irritating in a way and I wondered why no one had bought her a shaving kit for Christmas!

"Here's your lunch" She would bustle in and deposit a tray heaped with enough food for an army beside my bed. She wasn't very strong at conversation but once in a while she would surprise me and chat.

"We've had word from your father today"
"Oh what does he have to say? How is he?"
"Yes he's fine, busy with his regiment and all that"
 "And…does he ask about me?

Mrs Knight was shifty and whilst her back was turned mumbled something about "Yes of course he does".

"Could I read his letter?" I asked.

"Sorry too late it went in the fire already"

I knew that reply. I always received that reply. I was sure that father had completely forgotten he had a daughter. I had only seen him about ten times in my life when he had been given leave. He wasn't affectionate and seemed to have an invisible fear of me as if I was someone that repelled him. I had put it in my mind that I was responsible for my mother's death and so as a result my father could not bear me. I was the murderess of his beloved wife. Stranger still there were no pictures of my mother, no framed portraits along with all the others around the house of my ancestors. I wondered about this but it was one of those things that I was too afraid to ask. Too worried that I would cause upset or offence. Too sensitive a subject to provoke any negative reaction in those around me that would be concerned by my prompting questions.

"You'll be getting glued into that bed if you spend any more time in there" muttered Mrs Knight

"Need to exercise those joints and get them working again" and she closed the door behind her.

Her words had gone over my head but several moments later I thought to myself" I wonder whether I can still move? Maybe I should see if I can get myself out of this terrible situation"

I bent my knees up and rocked them gently feeling the strain in my hips. I then leaned to the side of the bed and slowly stood bending my knees and hovering. There, I was standing. With jubilation I drew a long and deep breath and had to steady myself on the bed frame as I bravely began to take a couple of steps before falling back into my bed with an exhausted smile on my

4

face. I had only just pulled back the covers when Nurse Dunn came in.

"Someone looks very smug today" She noticed the gleam in my eyes.

I pondered over telling her my news but decided instead that I would wait until I had mastered at least the breadth of the room before I showed her what I was so excited about.

"Time for your bed pan"

My expression dropped. I hated this undignified moment. But reassured myself that soon I would dispense with all this as well as all the other things that my nurse did for me.

"Bit of news in the papers" Nurse Dunn began

"Prince Albert is very ill with pneumonia and his new fiancée Mary is by his bed side distraught. Some are saying that she will never be a bride. Prince Edward and Princess Alexandra are in a right state. It's terrible news from the palace.

"But this is 1892 and the prince is only a young man, they must have the best doctors in the whole empire. He'll recover Mrs Dunn don't you worry".

Every day when no one was looking I would get out of my bed for a few minutes and walk around the room. I felt stronger and happier all the time. Then one day when the sun was high in the sky and the bees buzzing was the only sound in the still air I did it. I walked a breadth.

I waited for Nurse Dunn to come in. Today was the day that I would show her what I had achieved. At last the door opened. Nurse Dunn was dressed in black, her face tearstained, eyes red.

"He's gone she whispered. Prince Albert Duke of Clarence died last night aged twenty seven".

The house was plunged into a state of mourning. What should have been a royal wedding turned into a royal funeral. The country was in a sombre mood and my being able to walk seemed very insignificant.

Chapter 2

I must have dozed off after my evening meal of broth and bread because when I looked at the clock it was only eight. My body felt refreshed. Quite awake, I was excited to get up, to try to move around a little and strengthen my frail bones. It was still quite light as the days were getting longer and warmer although in the evening, it seemed more like the afternoon. I slipped from beneath the warm sheets and blankets and sat up in my bed. I stopped for a second to recover my breath, everything seemed such an effort; I felt like a rag doll. I looked around the room to where my bedside chest stood large and grand in chiselled oak, engraved with emblems of a yester year. I knew that somewhere within would be my dressing gown that I had not worn for ages. I stood, my legs still weak and trembling. I looked down at my feet so pale peeping out beneath my nightdress and took two steps like some tin soldier just out of a wooden box. My knees felt devoid of joints, my muscles tight and rigid. I tried to bend my knees. It took me back to many years ago when I had been to my first dance class and been instructed by my teacher to do plies, something which had felt very strange and uncomfortable. My knees bent stiffly and awkwardly but after several attempts it felt freer if not exhausting. I continued with more ease to reach the other side of the room. Successfully there I opened the cupboard door and pulled out my blue silk gown that I had nor worn for many years. I slung it over my shoulders and turned to the door, which seemed as daunting as reaching the top of Mount Everest.

I reached the handle and with a great sigh opened my bedroom door for the first time in nearly twenty months. My breathing was becoming quite laboured and I toyed with the sensible idea of retiring and heading straight back to bed. My head was ready to move forward even if my body wasn't. In the end it was my mind that won.

Beyond the door lay another world. A hidden forbidden world if you were an invalid. The hall was large. The complex network of rooms that meandered from each other to reach other wings and annexes baffled me slightly as I tried to recollect where everything led.

The house seemed very quiet. The old grandfather clock on the landing ticked with authority as if a sentry guard watching the household. I wondered if it could see me; hear me creeping around like a burglar on the top floor.

The staircase seemed very wide and grand in polished cherry wood. Its banisters curved and rounded, its ambience depicting the many grand balls and parties that would have been held here during the eighteenth century when lords and ladies danced through the night and princes would come here to find suitable debutantes and young ladies fresh from finishing schools.

At least that's what my father had told me many years ago. This manor had been in my mothers' family for hundreds of years and one day would be mine.

However, there was a neglected feel to this home. The curtains hung heavy and faded the floors needed to be stained and polished. I sat on the top step. Dare I go down? I glanced back to my bedroom door, my cell. I was free and ready to enjoy this new found liberty for just a little longer. I wouldn't return just yet. There was a faint sound coming from the dining room at the bottom of the stairs. As I bumped down from stair to stair the voices become louder and clearer. There were at least five people in there. It was late why were they still here? But then what did I really know about the comings and goings in the house. I was so unaware of anything in my room upstairs.

8

I reached the bottom step and tiptoed to the slightly ajar door. Peeking in I saw the housekeeper Mrs Knight, the gardener and odd job man Mr Shepherd, Dr Emanuel, John the grounds man and sitting facing the door my own special Nurse Dunn.

"It's going to be very tough on the child"

"She should be told immediately!"

"It's not right to carry on lying to her about this for so long" What child I wondered. Surely it wasn't me! I wasn't a child I was seventeen. What were they talking about? What was happening that I had been shielded away from?

A floorboard creaked under my foot. I stopped breathing for a moment paralysed with the fear of being caught. The voices ceased within the room. I held my breath, retracting the blue sash that had slid from the side of the gown. I could feel my heart thumping in my chest; it felt like it was beating so loud that they might hear it. It seemed like forever, anticipating some terrible reaction like the silence waiting for a stone to fall down a well, then eventually the splash at the bottom.

The voices continued. I breathed a sigh as I moved stealthily away from behind the door my dressing gown gripped tightly around me. I had to get back to my room but the stairway back really did feel like climbing a mountain. I felt extremely weak and anxious. I crawled up the first few steps then stopped for a rest then continued. By the time I had got to the first landing I was depleted of all energy and huddled myself into a shadowed doorway to rest before undertaking the remainder of my journey. My head was spinning. The conversations I had overheard downstairs whirring in my mind until it all became a complete blur and I collapsed with exhaustion.

I awoke in the morning, stretched out and noticed how bright the light was. My curtains had been drawn and the cup of tea beside

my bed had a skim on the top. I reached out, it was cold. It must be quite late, I wondered. My breakfast wasn't usually brought to my room before nine. It then dawned on me that I was in my bed. Had I got back here on my own? I didn't have any memory of moving any further than the doorway. Something tight and uncomfortable snagged around my waist. It was the sash from my dressing gown, which I was still wearing. I quickly fumbled and removed it fearing that if someone saw it they would know that I had been out of my bed and downstairs. I heard a tap at the door. Quickly I hid the dressing gown under the covers.
Nurse Dunn opened the door.

"Morning love" She quipped in her normal jovial tone.

"You've had a good long sleep this morning it's just past eleven, never known you to sleep so long!"

"Mmm" I nodded still confused as how I had got back to my bed the night before.
Nurse Dunn turned to face me her expression changing to one of astonishment as she stared at the side of my bed where part of my blue gown hung errantly from beneath the sheets. She thought she had seen something of that colour skim past the door last night but how could it be?

"Better take your medicine now" She suggested refocusing.
I smiled took my potion and Nurse Dunn left the room.
After she was out of earshot I leaned to the side of the bed, folded up the gown, took several achy steps to the cupboard and put it away. Then retreated to my bed pulled the covers over me as the door reopened and Nurse Dunn came back in.
She still had a strange expression on her face. She looked down the side of the bed again and I suspected that she may have previously seen the blue material of my dressing gown. She then went to the cupboard and opened it. There was the gown. Nurse Dunn pulled a face and muttered

"I must be getting old".

"Are you well?" I asked politely, smirking, considering that I knew that I had just baffled her.

"Yes child, everything's fine"

Child she called me child! The conversation that I overheard the previous night had been talking about a child. Not me? I was no child! But then they could only have been talking about me because there was no one else that it could be. I felt that I would soon be the recipient of some very bad news and wondered whether I should just confess that I had eavesdropped and have her tell me what was going on.

Before I could consider my question she had left the room again. The medicine made me feel sleepy and after eating a new tray of breakfast that was brought to my room I fell asleep again, still completely exhausted and confused by the previous night. The next few days were very quiet, no one seemed to say much, the mood was still sombre following the death of the Prince of Wales' son. Lots of thoughts and strange feelings surrounded me. I felt I could not trust anyone. They were all harbouring some big secret about me, which they were not prepared to share. I was determined I would uncover the truth. I wasn't going to tell anyone that I could walk. I was suspicious that someone must know though because how did I miraculously materialise back in my bed? Who was it? Would they betray me? I watched everyone with enquiring eyes but no one seemed any more interested or inquisitive about me than usual. I was perplexed but confident that I would know all the answers soon, somehow.

Chapter 3

My door had been left slightly ajar; the cat sauntered in, sniffed around my bed. Pounced up and starting pawing her way towards me.

"Hello Tabby" I announced excited at my unexpected visitor. I stroked her long pepper coloured fur. She purred and snuggled down beside me.

"I haven't seen you in ages, nice of you to come and see me, no one else does"

The cat looked up at me as if interested in my conversation, then began to preen herself.

"So what's been going on downstairs with all those plotting people? I wish you could talk. I wish you could tell me what is going on and what they have planned for me"

The cat closed its eyes under my gentle touch. I tickled her under her chin and ran my fingers through her long fur feeling the roundness of her body. I was suddenly aware of a shuffling behind my door. Between the crack of the door I could make out someone whispering.

"Tabby! Tabby! Come out here at once!" she voice urged softly.

The cat on my lap looked up for a moment then closed her eyes. A blue ribbon then appeared under the door and proceeded to wiggle around quite comically. Again the cat took no interest.

"Hello!" I called out.

"You can come in. The cat is here but she is fine you don't need to take her"

"Oh I must miss" Came a reply

"I'll be thrown out on my ear if I don't bring her back downstairs. She is near to kittening miss" The reply still came from behind the door.

"You can come in" I insisted.

"Oh no miss I daren't"

"Don't be silly I don't bite!"

"Yes but on account of the illness and that miss"

"Its fine it's not contagious Mrs Knight, Mrs Dunn and the doctor visit me regularly and they are all alive," I suggested invitingly.

There was silence.

"Well you won't get the cat then!"

"Oh miss I'm to find her and bring her back right away"

"Well you'd better come in then."

The door slowly began to open. A young girl about my age wearing a dark smock and white apron stood behind the door. Her red curls escaping under a cloth bonnet. Her eyes scanned across the room and intriguingly came to rest on me.

"Sorry to interrupt miss"

"Its fine I don't get any visitors up here and now two" I patted the cat.

"What's your name?"

The girl hesitated as if she would be rebuked for being here in my room and engaging in chitchat with me.

"I'm Maud miss and I shouldn't be here"

"Don't worry I won't tell"

She smiled.

"You talk strangely where are you from?"

"Oh we're from the west country from a village called Plympton"

"We?" I questioned

"Yes I'm here with my brother Tom he's eighteen and I'm
sixteen I'm the parlour maid and Tom helps in the stables and
runs errands around the house"

"How long have you been here?"

"Bout six months nearly. I really must go miss, Mrs Knight will
have me if I don't go downstairs shortly and I'm not allowed to
be in here. I've been told that I wasn't to disturb you miss in your
condition under any circumstances"

Her expression showed worry and edginess. She came forward to
pick up the cat.

"No!" I exclaimed

She shrunk back.

"You can't have the cat unless you promise that you will come
back tonight when the lights are out downstairs"

"Oh no miss!"

I held the cat tightly till she was prepared to agree to my terms.
She stammered

"But why miss?"

I pondered. I supposed she was my only link to the outside world.
She was the only one who could help me throw any light on what
was being plotted for me by all the adults and I so wanted a
friend. It seemed that since there was another girl of my age
living under the same roof as me, why not?

"Because if you don't come back I will tell Mrs Knight
everything and you will be sacked on the spot!"

"All right miss I'll be back at eight thirty"

I handed her the cat. She left with a curtsey and closed the door
firmly behind her.

I justified my harshness with her by the fact that if I had not been
firm then she would have gone and I would most probably never
have seen her again. After all she had been here for six months
and I hadn't even known.

I lay back on my pillows and began to plan how I was to discover the answers to the many questions bombarding my head. I would make Maud my little spy and together we would bring a resolution to this hopelessness and despair, which was hanging over me like a very black cloud.

Chapter 4

The minutes of that day passed like the heavy cogs in a wheel resisting the pull to turn. I was excited anticipating the return of Maud the parlour maid but at the same time unsure as to what I expected from my chance meeting with her. This truth that I sought left me with a heaviness that I was sure would bring me heartache. Secrets were always like that. The more it was delayed the more I dreaded the answers that I yearned for.

By mid afternoon I was so high on adrenalin that I had to get up from my bed and move around my room just to dispel some of my pent up nervousness. I stumbled at first as I always did but eventually it got easier and I was bending stretching and able to move freely. I glided like a swan, my fingers tracing along the wood panelling and the smooth cloth lined walls decorated in rich woven tapestry, now partially faded by the passing of time. My furniture of heavy inlaid wood probably took craftsmen years to achieve all its intricate detail. I pulled open my cupboard. My dresses and clothes hung untouched for the last year and a half now all looked so small. I realised I must have grown considerably despite my illness as I pulled out one of the dresses that when it had last been worn had swished and trailed on the floor but now barely fell past my knees.

I knelt over my bed and threw open my window. Sunlight streamed through, warming my face and I felt a comfort in the glow of its rays. The smell of freshly mown grass lingered in the air and I took a deep breath of this freshest of days savouring all the aromas as it filled my lungs. I suddenly realised that I could take a deep breath without that awful tightening and pain in my chest and knew that very soon I would be completely recovered.

In the distance a peal of bells cascaded from the steeple of the church. It wasn't the solitary ding-dong for Sunday morning worship but the happy peal for a wedding day. I strained to peer beyond the rooftops and fields to see the bride but it was all too far so I just sat back and revelled in the music of the bells trying to compose fictitious words that might make a fitting wedding bell song.

The freshness of the air must have made me feel lightheaded as I lay back and drifted into sleep. I was soon stirred by a scratching on the door.

"Come in" I called anticipating that it was Maud although it seemed a bit early as the sun was still dropping in the sky.

The scratching continued. I got up with considerable ease and opened my door. Tabby the cat ran in her soft fur brushing past my legs. She sniffed around the corners then settled under my bed. I tried to coerce her out but she was adamant to stay put.

"All right little friend come out when you are ready then"

I then climbed back into my bed aware that had it not been the cat at the door I may have been tricked into revealing my secret that I could walk. I made a mental note not to fall into that ditch again.

My dinner tray was brought. My food was eaten almost alone as I threw scraps of meat to Tabby who was still hiding under my bed. My tray was then retaken. I watched the sun set and darkness filled my lonely bedchamber. I waited. Voices and sounds within the house began to dissipate. Soon Maud would come. Soon I would at last have someone to talk to, an ally.

It grew very dark. The house was very still. No one came. I waited and waited until eventually I fell asleep on a tearstained pillow.

As dawn broke I awoke to a strange whelping sound. I stretched and pulled myself up in my bed. The sound became stronger. I got up and lifted my bed skirting. Beneath the bed Tabby was looking hot and sweaty, around her a pool of mucousy blood seeped over the floor and beside her lay four tiny kittens that she was licking and grooming. I reached out and stroked the soft little bundles of fur and Tabby began to purr loudly as they nudged beneath her and began to suckle.

I watched in amazement.

"Don't worry Tabby I won't tell anyone you're here"

How lovely they all looked, so peaceful, mother and babies. Completely absorbed I forgot the disappointment of the previous evening and curled up on the floor beside the kittens till I eventually fell asleep again.

A piercing scream woke me.

"The poor child has fallen from her bed"

Mrs Knight was in my room fussing and shouting. I was still on the floor where I had lain the night before.

Mrs Knight began tugging at my arm.

"Are you hurt? Is anything broken? Oh my lord how am I going to lift you back to your bed?"

She ran from my room leaned over the banisters and called.

"Maud! Maud! Get up here at once the Mistress has fallen from her bed! Come and help me"

She came back into the room running in circles and fretting.

"I'm fine Mrs Knight"

"No child lay still! Don't talk! You may have broken bones and internal bleeding" Hush be still be still! "Look at the blood!"

The door opened. Sheepishly Maud came in trying to avoid my glare.

"Help me get her back to her bed!"

"No!" Leave her call the doctor!"

"But Mrs Knight I am all right"

"I said hush!" She hissed.

I was in a dilemma. Do I stand and casually return to my bed and give away my secret?

I decided not. Mrs Knight was calming down a little. It was Tabby or me. I had to decide.

"This isn't my blood"

"What!"

"It's Tabby. She came in here in the night and gave birth to her kittens. I tried to see what was happening and slipped from my bed. I'm only a little sore but it's nothing serious please just help me back I will be fine"

"Oh child" Exclaimed Mrs Knight relieved.

"Maud take that arm I'll take this, now lift"

They soon had me back in my bed.

"I'd better get some towels" muttered Mrs Knight and she scurried from the room leaving me alone with Maud.

"You missed our appointment" I scowled not wanting to waste a precious second of time"

"I'm sorry miss" Maud still looked at the floor.

"Didn't think you'd have to see me then did you?

"No miss"

"I waited all night!"

"Sorry miss"

"I'm going to tell Mrs Knight you were in my room yesterday disturbing me"

"No miss I'll be sacked"

"Well you shouldn't lie about returning then"

"I didn't miss"

"I'm telling!"

"No miss, please miss, I promise miss. Please. Please. I will come to night on my life I will"

"I don't believe you! Mrs Knight!"

"No! Please. I swear I will come"

That was it. Now she was truly bound and I knew for sure that she wouldn't go back on an oath.

Mrs Knight returned.

"Yes. You called me?"

Maud shot me a glance to which I raised an eyebrow.

"Oh nothing, just wondered if Tabby could stay in my room it would be such good company for me"

"Nonsense!" She replied

"Whatever would the doctor say?"

They scooped up the cat and kittens in a box cleaned up and left. As Maud closed the door she mouthed the words "I promise" and she was gone.

Chapter 5

She came back exactly on time. I knew she would and I wasn't in
the least anxious throughout that day. I could tell that she was
nervous and a little worried about what I wanted with her, but
that suited me. At last I'd have an outside view from this little
prison of mine.
Over the last year and a half I had read almost every book from
the grand library downstairs. Mrs Knight had worked her way
around just grabbing handfuls of books for me whether they were
appropriate or not. As a result I had been living in a cocooned
fictitious world of heroines and villains where good triumphed
over evil in succinct and eloquent terms. I was in fact quite well
read in all subjects as Mrs Knight had not discriminated between
reference books and so I continued to be fascinated by a very
diverse core of subjects. This was my education; I excelled in it
since I had little else to do all day. I even read a little French and
Latin as I had been taught by my tutor and governess until the
time that I was confined due to my illness.
The thought crossed my mind that I would ask if my teachers
could return since I was feeling better and my mathematical skills
certainly needed improving. That was probably one of the only
things that I couldn't learn by myself.

So now I was faced with a freckle faced carrot haired girl who
was bobbing up and down in front of me curtseying and
apologising and to be quite frank I found it a little irritating.
    "Do stop that and keep still"
    "Yes miss. Sorry miss"
    "And stop saying sorry!"
    "Yes miss. Sorry miss" she bobbed.

"Why don't you sit down" I mellowed

"Tell me a little about yourself and where you are from"

She looked around. I patted the bed and indicated that she should sit. Suddenly she turned from a parlour maid to a girl again and jumped onto the bed her strained expression being replaced with a wide beaming smile.

I replied with an equally broad smile and we both erupted into giggles the ice having being broken.

I found out that she was one of nine children and that she and her elder siblings were all in service, she hadn't seen her parents for over six months.

"Don't reckon I'll be seeing them for a long time now, haven't seen my elder three sisters for at least four years. There's just me and Tom here and he looks out for me but don't know how long that might be for."

I questioned her about her mother. I always wanted to know about other people's mothers not having had one myself.

"Is she pretty?"

"Is she fat or thin?"

"What is her voice like?"

"Does she tuck you in at night and sing to you?"

Maud looked at me as if I was mad.

"Naaw! She just a mam. Short and round and always scruffy. Smells a bit when she's just come in after milking the cows. Helps me da with the farm and never sings!"

"What a shame" I replied.

"Well, when she's not working she's always busy with the babies and little ones although we all have our chores and help look after each other."

I imagined what it might be like to have a house buzzing with the chatter of lots of brothers and sisters. I supposed that the loneliness and tranquillity that I hated would be completely alien to Maud.

"What happened to your parents?"

I was taken aback. Somehow it seemed insolent of this young maid to be asking me such a personal question, but then I realised that I had grilled her tirelessly so maybe it was only natural for her to ask a question back. We had been getting on so well that for a moment the class divide seemed to have dissolved. Maud saw the expression on my face and realised that she had stepped over her boundary.

"Sorry miss" She blurted.

"Didn't mean to pry miss, keep forgetting myself miss"

I realised her genuine anguish and supposed that since I was treating her more as an ally than a servant then it wouldn't be out of place to divulge a bit of my life to her.

"No its fine Maud, you're my friend now" I reached to pat her hand.

I would have to gain her confidence somehow otherwise how could I expect her to go downstairs and try to find out all the dark secrets that the senior staff were hiding from me.

"My mother died when I was born and my father serves overseas with his military regiment. He doesn't get leave to these shores very often so I rarely see him…but he does write quite often."

I knew that I had just lied. He didn't write often, perhaps twice a year for my birthday and Christmas and even then I was only told that he had written and never actually allowed to see any of his letters. Since I had been ill he had not been to see me even in the critical days when they all thought I was dying. At the time I was too ill to ponder on it but now that I was stronger I was quite dismayed that he hadn't been given compassionate leave to come and visit his poor sick only daughter. He must really hate me.

Perhaps when the next letter came and was left lying on the kitchen table Maud could quickly glance over its content and keep me really informed as to what was written.

"Oh I'm sorry bout your parents" Maud whispered.

"I'm sure your father misses you very much, no wonder you were so wanting to know everything about my family. Anyway it's much grander to be a lady in a big house and have servants waiting on you everyday and not rubbing your poor hands away by scrubbing floors at five every morning"

"Five in the morning!" I exclaimed.

"Oh yes miss without fail or Mrs Knight will be boxing my ears!"

"You poor thing!"

Maud nodded

"We can't all sit in bed reading fancy books"

"No" I nodded and realised that every life has its advantages and disadvantages.

Maud was looking longingly at the books scattered over my bed and bedside dresser.

Realising my manners I interjected.

"You are very welcome to borrow them if you like".

Maud threw her head back and laughed.

"And what would I be wanting to do with them then?

I realised my stupidity. Maud was a servant from the country. She had never been inside a school or probably never even met a teacher or tutor.

"I will teach you to read"

Maud looked startled.

"Don't worry it's not as hard as it looks. You would like to read wouldn't you?"

Her face crinkled like the soft paper used to line hat boxes.

"Oh yes! Thank you miss. I never thought I would ever get to be learnt anything"

"Taught" I corrected.

"Oh it would be wonderful, oh miss!"

She leant over and gave me a hug. Surprised but fascinated I hugged her back.

"We'll start tomorrow. Eight thirty sharp!"

"Yes miss, goodnight miss" she was now bobbing and curtseying again her excitement spilling out of the seams of her smock.

She turned to walk out of the door her face alive with new promises and hope.

"One more thing Maud"

"Yes miss"

"Call me Alice"

Chapter 6

The days seemed to drift quickly from one to another now that I
had a friend. There seemed to be some purpose to my life now
that I was a teacher too. Maud was becoming a very able student.
Not only was she picking up how to read but her curiosity about
everything seemed to be expanding like an ever-absorbing
sponge. She would tirelessly ask questions and if we didn't know
the answers would skim the shelves in the library till we found
them. I found that I was sleeping more in the day since I was so
active with my nocturnal pursuits. I had become braver and more
audacious and now crept around the house like a thief darting into
shadows whenever I heard a creak and always made it back to my
room and the safety and comfort of my little bed. I never gave
away any clues as to my secret activities. Mrs Dunn and Mrs
Knight seemed duly concerned with my lethargy and summoned
the doctor more frequently who just suggested that sleep was
good and beneficial to my health. I felt quite smug that I was
fooling them all. It was almost as if I was telling them that if they
had their secrets then I could have mine too. Most of my evenings
were spent searching for any kind of information that would tell
me what they were all up to. I dearly wanted to find a picture of
my mother and still found it strange that in this grand house filled
with portraits there was not one of her.

I wondered about my mother frequently. I imagined her smile,
her warmth, the softness of her skin. I didn't even know if I
looked like her. I certainly didn't look like my father with his
dark hair and piercing blue eyes. When I had asked where the
portraits of my mother were I was always given some feeble

reply about them being in storage or away to be reframed. I knew none of it was true.

I did know that my mother had been an only child whose own mother had died in childbirth with her. I wondered if that was to be a family trait and vowed never to have children of my own because my fate would be almost definitely sealed. My mother had been brought up here at Sparrows Hawk Manor by her endearing and overpowering father. My grandfather had died when I was about two and everything had been left to me to inherit when I reached eighteen years of age. My father had always been serving in the army and had never been back on English soil for more than a week at a time over the last fifteen years.

My father's history was also very vague. He had once mentioned a sister up in Norfolk but I never knew whether she was married and whether I had any cousins or relatives. Sometimes I felt like I was a misplaced person. A child that never really belonged anywhere, in a world full of adults that were all preoccupied with themselves. I didn't know what was to become of me although I assumed I would probably be sent to a finishing school and married off at the first possible opportunity. Somehow I didn't think that I would be short of suitors as I was sure that I stood to inherit a fair amount as my family's only beneficiary.

The door opened. Nurse Dunn stood in the doorway her cheery face lit by the glow of sun. Somehow she broke my sober train of thought and restored me to the present.

"Morning little one"

"Morning Mrs Dunn"

There had been something that I desperately wanted to ask her and somehow now seemed the right moment to ask.

"Nurse Dunn?"

"Yes my love"

"I was wondering if...perhaps... it would be possible for me to...er... possibly... go out?"

She stopped and her face broadened into a concerned smile.

"Well it's almost the end of the summer and there won't be too many warm days." She stroked the side of my cheek.

"Yes why not! A little sunshine will add rosiness to those pale cheeks perhaps you should be out with all the other children spinning your tops and playing hopscotch!"

"I think I'm a little old for that" I chuckled.

She reached over and hugged me.

"Of course you are. You're practically a young woman now. I forgot that whilst you were lying in that bed all this time you were actually getting older and wiser"

She nodded to the pile of books by my bed.

"You'll have read the whole library by the time you're completely well"

I sat up.

"Nurse Dunn?"

"Yes?" She was smiling anticipating my next request.

"I don't think I will need much help to get down to the garden, can I show you something that I've been teaching myself"

I pulled back the covers and stood up. Instinctively Nurse Dunn reached to aid me but I shook my head and she could see that I was standing without the need to steady myself on anyone. I then took several strides and walked across the breadth of the room.

"My goodness!" She exclaimed

"What other tricks do you have up your sleeve?"

Suddenly my confidence diminished. I felt awkward that I had shown her my trump card and worried that I had made her suspicious of me. I walked slowly and feigning pain uneasily went back to my bed and slumped back against the pillows.

"That's it!" I announced.

"I wanted you to be the first to see"

"Excellent! Well certainly we should go outside but you need some outdoor clothes"

She turned to my cupboard and flung it open. The dresses inside looked very small and dusty.

"Well these won't do. I will send Maud to go to the dressmaker and get her to come and fit you for some new clothes then perhaps in a few days we can see about going outside and sitting on the bench under the trees in the shade."

"That would be so lovely Mrs Dunn, thank you so much"

When Maud came that evening I told her excitedly about my new clothes and that I had shown Mrs Dunn that I could walk again. Unfortunately she didn't share my enthusiasm.

"What's the matter Maud you seem very glum?"

"Its Tom miss"

"What is?"

"He's asking me lots of questions about where I'm going in the evenings and why I'm not in my room and what I've been up to. I've done something really silly and I read the newspaper headlines on the stand in the village. Well he asked me how I knew what it said and I didn't know what to say so I said that I heard someone else say it but I think he knew I was lying because the old fool that was standing near me definitely wouldn't be able to read!"

"Why are you ashamed to be able to read" I enquired.

"Oh miss, it's not right for someone like me to have ambitions above her station. People will think that I am being too cheeky for a simple parlour maid. I'll be sacked and have to go back to the farm."

"Don't be silly Maud!"

"No its true miss girls like me are two a penny and all I have to do is put one foot wrong and I'm out on my ear. Tom said."

"Well Maud don't you listen to that ignorant brother of yours. What does he know about education? He's probably just jealous that you can read when he thinks only boys are privileged enough to go to school. Take no notice of him he's just a bully!"

The door swung open. A tall dark figure stood in the shadows of the doorway. Maud and I shrunk in fear. There was a momentary silence in the room.

"I'm just a bully am I then? Ignorant and jealous am I?"

I recoiled. I was being chastised by a servant. How dare he! Tom stepped into the room. He was fairly tall with a roguish sweep of chestnut hair. His eyes were the same blue as Maud's but instead of being slight he was quite stocky and broad.

"Leave my room at once!" I managed to spout. "How dare you enter a lady's room unannounced?"

His eyes squinted and I feared that he might lose his temper and wake the whole household. However instead his voice lowered in a husky brogue.

"You have no right to keep my sister" He began.

"She has to be up at five every morning. She gets hardly any sleep as it is without you keeping her up till all hours. The likes of you are not like us! You with your fancy house and fancy ways, think you own us, think you can order my sister to keep you company half the night and filling her head with stupid ideas that she will never see come true"

His voice turned even more sinister.

"Who do you think you are? Invalid!"

With that he grabbed Maud's arm despite her protests and thrust her from the room.

"Don't you dare bother my sister again!"

The door closed with a thud and I realised that once again I was completely alone.

 I pulled the covers over my head and eventually fell asleep shaking and sobbing.

Chapter 7

I was in urgent need of new clothes. My old dresses from before
my illness still hung untouched in my wardrobe. The dressmaker
was summoned, measured me, and exclaimed quite
embarrassingly that I was now more filled out than when she had
last fitted me for dresses and that she would have to be more
generous with material in the hip and bosom areas. Within days I
was the proud owner of three exquisite new dresses. I should
have been more thrilled about their rich colours and fitted bodices
which were more becoming for ladies rather than young girls but
I wasn't. I was feeling quite sad about having no one that I could
talk to and have as a friend. I missed terribly being able to just
throw back my head and laugh as I had done with Maud.
Mrs Dunn had taken me down to the garden where I had sat in the
early September sun basking in the rays that glistened and
sparkled in my fair hair. The sounds of cuckoos in the distance
and the ruffle of leaves in the breeze reminded me of all the
wonderful things that I had been missing whilst confined to my
room.
Mrs Dunn sensing my need for company had invited a very
insipid girl from her church choir to take tea with me one
afternoon.
Rose Mcfarrel was a very prissy sort of girl with her thin dark
hair styled short with an even shorter fringe that was at least two
inches above her bespectacled eyes.
Her voice was quite high pitched and squeaky and she glared in
amazement at the most ridiculous botanical things exclaiming.
　"Oh look a crataegus oxyacantha!"
　"Oh look a wisteria sinesis!

I could only respond by looking at her pointed weasel face and say.

"Oh look a blade of grass"

But she didn't laugh or get the joke. Her face never creased at the sides of her mouth to reveal her smile.

When she ate her biscuit she nibbled it like a rabbit and I was so bored after an hour of trying to be so terribly polite and dropping hints like:

"I am so tired"

"I must go for my rest"

That eventually I resorted to,

"Oh no! My nurse will have to change my incontinence pad now!"

At that she hastily got up, said she had to leave and scurried down the path.

Mrs Dunn who had been witnessing this whole spectacle came over and sheepishly apologised.

"You're a very special girl Alice one day you will find equally special friends"

Left alone again in the garden I savoured the cool air as I drew in a heavy breath.

Behind the bench the rose bushes were filled with the sweetest smelling red and yellow roses, into which the last of the summer's bees hovered, hoping to pick up any lingering nectar.

At the end of the garden filling a wheelbarrow with weeds I spied Tom but when he stopped and looked up, I very obviously turned so my back faced him. I was not going to favour him with my countenance, not Tom that impudent servant.

But Tom obviously had other ideas. Once he had seen me he seemed to try to distract me so that I would notice him. I would not. I refused. However when I turned to the right there he was wheeling his barrow and plucking weeds. When I turned to the left the creaking barrow wheels moved again with an annoying groan. I didn't want to see him ever again. He was the cause of my present sombre spirit and I would not forgive him. I had seen Maud briefly this afternoon when she had brought out the tea tray. She had been acting quite strangely nodding at my cup without speaking. I had just smiled and said

"Thank you Maud"

But she persisted with her nodding until eventually she had left. I now noticed on the tray beneath my teacup of cold beige tea there was something sticking out that I had not seen before. I lifted my cup and pulled out a small piece of ivory paper. Upon it was the unmistakable childish scrawl that I immediately recognised as Maud's new found handwriting.

Miss Alice
Tom is very sorry. He wants to pologise for intruding into your chamber the other nite.he is pleased you tawt me to rite and maybe if I rite I can get a better job like a lady's maid
Maud

I refolded the letter and carefully slipped it into my pocket mumbling under my breath

"I should think so too, arrogant fool"

My thoughts were interrupted by the rustling of the rose bushes behind me. From the foliage came a harsh whisper.

"Miss Alice?"

I recognised the voice at once. Resigned myself to ignore it and stuck my nose high in the air.

"Miss Alice?" The voice persisted.

I began to hum loudly so that it would drown the intruder.

"You've a lovely voice Miss Alice"

I could not believe his impertinence.

"I do not wish to speak to you leave immediately" I snarled.
"But I must tend to the roses miss"
"Well tend to them then without disturbing me"
"I would like to apologise miss. It was wrong of me to barge into your room like that and say those things to you. I am really very sorry. Please forgive me?"
"Never!"
There was a sharp gasp and the ouch sound of wincing pain.
"Ha got a thorn stuck in your finger" I smirked "Good I hope it hurts," I added.
"It don't hurt as much as your scorn," he muttered.
"Well I won't forgive you and that's that." I retorted to the bush. But there was no reply and I assumed that he had gone with his tail between his legs.

Mrs Dunn who had been sitting on a rocking chair on the canopied porch at the back of the house now looked up at me. The sun was beginning to fall heavily behind the rows of tall trees in the distance. The air was now quite chilly; she put down her sewing and came towards me with a large blanket.
"Better put this around your shoulders or you'll be getting another ailment and that won't do now that you're on the mend" She smiled as she wrapped the soft woollen blanket around me. I looked up into her blue eyes appreciatively.
"We ought to get you upstairs now anyway. It's been a long day for you out here for so many hours."
She reached to help lift me from my seat but the stillness of the evening was suddenly broken by the sound of hooves galloping on the gravel around the front of the house. Sounds of commotion and voices were raised above the whinnying of the horses.
"Sounds like a carriage has arrived" Exclaimed Mrs Dunn.
"Will you go and see what's going on?" I asked.

"Yes, you wait here I will not be long"
Mrs Dunn lifted her petticoats and hurried up the steps that led from the back of the house. There were male voices and there seemed to be quite a flurry of excitement going on within the hallway and entrance of our house.

I waited patiently curious about the cause of so much fuss. The voices got louder as if almost all the servants seemed to have rushed out to meet the unexpected guest.

I pulled the blanket tighter around me as it was now becoming very cold and dusk was definitely setting in. I wondered whether Mrs Dunn had forgotten about me, as it seemed an age that I was sitting here alone in the garden. Eventually I saw two figures emerging from the large conservatory doors. As they came closer I saw that Mrs Dunn was being followed by a man of medium to tall stature with a dark cape over his shoulders that hung almost to his knees. As he approached I recognised his distinctive penetrating look and his deep blue eyes. His hair was a little greyer than I remembered and his complexion seemed sallow and pale. He seemed thinner but still walked with the same strong stride. He stopped when he reached several feet from my chair. I stood to greet him in excitement and awe. Mrs Dunn smiled at us both and announced simply

"Alice you have a very special visitor."

Chapter 8

My father was very overpowering and I never knew quite what
was expected of me when I was in his company.
It had been such a long time since I had last seen him and now he
appeared as if he was shorter than I remembered or perhaps it was
that I was so much bigger. He had a tiredness about him and in
my memory a vulnerable soft centre to the hard façade that he
presented with. My instinct was to run over to him and let him
enfold me in his strong arms. That was how I always imagined
and play acted these scenarios with my loving father stroking my
hair and calling me his cherished daughter.
 In reality it was nothing like that. We were standing at arms
length in the garden like strangers or at the very best a niece
meeting an old long lost uncle from overseas. There was no
warmth from him. He reached out to shake my hand most
formally and in response I bobbed a curtsey and lowered my
head.
The coolness of the evening now enfolded around us despite my
advantage of having a warm blanket draped over my shoulders.
We walked slowly inside and towards the drawing room where
Mrs Dunn tactfully made her excuses and left us alone.
    "How is your regiment father?" I asked trying to make polite
conversation with this man whom I hardly knew.
    "Oh!" He seemed confused.
    "Yes it is fine thank you"
    "Where have you been based?" You must have had a terrible
time in the Sudan. I read in my geography books about the awful
heat and sweltering conditions. Its central Africa isn't it?
He looked at me sternly and I was almost afraid for a moment.

"Why do you ask so many questions girl? They told me that you were very sick. I thought I would find you confined to your bed and in a much frailer disposition than this."

"I'm sorry to disappoint you sir!" I retorted.

"And rude! Has no one taught you how to behave?"

"No sir" I replied indignantly.

I glared at my father. He was cold and totally disinterested in me. I felt angry that I had expected so much from him even though I knew it was all futile and I would never be loved like a daughter by this man. This was not going well. I was annoyed that it had taken him two years to come to see me and that now he was here he thought it unreasonable of me to ask him questions. I had always felt that I was an inconvenient child to him. Someone that he despised for my mothers death. Now I knew that I was right. However he was here now and this may be my only opportunity to try to make him realise what an intelligent and dutiful daughter I really was and that maybe, possibly he could be proud of me and love me.

"I am sorry father" I back peddled.

"You must be very weary from your travels".

He looked at me. A look that made me feel quite vulnerable and alone. It was the kind of look a butcher might give to a lamb he was about to slaughter. A mixture of pity and indifference. I could feel a tear beginning to well but I fought and managed to retain it.

"Yes I am very tired I shall eat and retire to my room. We will talk tomorrow before I leave."

"Leave?" I wondered.

"Yes I have important business to return to overseas. Goodnight Alice"

My heart was sinking rapidly as I closed the door behind me and slowly began to take the long staircase back to my room.

38

"That was quick!" Mrs Dunn's voice was behind me.

"Yes" I didn't turn to look at her.

She swung around me, stood on the first step and lifted my chin towards her. The redness in my eyes could not lie to her and she immediately linked her arm through mine and escorted me up to my room.

"Get changed Alice whilst I get you some supper and some warm milk!" Her voice was tinged with an inkling of rage even though she tried desperately hard not to show it.

"I shall be back presently"

I began to pull off all my beautiful new but restricting clothes and laid them over a chair. I poured out some water from my pitcher into a bowl and began to splash cool water over my face and stinging sore eyes. I could not contain myself any longer and within the privacy of my little room allowed myself to cry. The tears came fast. Warm streams that mingled with the coldness of the water but the sadness within me seemed uncontainable and I truly wished that I had died from my illness and that all there was for my father to remember me by was a plain tombstone in an overgrown cemetery.

I finished washing and dressed for bed. I was quite drained as it had been a frightfully long day and I was worn out.

A knock on the door and it opened. Maud stood there trying to balance the tray with one hand whilst she opened the door with the other.

"Here's some nice thick broth and chunky wedges of bread for you" she smiled kindly.

I turned away so that she wouldn't see my sad expression.

"There's an awful commotion going on downstairs miss between your father and Mrs Dunn"

"Really?" I looked up forgetting that I was trying to hide.

"Oh yes miss! Lots of shouting! I think Nurse Dunn was quite upset about something."

"Do you know what it was about?" I asked secretly knowing that my wonderful Nurse Dunn was probably saying things to my father that I had no courage to say.

"No I don't know yet miss but…" She put down the tray beside the bed grabbed my arm and said.

"Come with me miss and we'll soon know what it's all about" Maud led me from my room along the corridor and into another small room that was directly over the drawing room where my father and Mrs Dunn were embroiled in their altercation. Maud led me over to the fireplace and beckoned me to lean towards the grating.

"Gosh Maud you are clever you can hear everything loud and clear from here"

"Shh miss" Maud fussed.

"If we can hear them then they can hear us too" she continued in a whisper.

I nodded silently and the two of us pressed our heads close together so that we were almost leaning over the cold charred coals and behind the fireplace.

"But Sir I implore you" we heard Mrs Dunn say.

"For the child's sake she should know"

"No!" Boomed my father's irritated voice.

"I expressly forbid it! She will not know! She will never know! I have decided that she should go to France she has some Gallic distant family there, she can continue her education and we will sell up this ghastly house and all these dead possessions!"

"You cannot do that Sir. She has had such a lonely life. You cannot take away the only place that she has ever known as her home."

"I cannot! I cannot" My fathers voice raised.

"How dare you woman! You speak above your station! Who are you to tell me what I can and cannot do? No wonder my daughter has such bad manners with people like you around influencing her with your ways. You are only a nurse and after having seen my daughter this evening I do not think that she is in need of a nurse! She seems to be in perfect health to me so a nurse is completely unnecessary. In fact madam, I think you can pack your things and leave we have no need for you anymore!"

"Alice needs me. She has been very ill and no one else bothered to care for her" Mrs Dunn replied accusingly to my father.

"You will not answer me back! You will not tell me what is best for my daughter! And you will leave this house by the end of the week!"

We then heard a door slam and there was silence from the darkness down the fireplace.

Maud and I pulled ourselves out of the cramped hole and scurried back to my room. By the time Mrs Dunn came in Maud had left and I was sitting up in my bed sipping the cold soup and eating the chunks of fresh loaf.

"Enjoying your supper? Mrs Dunn asked pretending to smile.

I nodded wondering whether I should let on that I knew about her argument with father but then thought better of it and said nothing.

Mrs Dunn approached me and gave me a strange look.

"What is that?" She asked

"What?" I replied.

"That black stuff on your face. Looks like soot. Didn't you wash before you got into bed?

She went over to the pedestal dipped in a corner of a towel and began to wipe my face clean.

"You have such a lovely face," she said tenderly.

"You will be a great beauty when you are older".

41

Instinctively I reached over and hugged her.

"Oh Mrs Dunn always take care of me don't leave, always stay"

"Oh child" She gasped. I could feel the warm tears dripping on my hair. She kissed my forehead and turned to leave the room.

"Mrs Dunn?

"Yes?"

"What don't I know?" I asked

"You don't know what an incredible girl you are," she said and she left the room.

Despite my chagrin and confusion I slept very deeply that night. In the morning when I woke I remembered the evening before and I realised that this nightmare was far beyond my dreams.

I was unsure whether I should go down for breakfast. I had been so used to having a tray brought to me every morning and languishing in bed with my books that that seemed the thing to do. However I presumed that my father would be waiting for me so I went down to the dining room. There he was already sitting at the head of the table a big plate of eggs, bacon and toast in front of him. Mrs Knight was pouring his tea.

"Good morning father, Mrs Knight."

"Morning Alice" replied my father.

"What can I get you for breakfast?" Mrs Knight asked.

"I'll just have some tea, toast and marmalade please".

I sat down beside my father still very much in awe of him but determined to try to appease him. I also knew that he had dismissed Nurse Dunn and I was determined I should have her reinstated.

"Did you sleep well father?"

"Yes thank you Alice and you?"

"No father" I lied.

"I had a terrible fever and sweats. I have them most nights and days too. I have only just begun to recover and I rely so heavily on my nurse to look after me. Sometimes I am most terribly sick and Nurse Dunn is there to tend to my ailing lungs and administer the most awful medicinal mixtures in order to soothe my aching chest. I don't know what I would do without her. I should surely not recover at all."

I then feigned a very convincing chesty cough, so much so that my father felt compelled to leap from his chair and pat my back.

"You seemed well enough yesterday"

"Oh no father I am still terribly afflicted"

Mrs Knight brought in my breakfast and laid it in front of me. I tucked in heartily and ate four slices of toast quite effortlessly.

"Well you seem to have an excellent appetite for someone so *afflicted*!"

"But I must father. I do try to eat well otherwise I won't recover quickly. Nurse Dunn is always reminding me how important it is to eat well and eat all my vegetables. She looks after me so well"

"I'm sure she does," echoed my father.

"Alice?" my father began.

"When you are completely recovered I thought it would be a good idea for you to go to Paris. You can be educated there and eventually in a few years time we could find you a good husband. I have made arrangements with some people that I know, they are distant relations but they would bring you up well and you will become part of the French gentry."

I gaped in amazement. Why did he want to send me away? Why could I not stay here in my mother's house?

"But what about this house? Surely this is my heirloom?"

"No Alice. We will sell this house. It means nothing. It is a sad house filled with ghosts and bad memories. You need a new life, a fresh start."

"But father what about you?

"I am to be permanently posted overseas. We probably will not meet again."

So that was it. He was going to get rid of me and abandon me in another country. What choice did I have? How could I fight this? Despondently I finished my tea.

"What if I don't want to go?"

"You will my dear. It a wonderful opportunity and it has all been arranged now anyway. We will wait for you to recover and by Christmas you will be a Parisian."

At that he patted my hand and I felt like I had shrunk into oblivion.

I returned to my room exhausted. I gazed out of my little window and watched the leaves that I had seen sprouting from the same branches in the spring now turn golden and red and prepare for the onset of autumn. I wondered if I would ever see those trees bare again with a sheet of winter snow or whether I would have been carted away to my new life by then.

There was a rustling from my fireplace and a brush turned and poked out from the flue, a head popped out after it.

"Hello Miss Alice" said a black boy with blue eyes.

I laughed for the first time in ages at the comical sight.

"It's me Miss Alice. It's Tom"

I stopped laughing.

"I know that you are still angry but please won't you forgive me?"

"No!" I said sharply. Still not quite sure what I was so angry about.

"Miss Alice I am going to make it up to you. I was wrong to behave the way that I did and you were only being kind to Maud but I didn't realise that, I was out of place coming into your room and saying what I said and I just want you to forgive me. I won't let your father send you away; he's not what he seems with his pale skin and soft hands. I've told Maud that she can come to you and carry on her lessons and it will be alright, I won't interfere." I turned to the fireplace with aloof stubbornness.

"I will never forgive you, now go away"
Tom disappeared and I realised how much like my father I sounded.

Chapter 9

I would like to say that Tom was completely excised from my
mind but he wasn't. At the strangest moments his conversations
would find their way into an unblocked crevice in my mind and
lodge there like an unwelcome tenant.
I wondered what he had meant about my father not being what he
seemed. I longed for Tom to come back and explain what he
presumed about my father's pale skin and soft hands.
My room began to darken as the skies filled with grey clouds.
How apt I thought that the weather reflected my own uneasiness
and sadness. A light drizzle began to fall. The lawns were
covered in a haze of mist through which I could make out the
figure of my father strutting around near the stables. His voice
rose. I could hear him instructing the stable lad that he had
brought with him to oil the saddle and fix the stirrups. The thud
of his feet on the gravel seemed heavy and harsh. As I watched
him I was aware that there was nothing that I could say that I was
familiar with and that I really knew about this man. He was a
stranger to me; as distant as my mother up in heaven. This
longing within to be part of a real family was just a fantasy and
soon I would be shipped abroad to Paris where I was to start a
new life as someone else.
My thoughts were interrupted by the smell of roast beef wafting
up the stairs. The rain had lifted and the skies were breaking
through in a deep blue hue.
I rolled over and began to fix my hair in the mirror opposite the
end of the bed. As I brushed the loose curls I wondered whether
now that I was to be a Parisian lady I should start pinning my hair
up like all the debutantes did down in London.
I straightened my skirts and began to proceed down the stairs. I
hoped that my father would be in better spirits than he had been

so far. I wondered whether his behaviour was as a result of his military training. Perhaps he had been the recipient of brutal mind manipulation by one of his superiors. Maybe he had forgotten the animosity and outrage that he would have been made to feel. Maybe he could understand this state of anguish that I was feeling.

By the time I came down there seemed to be an atmosphere of apathy in the air. I assumed that my father must have had words with the staff because everyone seemed most disgruntled and serious. I presumed that if he could be so cold and heartless with me then he wouldn't behave with any more compassion towards anyone else.

When I entered the parlour Maud was sitting at the large wooden table surrounded by rags and oils and frantically polishing the silver candelabra. She knew I was there but continued to gaze intently at her chores. I walked through to the kitchen, my heels tapping the cold limestone tiles on the floor.

Mrs Knight was just taking out a roast from the oven. The kitchen was filled with the wonderful aromas of browning gravy and crackling crispy potatoes and onions.

"This should make him less foul mouthed". Mrs Knight muttered under her breath.

"Can't imagine why he even bothers to come here with his temper tantrums and nasty manner!"

I coughed. Mrs Knight looked up startled when she realised that she was not alone and that I was within earshot.

"Sorry Miss Alice! She exclaimed.

"Lunch will be ready soon! I've made a vegetable pottage, roast lamb, parsnips, roast potatoes and fresh peas followed by your favourite rhubarb crumble with lashings of vanilla custard."

"Ooh excellent!" I cooed.

"It sounds absolutely delicious Mrs Knight and hopefully will cheer him up a bit. I'm sure that father will be most impressed!" I smiled reassuringly.

"Oh I do hope so dear, he seems like he could do with a nice lunch" Mrs Knight replied kindly although I imagined that she was probably thinking rather more unkind thoughts about my brutal father.

"Well!" Mrs Knight declared

"I think we are ready to serve up!" She stuck a fork in the lamb and the juices ran clear, steam rising from the forked wound. Loud voices from the hallway broke the tranquillity.

"Wonder what the rumpus is about?" Questioned Mrs Knight. The door flung open.

"Oh there you are!" Announced my father.

He was wearing his riding clothes and had his cape draped over his shoulders.

"I'm leaving! Just came to bid you farewell"

Mrs Knight and I exchanged confused and disappointed looks.

"But Sir!" I protested.

The cold eyes descended upon me. I recoiled at the intensity of the anguish that was spearing through me.

"I apologise Sir but Mrs Knight has made the most delicious lunch in your honour father and we were hoping that you would tarry a little and enjoy this wonderful feast first."

He didn't answer. But perused around the piping hot dishes displayed and the lamb oozing succulent juices. I smiled trying to pacify his simmering temper. He returned my smile with an indifferent look and declared.

"No! We have to make haste. We will stop at a very nice inn for some lunch"

Mrs Knight shot him a very insulted look then hastily turned her eyes downward so not to be further insulted by one of my fathers "looks".

"But father" I implored.

I need to talk to you about the arrangements for my future?

He shook his head and waved his hand at me.

"No, I have said all there is to say on this matter. There is no more to discuss."

"But I need to know…"

"There is nothing you need to know." He cut in and with a grand sweep of his cape turned and walked towards the door.

"Goodbye father" I whispered.

He turned and looked back at me. The etched horizontal lines on his brow softened and creased as he attempted to smile.

"God bless you Alice. You will be a lot happier in your new life. Forget me I was never a true father to you as I know how a true father should be."

At that he closed the solid oak door behind him with a thud.

I waited till the sound of his heavy boots had left the wooden floors of the hallway. I waited till they had marched over the gravel in the courtyard. Then I waited till the sounds of horses' hooves thundering through the cobbled streets became no more than a rustle in the trees.

I felt Mrs Knights hand on my shoulder. I lifted my head then shook it.

"It's all right. I am not sad. He's right. He isn't a good father. I think he cares a little about me though otherwise why would he arrange a new life for me in Paris? He never really loved me despite my years hoping he would."

I stopped and almost felt embarrassed at my impromptu confession. Mrs Knight made no comment almost as if I had said nothing at all. She turned and went back to her oven and began to stir at the simmering vegetables.

"Such a lovely dinner picked the vegetables fresh from the kitchen garden myself this morning. There's just no pleasing some people. Stopping at an inn! No inn keeper can make a feast like this" Mrs Knight mumbled to the cooling food.
Sensing her distress I tried to cheer her up.

"Come on Mrs Knight. This looks like the best meal you've ever cooked. Call in everyone else and let's all sit in the kitchen and eat. Shame to let it go to waste. Come on" I smiled reassuringly.

"Do you want yours bringing up to your room?"

"No Mrs Knight I'll eat with you down here."

"With the servants?"

"With the people that work so hard to look after this place" Mrs Knight smiled and her anger and frustration seemed to dissipate like the smoke steaming from the food.
I sat beside Maud. At first she was surprised that I would want to eat with all of them but I was desperate for company. I knew that my mind would only go sauntering down that path of sadness again and I was happy for any excuse to delay that inevitable grief that I knew would trap me sooner or later.
After an hour we were all patting our stomachs and praising Mrs Knight on her tremendous efforts. There had been laughter and chatter at the table, it seemed that this was like my only family, with gardeners, cooks, maids. There was one face missing from this strange pot pourri of characters and in a way I was quite relieved. Tom was nowhere to be found. They had called him but he didn't reply. Everyone seemed to have seen him within the last half hour but then he had disappeared in the same puff of smoke that my father had ridden out in.

"Probably in a haystack with some girl" Joked the gardener.

Maud shook her head.

"He's not like that" she whispered.

I could see that she was worried and uncannily I found that I was concerned too, for her sake of course.

Chapter 10

Days rolled from one to another. The cock still crowed early every morning and the servants woke and worked following the same routines; a clockwork existence that they never tired of. Meanwhile my life was about to change. I had no choices; my life was destined to me by my father. Perhaps life in Paris was to be better; maybe there I would find some contentment and solace. It saddened me though to think that I would never see my father again. How I had hoped that he would be different and more like the fathers in the books that I read…but alas that wasn't what god had planned for me. There would probably be more purpose and meaning in my new life and now that I was becoming a woman maybe there would even be a marriage in the not too distant future.

I was resigned to this change and now anticipated it with a hunger and eagerness that I had not previously envisioned.

The dressmaker had come and measured me for new leaving dresses and I had began to sort out things, mainly books that I would be taking on my journey.

Maud came to my room every day and I taught her a few words in French, which quite amused her.

"But why would they want to talk different?"

"They don't" I assured her but it's God's will. You've heard the story in church about Babel and the great tower that the people tried to build up to reach heaven. That's when god created languages and made us all speak differently."

Maud looked pensive as if great thoughts were skimming through her young mind.

"But we say our prayers in English, is that not what God understands?"

God understands all languages but of course English is His first language.

"Really?"

"Oh yes Maud even though I suppose the Pope would expect Gods first language to be Latin or maybe Italian….but it couldn't possibly be."

We both laughed. The thought of God speaking to Moses all those years ago in Latin seemed almost bizarre.

"So you're sure that God hears my prayers?" Maud was fretting and looking quite anxious.

"Definitely. Why what's the matter?"

"It's Tom miss. Something has happened he's been gone a week and that's not like him. He left the same night as your father went and for him to disappear like this means that something has happened, something bad."

I needed to reassure her, even though I felt completely relieved by Tom's departure. Good riddance I had thought to that young upstart that dared to have come into my rooms and told me what to do. Yes he had apologised but I was the kind of person that once my mind was made up about someone that was it. I would not go back.

"Miss Alice do you think he's been murdered or captured or taken as a slave overseas?"

Maud was a very simple girl deep down with a racing imagination.

"Maud who would want to take Tom? I laughed. "Pirates?"

"Oh no! I didn't even think of pirates. Oh my I've heard that they are wild and barbaric and…" She lowered her voice and whispered.

"They aren't like us….they eat people! They may have eaten Tom!"

At this point her face crumpled she had obviously been told some very strange stories.

"Oh Maud all of that is nonsense. Tom has probably just found something better to do. He's run off because he knew that he had acted inappropriately here."

"But miss he apologised to you. It was all sorted, I mean that incident."

I looked at Maud's tearstained face, knew that it would be inappropriate to say anything more to her on the subject, she was too simple to understand the implications of the way that Tom had acted a few weeks ago, when he had barged into my room to complain about Maud's reading lessons.

"We haven't seen the last of him Maud. Trust me he is like a bad penny he will turn up soon."

Another week passed. Then one day Maud burst into my room unable to contain herself and began squeaking like a rusty gate.

"He's back, he's come home! Oh Miss Alice I'm so relieved I cannot tell you how worried I was. I thought he had died and something terrible had happened but he's back now!" She took a deep breath.

"Good I'm so pleased for you" I replied between gritted teeth. "See I told you that everything would be all right and that he would turn up"

"Yes you did miss but I didn't believe you miss. Thought you were just saying that to make me feel better miss"

"No I wouldn't do that" I shook my head. "I knew" I said with the authority of someone that obviously had control over the fate of others or so Maud believed.

"I've got to go now and sort out some food for him. He looks half starved and I don't think that he's had a decent meal in all the time that he has been away. Oh I'm so happy miss I think I could explode!"

"I can see that Maud. Now why don't you hurry along and catch up with your brother instead of standing here?"

"Yes of course miss it was just that I was so excited that I had to tell you because I knew that you would be excited too."

I nodded and smiled as she left the room. I didn't have the vaguest notion where she could have possibly got the idea that I would be excited about some upstart gardener having returned from some erstwhile jaunt.

I reopened the page in my book that I had been reading until she had interrupted me and tried to curb the disappointment of his return by distracting myself in the pages of my novella.

Chapter 11

So where had Tom been? Maud in all her excitement and fluster had quite forgotten to mention that minor fact. He obviously hadn't been eaten by cannibal pirates or maybe he had, and had tasted so vile that they had spat him out and cut him free! Either way I was sure that sooner or later Maud would come bustling in and finish the story. It was very early and I was not accustomed to waking at the crack of dawn. I had not slept well, probably because I would once again have to encounter the tiresome Tom hanging around the place. I did try to go back to sleep but my mind was already racing through the tasks of the day so it was inevitable that my tired slumber filled body would have to struggle to get through this day.

After washing and dressing in one of my new outfits, a pretty blue embossed cotton skirt with white ruffle collared blouse I began pinning up my hair. I had never pinned my hair before but assumed that the time was right for me to learn and master the technique because surely all the ladies in Paris would be wearing their hair up and I didn't want to appear inadequate beside them. My locks were thick and heavy and no sooner had I wound the strands around my fingers and fixed them into place with at least ten clips than the pieces of hair would start unravelling and falling over my shoulders. It was becoming increasingly frustrating and after an hour or so I threw the box of pins on the floor defeated and began brushing out my hair. My brow frowning furiously in the gilt edged mirror opposite me.

"Good morning Alice" The door swung open and Nurse Dunn stood there.

"Oh hello nurse" I turned to greet her, my smile beaming as it always did whenever she was around.

"I've missed you so much for the past few days are you well?"

"Yes Alice. Thank you. I was just having a little break to spend some time with my boys and try to sort out another job"

"And? Did you find anything?

"Well it wasn't difficult but I managed to find a job at the hospital. They are looking for a senior nurse there and the hours are perfect for me to spend time with my children and family. You know that your father wanted me to leave but then suddenly relented and said that I could stay till Christmas when you depart for France..."

"Yes" I nodded

"Well you are so much better Alice and truthfully you don't really need me as you have done in the past......."

"Yes" I agreed

"Well they will only take me if I start immediately otherwise they will have to advertise and find someone else for the post."

"No!" I shook my head.

"Nurse Dunn you have been one of the only people that cared for me when I was so sick with fevers that I didn't know what day it was or whether I would even ever see another day! You were the one that brightened my life with your touch, with your optimism and your smile. I had hoped that you could come with me to Paris as my companion."

She looked me in the eye and I could see that she was wounded like a little bird caught by a cat and unable to fly.

"You are the sweetest child and I am really touched that you think so highly of me. If I ever had a daughter I would have wanted her to be just like you."

I lowered my lashes embarrassed by her gentleness.

"I cannot come to Paris. I have a husband and children here. You will have a wonderful life"

I knew that she wouldn't have been able to come. However I was still daunted by the fact that I would have to travel so far all alone.

"Mais oui Madame Dunn. D'accord."

"Yes and there's that too! You'll have to learn those fancy words so that you can speak with all your new friends out there. I could never do that, imagine me speaking all those funny words what would my children think?"

I laughed. It did seem quite ridiculous to think of Nurse Dunn speaking in French. Most of my French I had learnt from a tutor but that had been quite a while back now and I was positively rusty. I made a mental note to call on Madame Delange the milliner as she was native French and I could probably brush up my skills by having some conversations with her.

"Nurse Dunn" I began.

"What do I do with my hair?"

I pulled my fingers through the unkempt mane cascading over my shoulders.

"I'm sure the ladies in Paris will have all the latest techniques for creative continental styles and I will turn up looking like I've woken up in a haystack!"

Nurse Dunn took the brush from my hand and began brushing my locks.

"You have lovely hair. There's no need to pin it and look like an old maid. Ribbons is what you need lots of pretty ribbons. I shall get you some when I'm next at the village shop."

"All right" I resigned. Together we went down for breakfast. At the bottom of the stairs Maud was pacing with a duster in her hand feigning cleaning the banisters. When she saw us her eyes darted around worriedly and she tried to attract my attention without Mrs Dunn seeing.

"Nurse Dunn I shall catch you up in the parlour" I called out.

"I have forgotten something in my room"

When the door had closed behind her Maud clutched my arm and gave me an imploring stare.

"Miss Alice? Tom's in big trouble. Mrs Knight and Mr Sheppard have been shouting at Tom something terrible. They say he should be whipped for disappearing like that and that he will be out of a job if he runs off again. He told them that he got drunk in the village and was injured and ill and couldn't return until now. I think it's all a load of tripe myself, Toms never touched ale and he's not one to go brawling through the streets. He hasn't told me where he's been but I know he's been up to something."

"Are they going to whip him?" I asked secretly smiling to myself and thinking that he deserved it.

"Oh I hope not Miss Alice, Tom has promised to work without wages to make up for this and they said that that was going to happen anyway!"

"Well Maud, I'm sorry but in this case I have no sympathy. Tom is just a stupid boy that should know better than to disappear and then to return with such a feeble excuse."

"So you won't stick up for him?"

"No."

Maud shot me an alluring glance. Then she lifted her skirt, raised her duster turned her back to me and marched up the stairs. I tutted loudly to let her know that I disapproved of her arrogance and blindly sashayed through the parlour door and sat down for my breakfast.

Why should I be worried about Tom? Why should it bother me if that rude chimney sweep got a beating? I blanked my mind and diverted my thoughts.

"Ah le petit dejeuner" I announced.

I ate my breakfast heartily whilst perusing some journals with news of events in London. There was one section dedicated to the ongoing war in Sudan and the terrible conditions that our boys were suffering in the appalling heat out there. My thoughts immediately went to my father and I sympathised with the terrible ordeal that he must be enduring in his military post. The morning was brightening and a lone robin perched on the window sill of the bay windows of the dining room. The grand windows that looked out over the rose garden.

"Poor little robin, are you hungry?"

I scooped up some crumbs and discarded toast and went over to the window. I pulled the heavy sash and the robin flew to the nearest bush. The fragrant scent of thousands of roses rushed into the room like it was being sprinkled with delicate puffs of perfume. It was late in the year. Most of the roses were heavy with fully ripened petals that had long since bloomed and were now browning with age. They were falling and carpeting the land beneath them. It reminded me of an aisle in a church awaiting the onset of a bride.

The robin sensing I was safe flew back to the sill where I had deposited the bread and began hastily pecking.

The air had a morning chill and freshness. Interrupting the silence a cuckoo called in the distance. There was a rustle to my left. I looked down but saw nothing more than the branches swaying.

"Miss Alice?"

I knew the voice immediately and froze.

"Miss Alice I'm down here" The voice whispered intently.

"I've not the slightest interest in where you are located" I replied in an even tone.

"Please miss" the voice urged "lower your voice or I will be caught."

"So?" I continued loudly.

"Am I to care about the likes of you? Go back to your haystack I'm sure your lady friend is waiting for you!"

"Miss Alice, I must speak with you very urgently there is something that I must tell you. Something that I have discovered whilst I have been away."

"Tom!" I scowled.

"There is nothing that you may have discovered on your drunken rampage that would possibly interest me! Rantings of ale filled men lining ditches at the sides of the road are of no consequence to me at all!"

The anger and tone in my voice was most clear. Even the little robin flew off in disgust with Tom. There was a prolonged silence and I thought that I must have made myself quite clear. Then out of the hedgerow he appeared. He seemed so much more man than boy like. The cut of his jaw was covered with a growth of stubble. His eyes searched for mine and even I could not avert my glare indefinitely.

"What is it Tom? Be quick I have much to do."

His eyes stayed locked on me.

"Miss Alice, I know that you still have not forgiven me for my intrusion into your room when I came for Maud all those months ago. I know that the sight of me repulses you. I know that I have not always behaved correctly. But........ you are still the mistress here and my loyalty is to you only"

"Hmm" I responded a bit astonished by his eloquence with words and quite impressed by his defiance to tell me what he felt must be said. His voice was soft and he seemed almost appealing with his rugged straw hair and strong shoulders.

"So miss I wasn't in a haystack with some girl! I wasn't getting drunk with the men in the village. I only said some of those things to avoid the real truth."

"And what is the real truth?" I asked flippantly.

"Well Miss" Tom coughed and spluttered. His eyes now left their fixture on my face and darted around the ground.

"This is very difficult to tell you miss, I knew that there were lots of truths hidden from you in this house but up till now it was just rumours and gossip and I didn't want to believe any of those things."

My heart was now fluttering like a bird frantically trying to get out of a cage. I knew only vaguely about the secrets that were being held from me. That had been the original motivation for befriending Maud so that she could be my spy and tell me things that were being spoken below stairs.

"Yes, yes Tom! What is it that you have to tell me please tell me quickly I must know"

Tom now realised that he had at last caught my attention and seemed almost reluctant now to continue where he had left off. My anxiety and frustration seemed to rise uncontrollably and I almost fell out from the window upon which I was perched.

"Tom meet me in the summer house at the end of the rose garden in one minute. It is not safe to talk here. I will be there presently."

I lifted my skirt and petticoat and tore through the parlour and out through the front door. I ran around the house and through the hedgerows that ran beside the roses. As I ran through the rose garden I could feel the briars reaching out and snagging my beautiful new clothes, but I didn't care. The heat rising in my gut was driving me like a wild animal to the place where I would find maybe one truth that would justify my existence. One answer to the grating mountain of uncertainty that tormented my mind. I could feel the sweat sticking to the back of my blouse and I knew that I was still really too frail following my confinement to be running in this state of complete lunacy.

I arrived at the summer house. The ivy and clematis had wound their way around all the windows giving us complete safety and privacy. Tom was sitting on one of the great slabs of grey marble stone. I stopped and tried to catch my breath supporting myself against a tall pillar. I looked a sight. My hair was loose and scattered with petals and leaves and my skirt hem was muddied by the early morning dew and snagged with bare threads hanging from the ruthless thorns of the rose bushes.

Tom looked up and I could see that he had been crying.

"I am so sorry miss" He began.

"This is not easy for me to tell you"

I worried for an instant that he would not tell me and had changed his mind. I was half relieved and half frantic.

"Tom" I went and sat beside him.

"Please tell me what you have learnt."

He looked up and for a timeless minute we stared into each other's eyes. I searched for my answers and he searched for his courage to tell me. His sadness made me reach to his hand and I held his rough palm and broken darkened nails in my own soft white fingers.

He looked away from me.

"Alice I followed your father to London. I followed him to a grand house at 14 Inverness Gate. I waited because he said he was due to set sail within the week to return to Sudan, but he never went. He left every morning and went to his place of work in the city and returned every evening to his home. There was no ship and no fleet and no army. Your father has not been honest with you. He has a life in London and he has resided there for over twenty years according to the servants of the house."

I sat numb. I stayed there till Tom had left. Till the day began to grow dark. I stayed there till I felt nothing just emptiness and a hollow ache.

Chapter 12

The following few days seemed to be a complete blur. My mind was sifting and digesting all the information. I wanted to run away and hide, to scream that it wasn't true. But where could I go? How could I hide from the torment that seemed to seep within me like the sap of some poisonous tree feeding through my veins.

I considered the possibility that Tom was wrong and that he had merely camped outside the wrong house. However I knew that it must be true because Tom would not have put himself into so much trouble in order to deliver a lie.

So was this the terrible secret that everyone had been trying to protect me from? Was this heart ripping pain the truth that I had struggled to find? In some ways I was pleased that I knew but at the same time I longed to cast this information from me and remain an innocent child alone in my room.

I had refused nearly all food in the last few days. Mrs Knight had been unperturbed by my lack of appetite but Mrs Dunn had sensed straight away that something was amiss and that I was acting strangely. I knew that I would have to react to this news and that it would have to be very soon but I was unsure as to the best method for my actions. I considered writing to my father at this new address 14 Inverness Gardens a name that I now had memorised from continuously repeating it to myself. I wondered why he had lied and how I could demand an explanation but resigned myself though to the knowledge that it would all be in vain as my father would not entertain questions from me at the best of times never mind by letter on such a delicate matter. There were moments that I was just so inflamed that I felt like rushing down to London to confront him but then thought that I couldn't possibly undertake such a journey as I was only a girl and there was no way that I could travel all that way unescorted. I came down for my meals and fussed around the house under the watchful eye of Maud who was paying very particular attention to me. She had definitely heard all the details of my news from her brother and now gazed at me with a glary inquisitive look as if to ask what I would do with my burdensome casket of information. I didn't wish to speak to Maud. I avoided her and resisted the urge to respond to her imploring gazes. I almost wanted to consult with Tom and get him to repeat his news over and over till it was so worn that it ceased to exist but he was not around. I didn't exactly search for him but I was always around the gardens or stables and he was uncannily nowhere to be seen. Sometimes when I heard his voice I leapt to investigate but when I arrived at the place where he had last been he was nowhere to be seen.

"Alice!"

I looked up from my untouched plate of dinner.

"Yes." I replied to Nurse Dunn

"This is ridiculous you haven't eaten for four days! What has happened to you? I hope you're not coming down with your illness again! If you don't eat then you'll be like Rosie McFarrell who ended up looking so thin that everyone mistook her for a little boy!" Now you wouldn't want to look like a boy would you?"

"Yes you're right Nurse Dunn!" A smile was creeping over my face. An idea dawning on me like the dying embers of a fire that had just been fuelled with new wood.

"No I certainly wouldn't like to look like a boy!"

My mind was set. I now was hatching a plan and there would be no stopping me. I needed to know what was really being hidden from me in London and I knew that I had to go. There was no point delaying. My mind was reeling with excitement and anticipation. I would find out all the answers for myself. I would take the stage couch and the money that was saved in my large chest and soon I would confront the tyranny of my father and find out exactly why he was lying to me. My fear was real and apparent but I knew that if I delayed it would be too late and I would be sent to Paris and forgotten.

That night I tiptoed down to the kitchen and packed a bag with meats and bread. I then went to the stables and took some old riding jodhpurs and a flat cap. I went back to my room and folded some clothes into an old tapestry woven bag packed in the meats and bread and settled down to sleep.

At first light I awoke. Carefully tucked my money into the side of my bag and crept down the stairs. The house was silent save for the ticking of the grandfather clock in the hall and the sighing of the dog in the parlour. I carefully lifted the latch at the kitchen garden door and crept out into the early morning haze. The air was chilly and the dew seeped into the corners of my shoes. My hair was tightly piled upon my head and the cap fixed well forward on my head so it covered my face. I kept to the grass so that my footsteps would not be heard on the gravel and wake anyone. Before I knew it I was down the path and on the main road that led to the village. I reckoned that I had at least a two-hour walk before I reached the next village and the town station where the stagecoach to London would leave. I had done this journey two years before at the beginning of my illness when I had been taken to London to go to visit a doctor so I knew where to go.

After an hour my feet began to pinch and were sodden by the wet roads. My shoes were not used to the constant pounding over irregular cobbles and I longed to sit down and have the luxury of my warm bed. The sun was rising and people were getting up. Chimneys began to smoke and large clouds of vapour began to loom in the sky. I kept my face to the ground and avoided the "Morning Lad" greetings that the locals were saying and replied with a nod afraid to give myself away with my feminine voice. It began to rain. I held my bag close to me and started to run. I kept close to the trees to try to get some shelter. It wasn't long before I was approaching the town. The rain had stopped but I was already soaked completely by the downpour and the early morning coldness. I walked down the vaguely familiar street and reached the stagecoach stop. There seemed to be quite a lot of people waiting for the coach.

"I need a ticket to London," I asked in the lowest voice I could muster.

"One way?" Came an unimpressed reply.

"Yes"

"That's four pennies for outside and six pennies for inside and the coach stops near Reading for the night so you'll need money for lodgings"

"Yes I know" I gruffly replied.

I pushed six pennies towards the teller and received my ticket.

"There's a coach in an hour then another two hours after that" The station master announced.

We waited for an hour and just on time the coach arrived. I stepped up into the carriage momentarily forgetting that I was a boy then stood to allow the ladies to take their seats first. With everyone aboard we began to set off and the horses began to canter on their long journey. Suddenly there was a whinnying of horses as they screeched to a halt. A wave of fear passed through me and for a moment I worried that someone had discovered my disappearance informed the police and that they had stopped the carriage to check the occupants.

"Sorry ladies!" The driver poked his head through the window.

"Just another young lad for the coach! Nearly missed it by a whisker"

I breathed a great sigh of relief and huddled my arms around my cold sodden body. It wasn't long before the rocking motion of the carriage had lulled me off to sleep. I slept deeply. I was wedged between a large round woman of around thirty who produced a scrawny ball of wool when we set off and began tapping her needles away as she knitted a blue creation. To my left was an elderly gentleman of about seventy with large hairy ears and a solemn stony expression.

I awoke shortly after one. We had been travelling for around four hours and we were making a rest stop for an hour. I jumped down from the carriage and eased out my limbs. I still felt shivery and my clothes now had a musty sodden smell.

Chapter 13

I stretched my legs and moved around the dusty street whilst the horses rested and my fellow passengers wandered into a neighbouring inn to drink some ale and refresh themselves. I kept my cap pulled tightly over my face and tried to look down so that no one would take too much notice of me. My clothes that had been soaked that morning had now dried a little. They still clung to me like damp rags on an autumn washing line, never able to get completely dried. I could feel the lingering wetness penetrating into my chest and I began to cough. I longed to pull my shawl from my bag and wrap it around my shoulders but I had only packed some girls clothes and desperately did not want to arouse any suspicion so left it undisturbed in my bag.

I went into the inn and ordered a bowl of broth hoping that the warm soup would stop any stirrings of fever before they started. I drank hungrily dipping some warm chunks of loaf into the thick meaty liquid. A fire roared in the corner and after I had eaten I went to warm and dry myself beside the glowing embers.

"Five minutes till the coach for Reading" The driver came in and announced. I shuffled staring only at the floor and found my way back to the coach and religiously we all found our seats and I wedged myself between the hairy ears and the blue knitting.

All aboard we set off, the hooves of the horses rumbling over the cobbles and taking me nearer and nearer to my destination and my truth.

Surely by now Maud would have discovered my empty bed. Mrs Knight would have sent someone to search the stables and the rest of the estate to see where I was and tell me that my breakfast was waiting. They would know I was missing but they wouldn't know why or where I had gone. Tom would have known. He would be the only one who would know. I wondered whether he would have told anyone. I wondered whether they would have contacted the police and whether there would be a search party on its way.

I fell asleep again but this time when I awoke I was shivering and my head hurt with such a pounding ache that it felt like a pulsating bruise. When I tried to lift it or move, the pain stabbed with such a sharp intensity that it felt like a knife piercing through my skull. I could almost hear Dr Emanuel's deep voice warning me.

"Alice you must take great care following your illness and stay out of the cold and rain. The pneumonia and ague will find your weak chest and you will surely be afflicted!"

I hated to agree but I knew he was right. Anyway there was no going back. I was on a mission and my way ahead was clear even if I had to stagger there.

Night had fallen by the time we arrived in Reading. We halted abruptly outside an inn and were told that there were several boarding establishments along this road and to make sure that we were back on the coach by the morning at eight otherwise it would leave and we would be stranded. Everyone nodded and mumbled acknowledgement and we all began to disembark.

The first inn had a sign in the window saying "No Vacancies" and most of the carriage were spilling into the next establishment. Desperate to rest my weary head and take some nourishment from the bread and meat that I had packed I walked down the narrow road dimly lit by one old gas lamp and found the next inn but the sign in the window said that it was also full. Several more guesthouses and all the same signs. I began to feel very weak and in urgent need of a bed. I turned down a dark alley and began to feebly walk towards another row of houses hoping that my luck would change and I would find somewhere to stay. Suddenly out of the darkness appeared a figure. He was large and bulky and blocked my way.

"Excuse me sir?" I announced boldly.

The shadow moved out of the darkness and I could see his face red and foul smelling of drink.

"What have we here little lad!" He taunted me.

I turned to avoid this most unpleasant character but another leapt out from the shadows and blocked my path from behind.

"Seems to be a young lad," He replied to the stranger in front of me.

"What do you have there? Nice bag for a young boy like you. What have you got in there?"

I clung tightly to my bag aware that all my money was tucked into the side pocket and without that I could not get to London.

"It's mine!" I scolded.

"It's his Seamus!"Laughed the boy behind me. I then felt two powerful arms reach over to my shoulders, as he restrained me the other grabbed the bag from me.

"Give it back," I screamed.

A hand came down firmly over my mouth to shut me up. I struggled to fight the rogue so viciously handling me. As I did so my cap fell off my head and my long fair locks tumbled over my shoulders.

"So what's this then Bill? I think our lad is no lad at all but a bonny lass!"

"Yes and a feisty one too" Bill agreed

"Well there's nothing better to finish an evening of good ale than a nice feisty lass! I'll be a gentleman Seamus and let you have her first"

"Why thank you good sir!" At that he grabbed my wrists and began to drag me to a doorway at the side of the alley. Trembling I wished that I had stayed safely at home. My heels were digging into the hard stone floor and the morning's blisters were swelling under the pressure of my efforts to restrain.

From the shadows another figure appeared and I heard a thud of fist on jaw and Bill fell to the ground and began moaning. Seamus let go of my wrists and I ran and hid further down the alley. I could hear the pounding of knuckles and the crunching of bones and then Seamus slumped into a dead weight pile on top of Bill. The dark figure of my saviour picked up my tapestry bag and began to approach me.

I felt giddy with my fever, my assault and the smell of urine and dead rats along the alley but I had been well brought up and I gathered the courage to approach my defender and retrieve my bag.

"Thank you kind sir" I began. As I approached I recognised the figure standing before me. I recoiled aghast but remembered that he had saved my bag and my honour.

"Here's your bag Miss Alice"

"Thank you Tom"

"And your cap Miss Alice best put that on quickly"

We hastily walked to the end of the alley and to the light of the street at the end. A little guesthouse had a sign with the magic letters that spelled out "rooms available".

"We'd better get those" Tom suggested the whole town seems to be full tonight.

I pulled my cap tightly over my face and we walked in. I was shaken and baffled by Toms appearance but so relieved at the sight of his friendly face.

"Two rooms for one night please" Tom asked.

A woman with a very large frame and several rolling chins looked at the pair of us.

"Brothers are you?"

We nodded earnestly.

72

"Fancy for brothers to have two rooms? Well I've only got one room left for tonight and you'll not get anything else around here for tonight as every where's full by now so you'll just have to share"

I threw a glare at Tom but knew it would look suspicious to protest so said nothing.

"Come this way" The round lady began to waddle off like a goose and we followed her like obedient cygnets.

"This is your room" Its sixpence for the night and there's a pitcher of water on the side and hot water if you want to fetch it from the stove in the kitchen."

I went to my bag and took out the money, which I handed to her and she left us in the small but clean little room.

I turned to Tom.

"How did you know where I was? How did you find me?"

"The gate miss"

"Pardon?

"I'd been waiting for you to do something like this and when I heard the kitchen gate squeak as you opened it this morning I knew it must be you so I got up and followed you. Kept my distance behind mind as I daren't be seen by you, so had to wait till everyone was on the coach before I got my ticket, so very nearly missed it but I didn't and I'm very glad Miss Alice that I was there for you"

"Yes Tom, thank you Tom. Thank you for saving me"

I hadn't noticed previously but a large bruise was forming around Tom's eye and his hand was bleeding.

"Oh Tom are you hurt?"

"No Miss, I'll be fine miss. I'll be off miss. I'll see you in the morning"

"Where are you going?

"It's not right for me to be here miss with you in this room"

73

My head was spinning and I was feeling very faint however I knew that it would be wrong to dismiss Tom after all he had done to save me.

"No Tom you will stay and be my guard. What if those rogues came and find me? No you shall sleep on the floor there's enough blankets."

"Thank you miss" He stammered

"You are very kind miss".

I poured some water from the pitcher and dipped in a cloth. I approached Tom and began to gently dab away the blood from his brow and over his cut eye.

"Thank you so much Miss Alice, but you don't have to do that". He looked up at me earnestly and our eyes locked for several seconds. His blue eyes so endearing like a grateful puppy. I smiled and withdrew my gaze. I reached to wash his hand and he held mine with the softest of touches that made me shiver with excitement. I didn't know what was coming over me and assumed that my illness was consuming my body and making my mind hallucinate.

I moved over to the bed and stripped off two blankets that I gave to Tom who duly pulled a cushion from a chair to the floor and proceeded to make a bed for himself.

"Are you hungry Tom?" I asked

"Just a little Miss Alice"

I pulled out the bread and meats from my bag and we sat together eating our little picnic. Tom ate hungrily and I assumed that he had very little if any money on him and so had probably not eaten all day long.

"That was wonderful," He announced wiping his mouth.

I smiled once again and we laughed like children.

"So will you return to the country tomorrow Tom?"

"No miss"

"Why not, where are you going?"
Tom looked at me and his eyes were creased at the stupidity of my question.

"Why London Miss Alice"
We laughed again and the tone in my voice softened till the class distinction between the stable lad and the girl dressed as a boy dissolved like a teaspoon of sugar in a cup of tea.

"I don't think it's right that a lady should travel all that way unescorted even if she does look like a chimney sweeps younger brother"
I bashfully lowered my lashes and a huge grin erupted over my face.

"You are quite right Tom. You are my saviour. I wouldn't like to think what may have happened to me if you hadn't shown up at the very moment that you did"
I shivered at the thought.

"This is all my fault" Tom began.

"I shouldn't have told you what I saw. I am responsible for any harm that could have befallen you. You wouldn't be here if it were not for my foolishness. I am just a stupid boy"

"No Tom, it is I who is foolish and stupid. I know better than to creep away in the night. It is my furtive imagination and my unrelenting curiosity that has brought us here, not you. You did the right thing to tell me and I thank you for that"

"So there are no bad feelings between us anymore Miss Alice and you forgive me for all my behaviour in the past?"
I threw Tom a cheeky smile and shook my head.

"No Tom there are no hard feelings but I still do not forgive you!"
In my mind I wasn't quite sure what the original grudge had really been about. I assumed that it was because of Tom's outburst when he had discovered that I was teaching Maud to

read. I had played it along over such a period of time that the whole thing was really disproportionate and inflated to a status far beyond its worth.

In my mind I forgave him and quite naturally, after all he had saved my life, but I still couldn't bring myself to actually say the words to his face.

"I think we should try to get to sleep" Tom suggested

"You have had a very hard day Miss Alice and we have the same amount of travelling tomorrow we won't get to London till quite late"

"You're right Tom. I am exhausted"

I washed in the little basin and then blew out the candle and closed the curtains so that the room was plunged into darkness. I undressed under the blankets in the bed and was relieved to throw off the still damp clothes. Tom lay in his makeshift bed on the floor very still.

My head rested on the pillow and all the insanity of the day began to whiz around in my mind till it was spiralling like autumn leaves on a windy day.

I snuggled into the pillow and soon drifted into the sweetest of sleeps.

"Goodnight Miss Alice and please wont you forgive me?"

I didn't reply.

In my mind I was far away dreaming of my father that I would find in London. A father that had not abandoned me. A father that loved me. Who had no intention of sending me off to Paris.

A dream that in my heart I knew was only a dream..........

Chapter 14

I woke to the sounds of birds chirping in the still air. The trees seemed to be filled with a chorus of early morning autumn life and awakening.

I got out of bed and went over to the curtains pulled the crack between the lining with my little finger and peered out over the dusky fields.

In the distance cows were walking to a barn to be milked and the farmer was blowing his whistle and signalling to his collies. The pane of glass felt cold to my touch and soon misted up as I lingered at the window watching the day unfolding before me.

Tom sighed behind me. I turned and saw him stretched out on his back, head tilted to one side, eyes closed and dreaming. He seemed peaceful. I had never seen him without the worried lines on his face and the constant expression of anxiety. I tiptoed over to him. The bruise above his eye had developed into a purple yellow tinge. Instinctively I reached to touch him like a mother reaching to touch her sleeping child. His skin was soft and his features bold. For a moment he didn't look like a servant but like a young man, handsome and strong.

Tom opened his eyes and seemed bewildered and confused as to why I was kneeling beside him.

"Alice?"

"Yes Tom" I replied bemused by the fact that he had called me by my name and omitted my title.

"Is it morning?"

Tom began to sit up and squinted his eyes at the sun that was flooding the room.

"It's a beautiful day. You can hear the birds chirping and the cows bellowing in the fields. I think we need to get up and prepare for the coach to London."

"Yes" Tom muttered. He got up wandered around the room and then uncomfortably turned to me and looked me square in the eyes.

"Alice, I think I need to take you home. You seem unwell and yesterday evening must have been a big shock for you. You won't like what this journey will bring you. You will not be happy. You are better off to go home where you are safe and cared for."

Tom had such a strained expression in his eyes. His genuine look of concern made me feel so vulnerable and especially at this moment alone in this room with only a flimsy shawl wrapped around my nightshirt. No one had ever made me feel like they cared for me and I wanted to respond to this unusual feeling within me by reaching for him. I knew I could not, which made it all the more difficult.

"Tom I thank you for your concern and somewhere inside me what you are saying makes perfect sense and I know that you are right. However all my life I have been dutiful and correct and have never ventured beyond the invisible barriers that restrained me. Now I feel that I have wings and if I don't fly now than I will never know the truth and I will never understand what my life is about and why I have been brought up in the way that I have. I cannot continue living with so many questions and so much uncertainty, I need the answers and I am prepared for them even if they prove to be damaging to me."

Tom turned his gaze from me almost afraid to look into my defiant grey eyes.

"You are a very brave girl Alice. You have a lot of courage to say what you just said. You have a lion's heart and I admire you so much for that"

"So do you understand Tom that I must go on? I must do this."

"Yes Miss Alice but I want to be there for you. You need to be protected."

"Oh Tom!" I sighed "Thank you for that."

Inside me I wanted to cry. No one had made me feel so special and in tune with my thoughts. No one had ever complied with my wishes as if they were their own and that felt very special to me. In a way I felt indebted to Tom for sharing this with me. He had not been invited on this unsolicited trip yet here he was sprung from the shadows, my ally and protector and I was so grateful that he was here and that he understood me.

Tom left the room and went down to the parlour to fetch some hot water for me to wash. He then discreetly disappeared again allowing me some privacy. When he returned he had my breeches and shirt with him.

"Thank you Tom" I said as I took them from him.

"Oh my gosh they are warm where have they been?"

Tom smiled at me sheepishly.

"I took them down and laid them over the stove. Wanted to get all the dampness out of them didn't want you getting any iller."

"Thank you! Oh they're lovely and warm"

Tom nodded and left the room again so that I could change. When I was suitably attired as a boy again I gathered up my things and we left to make our way back to the coach stop for our final journey to London.

Throughout the journey with each clip clop of the horse's hooves I thought of Tom sitting above the carriage. I thought of his fair hair scattered in an unruly fashion around his face. I thought of his protective arms fighting off my assailants. Tom was my hero and now he was accompanying me on this most horrible of journeys so that I could find my answers. There was no motive for Tom. When he had left unannounced the last time he was told in no uncertain terms that he would be out of a job if he ever disappeared again and now he was risking he livelihood for me. How could I repay him? I had a little money but I knew that he deserved far more than that. Lost in my thoughts I took little notice of the fever that was creeping over my body and the heat that was gently rising and making me feel giddy and light headed. The carriage rocked and I slept gently fighting dreams of disappointment and sadness.

It was dark when we arrived in London. The air was different. It smelt like burnt chestnuts. The streetlights seemed to twinkle in a different way to Somerset. Noises on the street from the cantering on cobbles to the corner vendors seemed to melt into one great explosion of sounds. Voices, cockneyed twangs, lights colours and enormous buildings. I couldn't wait for the coach to arrive. I was jumping around in my seat eager to drink in all the wonder of being in London.

"Never been to London before?" Said the elderly hairy eared man to my left as he sensed my excitement and anticipation.

"Not for a long while" I replied with a smile. Then buried my face down into my lap for fear that my voice had betrayed me. He spoke no more and it was not long before the carriage ground to a halt and everyone began to disembark. I grabbed my bag and stood beside the carriage. Tom jumped down from the top and we retreated hastily into the darkness.

"Where do we go Tom?"

"We go and find you some lodgings for the night. You look so pale and fatigued Alice I am most worried."

"Oh Tom you fuss so much." I coughed.

"Can you not see that you are not well."

"Won't we go to try to find my father now?"

"No Miss Alice it is much too late and you must rest we have all day tomorrow and you will need your strength to face the answers that you will find."

I looked at Tom with that acquiescing look that told him that I knew he was right. We found lodgings almost straight away and without the problems of the previous night. I paid for two rooms and I ordered hot water for a bath. We ate quickly finishing off the breads and meats that I had brought with.

Once I had soaked in my lovely warm bath and then climbed into my bed my mind began to sift through the absurdity that was the last two days until I drifted into a much needed and restful sleep. However my body had received a deep chill on the previous day and when I awoke in the morning I was feeling most peculiar and unwell. My throat felt raspy and dry and my body ached whilst my head throbbed.

"Are you feeling unwell again?" Tom asked as we partook of our breakfast.

"No I feel fine" I lied.

I smoothed down my skirts and swept back my freshly washed hair. I had made a real effort this morning getting dressed and was quite pleased to be back in pretty girls clothes after my two day journey dressed as a shabby boy.

"So, will you escort me to this address "14 Inverness Gardens"?"

"If you would like me to" Tom nodded.

"Do you remember how to get there? I enquired

"Alice surely you will want to take a carriage, it's not befitting for you to go trawling around the streets in your fine dresses."

"Yes I forgot Tom. It's not like back home where everything is only five minutes away. This is London the big city"

"Its enormous Alice and so many grand houses and shops and everything you could imagine in the world."

"I don't care about any of that. I just want to get to my father. Will you take me? Can we go now?

Tom could see my impatience. He could also see that I was really becoming quite unwell as I kept relapsing into fits of dry chesty coughing.

"Well what are you waiting for?" He teased.

I grabbed my bag and we went out into the street. It was still quite early but unlike back home where maybe only a few people would be venturing out at this hour, there were hundreds of people up and down the streets on their way to work and school. We hailed down a carriage and leapt inside. Tom held his hand out for me to step up and I accepted it gratefully. Soon we were out of the bustle and the horses were trotting down some leafy lanes beside a big park. We turned into the street that I had been trying to imagine for almost a week. It wasn't what I anticipated. The houses were close together and were surrounded by huge wrought iron gates.

We alighted from the carriage and I paid the driver.

"That's the house" Nodded Tom as we stood on the corner of the street.

I stood quite petrified my feet seemed rooted to the place where I stood. I could feel myself trembling and my heart beating faster and faster.

"I'll not come any further," Tom said.

I look very scruffy and would be an embarrassment to be near you. Also if your father saw me and found out that I had led you to him he would kill me, of that I am sure!"

I didn't disagree with Tom and picked up my bag and began to walk towards the house. As I approached the heavy oak door opened and a young boy emerged. I watched him unaware that I was standing alone in the street now staring at him. He saw me and began to approach. There was nowhere to hide.

"Good Morning miss." He announced with a sharp crisp accent and a glowing smile.

"Good morning" I curtsied.

"May I be of some assistance to you?"

I hesitated unsure as to what to say to this stranger. My head was beginning to spin a little and my fever was rising.

"Yes I am looking for the home of Edward Sinclair"

"You mean Sir Edward Sinclair?"

"Oh of course" I replied shocked at the news of the knighthood. The young man smiled and shook his head at me.

"I'm sorry you have just missed him he has left already for the day but my father should be home by six tonight. Might I enquire as to your name?"

My knees were rapidly buckling under my weight. My mouth had turned dry and I was trying to suppress the urge to cry out.

"Your name miss?" He enquired again.

"Alice. I am his niece Alice." I quickly lied.

The road began to spin. The sky began to fall and crush me until I could no longer hear his voice or the mention of his words "my father".

Chapter 15

I opened my eyes and quickly closed them again. My ears seemed
to be blocked and the sounds that I could hear were all muffled
and distorted. My head a heavy weight like a boulder lay on a
great array of pillows.

My body was numb. As I lifted my head a huge wave of nausea
overcame me and I fell back quite helpless.

"Who is she?"

"She's our cousin silly!"

"What cousin?"

"Fathers sister's daughter in Northampton!"

"Oh the one we have never seen?"

"Yes Emily!"

"Is she dead?"

"No Jane she's just sick!"

"Why's she sick?"

"Because she has travel sickness of course!"

"Where did she come from Charlotte?"

"Bertie found her in the street and she fainted so he brought her
in."

"Mama! Mama! Look Bertie has found our cousin Alice and
she is sick! Come mama quickly!"

I could hear a ruffle of skirts. I felt a soft hand gently touch my
cheek and my forehead.

"Charlotte call for the doctor immediately, this poor girl is
burning up. Hurry Charlotte!"

"I found her in the street Mama. She was just standing quite
alone with no carriage and just this old cloth bag. She was
looking for father and she told me she was his niece."

"This must be one of Mary's girls although I thought they were much older than this girl. She looks around seventeen the same age as Charlotte."

"Yes Mama she does look quite young!"

The voices faded again and all I was aware of were hands holding mine, wet flannels soothing my aching brow.

"Oh Doctor Gibson thank you so much for coming so swiftly. This is my niece she has just arrived and she appears to have a fever."

"Yes Lady Sinclair. Of course. What is the girls name?"

"Alice doctor, her name is Alice."

I felt a warm but heavy hand gently touch my arm.

"Alice?"

I stirred a little unable to fight the ague that had captured my feeble body and was holding it, bound and restricted unable to move.

The hand moved to my head. It was firm and the palm felt slightly callous and rough.

"Sit her up Lady Sinclair I need to listen to her chest."

I could hear the older woman, her voice soft but firm asking all the children to leave the room. She then gently leaned towards me and whispered

"Alice I need to remove your clothes so the doctor can listen to your chest"

I nodded in acquiescence unable to form any words or create any sounds. She unbuttoned my blouse and I felt the hard cold metal of the doctor's stethoscope being pressed between my ribs. I began to cough. A deep rasping cough that I could not contain. The doctor pulled a handkerchief from his bag and told me to spit into it. He then turned to Lady Sinclair and shook his head.

"This girl is quite seriously ill. Her lungs are very congested and it has travelled quite deep. She must stay in bed and not

85

move. She is to only eat broth and I will bring a physic that she must take five times a day. Winter is coming and the air is very cold. I have seen people die from less than this girl has. We must exercise extreme caution with her if she is to survive!"
Lady Sinclair called to her maid to bring fresh nightwear and to warm it over the warm plates on the stove first. I felt her lift my arms and wrap me in the soft linen then gently I felt myself being carried up to a bedroom where I was laid in a great canopied bed swathed with silk curtains. A fire roared in the corner and the great shutters on the long glass windows remained tightly shut obscuring the world from my present state.

"May we see her mother?" Voices asked.

"Of course my dears she is your cousin she will be grateful for your stories and laughter. Only don't tire her too much otherwise she will not regain her strength"

"Will we get word to father?"

"No we will have to wait. Father has been called away on urgent business to Somerset. Must be some political business. He will be away for a few days. This will be a surprise for him when he returns."
Despite my position I felt fear and angst. In between my states of consciousness I knew full well what business my father had been called away on. A missing daughter would be good reason enough for him to go. I ached. The pain I was feeling was cutting enough to slice right through me. My head pounded and my heart felt like it had been ripped from my chest chewed by a dog then thrown back into my twisted body. I had never known deception. I had read about it in books but never believed that it could be so. My father whom I adored but feared was father to another family. It could not be. Was I hallucinating? Was my mind sick along with my body?

"Here is your physic Alice" Lady Sinclair lifted my head and pressed a teaspoon of dark liquid to my lips.

It smelt foul. It reminded me of the smell of rotting dung in the summer heat. I opened my mouth and obediently swallowed the potion. The dreadful liquid slipped down my throat like thick oil. I shuddered tasting the revolting residue on my lips.

"It's alright Alice. It will make you well"

I slept. I thought for the first time. My mind had little activity to take me on any more bizarre journeys. The sedative mixed with the medicine numbed my brain and quite happily I succumbed to the power of the vile liquid that could remove me from this painful reality.

I drifted for what seemed like minutes but the room changed from light to dark and I assumed that days must have been passing. My only knowledge of what was going on was from the excited burble of the children when they came to my room and attempted to stir me with their chatter.

Lady Sinclair was very kind to me and spent time with me every day making sure that I drank my medicine and that I had a little soup. There were five children. Albert eighteen, Charlotte at seventeen was only a few months older than me. Then Emily fifteen, Jane twelve and Archie who was ten. They were all very vociferous and secretly I loved being in their presence. They kept calling me cousin but I knew that really they were my brothers and sisters and I was warming to them so much because maybe in my dreams that was all that I had ever wanted. I never let on that they were any more than cousins to me. I knew that my solitude and loneliness had brought me a gift of wisdom that my siblings did not have. They would not be able to face the truth. This dreadful truth, which had been hidden from me for so long.

I wondered what had become of Tom. I felt very guilty because he had helped me so much and now I had abandoned him. Had he gone back home or had he lingered around waiting to hear of my progress? I hoped that had he returned he would not be in too much trouble due to his second disappearance.

Lady Sinclair unfolded the shutters and let the dim light into the room. The days were cold and my fire was stoked almost constantly to stop it going out. The colour was beginning to return to my cheeks and I was attempting to sit up in my bed a little.

"Lady Sinclair" I began.

"I must thank you so much for your kindness and hospitality. I feel I have imposed on your family and taken you all away from your lives. I shall be leaving soon and returning to my home."

Lady Sinclair turned to me shaking her head and came and took my hand.

"This is nonsense Alice! You are family and you are ill. It is our duty to look after you and care for you. We wouldn't have it any other way. My husband has always been so distant about his family and his sister Mary and her children and it has been a great shame that we have not met before. We are genuinely happy that you are with us and that we can care for you. We wouldn't have it any other way."

I smiled graciously at the sincerity in her voice but knew that I must get out of this house quickly before my father returned. In my mind I was thinking of all kinds of ways to escape, from skimming over the balcony in my night clothes to tiptoeing out in the dead of night. Physically I knew it was all impossible but mentally my bags were packed. What would happen when father came home? What would happen to me? Would the truth all come out? I didn't want to think of the consequences. I felt too weak to deal with the next nightmare in this never ending night of demons.

I wondered where and how I had come to be. My father was a politician and not the military man he had professed to be. Maybe it's true what they say about all politicians being liars. Tom had been right about my father's pale face and smooth hands. Soldiers in the Sudan had weathered complexions and hard hands. I wondered why I had never doubted him. I was not stupid and had read many journals about the war to know that my father lacked any experience of action. Who was my mother? I had always believed that my home belonged to my mother's estate but was that true? Was anything real? Was the only reality, that I was the bastard daughter of Edward Sinclair?

A clip clop in the road and the halting of a carriage. The heavy brush of feet over the entrance porch way and then the voice that I thought I knew so well.

"I am home my darlings."

I could hear the scurry of the children as they raced to their father downstairs. I could hear them embracing and kissing, the girls dresses floating around them as their father, my father spun them around.

"There's a surprise father!" Emily's voice giggled.

"Oh I like surprises my little poppit. Where is mother?"

"She's upstairs with the surprise" teased Archie.

"Well lets go and see what you have for me" Replied my unwittingly keen father.

I felt my heart thud with every step that my father took up the stairway. As he walked along the hall the perspiration was rising. I felt like I would burst if I did not wake from this terrible scene. As the door opened I wanted to hide beneath the covers and scream. I was frozen in fear. I prayed that my illness would overcome me and I would die right now in this instant.

"Father" the children chanted.

"Father this is your surprise! This is Alice!"

The jubilant face of the homecoming father who had walked through the door dropped like a heavy stone and the expression of harshness that I knew to be *my* father pierced me with cold angry eyes.

Chapter 16

There was a frozen moment in the room. It was like the stillness of death. Even the trees outside ceased to rustle their autumn foliage. The ice on the window panes seemed to be seeping under the sill and blanketing the room.

"Father you are so rude!" Emily sighed.

"This is our cousin Alice your niece? She prompted.

"Don't greet her so formally she is your sister Mary's daughter!"

The hardness in my father's face was exchanged with a look of relief and surprise. So his game had not been exposed and he had me to thank for that.

"Of course Emily" He smiled rigidly, came over and pecked a kiss on my forehead.

"Welcome Alice" He announced with a note of distain in his voice.

"Alice has been unwell Edward. She arrived here a few days ago and collapsed in the street outside our door. Albert brought her in and we called the doctor who says that her lungs are very weak and she must stay in bed and rest till she is completely recovered. The children have been excellent hosts and have welcomed their new cousin to our home"

Lady Sinclair smiled at her husband and he raised her hand to his lips and kissed it tenderly. She laughed almost embarrassedly and retracted her hand. The younger children had their arms wrapped around their father and he exuded warmth with them all that I had never seen in him before. I felt jealous. I felt angry that the love and laughter in this house, the love from him, had been denied to me for all these years. Why was I so hated?

My father turned to me and caught a glimpse of my pursed brow and curious expression that questioned his actions and his contempt of me.

"I wish to speak to Alice, I would like to hear news of my sister and her family."

"Alice must not have too much excitement dear" Lady Sinclair interjected.

"We all would like to find out more about her but have refrained from asking her too many questions on the advice of the doctor. She is not to be strained. Her lungs are very weak. We are most concerned for her."

My father turned to his wife and nodded.

"Of course Eleanor, don't worry I wish to only spend a few moments with her. I will follow you all down presently to the morning room and I will hear your news during my time away" He rose and opened the bedroom door. Without question everyone left knowing full well that he would speak to me if that was his wish and no one could stop him. I lay still, watching with fearful eyes as everyone filed past and through the door. It was as if all my armour, all my protection was leaving and I would have to face his wrath alone. He turned to me. I tried to keep my gaze direct. Stop myself from being vulnerable, from being just another silly girl that couldn't keep her head high.

"So Alice, you found me. What a clever girl you are!"

There was a definite note of malice in his voice. I said nothing and kept my eyes focused.

"How did you find out? Mrs Knight? Mrs Dunn? Which of those damned servants that cannot hold their tongues! They have all been paid handsomely for their silence yet a word has surely been spoken otherwise you would not have found me!"

So they all knew. I knew that they had been hiding secrets from me. I knew that they all considered me locked in my childhood and innocence. Little did they realise that I had grown up. I had questioned, and now I had found out of my own accord the terrible secrets that they were hiding from me.

"You have no rights here Alice! You should not have come to this place! This is my home and you are just nothing, nothing do you hear!"

His voice was rising and the redness was breaking through the little capillaries in his face. I could feel my palms tightening beneath the bedclothes and I longed to jump from the covers and slap him hard round his face for his cruelty and harshness towards me.

"You will not blackmail me Alice! There is no financial gain for you here. If you came to seek revenge and fortune than you are getting in far too deep for your position! Why could you not just obey my commands and go quietly to Paris and live your life there as you were told? Why are you so disobedient? You are a thorn to me. A poisonous thorn intruding into my life. You must leave! You disgust me!"

He turned and thumped his fist onto the marble mantelpiece. Then stood breathing heavily whilst I digested his venom. Still I said nothing. There were no words that could express my deep shock and hurt. How dare he think that I had come here looking for financial gain. How strange that the real reason would never be known or comprehended by him. The greying flecks at the sides of his dark hair reminded me of silver worms like the snakes and worms in a picture that I had of Medusa. Snakes weaving and twisting like this man who was destroying me from the inside leaving my heart like a charred lump of coal. I felt crushed but nevertheless still defiant.

"Father?"

He turned to me arrows still shooting from his eyes.

"I am not a child! I am not a thorn! I am your daughter, your flesh and blood! We share the same characteristics; you will not treat me in the way that you have all my life! I am not here to try to extract your money and I do not understand why you would even think such a thing from me. I can only imagine that this thought comes from some other consequences of your actions. Nothing surprises me with you anymore. I am here now and intend to stay till I am well. I will not leave; I still have much to find out! Your wife and other children have been most kind to me and I wish to repay them but not by upping and leaving in this state. I will recover first. I know what I must do and no one will stop me. I will not betray your secret. I will not tell the world your lies but you will treat me with respect!"

My father turned, his eyes glaring, his cheeks ablaze. He marched towards the bed his fist raised.

I sat up firmly.

"Yes father, strike me, I dare you! It will be nothing compared to the unseen bruises that you have already given me."

He stopped and snorted loudly. His countenance showed he was confused by my audacious outburst. He lowered his fist and stormed from the room slamming the door behind him.

I lay back on the pillows. I did not cry which surprised me. I felt very strong and bold. I was replaying the whole episode in my mind over and over and wondering how my father would respond to the new Alice, the new me that he had never encountered before. In fact I wondered what the new Alice was going to do next. I felt that I now had some power over my father and it felt very reassuring that I could dictate a little the pathway of my future. I was so deep in my thoughts that I didn't hear the gentle tapping on the door.

"Alice may I come in?" I heard a voice behind the door

"Yes Albert, of course you may" I replied.

94

Albert entered the room. He had the same stature and physique as my father but he had the gentle eyes soft features and light brown hair of his mother. He pulled a chair beside the bed and held a newspaper journal in his hand.

"I have come to read to you Cousin Alice, if I may," He corrected himself.

"Of course cousin Albert" I smiled. I would love you to read to me.

"Oh anything to get out of that sombre room downstairs. Father is not usually so antisocial and distant"

"Isn't he?" I questioned amusingly

"Oh no he is quite timid really; he is responsible for so many political decisions so his communication skills are most superb"

"Really" I nodded, trying to stop my absolute amazement showing in my face.

"Yes, I think father must be troubled with a lot of work issues as well as some unpleasant issues in Somerset that he has just returned from attending. He is in a growl of a mood and has dismissed everyone from the room whilst he drinks his whisky. He doesn't often drink whisky so it's probably something terrible."

Albert caught the concerned look on my face.

"But please don't take any of this personally; it is nothing to do with you. I'm sure when father gets to know you he will adore you as much as we all do."

Albert's hand gently came to rest on top of mine and in the brief second of silence that followed we exchanged smiles.

"You really are the most charming cousin I have ever had the pleasure to know Cousin Alice. I am very honoured that you have come to stay with us"

"Thank you Albert, I am so glad that I am here and I am grateful for your kindness. It is very reassuring for me at this difficult time. Now tell me what was this unpleasant business that my f....uncle had to attend to in Somerset?"

"Oh some terrible business! I don't really know exactly what it is but father is terribly encumbered by some burdensome business that he wishes would be eliminated altogether. Only recently he mentioned that the troubles in Somerset had all been resolved and that he could wipe his hands of them but now they seem to have resurfaced again and it is really quite awful to see father afflicted so badly by this."

"Oh dear Albert, what a shame for your father to find that he can't wipe his hands of this terrible thorn in his side!"
Albert looked at me questioningly.

"That sounded a little sharp Alice, are you mocking?"

"No. Now why would I do that?"

"I apologise Alice of course you wouldn't do that, you must only want what is best for your uncle too, don't you?"
I smiled and gestured to the journal.

"So what is happening in the country?"
Momentarily distracted from my rather cynical behaviour, Albert sat back and began to read the news to me. However my mind was wandering quite carelessly and going down routes that I had never dreamed I could venture. I still had so much to discover about my father. He obviously had more skeletons in his closet than I had assumed and here in his cosy little home they were all oblivious to the deceptive lying man whom they called father. I still believed that there was so much more to learn and I would have to get my father to tell me what I needed to know. It would not be easy but if my father was a manipulative liar than surely I must have inherited a little of those traits from him, otherwise I could not lie here in his house and plan the things that I was planning. I wondered about my mother. I desperately needed to know what she was like and whether she had loved me. What had

she intended to do with me her illegitimate daughter? I suppose all her decisions would have been voided by her death at my birth.

"Isn't that quite fascinating Alice?"

"Oh yes I nodded at Albert" Completely unaware about what item of news he had just read to me.

"So there will be a royal wedding after all."

"Who's?"

"Were you not listening at all?"

"Prince George and Princess Mary of Teck! He is to marry his deceased brothers fiancée!"

"Yes quite fascinating, very fascinating."

But my mind was focused far away on a very different agenda.

Chapter 17

Albert was becoming a very attentive cousin. He came and sat
with me every day and read to me or sang to me. He had
wonderful books of poetry that were quite modern and very
unlike the library of dusty books that I had all but read at home
back in Somerset. I loved Albert's charm and the consideration
he showed, if I so much as winced in pain or coughed. He would
fuss over me so and sometimes being the girl that I was, I teased
and let him think that I was in a far worse state. Albert would
respond by being quite offended and I would have to apologise
for my temporary lapse. Of course I lapped up all his attention
like a kitten that had just been introduced to cream. Not only
from him but from all my new brothers and sisters. To me this
was the happy families that one read about in books. This was too
good to recover from and go home. I wanted to stay in this house
of laughter forever, but I knew that could not be. I had heard my
father's voice in the corridors but he had never shown his face
back in my room since that day of his return. I sensed his
irritation but dismissed it in favour of my well being and revenge
for all the years that I felt I had to make up.
My sisters loved to fuss over me like I was some kind of life size
doll that they had just been given for Christmas. They combed
my hair and pinned it into all manner of bizarre styles till I was
quite exhausted by their tireless energy.

"Come now children Alice need her rest so that she can recover
quickly" Lady Eleanor would say.

"When she is recovered will she go home?" Enquired my
youngest sister Jane.

"Yes of course dear, her family will be very worried and will
expect her home as soon as she is well. Father has been in touch

with her mother who is unwell herself and so is unable to travel down to see her."

I smiled an uncomfortable smile. It was almost as if I needed to confer with my father and spin tales that concurred so that neither of us was caught out by this unsuspecting family. Secretly I was quite frustrated at the deception that was being spun. I wanted to announce my true self but I knew that I could not and that I would risk everything as well as being the victim of shame and humiliation. I was angry that my status was such that I would always feel inferior and degraded. I felt that my father owed me some compensation for putting me in this predicament. In fact it incensed me so much that I intended to confront him with it when I next saw him.

"Cousin Alice?" Albert was by my side.

"Yes"

"I was wondering if you might like a change of scenery. The crocuses and hyacinths are in bloom in the side garden and if I escorted you down to the drawing room then you would be able to see them and possibly we could open the window slightly if the doctor agrees and you could even smell their lovely aromas."

"That sounds delightful Albert. Yes it would be so nice to get up from this sick bed and stretch my legs a little."

It had occurred to me that I had now been confined to this pretty room for nearly three weeks since I had arrived. I did love this room. It was west facing so that the sun peeked through the curtains quite early in the mornings and woke me with the rays that formed triangles of light over the darkness. The room was decorated with pale blue wallpaper and had matching silk curtains with gold ties. Large sash windows enclosed the south aspect of the room in a sort of bay that was framed with a window seat Pictures in miniature frames around the walls were all of the children as babies and young children. I would smile at their happy faces that seemed to gleam at me when I was alone. I often wondered why I had never seen a picture of myself in my home, but I assumed that it was obvious that no one would want to take a picture of an illegitimate motherless bastard like me. Who was there to derive any pleasure from it? What parent would cast his eyes over my smiling countenance and praise me? There was no one. Once again I realised how very alone I really was in this counterfeit world that I had stumbled into.

"Alice you do frown quite a lot!" Albert scowled. "Please do tell what is vexing you so?"

I looked across at Albert whose presence I had quite forgotten and had ignored.

"Nothing is vexing me, Albert. I am just so grateful for all your kindness that I was just a little overcome."

Albert's face relaxed into a cheeky grin and he even seemed to blush a little. He took my hand in his and gently pressed it to his lips.

"You are so special and so lovely cousin Alice. I have become so used to you being here with us in the house. I know that this will sound most selfish and unkind but I really hope that your recovery is a slow one, so that you will not have to leave too hastily. In fact everyone loves you Alice and wishes you to stay."

"Everyone?" I asked

"Well nearly everyone. Father seems to be very concerned that your family up North are greatly troubled by your departure and he seems quite insistent that you should leave the very instant that the doctor says you can travel so as not to cause your sick mother any more worry. I do understand that you will have to leave eventually but I do so enjoy talking and reading together and I will miss you so much. Father has been very strange and dismissive about you and says that once you leave you will not return. When we asked if we could travel to see you he said that

that was quite out of the question! I don't know if there was a family dispute or argument but it does seem very strange that we are cousins and have only just met!"

"Yes Albert, there are many strange things that we will never understand. However I would like to smell the flowers in the drawing room garden. That would be very nice. I do think you should consult with your mother first before I leave the room as I would not like to go against her wishes and she did request for me to stay confined to my room."

"Of course Alice. In fact I will go and ask her straight away before she goes out to town. I shall be back shortly."

The door closed and Albert was gone. I sank back into my pillows and contemplated what my next move could be. There would be a point when I was recovered and would have to leave, although it would not be uncommon for a niece to live with her aunt and uncle especially if they were connected with London society and that would guarantee a better social status for the "niece". It seemed the better option rather than going back to Somerset and then being carted off to Paris. I knew that French society were far more liberal about ones parentage and that small issue of legitimacy, but even so, it seemed such a long way from what I considered home and those familiar things like newborn lambs bleating in fields and the clatter of hooves over the cobbled roads. I assume that there are sheep everywhere but how comforting when one knows that they are English and in a green lush field rained on with English rain.

"Alice! Mother says it is fine but only for half an hour after which you must go straight back to bed!" Albert had burst back into the room like an excited child.

He fetched my dressing gown from the closet and wrapped it around my shoulders as I sat up and swung my legs over the side of the bed and put them into the furry slippers.

"This is so exciting!" He exclaimed." You are leaving this room for the first time!"

"Albert calm down. You would think that I was a puppy being taken out for his first walk! I am not so fragile, I won't break!"

"I'm so sorry cousin Alice but it seems that I have only known you to be ill and in bed and now this is such a major turn of events that I cannot contain myself."

I chuckled to myself at his genuine excitement.

"You really are quite funny!"

Albert took my arm and led me down to the top of the heavily ornamented sweeping staircase. The cherry wood reminded me of home the only difference was that my home was old and sad. The wood and furnishings in my home were aged by time and worn carpets underfoot stood threadbare and lustreless. Everything here was new and plush. The colours were vivid and rich. The old musky smell that I knew from my home was replaced by the pungent smells of new leather bound books.

"Let me help you down the stairs. That's right one foot then the other."

"Albert!" I scoffed.

"I am not a baby I have walked before!"

"Have you? Yes of course you have. I am just so worried that you may fall cousin Alice that I feel I must cling on to you and protect you."

"Thank you Albert. I do appreciate what you are doing but you really must not fret so!"

We made it down the stairs with Albert guiding every step. We then walked the few steps over to the drawing room where a chaise long was positioned beside the window and to which I was directed to go.

"Well done you've made it!" Exclaimed Albert as he thrust open the windows.

The cool air came rushing into the room and I folded my arms around myself. Instinctively Albert came over with a large rug and wrapped it around me.

"There you go, can you smell the crocuses? Look at those pinks and blues aren't they quite exquisite?"

I drank in the sweet smells as they bathed the room. The fragrance of lily of the valley and snowdrops, pretty as they broke through the hard crusty ground outside.

"This is so lovely Albert, thank you for bringing me downstairs.

Albert came to sit by my side his eyes bright his face all-aglow.

"Yes this is lovely Alice, but you, you are the loveliest of them all. There is no flower as sweet as you. You are the most precious rose in my garden Alice."

He took my hand and I found that I could not look at him. He was staring at me quite intently and I was feeling a little unnerved.

"Alice I do believe that I love you…….."

"As a cousin" I continued.

"Yes of course as a dutiful cousin Alice."

We sat for a while and Albert made sure that my lunch was brought to me here. I breathed in deeply all the crisp fresh air and felt my lungs ache a little, as they were flooded with so much oxygen. We stayed until I felt the weariness returning to my body and the sounds of Albert's voice began to drift over my head till I could no longer comprehend the words he was saying to me. My over attentive cousin then helped me back to my room and the maid came and took over to attend to me and tuck me back into my bed. I nestled back into the snug comfort of my feather pillows and before they had left the room and closed the door I had fallen into a deep undisturbed sleep.

Chapter 18

I awoke to the sounds of rustling around my bed. I stretched my body like a cat uncurling from a long nap and rolled over to see who was there.

"Oh I'm sorry miss didn't mean to wake you"
A young maid stood in my room dusting the tops of the cupboards with a long feather duster. Unlike the staff at home she was dressed in a neat black uniform covered by a white pinafore.
"No that's fine, you carry on and do what you need to do" I replied.
The girl stopped and looked at the floor.
"Is everything all right?" I asked inquisitively.
The girl approached the bed and pulled out a dirty envelope upon which the name Alice was carefully printed. She handed the envelope to me and I noticed that it was unsealed.
"I was asked to give this to you"
"By whom?"
"By a lad that was hovering around the kitchens. Nice lad, handsome and cheeky eyed, he said to give this to the young lady who was unwell and to make sure that no one saw me doing it."
It didn't take too much guesswork to work out who the lad was. I turned the envelope over in my hand and took out the note that was within.
"Have you read this?" I asked sharply
"Oh no miss. I wouldn't do that miss. I couldn't do that miss."
"Can't you read then?"
"No. But I do know some letters, but not how to put them together to make a word."
I read the note, reread it and then put it back into the envelope.

"So where is the lad that brought you this? Is he waiting?

"No miss. He was waiting around for several days and I brought him some food and left over bits from the kitchen. He was so thankful. Lovely boy he was. Although he did talk a bit funny said he was from the West Country wherever that might be. You see I've only been to London, born here and never left. Never had anywhere else to go but the poorhouse and I ain't going there."

"So when did you receive this?"

"Oh, maybe about two or three weeks ago when you had just come miss."

"So why have you only just given it to me?"

"Because he said it was a secret. He said that no one was to know. He said that I had to make sure that you were quite alone when I gave it to you."

"So where have you kept it till now? How do I know that no one else has read it?"

"Because I kept it under my pillow, inside the pillow case where I knew no one would find it."

The girl seemed honest enough and she seemed to be quite loyal to the author of the note. Her gaze never left the floor and when she did look up she looked at me directly without a trace of a flicker.

"Well thank you. What is your name?"

"I'm Sarah miss."

"Well thank you Sarah for delivering this note to me and when I am able I will repay you for your discretion."

"Oh there is no need for that miss, I have already been repaid by the young man who delivered the note."

Sarah smiled a sheepish smile and I felt myself instantly recoiling at the thought of what her repayment might have been.

"Very well then, and you're sure that no one knows about this note?"

"Yes of course miss. I might only be a servant but I know how to keep my word."

"Thank you Sarah."

After she had left the room. I took the letter from under my pillow and reread the rough scrawling words. I wanted to smile and revel in the undercurrent of concern between the lines but deep down I was quite distressed and maybe a little jealous of Sarah the maid, who had obviously been given something worthwhile in order for her to have gone to the trouble of delivering this note. I wondered if he had looked into her eyes with his deep blue ones. If he had looked at her the way that he looked at me. I wondered if his smile made her gasp the same way that I did.

There was a knock on the door. I carefully replaced the letter under my pillow and sat up.

"Yes come in" I responded.

The door opened and there was Albert. Good old reliable Albert with a glint in his eye and a spring in his step.

"Good morning. Wondered if you would like to come down for breakfast and smell the flowers again?"

I pondered for a second then nodded and agreed to what seemed like a fairly good idea.

"Absolutely. That is most agreeable and I felt so well yesterday after I came down that I don't see why not."

"I have already received a positive response from mother, I told her how much you enjoyed yesterday afternoon and she said that as long as you had no bad effects from it that it would not do any harm."

Albert took my arm and led me down the stairs and I walked a little more confidently then yesterday.

Downstairs in the dining room everyone was sitting eating their breakfast, laughing and squealing. The room was bursting with chatter. As we entered the room fell silent and everyone looked up.

"Alice. How wonderful my dear. You look positively radiant. I do believe that you are recovering very well!" Exclaimed Lady Sinclair.

The girls began to offer me breads and jam and argued as to whom I would sit beside.

My father peered over the top of his newspaper and frowned. In reply I tossed back my head and made myself comfortable between Jane and Emily.

"This is so lovely to come downstairs and have breakfast with you all. Thank you so much Aunt Eleanor I am so grateful for your hospitality."

"Nonsense Alice. Don't thank us we are only too pleased to have you here aren't we Edward?" She looked up over her teacup to her husband at the opposite end of the table.

My father didn't respond and continued to look at his newspaper.

"Edward?"

"Sorry my dear"

"Tell Alice how pleased we are that she is making such good progress."

My father turned to me. His cold eyes trying to hide the obvious apathy that he had for me.

"Yes Alice we are so happy that you are making excellent progress and that you will very soon be reunited with your own family."

I threw my father an equally cold look. I was aware that our dislike of each other was becoming a little too profound and would probably be looked upon with curiosity by the rest of the family and so smiled sweetly and replied.

"Yes Uncle Edward I cannot wait to be with my real family."

"But we are your real family Alice." Quipped Albert. Not realising how very true his words were.

"Uncle Edward?" I began.

"What is the news in the paper? How are our troops doing in Sudan? It must be so hard for all the soldiers fighting so bravely for our country."

"Yes." Replied Albert

"I wanted to go and fight but father insisted that there are more worthwhile things to be done right here at home."

"I'm sure there are." I agreed sarcastically directing my answer to Albert at my father.

At that my father folded his paper and rose from his chair.

"I must be off to The House of Lords we have some very important debates today. Good day everyone."

After my father left the atmosphere lifted like clouds that drift away revealing a perfect blue sky. The girls insisted on showing me around the house and into practically every room until I was so exhausted and confused that I had to retire back to my room. Albert had gone off to his academy but promised to come and see me as soon as he returned home.

After I had rested I slipped my hand under my pillow and retrieved Toms note. I then took it and placed it inside my shoe in the cupboard.

The cupboard was filled with the girls' old dresses. I had only worn nightdresses since I had been here and so it seemed strange to touch all the fine silks and velvet materials.

"Don't look at those they are all old."

Charlotte was standing behind me; she took my hand and began to lead me towards her room.

"I've got so many beautiful dresses Alice and we are the same age almost and the same height and build. I would love you to

108

share my clothes with me. My sisters get all my old dresses but you could have one of my new ones."

"You are so kind Charlotte" I could feel tears welling behind my eyes. It seemed so strange yet so natural to have a sister that I could share clothes with. I was revelling in the excitement of not only the dresses but of Charlotte's genuine warmth and love. She noticed the sadness in my eyes and leaned towards me throwing her arms around my neck and embracing me.

"Cousin Alice I feel that I have three sisters now. Please don't be sad we are very lucky that you have found us and don't let your uncle upset you or let you think any differently because we all feel the same."

I couldn't help it. The emotion began to spill over and Charlotte had to give me her handkerchief to dry my tears.

Before long we were trying on dresses and laughing again. Lady Eleanor came in and remarked how well the dresses looked and how similar we both were in height and stature. I smiled secretly and nobody realised the secrets that I knew and kept hidden. Charlotte gave me three dresses and I swished around like a princess in my new gowns.

"Alice I think you should rest again dear. You have had a very busy day and have hardly stayed in your bed at all." Declared Lady Sinclair.

"But I feel so well and I really don't mind being up I am having so much fun."

"Very well rest for an hour and then you can come down and have dinner with us all."

An hour later I came down to the drawing room where everyone was assembling before dinner. I stood before the large glass windows and looked out onto the lawns that seemed to cascade down the hills and backed on to the parklands beyond. The door opened behind me and I heard my father enter. I heard him embracing his wife and all the children and then he was behind me and his arms were enveloping my shoulders. For a moment my heart skipped a beat and I imagined that my father now did love me and accepted me as one of his true children.

"Charlotte" He whispered in my ear.

My heart sunk and I realised that the dress had confused him. I spun around and his happy relaxed countenance changed to one of horror and hatred.

"Why are you wearing my daughters dress?" He shrieked almost hysterically.

"Edward!" Exclaimed Lady Eleanor.

"That is not necessary! How dare you frighten the poor girl!" I took two steps back and slumped into a chair. Albert was by my side in an instant.

My father diplomatically tried to recompose himself, whilst I was left feeling shunned and distanced from my father once again. How easy it would have been for him to let me in and warm to me, but how hard he tried to fight and hate me. I would have loved him in an instant if he let me but his ice barriers were firmly constructed against me.

"Apologise Edward!" Demanded Lady Sinclair.

My father looked at his wife and mumbled an apology under his breath. He then gestured to the dining room and we all took our seats in silence. We ate dinner with little conversation. Every time I looked at him he turned to look the other way. It was horrible. Even though the rest of the family seemed to have forgotten the incident I had not and when eventually I retired to my room I went straight to the hidden note in the shoe and eventually through all the tears fell asleep clutching the little note of hope.

Chapter 19

The next few days came and passed without incident. My father seemed to ignore my presence even though I was very visible in every part of the house and enjoying the company of my new family. Within myself I was feeling much stronger and more able. The doctor had been several times and had been quite content with my progress, enough to allow me to venture outside if I wished, as long as I was quite warmly dressed.

The weather was crisp and the short January days were gradually getting longer as we went into the early days of February. Still I knew the dangers of catching cold and how it affected me physically. I had to keep well. After all I had so many secrets yet to uncover. Mentally I was becoming bolder and felt that I would have to start making major decisions soon about my future. This is where I was in a different world from my siblings. They only knew a world of silver spoons where their whole lives were played to cues, every step carefully rehearsed and following ready-made pathways. My situation was very different. I didn't have the luxury of a normal family and a loving cocoon in which to envelope me. Despite my tender years I knew that there was only one person that I could rely upon to have my best interests at heart and that would only be me.

Sometimes I hated my isolation and the desolate way that I felt. I hated the unnatural way that I had to behave. I knew it was a compromise and that if I wanted to stay here that I had to keep painting a clowns smile on my face. I longed to be off guard, to have no worries, to wake up without a frown on my brow. But that was not my fate, not what life had in store for me. I had been given challenges and I had to conquer them. I was living in a society where status meant everything and illegitimate children were treated like lepers and shunned. But I could pretend. I could overcome this and I was determined that I would.

My sisters had decided that I was to join them in their sewing circle and I was to stitch all the browns and blues on the large tapestry that was being made. It was quite good fun and I was learning all sorts of new techniques that I had not even dreamed about having an interest in before. They had already progressed quite significantly and it was beginning to look very good.

"Alice you sew so slowly." Laughed Jane.

"Well some of us had to spend time reading books and learning about the world" I retorted.

"All right then miss clever!" She giggled

"Yes Alice is so frightfully clever" Emily added.

"So are you going to tell us about your family then?"

This one always stumped me. Up till now I had only admitted to having lived in Northampton with my sick mother. I had much older sisters that were married and lived even further north.

"But what happened to your father?"

"He died."

"So why did you come to London?"

There was no answer that would readily satisfy their hunger to know the answer to that question.

"I wanted to see my uncle and meet my delightful cousins."

"Yes but why did you not write first and say that you were coming?"

"Because I knew that there had been some dispute between my mother and my uncle many years before and that was why they had not seen each other for so long. I was afraid that if I wrote first I might be rejected and therefore unable to come ever and I didn't want to risk that possibility."

"Oh that is terribly clever Alice. How pre-emptive of you to consider that possibility."

"…and then we could never have met!"

"Yes absolutely! You do think about things very deeply don't you Alice?"

I nodded at my youngest sister and thought to myself that she only knew the surface of what really lay deep in my thoughts.

"So what is the argument between father and your mother Alice?" suggested Emily.

"I still don't know." I shrugged.

"I shall have to find out later when I have a chance to speak to m…your father."

The rest of the day I was very distant in my thoughts. I declined to chatter between the sewing and it wasn't until we heard the great thump of the front door that I finally recovered from my semi coherent state.

"Father must be home!"

Emily went to go out to the hallway to see her father.

"No it's not father its Albert and he has brought his friend William home from the Academy. William is gorgeous and we all absolutely adore him. But alas William has eyes for one girl only and that is Charlotte."

Charlotte looked down bashfully and signalled for her younger sister to hush.

"It's not true Emily! He is far too young as am I, for any flirtations and please do keep your voice down it would be most embarrassing if he could hear you."

The door opened and the two boys walked in looking quite gallant in their uniforms.

Albert scanned the room and on seeing me turned to William.

"William, I do believe that you are very familiar with everyone here except our new guest. May I take this opportunity to introduce you to my most wonderful cousin Alice."

William came over to where I was sitting and gave a very deep bow. He kissed my hand and I couldn't help feeling flattered by his over gentlemanly behaviour.

"I am so delighted to at last be having the pleasure of meeting with you Miss Alice. Albert has done little else but talk about you all day when we should be pursuing our studies. It's almost as if he wishes that he could be studying you and now that I have at last met you I can see exactly why. You are most exquisite Miss Alice; it is a great honour and privilege.

Unable to contain myself I let out a little chuckle.

"Does something amuse you Miss Alice?" he asked sweeping his shoulder length hair back off his face and directing his brown eyes straight into mine. His eyebrows quite thick and dark, shadowing over his very angular face.

Before I could answer Albert was directing William away from me and out of the room.

"Alice has been very unwell William. We must go now and leave the girls to their sewing. Alice must not tired by too much conversation."

William appeared rooted to the spot and reluctant to move. Charlotte coughed and distracted Williams gaze from me.

"Oh Charlotte I am so sorry. I have failed to wish you a good day."

He nodded his head in her direction and then followed Albert who was pulling on his sleeve out of the room.

"Well well!" commented Emily

"That was charming!"

"What do you mean?" Asked Jane.

"Well William has always been completely in awe of Charlotte. It's always Charlotte this and Charlotte that and then he takes one look at Alice and doesn't even notice poor Charlotte!"

"That's nonsense!" Scoffed Charlotte. "Button your lip Emily! What do you know about what William is thinking?" She continued.

"I think we all know what William is thinking. Even Albert knew what William was thinking why do you think he dragged him out so hastily? He didn't like his precious cousin being flirted with. It was very obvious to me!"

"Emily stop!" Shouted Charlotte.

"Please don't argue." I intervened.

"I am sure he was just being polite, I really don't think there is anything more to it than that. He is very charming Charlotte and I am sure his affection for you is unaffected."

Charlotte threw me an icy look and turned to pick up her sewing. The door then reopened and William re-emerged.

"I've escaped momentarily from Albert. I just wanted to come back and tell you Alice how charmed I was to meet you and would like to know if you and your chaperone would like to go out riding when you are feeling a little better?"

I was stunned. Charlotte glared at me and I could see the redness welling in her eyes. I didn't wish to appear impolite yet I could not knowingly cause any pain to my sister who was clearly being rejected on account of me.

"I could not possibly go out as I have been advised against it by all my doctors. However I am sure that Charlotte would be available to accompany you for a drive whenever you should wish."

The door opened and there stood Albert with his hands on his hips and looking most displeased with his friend. William in response threw up his hands and shrugged his shoulders.

"I am so sorry Alice for the rudeness of my friend." Albert began.

"William has just asked Alice to go riding with him!" Declared Emily.

"He what!" Said Albert amazed.

"Sorry Albert. But you can't keep this delightful cousin all to yourself."

"Oh yes I can! Now hurry up and leave this room immediately otherwise you will not be invited here again!"

The two boys left the room. As William left he turned around and gave me a discreet smile. All the girls saw and at that point Charlotte burst into tears and hurried from the room.

"Now look what you've done!" Exclaimed Jane.

"Me?"

"Yes!"

I dropped my sewing and let my skirts swirl around me as I climbed the staircase and went directly to Charlotte's room. Charlotte was lying across her bed sobbing. When she realised that I was there she turned like a wild cat and hissed.

"How dare you come into my room without knocking!"

"I am sorry Charlotte. I didn't mean to upset or offend you in any way. I am so sorry that you are upset. I apologise if I have been the cause of any distress to you."

"I saw you fluttering your eyelashes at William! I saw the way he looked at you!"

"No dear Charlotte!"

I went and sat beside her on the bed. The last thing that I wanted to do was to cause any unhappiness to my dear sister. I was trying very hard to do the right thing and console her even though I knew that I had done nothing to cause this outburst. It also occurred to me that it was all being dramatised and blown out of proportion and it was such a little thing anyway. It seemed that Charlotte was overly sensitive and this in some ways frustrated me when I thought of my own situation and the trials and tribulations that I had to face. Nevertheless I had the tact and diplomacy skills to remedy this situation.

"Charlotte I have absolutely no interest in William. I find him quite distasteful and overly audacious. I have no interest in someone that displays qualities such as those. I have not flirted with him in any way and never intend to do so in the future. He is yours Charlotte and I shall always dismiss his advances towards me, be assured of that."

"Do you mean that Alice?"

"Of course Charlotte!" I enforced.

Charlotte thought for a moment. Then she dried her tears.

"So you think he is rude and distasteful?"

"Yes of course."

"Well I don't think lightly of your comments about William. Who do you think you are making judgements about him? You have only just met him!"

"Well I am sure he is very nice." I was trying very hard to appease.

"So you do like him?"

"No of course not."

"Alice you are very tiresome. You cannot make your mind up if you like him or not?

"Charlotte I am sorry once again. I will go to my room now. I will see you later at dinner." Charlotte did not answer and I knew that this was one battle that I would not and had no desire to win. In the hallway I bumped into Lady Eleanor.

"Oh I was just calling everyone down for dinner. Are you well enough to join us again?"

It would have been correct of me to go to my room and let everyone recover from this overblown situation. However I was unconventional and in some ways incited trouble.

"Of course I will join you for dinner. Thank you Lady Eleanor."

Lady Eleanor tapped on Charlotte's door and announced dinner. She then turned and proceeded to walk down the stairs to the dining room and I followed dutifully. In the hallway Albert was just bidding farewell to William at the front door.

"Hello Lady Eleanor a very good evening to you."

"Why hello William. We are just about to sit down for dinner wont you stay and join us?"

William shook his head, then glanced upwards and saw me coming down the stairs.

"Yes thank you Lady Eleanor I would love to be your guest." Albert was clearly put out by this situation and wanted rid of his friend.

"Didn't you tell me William that you were in a hurry to get home?"

"No I said no such thing!"

"Oh yes you did!" Albert was practically pushing William out of the door.

"I want to stay and your mother has very kindly invited me it would be rude to refuse."

Albert had to admit defeat and allowed William to push past him and close the front door.

In the dining room William insisted in sitting beside me but thankfully Albert muscled in between and this time was most adamant so that William had no choice but to concede. Charlotte entered the room and looked at everyone with suspicious eyes. She seemed pleased though that I was seated beside Albert and that the empty seat was on the other side of William.

We ate. We laughed. We conversed in the most genteel manner. In fact everyone behaved very well, although I knew that once dinner was over the previous hostilities would resume. I couldn't make up my mind about Charlotte. One moment she was very kind and loving and the next she was moody and strange.

"Sisters!" Replied Emily without even being aware of the question.

"Sorry?" I questioned.

"Well you know, one minute they are great and you love them completely and the next they are impossible. All sisters fight its quite normal. Didn't you fight with your sisters?"

I was stumped. Being an only child meant that my knowledge of family relationships was very limited. There was so much that I didn't know and seemed oblivious to. There was still so much but maybe if I was not careful, there would only be so little time.

Chapter 20

It seemed that I had a lot to learn about families and siblings. Not only did I have a rather confused attitude to the way that they all behaved but also I was being introduced to the concept of sibling rivalry. Why did they have to fight and argue so much? What was wrong with taking on their own responsibilities and sorting out things independently? The situation with William had really led me to believe that they were all quite selfish in their attitudes. I could neither do right nor wrong as far as Charlotte was concerned. If I made a positive comment I was chastised and if I made a negative one I was rebuked so I tried very hard not to bring up the subject or to discreetly change the subject when someone else brought it up. Meanwhile Albert had announced that William was no longer his friend and so would not be visiting again. That seemed to solve some problems although Charlotte always looked at me warily whenever his name came up. I resigned that I was going to have to declare my disinterest in William once again in order to get her to really believe me. However though he was very charming and gallant.
My future situation also greatly concerned me. Although I loved being here it was also becoming tedious and hard work at the same time. My younger siblings were all quite loud and boisterous and always asking the most annoying questions. Charlotte on the other hand swayed from very complicated to incredibly easy and Albert was just a little overwhelming at times. He was always following me around and fussing over me with a little too much cousinly attention. Lady Eleanor sometimes looked at me as if she was looking right through me and I felt a bit intimidated by her penetrating eyes that seemed to ask never ending questions. At times I had been a little homesick. I

wondered how everyone was, back at the old house. I wondered how Maud was and whether she was still continuing with her reading and studies. I was unsure what arrangements my father had made when he had returned. Obviously the whole upkeep of the house had been for my benefit and now that I was not there, had he dismissed all the staff? My father had not mentioned my return in fact he had hardly talked to me recently. I had also briefly thought about Tom. I had tried to fill my head with negative images of him but they kept being brushed aside in favour of those wonderful sentimental ones of him coming to my aid on the way down to London and all those special moments that we had laughed together. It all seemed so long ago. So much had happened and even though the pace of my life was painfully slow it still seemed to be racing ahead of me.

"Alice?"

I spun around to the voice of my father. He was standing there with the usual frustrated look etched on his brow. I assumed that the talk that I had anticipated with him would come sooner rather than later.

"Yes father." I smiled sweetly to try to quash some of his animosity towards me.

He stood for a few moments the coldness turning to iciness in his eyes. It saddened me greatly because I knew what a warm and caring father he was to the rest of his children and longed so much to have just a little remnant of that love.

"You have outstayed your welcome in my house." He declared as if he was talking to a stranger.

"You think that you have a place here and you do not. You wear my daughter's clothes and act like you are one and the same. Your time here must come to an end immediately. You must leave!"

In my mind I thought it then barring all etiquette let the words spill from my mouth

"But father I am one and the same! You chide me for wearing Charlotte's clothes but I am your daughter too."
I paused and looked him in the eye.

"Or had you forgotten?"

"I constantly try to forget but like a bad smell you continue to linger Alice." He threw back callously.
I quashed the tears. I would not be intimidated by this bully. This was my opportunity to speak and I would not be silenced.

"No father I will always linger! I shall not be brushed under the carpet. I am not like your London children. I have a hard heart. Your words can bruise but they will not crush me, I wish to have some input into my life. I do not wish to be pushed about like a piece of dirt. I will have a say in my future or I shall expose you for the liar and scoundrel that you are!"

"I should have dumped you at the workhouse like a beggar! Then where would you have been? You have been very privileged to be brought up in a big house with servants and tutors. It would have been so much simpler to have got rid of you long ago instead of having to endure this nonsense from you now!"
I was stunned and momentarily speechless. Yes I suppose it could have been worse for me even though I had not considered that I would have had any other options.

"I thank you father for your kindness to your poor illegitimate child. I suppose that life would have been simpler for you under those circumstances but that is not the case now and I have found out your sordid little secret whether you like it or not, so there is no going back on that!"
He shook his head. His greying hair slightly long at the back and curling over the nape of his neck.

122

"So feisty! So much like your mother! Think that you can change all the rules. Think that you are in control! This isn't a world for a woman or a mere girl like you. You are bound by mans rules and a male dominated society to whom you will always be subservient. Had you been a boy then maybe your life would have been different but that is not the way it works. Will you challenge God next for making you what you are? I am sorry Alice but you have no voice and especially not in this household."

Once again he had the upper hand over me. By mentioning my mothers name he knew that I would be fazed and however hard I was trying to overcome my inferiority I knew that he was winning, after all he was the politician used to lying under pressure and having all the answers on tap.

"So I am feisty like my mother am I? What other qualities did I inherit from my mother? Why have you never mentioned her before? Did you destroy her too? Did she really die of childbirth or was it a broken heart?

He turned his back on me and began to walk away.

"Stop!" I shouted. My anger and frustration rising like the heat from a roaring fire.

"I do not wish to talk about your mother." He replied simply.

"Why! Why!"I began to scream hysterically.

"Nobody has ever spoken to me about my mother! There are no photographs or portraits of her in my house. I don't know if I look like her, I don't know what she did in her life. I know nothing!" The tears were now streaming uncontrollably from my eyes. Even though I had vowed to myself that I wouldn't show any weakness in front of my father he had still managed to find that flaw that lay within me and with which I had absolutely no control. My father was the only one that knew my mother and now he was defiantly telling me that he did not wish to talk about

123

her. He would talk about her and he would tell me about her! He had to otherwise I would never know, and I could not bear that.

"Alice, your mother is in the past. That part of your life is over now. You do not need to know anything about her other than she had some means, which is why you were left your grandfathers house where you currently live. I am officially your guardian and so it is my decision to dispose of the house and send you away to a country where you will be able to have a good life and maybe find your place in this life. You will find a suitable husband and have some financial means of your own from the sale of the Somerset house. I have considered your life Alice even though you think I have not and for your mother's sake have done the best that I can under the circumstances for you. As far as looking like your mother you have her eyes only and that is all."

Yes I supposed that I did look more like my father. Charlotte also looked like father and that's why we appeared so alike and could confuse those around us that we were more like sisters than cousins. My father seemed more at ease and less irritated with me. I think that was because he knew that he had the upper hand and that all cards were dealt in his favour. It seemed that I had no say in my life but regardless I thought I would give it one last chance.

"Father, I apologise for seeming ungrateful for your courtesy towards me and yes of course if you had seen fit to allow your daughter to be brought up in the workhouse than you were completely at liberty to dispose of me there. However I feel that there was more to it than that and I would like to know what part my maternal grandparents had in all these decisions. Surely they didn't want their only heir discarded into a workhouse heap. Where were they? Where is my mother buried? Why does no one mention her?" Why should I go to Paris? Why can't I just live here?"

"So many questions little Alice. My decision is made with your best welfare at heart. You cannot live here. Your parentage would eventually be examined if you should meet a suitor and that would discredit all my family and me. They would all be ruined and it would be your doing Alice."

Yes I thought to myself twist this so all the blame falls on my shoulders.

"But this is your mistake father?"

"No you are the mistake Alice and that is why you have to go."

I was seething, but powerless. I hated the way he could manipulate every word he uttered and leave me confused and rummaging in the dark.

"And my mother and her family?" I questioned.

My father went and sat down in his dark brown leather Chesterfield chair. He shook his head and placed his hand under his chin in a contemplatory manner.

"I suppose you have some right to know. When your mother was with child she was sent away to a convent. It was a disgrace for the family and in some way a relief to their shame when she died. But then there was the problem of you. Your grandfather was a widower and when you were presented to him he agreed that you should be brought up in his home and should inherit his estate since his daughter was an only child. You were to be told that your father had died whilst married to your mother and there was to be no mention of illegitimacy. You were then to be sent abroad when you came of age so that no questions would be asked and you would be protected."

My father fell silent and I watched his troubled expression and the way the lines on his face creased around his eyes.

"So how come you came back?" I asked curiously.

"When your grandfather died he appointed me guardian. You were only two years old and had never known a mother or father.

I felt sorry for you and confessed one drunken night to being your father. Once you and everyone in the household knew I had no choice but to continue to be your father, but from a distance. I never thought that you would question or be nearly as headstrong as you have turned out to be. I thought you would just comply with all my instructions and not turn up here on my doorstep!"

"I am my father's daughter!" I retorted fiercely

I was beginning to see my father in a different light. He was vulnerable in a way that I had not anticipated. Maybe he had loved me but had just been unable to do so and so blocked me from his life. Maybe his hostility was just a facade. I wondered if he had loved my mother. I wondered if he loved me now.

"Alice you must go. I will make the arrangements and you will leave at the end of the week. There will be no more discussion. There will be no more arguments. You will obey me. I will tell everyone that your mother has recovered and that she is expecting your return."

He left the room and I knew that he was right. By the end of the week I would be back in Somerset.

Chapter 21

Even though the conclusions to my stay here in London were inevitable I was neither unhappy nor sad at the decision. This bewildered me somewhat as I considered myself a fairly level headed person. I had loved being here but it had also irritated me too. I loved my new family but at times their complete lack of rational thought frustrated me. I was beginning to realise that the solitude that I thought I had hated, I actually enjoyed. Yes, I liked my own company immensely. I enjoyed reading my books and thinking deeply about things. Perhaps if there was anyone who was on the same intellectual plane as me then we could have had some stimulating debates, but my brothers and sisters were unfortunately quite shallow in that respect and so bored me. There was however one interesting person. It was a shame that all I could do with him though was fight. I tried to imagine the deep and meaningful conversations that I could have had with my father. I would have loved to hear stories about the policies being debated in parliament and the problems being faced by my father's constituents. I could have been such an asset to him. How much we could have enjoyed being father and daughter instead of the fierce enemies we had become.

I had never considered that I may be homesick but I was. I missed being woken by the cockerels in the roosts. I missed the smell of green fields and being able to open my window and gaze out onto mile upon mile of fields and pastures. I missed the sounds of the carts rolling on cobbles and the dogs barking at the horses in the barn. I missed the servants and Mrs Dunn especially. I wondered if she had gone and taken up her position at the hospital, the one that she had told me about before I left. It was funny that it seemed like years before that I had eagerly anticipated her arrival every day and longed for her tender care during my illness and now I had been away weeks and hardly given her a second thought. I remembered her smiling face and wondered if indeed I would ever see her again.

I had to tell everyone that I was leaving. It saddened me that I had to leave like this and despite all faults I did still feel some connections and bonds with these people.

"Charlotte?"

I knocked gently on her door hoping that she would be in a good mood today and make my news that much easier to break.

"Yes come in. Oh it's you what do you want?"

I sighed at her attitude but realised that this was how she spoke to her other brothers and sisters so in some ways it was a compliment to my familiarity.

"Charlotte I have some news for you?"

"Oh what's that then? Has William asked you to go out riding with him again and have you accepted this time instead of substituting me like last time?

"No Charlotte. This has nothing to do with William. My thoughts about William are the same as always. In fact I doubt that I shall ever see William again in my life."

Charlotte turned to me with a curious frown on her forehead. I smiled and took her pale hand in mine.

"I have some news that bearing in mind your animosity towards me will probably be most welcome."

She looked up and retracted her hand from mine. We went and sat down on the window seat and I began.

"Charlotte as you know I have recovered greatly from my ague and the doctor is quite pleased with my progress. My mother in Northampton has been unwell too and so has been unable to come down to see me. It is right that now that I am recovered that I should go home as soon as possible and tend to her."

"Oh" Charlotte was speechless.

"I will be leaving by the end of the week and then you can have William all to yourself."

"Oh Alice. I am sorry. I have been most childish in my behaviour towards you. Must you leave? When will you return?" There was no point pretending with Charlotte and I thought it best to explain to her the finality of the situation.

"Charlotte, I think that this will be the last time that we ever see each other. My mother told me before I left that we would be travelling to France in the spring and taking up residency there. The climate is better for her health and mine and we have connections there. I doubt that I will be returning to English soil so we will never meet again."

"No Alice!"

Tears were beginning to form in her eyes and hung like heavy globules in the corners till they eventually spilled over and traced their way down her smooth curved cheeks. She reached into her pocket and pulled out a kerchief and began dabbing away. Seeing her so upset touched me deeply. No one had ever cried for me before. No one had been so sad on account of me. Instinctively I put my arm around her shoulder and told her that it would all be all right.

"You will come to visit us though Alice? Maybe some time in the future you could make your way to England and come to see us?"

"I don't know Charlotte. I believe that I am to be found a suitable husband as soon as we arrive and then I will be bound to his rules and that would mean that I would surely be unable to make the journey back here."

"Oh but Alice we have only just found you and now you are to disappear as if you had never existed! This is terrible! You will write though? You will still communicate with me?"

I knew that my father would wish me to break all ties and stay away permanently from this new life that I had found but I did not know how to tell Charlotte without appearing to be terribly callous.

"Yes of course I will write." I lied

"Just as soon as I know what my new address will be."

There was another knock at the door. Albert poked his head around the door.

"Just calling you girls down for dinner," He piped.

He couldn't help but notice Charlotte's tearstained face.

"What up sister dearest? Has Alice been upsetting you again? He threw me a cheeky grin.

"No." Charlotte replied

"It is worse than that!"

"Nothing can be that bad." He remarked stepping into the room.

"Alice is leaving!" Charlotte declared.

Albert's faced paled. He stood quite still and stared hard at me with an almost insulted expression on his face.

"Why? What's wrong with our family? Why do you have to leave so suddenly? You arrive here quite unexpected then decide to up and leave whenever it suits you?

"Albert?" Charlotte chided.

"That's a little uncalled for!"

"Well it's true! Why is she just leaving?"

"Can I answer some of these questions since I think this involves me?" I interrupted.

They both respectfully allowed me to speak.

"I have just explained to Charlotte that I must leave because my mother needs me and I am expected to return home. I do appreciate all the hospitality that your family have shown me but it really is time for me to leave."

"Tell Albert that you are moving to France!" Added Charlotte.

Albert's eyebrows lifted and once again I felt open to scrutiny.

"Thank you Charlotte. Yes Albert, we are leaving to go to live in Paris where the climate is better for my mothers' health."

"And…" Charlotte prompted.

I shrugged my shoulders at her; unaware as to what further news she wanted me to tell.

"That you will be married to a Frenchman!"

Albert glared. I suddenly felt quite battered by the conversation. I could not look at him. I stared at the floor and then announced.

"I think we should go down for dinner then. Won't they be waiting for us? Won't the food be getting cold?

"Married! Albert's voice was getting louder.

"Yes Albert. It is what is to be expected of a young lady."

"Yes but to a Frenchman! What Frenchman? Do you know this fellow to whom you are betrothed?"

"No of course not, and it's not going to happen straight away but yes it is my mothers intention that I am to be wed."

The look on Albert's face told me that he needed something more to convince him that it was true.

"…And your father has approved of all these matters and that is why I am to leave with such urgency."

"I knew that father would be involved in this!" Albert raged.

"I don't know why but he has not liked you Alice. Maybe it is because of the feud between your mother and him but he is wrong to take it out on you. I cannot believe that he wants you to leave us and go abroad. We would probably never see you again."

"No we won't, but she has promised to write." Charlotte interjected.

"Well we will see!" Shouted Albert as he left the room.

Charlotte and I went down to dinner. I regretted that I had involved my father into the conversation. Albert had seemed so upset and I didn't know what he was going to do or say.

We all sat at our places for dinner but Albert was missing. Father being in one of his "well he can go hungry" moods insisted that we did not wait and so we started with our soup.

"Alice is leaving us at the end of the week." Charlotte announced quite casually.

"Oh my dear!" Exclaimed Lady Eleanor.

My father just sat at the head of the table a smug look hanging over his face.

"Yes Lady Eleanor. My mother is ill and I must go home as quickly as possible. I am very grateful for all your kindness but it is really time for me to leave."

The children began to whine and moan. They were pulling on my sleeves and begging me to stay. Charlotte remained silent but the look on her face told me that I would be missed by nearly everyone. My father's eyes met mine and he gave me a silent nod.

"I will be travelling to Paris shortly and will be embarking on a whole new and exciting life." I added.

The door behind me clicked shut. Albert stood motionless his back to the door. His face was red and flushed and an odour of whisky reeked from his breath.

"Father." He began

"I am not happy about Alice's news and I am most unhappy with your involvement in it. You are her uncle yet you have been very distant towards her. I understand that it is a family dispute but there is no need to involve Alice....."

"That is enough Albert!"

"No father. I will have my say. You wish Alice to go abroad and marry well I have a better plan why does she not stay right here and marry. She is your niece she is from good stock there will be no problem marrying her to a suitable man. In fact I have a very suitable bachelor in mind. Someone that loves her completely, someone who will be an honest and faithful husband."

We were all standing, witnessing Albert's outburst with absolute amazement but when he actually rushed to my side and knelt on one knee the whole room was aghast.

"Alice will you marry me?"

"What!" I gasped in shock.

"What!" Echoed my father his face turning red with rage.

My father leapt from his seat and paced around the table pulled Albert by the scruff of his neck and dragged him from the room.

"You are drunk my boy! You are a disgrace! What has possessed you?"

When the door had closed on the two men Lady Eleanor quite calmly announced.

"I think we are ready for dessert now"

We ate our custard pudding trying to be oblivious to the sounds of yelling coming from the drawing room down the corridor.

I was trying to digest the absurdity of the evening whilst at the back of my mind trying to plan how I could turn all this to my advantage.

Chapter 22

"Alice I wish to speak to you!"
I could tell by the tone in my fathers' voice that all was not well.
Since the episode with Albert the night before, I had been
expecting my father to have words with me.
I had lain awake most of the previous night wondering what tales
my father was telling Albert as to why he could not marry me. I
was half expecting my father to come to my room late after the
incident but he never came. As a result I woke feeling quite
fraught and irritable and desperately needing sleep.
He closed my bedroom door and sat on the chaise longue beside
the window.

"Alice you must really leave immediately. This situation is now
completely out of hand and you are just complicating matters
more and more with every day that you stay here.
Albert is completely out of control. He thinks that there is no law
to prevent cousins marrying as he does not know what we know.
You must go. I cannot have you under my roof for one minute
more!"
I looked at my father who was clearly very disturbed and seemed
to have lost his reins on the matter. Despite my fatigued state I
knew that I could possibly have a method of moulding this to a
way that suited me.

"Well father, I think it is an excellent idea to marry Albert. I
could stay here and you could buy me a house and I would have
all my family close at hand. It would be so idyllic don't you
think?
I hadn't anticipated the hand that rose and then came down hard
across my cheek. The sting and shock of the pain made me
freeze.

"You stupid little bitch! How dare you demand anything from me! How dare you cross me!"

He raised his fist again and I ran and cowered in a corner.

"I would rather kill you than have you destroy me! I will not tolerate this from you! This will be your last mistake my dear!" He pulled me from the corner of the room and began to lash his fists at me uncontrollably. I tried to fight back but his strength far superseded mine. Deep within me all I could feel was contempt for this monster. I hated him and I wanted to run as far as I could away from him.

When he had overcome his rage he threw me like a discarded sack of rags onto the floor.

"Be ready to leave in five minutes. Do not dare ever speak to anyone about who you are or I promise you will be dead! Dead do you hear! And when I find out who told you the whereabouts of my house they will be dead too!"

After I heard the door slam I pulled myself up from the floor. My body ached. My face was now swelling with bruises. My lip was split, as was the area above my left eyebrow. I staggered over to the mirror and saw what had become of me. I wiped the tears from my eyes and defiantly washed the blood from my wounds in my pitcher.

How dare he hit me! I was no servant that he could beat. I was his daughter.

The swelling over my eye was growing by the second. I could feel my face throbbing. My eyes stung with a pain that was completely foreign to me. Nevertheless I stood defiantly and swore that I would take revenge. But how? What could I do? How could I fight this animal? I really did believe that he would kill me. He had shown me just how brutal he could be and I dared not say a word.

I went to the cupboard and pulled out my tapestry bag. I did not have much to pack. I would only take one of Charlottes dresses the one that I was wearing. The one that now had blood stains dripping over it. It did not seem right to take anything more. I had arrived here with nothing as I had been wearing only one of my dresses and the rags that I had worn to disguise myself for my journey down to London.

As I took my boots from the cupboard I pushed my hand down deep into the foot and took out Toms note. I uncrumpled it and sat on the edge of my bed reading his amateur and scrawlish writing. Every word showed concern. Every word echoed his sentiments about my good health and welfare. Tom was only a servant yet he displayed a warmer attitude towards me than those who considered themselves family. Everything with Tom was unconditional and meant from the heart. When I thought about him and the way he looked at me my heart just wanted to melt.

The door flung open. My father stood there red faced and angry. He seemed slightly shocked for a couple of seconds when he saw the puffiness in my cheeks and the way my top lip overhung my bottom with soreness and congealed blood. His focus was then diverted to the note in my hand and once again he was ignited.

"Thought you would leave a little farewell note did you? Thought you would tell everyone what I have done to you?"

"No!" I shrank back in horror and fear. The memories of the pounding still ringing in my ears.

"Give me that," He demanded

"You won't be leaving any farewell notes here!"

I grabbed the note tightly in my fist. I knew that I could not incriminate Tom. I could not let my father know who had led me to him.

At my reluctance, my father pounced over to me and began to unravel my fist. His sharp nails dug into my hand and I squealed

136

in pain. Once again he was too strong for me and I was powerless and weak. He grabbed the note half ripping it as he did so.

"No!" I yelped but it was too late he was reading it and learning all the details that I desperately wanted to hide from him.
I panted breathlessly from my tirade whilst my father stood smugly absorbing the information in the letter.

"So, you have a little servant clambering at your skirts. You are a filthy wench Alice. You are no lady! No child of mine! I will see that this Tom is found and receives the just reward that he deserves. He will not get away with this."

"Tom has done nothing!" I screamed in his defence.

"All he has done is shown me the truth that you have denied me all my life. He has done no harm."

"No harm! He is a thorn in my side! He is the cause of all my troubles and he will pay!"
I turned to my father with utter contempt in my eyes and spat at him. He raised his fist again then grabbed my arm and my bag and began to bundle me down the stairs. I said nothing but allowed him to push me out of the front door and into a waiting carriage.

"I will take you back myself!" He declared

"Can't trust anyone else with the responsibility of getting rid of you!"
He climbed up on top of the carriage and took the reins and whip. The horses whinnied and raised their hooves. I looked out of the window to look at what had been my home for the last few months. I was sad to leave like this without the hugs and embraces that I thought would bid me farewell.
Alone in the window of the drawing room stood a tall elegant figure in the shadow beside the curtain. I was sure it was Lady Eleanor. As the carriage pulled away she moved and for a split second our eyes met and I saw her regret and sadness. I wondered

if she had seen my face. If she knew what her husband had done to me.

I sank into the back of the carriage and watched my new world fleeting past me. Trees, houses, vehicles. The enormity of this new place astounded me. Even though I had been here quite a few weeks now, I had not really ventured out and so hadn't really appreciated what was around me. The buildings seemed to stand like huge ogres ready to fall on me and crush me. I felt very small, very scared and once again very alone.

My father drove like a madman. He swerved around corners and whipped the horses, grunting and uttering curses into the rushing wind. It was not until we had left the streets and sounds of the city that he pulled the horses up a little and allowed them the freedom of a gentle cantor.

It was hours before we stopped. My father must have been hungry and the horses definitely needed fresh hay and water. It was a two day drive back to Somerset and even though my father was quite keen to keep going all through the night there was no way that the horses could keep up that pace.

I heard my father dismount from the top of the carriage. He went around to the horses and unshackled them. I heard him speak to the servants at the inn where we had stopped and give them orders to tend to the horses. I didn't move. I sat very still imagining that if I were silent he would forget that I was there. I don't know whom I was trying to fool because it wasn't long before the handle of the carriage turned.

The cold eyes met mine.

"We will rest up here for the night! Then we will leave at the break of dawn!"

I moved from the shadow and the gaslight from the lamppost lit up my face. My father gasped and pushed me back into the carriage.

"Stay here until I have the keys to the rooms. You cannot be seen looking like that!"

I silently slid back into my seat. Soon he had returned. He held a blanket and wrapped it around me. He took my arm and led me through an old brown door and into a crowded inn. It was noisy and rowdy but no one seemed to take any notice of two figures that weaved their way past the crowd and filed up the stairs at the back of the bar. My father opened the door of my room. It was small and sparse with only a narrow bed and a table upon which was a pitcher and jug.

"I will bring you some dinner." He announced and left, locking the door behind him.

When he returned he was carrying a tray upon which was a bowl of soup and some bread. On another plate there seemed to be a kind of stew with great big lumps of potato and carrot.

I didn't look at my father. I sat obediently on the bed staring at my reflection through the darkened window. A candle flickered beside the bed and I realised that I could be snubbed out just as easily as it could. I was worthless, an inconvenient package of skin and bone that was now being removed and returned whence it had come. I heard the door close and the key once again turning in the lock and imprisoning me in this hole.

The food on the tray beside me smelt good but I could not eat. I felt so numbed by the day that I was not sure if I would ever be myself again. I warmed my hands over the rising steam from the plates and reflected on my nightmare. Perhaps I should try to cut my wrists and be done with all this, but they had only brought me a spoon on my tray. I looked around for a beam upon which I could tie my sheets and hang myself but there was none in this very low ceilinged room. In despair I picked up a morsel of bread and put it to my lips. I didn't have the will to actually open my mouth. Eating was staying alive and I so wished to be dead. I dropped the bread to the floor and a little mouse scurried from under the bed grabbed it and retreated.

I sat there for a very long time. My candle had long burnt out by the time I actually lay on the coarse pillow and allowed myself to close my eyes. I wondered what my brothers and sisters had thought when they had realised that I had gone. I had left like a thief and I felt great sadness for having not been able to say goodbye. It was a terrible feeling and almost like a dream that I had actually lived like a real lady, I had lived as my father's daughter in his house and for a few moments had been nearly somebody.

I wondered how long it would take for them all to forget me. Maybe they had forgotten me already. Perhaps I had imagined it all and nothing had been real. I had never felt such melancholy, never ached so, both mentally and physically. I had seen my brothers and sisters when they were sad yearning for the comfort of their mother. I had never known that feeling, yet now I wanted my mother. Yes, I wanted some faceless woman that I had never known to come forth from the shadows and comfort me.

It occurred to me that before I was to leave for France I must find my mother's grave.

That would be the last thing that I did before I left.

Chapter 23

I woke and sat on the corner of my bed reflecting on the last few days. Dawn had only just broken and I had only slept for maybe an hour or so. I was sad and deflated, of that there was no doubt and because all these feelings were so new to me I didn't know how to cast them aside and bounce back to my normal self. No one had ever laid a hand on me and I was genuinely scared.

I scratched at my skin that was already looking raw and chaffed from the coarseness of the blankets. My ankles itched as well and I suspected that I had shared my bed with many little creatures and mites that had all decided to feast on my delicate skin.

I stood and stretched and my body immediately twinged with sharp pains as my bruises and battered joints heaved into wakefulness. I dragged myself over to the other side of the room and to the full-length mirror on the gilt stand that stood beside the basin. I glared at the remnant of myself that reflected back at me. My face had a purple and yellow hue and my eyes were bloodshot and red. I brushed my hair, pulling the knots from the tangled strands. I wouldn't cry. Couldn't. Here I was like a lost puppy being taken back to a life in which I could make no decisions or choices. It was my own doing. I had thought that I was invincible and now had sadly learnt a harsh lesson.

I was aware that at any moment the door would open and my father would come and get me for the final part of our journey back to Somerset.

I really missed Somerset. It was the only real home that I had ever known. The smell of the cherry wood banisters and the fresh cut grass in the meadows enticed me like a cat to a bowl of cream. It was the only place where in this world of lies and betrayals I could really feel safe. Those smiling eyes would be there to welcome me home and those strong arms would make me feel like the queen of my little world once again. I couldn't wait to get back and to see Tom. So what that he was a servant? Who cared that he was of a lower birth than me? I was illegitimate. I was substandard and of inferior quality so it didn't matter any more about status. I had been in the company of gentlemen like William and Albert and I knew that Tom possessed a strength and sensitivity far more appealing than any quality that the other two had. Tom had shown me that he was devoted to me. He had risked his life to follow me to London and ensure that I was safe. He had written and declared me to be the most precious thing in the world and now suddenly I was realising that if he were by my side I would have the strength and determination to conquer all, even my father.

I heard the key turn in the door and my father slowly pushed the door open.

"Morning Alice, are you ready to leave?"

His voice was soft. He avoided looking directly at me and I knew that he was probably afraid of what he might see.

"Yes father I am ready." I replied.

I gathered up my bag and followed him down the stairs and through the deserted inn and outside to the carriage that was waiting. The air was cold and biting at this unearthly hour and I plunged my hands around my shawl to keep them warm. The horses were scraping their hooves on the gravelled floor and were quite eagerly waiting to begin their journey, following their rested night.

I stepped up into the carriage without a word.

"This is for you to eat on the way." My father thrust a loaf and some wrapped cheese and meats into my hand. Once again he avoided my eyes and turned away like a coward.

He climbed up and took the reins and once again we were racing through the countryside, hedgerows and trees fleeting past us. Rabbits scurrying to avoid being run over by the perilous wheels of the carriage as it swayed and swerved on its unrelenting journey.

I counted the hours by watching the sun rising in the sky and then slowly and heavily sinking again so that the darkness once again engulfed this sleepy part of the world.

I fell asleep frequently. I was so exhausted both mentally and physically that it was welcome to escape into that subconscious paradise state.

It wasn't long before I recognised the gentle pull of the hill and the wide cobbles as the horses clip clopped their way up to the old house. Excitedly I looked out of the window and a tear found its way into the corner of my eye when I realised that we were home.

The lights were only on downstairs and a stream of smoke gently dissipated from the chimney and into the grey sky.

"Tom" I whispered out loud and wondered where he was and whether I would be able to see him tonight and warn him to stay away from my father.

As the horses turned to the courtyard at the back of the house Mrs Knight opened the back door and came out. She saw my father sitting aloft on the carriage and when she peered in she saw me and her whole face lit up.

She rushed to the door and before the carriage had even drawn to a halt had opened the door and was calling out.

"Miss Alice, oh Miss Alice we have missed you so much."

It felt good and warm to be home. I hauled myself from the back of the carriage and took her hand as I stepped down and out into that familiar place.

The moon was full in the sky above and shone down like a globe lighting us like we were on a stage.

Mrs Knight shrunk back.

"Oh Alice! Oh my dear!"

"It's nothing Mrs Knight. Alice fell down some steps and bruised her face. She is well, it is nothing. Tell Mrs Knight that you are well Alice." Encouraged my father.

"Yes Mrs Knight. Please don't worry. I am extremely well."

"Take Alice to her room Mrs Knight and you can bring her up some supper she is very tired from her long journey, she needs to rest."

"Very well Mr Sinclair. Come along Alice."

She took my bag and I followed her through the parlour and into the hall. We climbed the large cherry wood staircase, which suddenly seemed so much grander and statelier than I remembered. I traced my fingers along the grain of the wood and savoured just how precious every aspect of my home really was. Even the ticking of the grandfather clock in the hall seemed to reassure me. When we reached my room it seemed like I had never left. Everything was just the same. Every item just as I had left it.

I collapsed onto my bed.

"Hello bed." I hugged my pillows

I opened my window.

"Hello fields"

Mrs Knight stood very still watching me.

"Are you really well Alice? We heard that you had almost died after your journey down to London. You really frightened us when you disappeared like that. We didn't know what had become of you. You shouldn't have gone off like that! You are only a child!"

Mrs Knight irritated me. One thing that I most certainly was not was a child. I don't think I ever had been, but now I most certainly was not. I wanted to turn around and say that in London a servant would never turn around to her master or mistress and speak to them in the way that she spoke to me. I was no kitchen maid that she could scowl. However I realised that she had always been like that with me and knew no different. She had been allowed by my father to talk to me so and have no respect for my status so maybe it wasn't really her fault.

"I apologise Mrs Knight for any distress I may have caused you. It was not my intention to cause you any worry but I needed to have some questions answered."

"Best to leave these things alone." She muttered.

I was riled. Best for whom to leave these matters alone? Certainly not for me! I could not explain my deep feelings of wanting to find my place and who I was. Neither did I want to share any of this with someone like Mrs Knight for whom I now felt some contempt for having lied to me for all these years. She still treated me like a baby and that would probably never change. I realised that in the time that I had been away I had actually learnt an awful lot about myself and even though that knowledge was painful I had taken it in my stride and accepted it. I had grown up an enormous amount and considered myself to be brimming with wisdom and a deeper intellect.

I had now only been safe within the walls of my house for a few minutes but the subdued and scared Alice was beginning to regain the confidence that had been knocked out of her over the last couple of days.

"Let me take a look at these bruises." Suggested Mrs Knight.

I sat at the end of the bed near to the light whilst she brought clean hot water and towels and began to bathe my bruises.

"Perhaps I should call the doctor?"

"No, that's not necessary!"

"Well you look frightful. Child like you not looking where she was going and falling so clumsily!"

"It was an accident Mrs Knight." I responded gritting my teeth.

"I'll go and get you some broth and then you should get some sleep child."

She left the room and I was quite relieved. Two seconds later there was a tap at the door and it slowly opened.

"Tom!" I had to stop myself from screaming his name out loud. Our eyes met and I could not help myself from running into his arms and clinging to him like he was the last person on the earth. I felt him hold me tightly. The warmth and strength he exuded made me feel like my inner fight was now returning. I could feel his hand run down my back till he reached a point over my ribs where the bruises were still very sore and I gasped. He pulled away and looked at me startled.

"Alice have I hurt you?"

"No Tom. You could never hurt me."

He stroked the bump over my eyes and traced his fingers over the welts around my face and over my lip.

"My poor Alice. Who did this to you?"

I looked to the floor. I didn't want to confess but my eyes told him the answer without me having to utter a word.

"Bastard! How dare he lay a finger on you, his own daughter!"

I didn't contradict him and he took my silence as affirmation of his accusation.

Heavy footsteps on the stairs broke the tension in the room.

"Quick hide in the cupboard! Mrs Knight is coming back with my supper."

As I closed the cupboard on Tom he leaned slightly forward and our lips brushed in the most tender but swift kisses. I turned to face Mrs Knight trying to conceal the most wonderful feeling that was sweeping like a tidal wave over my body.

"Drink this good soup." Declared Mrs Knight oblivious to my exhilarated state.

"Yes Mrs Knight, you are so kind to me."

Mrs Knight gave me a confused look.

"Good I'm glad that you are seeing sense. Are you sorry that you caused us so much trouble?"

"Oh yes Mrs Knight. I have been very reckless and stupid and have learnt my lesson well. I shall always behave from now on." My smile was broad and I didn't really care what I was saying or that it was so out of character with the way that I was generally feeling.

I began to drink my soup knowing full well that once Mrs Knight had gone I would be left alone and undisturbed for the whole night.

Chapter 24

I was floating on a cloud so high that I thought I could see heaven. I had never known a feeling that could completely turn your stomach and head so that you were catapulted into another realm of the universe. I was spinning like a top but regardless of how giddy I was feeling I didn't want to stop.

Was this love? Was this complete total utter feeling of whoosh, love?

I grinned to myself and pulled the covers up to my chin. Maybe I was just hallucinating? Perhaps it had all been a fantastic dream? I rolled over and my skin brushed against Toms. No, I wasn't dreaming. There was no remorse. No sense of guilt or immodesty. I felt no shame, no feeling of regret.

Tom had shown me completeness. He had betrothed himself to me. We had promised each other nothing more than an open and honest heart that would always beat for the other. Tom had asked me to marry him and without doubt or reflection I had agreed.

I was swimming in a large ocean but the current held no fear for me, I knew exactly what I was doing and I wanted this more than anything I had ever yearned for in the past.

Tom opened his eyes and looked longingly into mine. His arm reached out and I felt him so strong yet soft and gentle reach out to me. He ran his hand over my back and I closed my eyes and the exquisiteness of his touch.

He enveloped me once again and we rolled like playful kittens till our bodies entwined once again and we were as one.

"I love you Alice."

"I love you too Tom."

"I'll always look after you. I will marry you as soon as we can get away."

"Yes Tom."

"Then you shall be mine and not even your father can cast aside a union blessed by god."

"Yes Tom"

"Alice you are so beautiful."

"Yes Tom."

I was in a semi dream like state. Neither coherent nor incoherent.

"Will we live here and you master the estate?"

"Oh Alice! I don't think I could do that! Can you imagine me telling the other servants what to do? No this house has always been a prison for you Alice; I wouldn't like to bring up my children here. We will find a little cottage somewhere, we'll get a good price for this and all its land."

"Your children?"

"Sorry Alice, our children."

A fresh smile crept over my face. I had never really thought about my children, about my own family. Having Tom was all I really wanted but now the prospect of my children, my family, excited me even more. Maybe the family that I had always secretly longed for was my very own family.

"How many shall we have? Will we have boys or girls?"

Tom looked at me and with all sincerity announced.

"We will have what we are blessed with, but maybe strong sons would be an even greater blessing."

"What's wrong with strong daughters? Girls can be equally intelligent and hardy!"

"Don't be silly Alice. Girls have their dolls and their kitchen chores it's the men that do the real work!"

The window had blown open and suddenly a shot of cold air seemed to be sobering me up. I sat upright and perused Tom who was laying on my embroidered French lace pillows.

"Girls are not stupid! Girls can achieve as well! For goodness sake we have a queen on the throne at the moment. A good queen that is ruling this country far better than any king. A queen that is building England into an empire!"

"Yes Alice but that's just an accident of birth. Don't you think that all her advisors and people around her in the government are men? It's men that make the real decisions not women."

I got out of bed and went over to close the window biting my lip all along. It was true that men considered themselves the superior sex and we frail women just acquiesced with all their demands. Why didn't women stand up to men? Why was there no rebellion to this unfair state?

The reason was simple. The government was made of men and they laid down the rules. They deemed that all that a woman owned belonged to her father or her husband. They shifted power from the gloved hands of ladies, and any woman who dared to stand and contest, was laughed at and either thrown into jail or into a mental asylum. Women were the silent force. Working behind their husbands. Urging them, encouraging them, sifting through their dilemmas and advising them. But always behind doors where no one could know that the man was really only the middle man.

Tom was the same. Conditioned to believe that he was superior, even to me. I was a woman now and further more a woman that wanted to change the world...somehow.

I closed the window. The dawn had long broken and the young lambs were bleating in the fields beyond. The crisp air rushed into my nostrils and cut into my lungs as I drew a deep breath. A reminder of the ague that had affected me so badly.

"Alice come away from that cold window. Come back to this warm bed."

His voice melted in my ears. Maybe I did want to change the world but not right this minute. I scurried across the cold floor and gently lifted the covers revealing Toms body. I blushed and turned my eyes, then climbed into the warm bed and allowed myself to become enveloped into that warmth that I was now becoming so comfortable with.

There was so much to plan and so much to do and it all had to be done swiftly before my father could interfere with my new revised itinerary. He would be furious but then what did I care. It was my life and I needed to take control if I had an opportunity, and Tom was my answer. This was my last chance before it was too late.

I knew I was safe now. Here with the man that I loved, my future was remapped. Nothing could touch me. At last I was safe and loved. At last I could relax and with that thought in my head I managed to drift off into the sweetest of slumbers.

I was awoken by a tap on the door. Tom had already leapt from the bed and was frantically pulling on his clothes. I was startled and scared, scrambling with petticoats over my head.

"Be there in a second" I shouted.

"It's only me Miss Alice it's Maud."

I sighed. A deep sense of relief, which only lasted for a moment.

"I'm out here with your father; he has come to talk to you when you are dressed."

My heart began pumping again. The sweat creeping over me like a damp towel. I pulled my skirts up and wrapped my shawl over my shoulders. Tom meanwhile was trying to rearrange himself back into the cupboard.

"Good morning Alice"

I tried to recompose myself as my father entered the room.

"Good morning father."

"I hope you slept very well, if not quite restlessly." He nodded to the bed, which was in the most terrible state of disarray.

"Yes father." I hastily tried to pull the covers into a neater arrangement noticing as I did so the bloodstained sheets.

"We will make the arrangements for you to leave straight away. You will pack up your belongings and anything else that you want or need from the house and by the end of the week you will go."

This wasn't the time or the moment to tell my father that I had other plans. It was easier to just agree with him. Packing my things wasn't the problem because I would need to pack my things in order to run away with Tom. We would probably head West find a small parish and then find a priest to marry us before returning to sell the house.

I wasn't completely sure if that was what I really wanted to do. This house had been in my family for centuries and my only link to my mother and her ancestors.

Maud who had been patiently standing in the corner after depositing her breakfast tray now carefully turned and tiptoed out. Her face had been brimming with anticipation to talk to me and hear all my adventures since I had been away. I could sense her annoyance at my father for standing so long and not giving her leeway to speak. Nevertheless she had given up waiting and was probably in awe of Mrs Knight downstairs in the kitchen who would be boxing her ears for not getting on with her chores.

"Of course father," I said humbly.

"I will get all my clothes and books ready. What will become of the house?"

"The house will be locked up and the servants will have to find other positions. It is too expensive to keep them here for nothing.

They will get good references and be able to find other jobs easily."

"Yes father."

"I will not sell the house just yet. It may come in handy as a dowry for you when we find you a suitable husband."
I smiled at the mention of the word husband and imagined myself in a little parish church in Wales, kneeling before the priest and taking Tom to be my lawfully wedded husband.

"Mrs Knight will escort you and once you are settled at your new home with Madame de Laraunt she will return home."

"Of course father, whatever you say father." I added facetiously.

"None of that cheek!" declared my father.

"You will have respect for me and for my position"

"I meant nothing father."

"Do you want new bruises to match those just fading on your cheeks? Remember I will kill you if you disobey me or cause me any more disappointment. I have had enough of you and your lip!"
There was a rustle from the cupboard. Under my breath I was trying to send a message to Tom to stay still and not to be riled by my fathers' angry tone with me. We had to weather that storm. We could not risk being caught now, not when we had made our plans and were so close to getting away and being safe.
The cupboard door flung open.

"How dare you speak to Alice that way? You are a big bully! No man would do that to the face of a young girl! Only a coward would do this and you sir are a coward!"

"Tom hush, no!" I pleaded.

"So this is Tom, I've been waiting to meet you! You are a filthy servant hiding in my daughter's closet. Alice you are nothing more than a whore letting every stable boy into your bedchamber!"

I knew what my father was capable of and I was genuinely scared for Tom. I stood quivering unable to speak whilst my father and Tom spat venom at each other.

My father was becoming more and more enraged. I had seen that look in his eyes before and I knew that it meant trouble. Suddenly he lunged and grabbed Tom by the throat. Tom struggled and fought back, landing a punch on my father's chin.

They fought like wild dogs, drawing blood and scratching whilst I, like the weak girl that I was cowered in a corner till Tom was overcome and panting on the floor beneath my father's breaches.

   "I'll show you what happens to imbecile servants that think they know better than their masters! I'll show you what will become of you!"

He dragged Tom by his collar pulling him so hard that Tom almost turned blue. He pulled him with the strength of a giant down the stairs and into the courtyard screaming at me as he did so, that I should stay in my room otherwise I would be next. He dragged him all the way to the stables. Then the great barn doors slammed shut.

Chapter 25

I didn't know what to do. I ran to the window flung it open and waited. Maud came into the room looking flushed and anxious.

"Miss Alice what's the master doing with Tom?"
"I don't know Maud. This is all my fault, but we must stay here or we shall be in grave danger."
From the open window came the sound of a lash of a whip followed by a loud piercing scream.
"Oh sweet Lord" Fretted Maud. "The master is beating him."
My hands clasped around my ears and the tears began to stream down my cheeks.
"I shan't hear it. I shan't listen!" I whispered trembling at the thought of what was happening to my sweet Tom.
"Miss Alice I am going down there, I can't stay here whilst my brother is being hurt."
Maud turned to leave the room. I could hear the swish of her skirts as she hurried to get down the stairs and out to the stables.
"No Maud!" I pleaded as I ran out after her. Despite knowing that we really should stay in the safety of my room, I did want to go out there and put a stop to whatever terror my father was inflicting upon Tom. This was my doing I had led Tom to my father's lair and now he was being savaged by this most ferocious beast.
Maud and I ran like lunatics out of the door around the courtyard and to the bolted stable door. From within we could hear the lashings of the whip and Tom's screams piercing the early morning skies.
"We must stop him" pleaded Maud.

"We can't he will beat us too!"

Maud looked at my face still tinged with the purple of my bruises.

"Did he do this to you?"

"Yes" I nodded humbly.

"Oh Miss Alice we have to get Tom out of there, he will kill him!"

Those words froze like ice on a pane. I hadn't even considered such a thing. Tom was my love, my future and my freedom. No one could kill him! He couldn't die. My father couldn't commit murder or could he? Yet he had threatened to kill me and I had believed him. He had broken nearly every other commandment in the bible so why stop at murder?

Tom's screams began to subside but the cruel whip kept lashing. My father was grunting and swearing, as Maud and I listened huddled like terrified mice outside the doors. Even the horses in the stable that had been whinnying and making all kinds of attempts to free themselves from their chains probably from fear and confusion had now remained silent.

There was then one large cry. The great barn doors began to be unbolted. I grabbed Maud's hand and we ran and hid behind a water trough.

My father emerged staggering from the barn. He was ashen faced and clutching his left arm. He walked like a drunken man towards the house from where Mrs Knight quite tactfully now appeared.

"Help me," he mumbled.

"Go to the village and call Doctor Emmanuel. Go now woman! What are you waiting for and bring him straight to me!"

Mrs Knight who was clearly shaken by my father's unsightly demeanour, obeyed and rushed to go to the village. She clutched at her skirts and made her way as fast as her arthritic legs would take her down the gravelled path and towards the doctors. My father turned to the front door and partially collapsed.

"Damn" he muttered. He crawled through the front door and into the house. Maud and I waited till he was completely out of sight then with one thought uniting our minds we ran into the barn.

The vision that met us was not one that we had imagined or anticipated. I don't know rightly what we had expected, but the lifeless body staining crimson the bundles of hay upon which it lay was very horrific.

Tom was half naked. His shirt had been ripped from his back. He lay on his front, his head turned to one side. His back was raw and oozing with his blood. Maud and I looked at each other, fear and desperation clouding our eyes. I felt nauseous, aghast at what I was seeing. Maud clutched at her stomach and instinctively I grabbed her and supported her.

"Is he dead?" She asked.

I breathed deeply and with great trepidation approached Tom. I knelt down and put my face next to his. His eyes fluttered and rolled then closed.

"I think he's alive!" I screamed.

"Oh thank you Jesus!" Exclaimed Maud.

"Get some water! Quickly Maud!"

I touched Toms face. He was ripped to shreds. There had been no mercy. No pity.

Maud returned with the water and we put it to Tom's lips. He made no attempt to drink. We dampened a corner of Maud's petticoat with the water and squeezed it into his mouth. His tongue lapped slowly although he made no sound. We then tried to wash the blood and dirt from his back. Grains of grit and gravel seemed to be embedded within the deep red wounds. Tom let out a pitiful moan and instinctively we stopped.

157

"Are we hurting him? Is this causing him more pain?" Maud asked.

"I don't know. I'm scared Maud, we must do something but I don't know what. We must move him and clean him but I don't know how." I sobbed.

"The doctor should be here soon. We will wait for the doctor. He will know what to do."

"My father called the doctor for himself not for Tom." I replied abruptly.

"He doesn't care about Tom it's not his concern whether he lives or dies. He stamps on people like they're ants. Tom is just another one." I added contemptuously.

Maud looked at me.

"And you, are you an ant too?"

I looked into Maud's grey eyes. Her wisdom shining through.

"Yes Maud we are all ants if we let ourselves be."

Hurried footsteps outside on the gravel faded as they reached the house.

"I suppose that Mrs Knight is back with the doctor. Hurry Maud go and get him as soon as he is available and bring him here, I will wait with Tom."

Maud got up to go then stopped and turned to me.

"Miss Alice, I am just a servant girl. The doctor won't listen to me, he'll laugh at me. I think it's better if you go and ask him, he'll listen to you."

I thought for a moment then realised that Maud was probably right. I didn't want to leave Tom but if I didn't fetch the doctor what chance might he have lying here in filthy horse dung, bleeding?

"Tom" I whispered in his ear hoping that he could hear me.

"I will be back soon my love. I'm going to get the doctor we are going to help you and then we will be gone from here. We'll leave and be married."

Tom stirred a little then tried to speak.

"Your…"

"Don't speak Tom it's all right everything will be fine"

"Find…"

"Find what Tom?

"Other" and then Tom closed his eyes again and began to breath softly.

"What do you think he was trying to say?

"I don't know, let me know if he says anything else. I'll be back as quickly as I can."

I ran into the house and into the hallway I could hear the doctor's voice coming from the library. I crept behind the door and listened, then pushed the door slightly ajar so that I could peek in.

"You must take great care Mr Sinclair and get to your bed. You seem to have had an attack of some sort and even though the numbness down your arm has dissipated a little, you must take all pressure off your heart or it could be bad."

"Nonsense!" Scoffed my father.

"You may think it's nonsense but you must be careful."

"A stupid servant caused all this. He's excited my heart and made it start racing. Young upstart. Don't you be tending to him doctor? I'm not paying you to waste your time with him. He can sleep it off in the barn."

"Whatever you wish Mr Sinclair but I do suggest that you take to your bed as soon as possible."

"Bed! I'll go to my bed when I am back in London. Everyone has their instructions and I have had enough of this forsaken place."

I wouldn't travel Mr Sinclair, not in your condition .You must rest!" Said the doctor horrified.

My father was looking ashen like the embers in the morning grate. He was holding onto his arm and lying propped up on the sofa. The doctor had all his instruments laid out over the desk but had clearly not been successful at persuading my father as to what was good for him.

"Good" I thought.

"Don't listen to the doctor, die you bastard."

The doctor began to pack up his belongings. He was shaking his head at my father's stubbornness.

"You had best listen to me Sir otherwise there'll be nothing more for me to do for you!"

He closed his bag bade my father farewell and began to approach the door. Hurriedly I raced to the bottom of the staircase so that I could not be guilty of eavesdropping behind doors.

Doctor Emmanuel closed the library door behind him and began to walk towards me.

"Doctor Emmanuel" I beseeched.

"I need your help most urgently"

"My dear" Dr Emmanuel looked at me and observed my dishevelled appearance and my discoloured face.

"Are you well Alice? You seem quite distressed."

"Yes doctor. I am just fine but there is a boy in the stables that is in urgent need of your medical expertise."

"Oh" Replied the doctor, looking away uncomfortably.

"Please come. He has been injured quite severely and I am afraid that he may die!"

"Alice, this is some drunken lout that has upset your father and caused him to have quite a severe heart palpitation. I am surprised that you haven't shown any consideration for your father or his condition. You seem to be more concerned about some servant than the person that you should be showing concern for!"

"But Dr Emmanuel that is just not true! Tom is not drunk. He has been severely beaten by my father and needs your care. Please come!"

"Alice, I am not in the habit of being ordered around by young girls. I am also not inclined to see this young fellow as it is your fathers express wish that he be left alone to sleep it off."

Dr Emmanuel nodded and bade me farewell. It was pointless to plead with him as he was completely disinterested in my plight and I could tell very much, under the influence of my father. I ran back to the barn.

"Maud how is he doing?

"Oh Alice he needs help. Where is the doctor?"

"He won't come." I said simply

"Why?" Maud was crying

"Forbidden to do so by my father!"

"What's wrong with your father?"

"Heart ailment…I hope he dies."

"Miss Alice you mustn't say such things"

"It's true. I don't care. Look what he has done!"

"We must get help Alice he's been mumbling and calling for his mother. We must get help. He's beginning to burn a fever"

"There's only one more person we can ask. I'll have to go to the village myself and get Nurse Dunn. She's always been there for me. She'll help. She'll sort this out. She'll help Tom if only for my sake.

I didn't waste another second. I turned and was half way down the hill before I had given it a second thought. I would get help. I would save Tom and then we would be gone.

Chapter 26

The road down to the village was paved with cobbles, which seemed quite slippery from the morning rain. It was all down hill and I remembered this route well from the last time that I had trodden this path, on the morning that I had ran away to London. On that occasion I had been unaware that Tom had followed me. Now I was following this same route, with the hope that I could find someone who could help Tom to recover from his ordeal with my father. The image of his wounds weeping and sore grated on my mind. I ran faster till I could see the little house where Mrs Dunn my nurse lived. It was a little red brick cottage with smoke billowing from the chimney and drifting into the grey skies. I hadn't seen Nurse Dunn for many months but she was the person that I most warmed to and the one that I imagined would be like the mother that I never had. She had cared for me during my sickest days and had made me well and strong. She had never let me down and I was confident that now in my hour of need she would be there for me and help me through my dilemma.

I lifted the brass knocker and struck it three times. I could hear a shuffling from within and then the heavy latch lifted and the door opened.

A small boy with dark hair and dark eyes stood looking at me innocently. I presumed that this must be one of Nurse Dunn's two sons.

"Hello is your mother at home?"

He shook his head.

"Do you know where she is or when she will be back?"

He eyed me suspiciously. I supposed that I did look a mess. My dress was covered in horse manure. I had Tom's blood on my skirt and my hair had not yet been brushed this morning.

"She's just gone to the hospital. She's the nurse there."

"Thank you" I responded gratefully.

He closed the door and I heard the latch being pulled down again. I turned and looked around for the outline of the hospital, which I could see about half a mile away in the distance. I began to run towards it. My feet were pounding on the cobbles and aching with each step. All I could think of was Tom who might be dying in that stable if I didn't get help.

I reached the hospital. I hurried through the Gothic arch entrance. The strong carbolic smell engulfing me as I walked into the entrance hall. I looked around and then suddenly a familiar figure came into view. Down the corridor I could see the back of Nurse Dunn. I ran breathlessly. My dress was clinging to me and the beads of sweat were rolling down my brow. She turned when she heard me and then instinctively opened her arms to me.

"Alice! Alice are you all right? My dear you look frightful what has happened to you?"

"Nurse Dunn, I need your help most urgently!"

She held her arm around my back and instinctively the story began to pour from my lips.

"My father has had the most frightful argument with one of the servants and has beaten him and whipped him. He is barely alive and I am afraid that he might die. I need your help. Please Mrs Dunn will you come and tend to him?"

"Does your father know that you are here? Have you called out the doctor?"

I felt ashamed to tell her the truth but felt that I had no choice.

"Nurse Dunn, the doctor has already been to the house, not to see Tom but to see my father. My father has told the doctor that he is not to tend to Tom and the doctor left without even taking a look."

Nurse Dunn appeared uncomfortable.

"If your father has forbidden the doctor to tend to this servant than I do not think it wise to do so."

I began to cry. I felt so hopeless.

"However" she continued.

"…Your father has not actually told me that I cannot see to the boy so I would not be actually disobeying him would I?"

"Oh thank you Nurse Dunn!" I threw my arms around her once again.

"I will just have to tell the other nurses that I have to leave for a while and then I need to prepare a bag of supplies. Wait here Alice I will be a few minutes."

I sat down. My head was spinning and I felt very light headed. It seemed like ages till Nurse Dunn reappeared in her coat carrying her medical bag.

We left the hospital together, walked through the village at a brisk pace and climbed the steep hill back to the house. The sun had dried the roads and the primroses and lilies of the valley lined the pathways up the slopes. Nurse Dunn asked few questions and I was grateful for the lack of intrusion. It would have been so difficult to fill in all the gaps and explain all the things that had happened since we last met. She had seen the urgency and need that I had and without too much thought had once again been there as one of the only adults in my life to actually support me. Just the touch of her hand gave me hope and confidence and I knew that if anyone could make this right it would be her.

As we reached the gates of the house my pace fastened and we began to run towards the barn. We entered. Maud was bending over Tom's body stroking his face and weeping.

"Oh thank you so much for coming. I hope it's not too late. Please help him. Please"

Nurse Dunn gasped when she saw the whipped bloodstained body laid out in front of her. She turned to me.

"Did your father do this?"

"Yes" I nodded ashamed.

She crept beside the body and lifted his limp hand feeling for his pulse.

"He's very weak"

She looked at Maud and me and asked.

"Can we move him to somewhere clean? Does he have a room where we can take him too? It's dirty in here and these horse flies aren't going to help him?"

"Yes." Maud replied.

"His room is around the back of the house in the servants' quarters. But Nurse Dunn how are we going to carry him?"

"I don't know but we must. This place is filthy and he will definitely get an infection if he stays here one minute longer. Alice you take one arm, Maud you take the other and I will take his feet. We have no choice this poor boy needs to be moved." Together with the strength of Hercules we pulled him, lifted and carried him around the barn and to the back of the house, through the mud room and down to his little room in the basement. This was a part of the house I had never been in before and never even knew existed. Of course I knew that the servants slept downstairs but I had never ventured into any of their rooms or even imagined what they looked like. The room was tiny and sparse. Just a bed and a plain wooden cupboard. When we tried to get through the door with Tom there wasn't even enough room to turn around and we had to let Nurse Dunn go into the room first then single file in after her whilst she supported all of Tom's weight.

We laid him on the bed on his front. His back was so badly injured that we couldn't put even the slightest bit of pressure on it. Nurse Dunn then sent Maud to get hot water and clean towels. She opened her bag and took out a bottle of dark inky liquid. She poured a few drops into the bowl of hot water making it turn a yellowish hue. She then got the towels and began to gently dab at the weals and burns and clean them out. Occasionally she would dip her tweezers into the liquid and then pull great pieces of gravel and dirt from Toms back. All the while Tom lay very still. Sometimes he groaned but generally he made not a sound. When she had finished cleaning his back and his face she turned to us and said.

"I have done all I can for him now. He has lost a lot of blood and his pulse is very weak. He seems to be a strong boy though and he should pull through. There is no more we can do but wait. Hopefully when he wakes we will see an improvement but now we have to let him sleep and pray that he recovers. Maud you must be responsible for checking on him and giving him water so that he can drink. Take this tincture and dab it onto his back as you have seen me do, every few hours. I will try to come back tonight to check on him."

"Thank you nurse Dunn" I acknowledged.

"We just didn't know what to do."

"You did the right thing Alice you came and got me." She put her arms around me and kissed my cheek.

"Now go and clean yourselves up and please don't tell anyone that I was here."

We both nodded in comprehension.

Nurse Dunn packed up her little bag and began to leave. We followed her to the gate and as we were about to bid her farewell Mrs Knight ran screaming from the house.

"The master! The master!" she yelled.

"Nurse Dunn thank goodness you are here. Please come quickly; the master is lying on the floor in the library!

Nurse Dunn shot me a look and then ran inside the house with Mrs Knight. I stood alone for a while listening to the footsteps as they scurried into the distance. The air was warm now and the sweet smell of the grass in the pastures and the spring flowers on the lawns wafted around me. I didn't feel the need to run anywhere. I wasn't even curious to know what had happened to my father. I had seen what pain he was capable of inflicting and all I wanted was revenge. I hoped that whatever he was suffering was tenfold of what he had caused. I had no sympathy. Far from it I wished that I could rub the pain of Tom's wounds into the weakened heart of my father. I wanted the gravel and dirt to stick in his lungs till he could not breathe. I wished him all ill that there was in the world. I wanted the fires of hell to burn him up.

I just stood till the rage had passed through me, until I felt calmed again and able to walk back to my room.

I stripped off my clothes and began to bathe in the cool water of my basin. I splashed the water onto my face and around the back of my neck. I then brushed my hair, pulling at the knots and teasing out all the strands. Then twisted it into a braid and pinned it neatly on top of my head. I dressed in a new clean dress then calmly sat at my dressing table and dabbed some powder over my fading bruises. Outside I could hear the clippity clopping of hooves and Dr Emmanuel coming back to the house. Down below I could hear the frantic voices of Nurse Dunn, Mrs Knight and Dr Emmanuel all conferring in the hallway.

I didn't move. I sat quite still and emotionless. I had no desire to see what was going on. I had no interest in the welfare of my father.

I took a book from my shelf and went over to the seat by the window and began to read. I was lost in the pages of the book, completely absorbed by the imaginary world which absorbed me. The pages turned, the voices diminished. I was alone like an empty vessel, one with a crack at the bottom that could never be filled.

I didn't want to think about my life. I didn't want those internal bruises to shadow me. I was a pawn to everyone, a chess piece with only one move. There was no benefit for me anywhere; I felt that I didn't belong to this world. Maybe I was just a very strange girl. Perhaps I should have been born as Cleopatra or someone like that who could do and live as she wished. What was I? I pushed all thoughts of Tom from my mind. Maybe if I didn't think of him I wouldn't feel so morbid and disillusioned. I didn't want to think of the worst but how could I not? Everything that was important to me I could not have, so maybe I should just accept it. Maybe I should join a convent and take a vow of silence. No one wanted to talk to me anyway and for some people it would be a blessing just to get me out of the way.

Would Tom die?

"No Alice" I told myself. Stop thinking like that. I tried to get back into my book but ended up gazing out of my window beyond all the rooftops at the grey spires of the church that reached out like a pointed dagger to the sky. The bells often rang. They were not ringing now, there was a hollow silence gagging the village.

Somerset was so different to the sounds of London. London hummed and churned. Bicycle bells, whistles, voices calling way above the clatter of horse's hooves. I could not imagine what Paris would sound like; if there was music in the air, if people danced in the streets to the sound of the accordion.

"Alice?"

I sat looking out of the window oblivious.

"Alice?" The voice was more urgent.

I turned to look at Maud.

"He's gone Alice, he's gone."

Chapter 27

Gone was a very final word. Gone meant forever and had very heavy implications.

I perused Maud's tearstained face and immediately felt a bolt searing through me.

She came into the room and put her hand on my shoulder. We had shared enough harrowing moments recently for her to feel that as a servant she could do that.

There seemed to be a confused and perplexing few seconds whilst I registered exactly what she was telling me.

"Did he say anything?" I asked.

"Alice it's your father who has passed not Tom."

I took a deep breath and then the tears of relief came flooding through.

"I am so sorry Alice for your loss."

I frowned at Maud. She had mistaken my relief with grief.

"I am not sad for my father. I have been wishing him dead since he did this to my face. I have no feelings for that man who spent his whole life lying to me and telling me fictitious stories. Why would I cry for him? He was the worst fraudster one could have as a parent!"

"But he was still your father Alice. You owe him your life."

"My life! What life? He stole my life and my childhood! Maybe I should be grateful to him though for dying."

"Oh Alice that is a terrible thing to say!"

"I don't care, its true."

The door opened and Nurse Dunn walked in.

"Alice I am so sorry. Your father's heart was just too weak and gave out. The doctor came and we tried to save him but it was all in vain there was nothing we could do."

I shot Nurse Dunn a look as if I had been betrayed.

"Well you shouldn't have tried so hard then should you? I thought you were on my side?"

"Alice!" Nurse Dunn was equally offended.

"This was a man, a human being! He was sick and needed care in the same way that anyone else in pain would be treated and be given care! He was a respectable man. It is disgraceful to have such an attitude Alice, whatever he may have done. If you were my child you would be punished for such insolence. He was your father Alice! Your father!"

I bowed my head. I had never seen Nurse Dunn so red faced and angry. It just felt strange to me that anyone would want to show any kindness to someone who was simply a despicable monster.

"Alice I think you should go downstairs immediately and see your father before he is moved. It is only the right and proper thing to do."

"Moved? Moved to where?" I enquired.

"Well he cannot stay here! He must be taken back to London. Your father cannot be associated with this place or there will be scandal and gossip. He will be taken back within the hour."

I was baffled. Surely they could not concoct a story so fascinating that Lady Sinclair would believe? But then they had all been part of this conspiracy for so many years that it was second nature to the servants of this household. I wondered what my position now was in this tangled web. Was I now free to do as I pleased now that I no longer had a taskmaster?

"I am sorry Nurse Dunn." I mumbled.

"I should think so too!"

We walked down the stairs and to the library. Before Nurse Dunn opened the door she tried to prepare me for what I was about to see.

"Have you ever seen anyone dead before?"

"Not quite" I replied with a hint of sarcasm, which thankfully was unnoticed.

"It may be a bit of a shock. I have smelling salts in my pocket should you need them. Now prepare yourself Alice."

At that she turned the handle and we walked in.

Dr Emmanuel and Mrs Knight were standing beside the body. My father was laid on the settee a blanket covering his face.

Dr Emmanuel turned to Nurse Dunn.

"Why have you brought the child here?"

I winced slightly at the word child but remained composed.

"She is here because this is her father, and she is no longer a child"

"Thank you" I replied in my head.

"Well I suppose so, but only for a moment and then we must prepare to take him back to London."

Dr Emmanuel pulled back the blanket. The face was blue and sallow, the eyes closed. The hair lank and almost white at the sides. Instinctively I stepped back, away from this figure that was greying before me. I could not feel any sadness. There was no feeling of regret. In fact no feeling at all. I pulled the cover back and turned away.

Behind me, the doctor was talking about what story they would tell when they returned the body.

"May I make a suggestion?" I interjected.

"Oh?" Replied the doctor.

"My father was supposed to be returning me back to my home in Northampton. I could say that he became ill upon the way and died suddenly. I think that I should return with him."

"...But I don't know that is what the master would have wanted."

"Dr Emmanuel. I know that you think of me as only a child but I assure you that I am not. I understand all the deceits that were

171

constructed to protect me and during my recent visit to my father's house in London I learnt the art of continuing the art of deception. I was able to pull it off brilliantly. I feel that my fathers' family deserve a little more than a corpse turning up on their doorstep and if anyone should deliver him back with a reasonable story than it should be me."

There was a stunned silence in the room.

"Umm,oh,erhum" Faffed the doctor.

Mrs Knight shook her head at the whole scene.

"How do we know that we can trust you Alice? We have all pledged our loyalty to your father and have done so for many years. What is there to stop you betraying him?"

"I am his daughter am I not?" I replied indignantly

"Furthermore, whatever my feelings for the man, I was still a guest of his wife and I have utmost regard for her and so would not jeopardise the trust that she has for me."

They all looked at each other with a mixed look of concern as well as relief. Of course if I took my father home it would be more convenient for all of them and they would not be the ones going out of their way to lie. My thoughts were with my brothers and sisters who had shown me every kindness and for whom I would perform this mission. It was not for my father. He deserved nothing from me. I also knew that if I did this then maybe I could convince Lady Sinclair that I could have a place in London society as her niece of course. Possibly she would take pity on the poor girl who had returned her dear husbands body back to London. Possibly my father-dying like this could be to my advantage after all. Maybe I could gain from this somehow.

"I think Alice has a point" Suggested Dr Emmanuel.

"It may look better coming from her."

I could see in the doctor's eyes that I was saving him a trip down to London.

"Well we are all busy aren't we?" Added Mrs Knight
Nods all around.

"Alice?" Nurse Dunn was looking concerned.

"Are you sure that you want to do this? Bearing in mind everything that you have been feeling lately and you must be quite exhausted anyway from your journey here. You've only practically just arrived."

I had made up my mind and nothing could stop me. I would sort out any business here when I returned. Life moved at such a slow pace that I could be away for weeks and nothing would really happen.

"Yes it is fine Nurse Dunn. I think that this is my responsibility and I should be the one to do this for everyone's sakes."

"I will prepare the carriage," said the doctor.

"Alice get ready quickly."

"I need no time. I will take my small bag. Mrs Knight you can pack some food. I shall be half an hour."

I left the room. Maud was standing in the corridor with a very soured face. I supposed that she had been listening behind the door and had heard every word.

"Why are you doing this?" She asked timidly

"Not here" I replied and we went quickly to my room.

"Doing what!" I demanded

"Leaving." She whispered.

"Because I feel that I should."

"But…"

"But what is it any of your concern anyway?"

"Miss Alice?"

"Maud, I am the mistress here now and I feel that it is right to escort my fathers' body back to his family. Whatever he may have done to me, they always showed me kindness and respect. I felt wanted and a part of a family for the first time ever. You

173

wouldn't understand that Maud. You have always had a family. I have not. My father was the only obstacle to my continuing happiness in London. Furthermore I don't see why I should justify my actions to you!"

Maud stood muted and shocked at my abrupt tone. I could see though that she was desperate to say something to me.

"Speak girl! What is it you want to say to me?"

"Miss Alice, what about Tom?" We need to care for him."

"Well you can do that cant you? You can get him repaired for me for when I return."

"Alice, why have you forgotten about Tom? Why are you acting and thinking so differently from the Alice this morning who would have done anything for Tom?"

I didn't wait to let her words absorb into my skin and sink deep into my heart. I was tired and listless. I hadn't slept for days and felt irritated easily especially by this simple girl that had no idea of how I could use this situation to benefit my status. She would always be a kitchen maid, yet I had the potential to be somebody, but it would only happen through my own ambition. I knew that very well. I hadn't forgotten Tom but at this moment he was of no use to me and I was certainly of no use to him.

"Maud I am the same Alice. However the situation is different now and I have to act accordingly. This is not my choice this is my duty and it must be fulfilled."

Maud bowed her head still not fully comprehending what I was doing.

I grabbed my bag. Took a couple of dresses folded them in the bag with some petticoats whilst Maud went to the other drawers and started putting other items into the bag.

It wasn't too long before I was all packed and ready. As I came down the stairs I could see that the carriage had been brought around to the front and my father wrapped in blankets had been placed in the back. I assumed that I could either share the carriage with him or ride up front with the driver. Mrs Knight handed a hamper to the footman who duly placed it under his seat.

"Well everything is ready for your departure." Said Dr Emmanuel.

"Thank you" I nodded at the small crowd assembled.
I stepped up to the carriage. Maud walked away in a huff. I realised why and jumped down.

"I shall be back momentarily." I announced.
I ran after her and followed her back to Tom's room.

"I thought you would go without saying goodbye."

"Oh Maud would I do that?"
She gave me an indignant look as we walked into Tom's room. Tom hadn't moved. His breathing was still shallow and his back had a weeping yellowish tone. He smelled repugnant. Was this the man I loved?

"Take good care of him Maud"
I returned to the carriage and with a crack of the whip was gone.

Chapter 28

The journey down to London seemed to pass quickly. I had taken several books and that seemed to help me pass the time. In my mind I kept trying to rehearse what I would say to Lady Sinclair. I knew that this would be very difficult for her as well as all the family. My mind was steadfast in the mission that I wished to accomplish and that was, to try to achieve some kind of status now that my father had been removed as my obstacle. Of course I had no experience with what was the correct or incorrect way in which to conduct myself. I could only follow examples set by those that I had read about. Who was to say if they were right or wrong? I knew I had to display a token of regret and compassion towards my family in order to appear sincere or they may well turn around and reject me.

Soon the sound of the horse's hooves on the cobbles changed so that I knew we were not on the dusty roads anymore. The scenery had changed too. The green endless fields were replaced with factories, workhouses and the endless buildings of London. We were back and before too long I would be going up the familiar steps of the house. The carriage turned the corner and we were here on the street where my father had lived.

As I stepped down from the carriage I took a deep breath. The air lacked the sweetness of country air and the soot of the chimneys seemed to settle and hold in the air. The body of my father was still wrapped in the blanket and was now beginning to have a distinct odour that wafted out into the street as the carriage door opened.

I stepped up to the house and pulled the brass bell lever. Sarah the maid opened the door to me.

"Miss Alice, what a pleasant surprise we thought you had left and weren't coming back."

"Where is Lady Sinclair?" I demanded brushing past Sarah and into the house.

"Why she's in the drawing room sewing with the young girls." I marched straight for the drawing room and inhaled deeply as I turned the handle. Lady Sinclair was sitting beside the window and Charlotte was to her left, Jane and Emily on the window seat to her right. As I walked in they all looked up in surprise and the younger girls bounced from their seats and began to run towards me to embrace me.

I felt a deep comforting warmth. It felt so right and so lovely to be here amongst the only family that I ever had or ever would have. I clasped my arms around my younger sisters, feeling there soft curls and velvet dresses so close to me.

Lady Sinclair and Charlotte rose from their seats and I knew that my dire task was upon me.

"Lady Sinclair" I went over to her and clasped her hand. She looked at me with confusion in her eyes and I knew that she was now very concerned.

"What is it Alice?" Asked Charlotte who also realised the apprehension in my tone.

"I am so sorry everyone, but I have the saddest news to convey to you."

In my pocket I grasped the smelling salts that Nurse Dunn had given me two days ago just in case I would need to use them now.

"What! What is it Alice?" Charlotte was urging.

I didn't like this moment. The worried and anxious faces looking at me. It occurred to me that maybe I should have spoken to Lady Eleanor alone to break the news but it was all too late now.

"Is it Edward? Is it my husband?" Pressed Lady Eleanor.

There was no going back now. I knew that she knew. Why else would I be back here? I wondered if she had seen me leave the week before. If she had been the one standing in the shadows behind the curtains. If she had seen me bundled into the carriage. Had she seen the bruises that marred my face?

"Oh Lady Eleanor, I am so sorry. I don't know how to say this but your husband became unwell on the road and we had to stop to seek assistance. He was told to rest and regain his strength but he kept insisting that he was well until his heart just could not take the strain anymore and he collapsed, fatally. I am so sorry Lady Eleanor."

She dropped into her seat like a heavy sack of potatoes and began to tremble, her lip quivering, her hands gripping to the sides of her chair. I pulled the bottle of smelling salts from my pocket and waved it in front of her nose. She coughed and sighed but said nothing. Her eyes vacant and welling with tears but her voice was choked. Her daughters rushed to her side and put their arms around her, the little one resting her head on her lap. They all had tears in their eyes yet all said nothing. I assumed that they didn't want to offend their mother by saying the wrong thing. I was scared that I had done wrong. Had I done this deed so badly? The grief and sadness in the room became infectious. Within minutes they were all crying profusely and swept into this unnatural tide I cried too.

After a while Lady Eleanor spoke.

"Alice I know that this has not been easy for you to bring us such bad tidings. We are very grateful though that it was you and not some stranger that brought us this news. This may seem strange but I am glad that he had a familiar face around him when he died. You must have been a great comfort to him in his final moments and for that I am indebted to you Alice."

She took my arm.

"Please take me to him. I need to see my husbands' body."

"May we come too Mama?"

"No, Charlotte you stay here with your sisters. We need to tell the boys, this will be very difficult especially for Albert, as he will assume the head of this family. Alice will escort me now"

"Of course Lady Eleanor" I agreed as I took her arm and linked it in mine.

We walked out of the room together. Each step seemed heavy and laboured. Her words were ringing and repeating in my ears. I felt like a fraud, like a cuckoo that had just laid an egg in some other bird's nest. I was with my step mother and she believed that I was the comforting face that had been with her dying husband and had helped him. How distant from the real truth could that be! This grieving family could never know what really took place. What lies and deceit had been spun in order to protect them.

We approached the carriage. The servants as well as the coachman stood with their heads bowed.

Lady Eleanor pulled back the blanket and I had to steady her, as she took in the sight of my father his body now very grey, cold and almost unrecognisable as the man who had once been her husband.

"Dearest Edward" She stroked his brow.

"We have always been there for each other but now you have finally left me. I always feared this moment but now my darling you really have left and I suppose I will not fear that which I have always feared, any more."

She pulled the blanket back over his face and turned to me. I was standing several feet behind her wondering about her words to her dead husband. It seemed strange but then I supposed that when in grief strange things are said and done. I did wonder though what she had meant.

"Lady Eleanor is there anything that I can do for you?"

179

She pondered for a minute.

"Yes Alice there are lots of arrangements to be made. I will need help. My children will be too consumed in their grief to help me but you Alice are almost like a daughter and I will be very grateful for your assistance."

We walked back into the house together as the servants removed their caps in respect. We went to the library where Lady Eleanor sat down and quite methodically began writing a list of things to be done.

"We will have to contact Edwards's secretary in the House of Lords. It will probably be a grand funeral but I would like to keep it as quiet as possible and mainly have family present. I hate these large affairs where there are just too many people and you have to open your soul in front of everyone."

"Would you like me to speak to her and make the arrangements? We must call on the undertakers and the vicar and see when the funeral can be."

"Would you do that too Alice?"

I nodded and Lady Sinclair then let out an almighty roar and began to cry. She was almost howling as she held on to my skirts. I put my arms around her and insisted that I escort her to her room where she might lay down and take some rest. As I closed the door of her room I breathed a great sigh. My task was done although I still had a great deal of work to do. All of this would not be wasted time. All these actions would be noted and Lady Sinclair would have no option but to be completely indebted to me.

I worked very hard for the rest of the day and for the next few days. There was so much to be done. Service books, invitations, press releases, flowers, seating allocations. The list seemed to be endless. The whole household were dressed in mourning and wore black. Kind gifts and flowers were constantly arriving at the house from distant well wishers and constituents.

Lady Sinclair emerged from her room periodically but every time seemed very red eyed and weepy. I resorted to bringing her trays of food but she barely touched a morsel. The girls were just as bad sobbing away and acting as bereft as their mother. I was a little perplexed by all this sorrow. My true feelings for my father could never be told. In my eyes he was the worst man in the world. How strange that I had ever longed for him, craved his love. It seemed so long ago that he was the man that I imagined to be the bravest soldier heading his regiment in Sudan and fighting to save the empire. So many lies for so long. How I had grown up! I watched the faces of my brothers and sisters and wondered if things had been different if I too would have felt such extreme sadness for the loss of a loved one. He had never loved me. That would always be my cross to bear.

Albert had been very strange towards me since my return. I wondered what conversation had transpired between him and my father the night before I had originally left after Albert had asked me to marry him. It did not seem the right place to ask what the conversation had been about but I could guess that some derogatory remarks had been passed that Albert must certainly have believed to be true.

In my moments alone I wondered about my future. I wondered about Tom and prayed that he was well and recovering. I wished him no ill. I was grateful to him for the part that he had played in my protection but I knew that he would probably not feature in my life in the way that I had planned. Was I callous? Was I just cruel? Tom had loved me in a way no one ever had and I had at the time believed that was all I needed for my happiness. Fate had turned her page though and now things seemed far more different than before. Was I the only one who could see it? Would I have to break Tom's heart? Maybe it would be better if he did die then that would be one less horrid task for me to perform.

Meanwhile I was strutting around the house like the mother hen that was in charge of all the matters that needed sorting. My natural common sense meant that everyone simply entrusted me with jobs that they knew would get done. In a way I had taken over Lady Eleanor's role as she was now mainly confined to her room.

The night before the funeral everyone seemed very tense and almost keen to get it all over and done with. It was as if it would be a release to actually get my father buried.

I sat with Charlotte in her room combing out her hair and trying to console her. We were so physically similar and yet she had no idea that we were sisters. We had inherited our father's characteristics and being almost the same age meant that we did have quite a few things in common.

"You didn't really know my father very well Alice."

"No Charlotte"

"But he was a wonderful man, so caring and warm, so affectionate."

I nodded but my thoughts of him which remained unsaid were very different.

"Alice if only you would have known him with us, holding our hands, running in the park, feeding the ducks. Its like we have lost the most special caring and wonderful man and our lives will be so empty and lost without him."

Two sisters, connected by one father, yet our memories of our lives with him were so diverse. I almost wished that I could swap lives with Charlotte and have her wonderful memories instead of my torn and ragged ones. I looked at my reflection in the long gilt mirror and realised that I too was crying... for my father.

Chapter 29

I woke to the sound of rain. That heavy patter as rain comes down, hits the slate tiles with such force that the raindrops bounce off and trickle down the brickwork at the corners of the gutters.

I rolled over in my bed listening to its rhythm then eventually sat up and pulled the curtains open. The glass was splattered with tiny raindrops all weaving their way down the frame like hundreds of tiny rivers. The streets outside were full of puddles and the great wheels of carriages were splashing passersby as they scurried through the streets. Hoods and capes were being held fast by white bony fingers.

My door burst open and Charlotte came in her expression vacant and sat herself on the edge of my bed.

"I couldn't sleep last night at all. I am so weary. I don't know what to do with myself, all I can think of is that this afternoon they will put my dearest papa in a box and then put him in that cold ground."

"Dear Charlotte" I smoothed my hand over her hair.

"Look at the skies they are dark and crying too!" She added.

"You must be strong for your mother today. You need to rest." She lay down on my bed and I stroked her temples till eventually she fell asleep. She had looked all red-eyed, white faced and terribly sad. I watched her sleep, her chest gently lifting and falling. She was so exhausted and seemed ill with worry. I wondered how Lady Eleanor would be. This would be a very difficult day for her and she had found the last week of this ordeal very distressing. Over the last few days she had hardly been seen. She had barely eaten and seemed to be deteriorating rapidly each moment. I tiptoed out of the room, leaving Charlotte sound asleep. Putting my own feelings aside I went to Lady Eleanor's rooms.

I turned the handle. I knew that I should really knock first but I didn't want to disturb her if she was sleeping. She was sitting at her dressing table. Her bed had not been slept in. She was staring absent mindedly at the rain.

"Lady Sinclair" I whispered.

She held her hand out to me and I came and sat on the floor beside her.

"Lady Eleanor, is there anything that I can do for you?
She shook her head and didn't even venture to try to change her expression. I glanced around the room her evening tray still untouched lay beside the bed.

"May I get you a drink? Some tea perhaps?"
She shook her head.

"You must try to rest. You need your strength to get through this day."
I went over to the sash cord bell and pulled it. A servant soon came and knocked on the door. I ordered a pot of tea and some toast with marmalade. When it came I poured a liberal amount of sugar into the tea and put the cup to the lips of Lady Sinclair. She shook her head like a stubborn child but I was persistent like a parent trying to feed a child and eventually she drank the tea and ate the toast. I then led her to the bed and bade her lay down which she did obediently realising that she could not argue with my insistence. I stayed with her till her breathing slowed and I knew that she too had fallen asleep.

"The mistress is not to be disturbed," I demanded as I left the room.

I went outside to the gardens. The rain had subsided and the ground was wet with puddles and slippery wet patches on the marbled slabs. I could feel the dampness seeping through my shoes and gently lifted my skirts so they wouldn't get wet and stained. A flock of geese squawked overhead as they flew to the lake on the common. Grey clouds were still looming in the skies but the bright outline of the sun was straining to tear through the dullness and brighten the skies.

I felt surprisingly strong and so much in control. Everyone around me had been very unbalanced by the death of my father and this had given me the opportunity to come shining through. I felt needed and wanted. I was the one making all the arrangements and almost holding the family together. My whole focus had now changed. I had turned from the hard selfish girl that I had been, to someone that enjoyed the dependency of others. My father's death had taken a great burden from my shoulders almost as if the tendrils of a strangling plant had been loosened from my neck and now I was free.

"Alice?"

I spun around.

"Oh Albert."

"I have not really spoken to you much since your return." Albert was eyeing me awkwardly and with a slight degree of discomfort.

"I am very sorry for your loss Albert." I replied

"Alice?"

"Yes"

"I don't know where to begin."

"What is it Albert?"

I was beginning to feel worried. Albert was looking so strained and was obviously finding it difficult to say what he wanted.

"The last time you were here before you left, I, er, um, I asked if you would marry me and my father told me some very distressing information about you that I had not known about. I thought that I would never see you again and that you were to be

deported to France and that would be the end of that. However you are here and the information that my father told me held lots of question marks that I thought I would never have the opportunity to have answered. It seems only fair that I should give you the benefit of being able to tell your side of the story and then for me to make my own judgements concerning you."
I stood wide eyed in disbelief.
"What did my father tell you?"
"My father" He corrected unknowingly.
I flustered and tried to compose myself.
"He told me that I could never marry you because both your mother and father are afflicted by terrible rages of madness. He said that it was due to one of these rages that your own father died and that the illness that affects your mother is also one of complete insanity and that your sisters are known to have the same complaint. I am sorry Alice but father said that you were insane too and I could never marry you. In fact you were going to be sent to an asylum in France from which you were never to be released."
I stood gawping like the idiot that I had just been accused of being.
"I think I need to sit down"
"Yes of course Alice lets go to the drawing room."
I sat down on the large wing chair that had been my father's favourite seat. The room seemed to be spinning slightly and I was trying so hard to contain my rage. Even from the grave my father had found the ability to incite me and cause me the most difficult of dilemmas. I didn't want to marry Albert because he was my brother but at the same time I could not let him think that I was an insane person who had a family history of madness. Perhaps there was some madness. My father's behaviour towards me had never been sane and rational. What could I tell Albert? I looked

up and scanned his eyes. He had a pleading look like a lost puppy waiting to be given a bone. I felt sorry for him. I wanted to ease his curiosity and give him a satisfactory answer. But what? What could I say? I could not admit to this madness because then all my chances of future marriage to anyone in society would be jeopardised.

"Alice, are you feeling well?"

"Yes Albert quite well. I am just a little shocked that your father would have told you such awful untruths."

"So it is untrue" Sighed Albert collapsing into a chair.

"I could not believe it but I knew nothing else. I have watched you over the last week with much confusion. How could you be quite mad when you have acted in the most courageous and honourable way? You have been indispensable to my mother and sisters, you have helped make arrangements and have been most sensible and level headed throughout, not the actions of a madwoman. Yet my father had said that you were!"
I squinted at him in an insulted way.

"Oh Alice I am so sorry if I have offended you."

"Albert" I said softly

"I am pleased that you had your doubts about this information. As you can see I am quite normal."

"Perfectly normal" He added.

"Yes, thank you and I can only think that the arguments that my mother had with your father many years ago that had estranged them from each other had led your father to believe that we were all mad. I assure you that that is not the case. My father died of an infection many years ago and my mother's illness is quite unrelated to any insanity."

"Oh thank goodness!"

"I beg your pardon!"

"No sorry dear Alice I didn't mean thank goodness to your fathers death or your mothers illness but to thank goodness for your healthy state of mind and your completely normal demeanour."

I nodded in acceptance of his grovelling statement.

Albert came over to where I was sitting and dropped onto one knee. I rose to try to divert what I could only assume to be what would follow. Albert was one step ahead of me and took my hand. Before a word could be uttered I intercepted.

"Albert, we have work to do today. Your father is to be buried in a few hours. This is not a time to do or say anything rash. You will behave with decorum and respect as befitting the eldest son. Is that understood?"

"Yes of course Alice. You are so wise Alice and so perfectly not insane. I am so angry with my father for having tried to taint my image of you because of his own past arguments. I am so sorry that I doubted you and..."

I have work to do Albert. We will not speak of this again. Today is a sombre day and we will behave with respect to your father whatever our personal feelings."

Albert nodded and I left the room. I was still in control and had managed yet again to rise above all obstacles. I had to maintain my composure; my whole future depended on being able to be a respectable and eligible young woman in this society so that I could marry well and achieve some sort of status. I had spent my whole life being shunned and more recently feeling ashamed of my parentage and now I had the opportunity to turn all that around, and I would.

I went to my father's office and checked final arrangements with his secretary. I went to the kitchens and made sure that the catering for after the funeral was all in order. I perused the seating plan for the church service and when I was satisfied that everything was as it should be I then went to dress the younger children before finally waking Charlotte and Lady Sinclair and helping them to prepare for the rest of their ordeal.

I never for one moment questioned my involvement. There were things that had to be done and it seemed a natural responsibility to ensure that they were done properly. I was assuming great respect from the whole household as well as my father's staff who were at some times consulting me when they were unsure as to what to do. Albert was observing me inconspicuously although I knew he was watching my every move.

Time was ticking by. The carriages were all lined up outside the house. Albert on my instruction led his mother and I followed with the girls. The time had come to bury my father. I felt no sadness and definitely no joy. I was now an orphan, on my own to fend for myself but.......maybe I had always been, I suppose I had never really had any parents. As they lowered my father's coffin into the ground, I felt that there were still so many questions that were being buried too. Questions that it was all too late to ask.

Chapter 30

Weeks have rolled by. There is some normality returning to the Sinclair household. The children have returned to their studies and Lady Sinclair is slowly beginning to receive visitors who are coming to pay their respects. My position within this house has remained the same; I am still given responsibilities far beyond the normal capabilities of a seventeen year old. I seem to be indispensable and I like that feeling of power and being wanted. My eighteenth birthday is soon approaching. I know that I am supposed to inherit all of my estate and I assume that the lawyer that deals with my father's probate will have the information that I need to complete those transactions. I am still unsure as to what arrangements my father made before he died. I assume that his urgency to send me away was due to my impending birthday and his reluctance for me to inherit. Things have all changed now and I am determined to secure my wealth. Luckily Lady Sinclair has asked me to go to see the lawyer and collect whatever forms there are that need to be transferred to Albert's name. I will use that opportunity to discuss my situation with him. I have been told that he is getting on and has a hearing problem. I hope that he will respect my privacy and deal with me regarding my affairs. Since the funeral we have had many well wishers coming to the house. Benjamin Ainsworth the son of some old friends of the Sinclair's has taken a shine to Charlotte and she is totally besotted. William is just a distant memory in her thoughts and after all the fuss that she put me through too! The house does actually seem to be swarming with eligible young men like bees to the two young ladies living under the same roof. I have not been swayed by any. I am not too fond of all the meaningless gossip and pointless chatter that they all are desperate to express.

Charlotte loves the attention and flirts shamelessly but I must admit that it bores me.

There has been one person at the back of my mind. Whenever I think of him I try to distract myself and occupy my mind with something else. I do sometimes feel guilty but however warm Tom's eyes are in my dreams, I know that he is from a different world to the one in which I now live and we can never be together. The thoughts however keep lingering in my mind and it takes great determination to banish them. I do hope he is well. I hate to think of him stinking of foul weeping wounds and hope that Maud has helped him to heal. I sometimes fear that when he is recovered he may come looking for me. Then what will I do? Will my rejection be another lash of the whip to which he very nearly succumbed? Tom is by far more of a man than these feeble suitors that have been flocking to the house but he has no place in my society, so it cannot be a match.

"Alice?"

"Yes Lady Sinclair" I replied with sincerity and a warm smile.

"Please call everyone for dinner in the dining room at seven tonight. I am feeling so much better and maybe its time that we all began to eat together again."

"Oh Lady Eleanor that is wonderful! It's been so sad that everyone has been eating alone in their rooms. I'm sure that when I tell them they will be very pleased."

"Alice, I haven't really had the opportunity to tell you how much we appreciate all the help that you have given to this family. You have been an incredible asset and I don't know how we could have managed without your unconditional support."

"I just want to be able to help and be a part of this family." I replied sincerely and honestly.

"But Alice, you are not a member of this family. You have your own family and people are asking why you have parked yourself here with us and why you have abandoned your own kin! Do you not think that you should be making plans to return to your own life?"

I was stunned. I could feel the colour draining from my cheeks. Could I seriously have thought that I could just install myself here indefinitely? There was obviously some suppressed resentment within Lady Eleanor.

She smiled sweetly.

"You will take the papers to the solicitor tomorrow wont you?"

"Yes of course." I replied unenthusiastically.

Dinner that evening was of great excitement to the family. Over the weeks we had all resigned to having our trays sent up to our rooms and there had been very little communication.

The younger children had eaten together in the nursery with their nanny but the rest of us had been very distant, leaving each other to grieve in our own ways.

"This is so lovely to be all together again." Lady Sinclair was directing her comment to her children and not to me.

"Yes mama" added Jane.

"Not quite all of us" Interjected Archie.

"Father is missing!"

All faces turned to him coldly. Archie froze and realised the stupidity of what he had just said.

"Why do you have to upset mama so? Why are boys so stupid?" Retorted Emily

"I beg your pardon?" Said Albert

"Not all boys are stupid! I know some fairly stupid girls too."

"Now, now children." Lady Sinclair was back to her normal matriarchal self.

"It would be nice if we could all try to be civilized and eat normally"

"Alice I am going to town tomorrow to get fitted for some dresses would you like to come with me? Asked Charlotte.

"Charlotte I would love to come with you but I have to run some errands for your mother tomorrow at the lawyers."

"Why are you suddenly in charge of everything? Why do you have to go to the lawyers, that's a boy's job, send Albert?" Charlotte's tone had definitely changed and had become more hostile.

"It's not a problem. I could go early and then meet up with you after and help you to pick out your dresses. I would love to help you. It would be fun to go out and do something like that after the month that we have just had. If that is all right with you Charlotte. What time are you leaving?

"I'm leaving at noon."

"Well I could meet you at the dressmakers at one?"

"All right but don't put yourself to too much trouble." She replied sarcastically.

I could not eat. I felt that I was very misplaced. This was a family reunion and I should not be here. Lady Eleanor didn't speak to me but I could tell from her glances that I had fallen from her favour. Perhaps I had been trying too hard to take over her responsibilities and she felt that I was treading on her toes. I didn't know. I made my excuses and left the table and the coldness that surrounded it.

The next morning I got up early and made my way into the city. The carriage stopped outside a tall grey building where lots of suited and hatted gentlemen were making their way into the large doors. I stepped from the carriage and a young lad walking on the street opened the door for me and helped me to step down. I politely thanked him and he tipped his hat towards me.

I entered the building. The ceilings were incredibly high and ornate. I stood overwhelmed by the enormity of such a fine place.

"Can I help you madam?"

An old bearded chap leaned across the desk behind which he was standing.

"Oh yes thank you." I stuttered.

"I have an appointment with Mr Pettigrew of Pettigrew, Foster and Jones."

"You need to go up to the sixth floor, the stairs are through the corridor and to your left."

"I'm much obliged"

"And remember to speak loudly he's a bit deaf!" He called after me as I made my way down the hall.

On the sixth floor there were several doors with names engraved upon them. I immediately saw the one that I wanted and gently tapped on it. There was no response.

"You'll be knocking for a long time"

A young man stood behind me. Briefcase in his hand.

"Allow me" And he opened the door for me.

"I'm James Foster who are you looking for?"

"Mr Pettigrew"

"Follow me. He's probably in his back office is he expecting you?"

"Yes my name is Alice" I considered for a moment and then gave him my correct surname.

"Alice Sinclair"

"Oh, such a pleasure to meet you." He took my hand and darted a twinkled look in my direction.

I followed him down the hall till we reached Pettigrew's office. He opened the door. The old man behind the desk didn't even look up.

"Pettigrew! Alice Sinclair is here to see you!

194

"Huh"

"I said Alice Sinclair is here to see you!" He repeated going up at least five decibels.

"Thank you" I said to James Foster as he left me in the room.

"My office is two away come and see me when you are finished here."

"Oh" I was surprised. "Yes of course." I nodded.

"Sit down young lady, what did you say your name was Sally Clair?"

"No Alice Sinclair."

"Sally Harris?"

"No Alice Sinclair" I practically screamed.

"All right Sally no need to shout. So why have you come to see me?"

Chapter 31

Mr Pettigrew wiped his brow with his handkerchief. His right hand trembled slightly as he held his pen and tried to take some notes. His office was messy and dishevelled much as his appearance. Books were stacked up in clumsy piles all around and dust sat in great thick clouds above every inch of the room.

"So Miss Clair why have you come to see me?"
I spoke loudly articulating every word.

"I have come to see you about my father's will and the papers that have to be transferred to my brother's name. I have also come to see you about another more personal matter which concerns my estate in Somerset being transferred to me. I think it is held in trust till I am eighteen and it is nearly my birthday."
He looked at me with a confused look then shook his head violently and began shouting.

"Silly girl stop mumbling! Can't hear a single word you're saying! What's that, you want to go to Somerset for your birthday?"
I sighed a frustrated sigh. Then repeated what I had just said practically shouting each word.

"That's better."
He dropped his pad of papers on the desk and a haze of dust choked the air.

"So let me see then, you want to transfer your father's estate to your brother in Somerset?"

"No Sir that is my estate and that is to be transferred to me."

"To you girl? Don't be so silly! Property belongs to a man and if you have a brother it shall be his."
He was muttering under his breath and trying to write this all down. His greying moustache that still held crumbs from his

morning toast twitched as he wrote. My protestations seemed to waft aside. I was becoming quite agitated and although I maintained my demeanour I was seething between my teeth.

"No Sir you do not seem to understand. My brother is only my half brother. There has been considerable secrecy over all these affairs because the property that I am to inherit belonged to my mother and not to my father. This has nothing to do with my fathers' family, this is my property."

Pettigrew stood. He was quite short and stout so had no great presence standing. He threw a book to the table, stirring the layers of dust and making me cough. I could feel my eyes burning as the dust stagnated in the air.

"Young lady! This is most serious. You cannot steal land from your brother's estate and expect me to keep it secret! Why do you call your brother only half a brother? Am I only half a man? You young lady…" He said pointing an accusing finger

"You are only a half wit! There how do you like that? To be called half of anything is an insult isn't it?"

"Mr Pettigrew this is a very sensitive matter. I am sure that if you dealt with my father in the past then you will know of the situation and the fact that my property belonged to my mother and was left to me in a trust. Now that my father is dead I need to secure that money for my future dowry.

"So your father doesn't wish you to have these funds?"

"No these are my funds. I don't yet know if there is any extra provision being made available for me in my fathers will but I very much doubt it!"

"So you doubt that you have any funds?"

"No, I doubt that my father has left me additional funds from his own private estate."

"So if there are no funds what do you wish me to do my dear, pluck it off the trees?"

197

I was getting nowhere. This old fool could not understand me and would certainly not be able to help me. In despair I wrung my hands, twisting them over and over. What else could I do?

"Don't know why they sent some half brained, half witted girl to see me? What does a girl know about men's dealings? Wasting my time!"

I smiled politely although deep within me I was raging. I brushed the settling dust from my skirt and rose to leave.

"Goodbye Miss Clair and tell them to send a boy next time."

I shut the door behind me and swallowed back my tears. Now what?

I began to walk back down the corridor. The second door on the left was slightly ajar and I could see James Foster sitting at his desk. He looked up and smiled at me. I stopped. Should I go in? Should I confide my circumstances to him? Realistically I had little choice. The paperwork for my estate was held within these offices and I really could not deal with that bumbling fool in the end office.

James beckoned me in.

"How did you get on?"

My solemn look told him all he needed to know.

"Oh that well then?" He responded jovially.

I nodded.

"Well can I help you?"

I perused his neat clean office. Files were neatly stacked and books arranged methodically on a large bookcase. Not a speck of dust in sight.

"Why is Mr Pettigrew's office so dirty?" I said out loud without thinking.

"Oh he won't let anyone go in there! Doesn't trust a soul. Thinks they might be trying to steal all his disorganised papers." James leaned forward and whispered.

"He should have retired years ago but just doesn't trust the rest of us to do the job properly and no one dares to tell him any different!"

"Oh" I nodded quite understanding.

"Well did you get anywhere with him or did he leave you feeling that he just didn't know what you were talking about and it was all a shameful waste of time?"

I smiled.

"Its fine Miss Sinclair we are used to seeing his clients and continuing with their cases. How can I help you?"

James Foster seemed so amenable and sincere. His brown hair had a fashionable wave. It swept off his face and revealed his very intense deep brown eyes. He smiled a lot making me feel very comfortable and safe. Yes I would confide in him. I was sure that he was the one that could help me with my delicate problem.

"Wait there." He instructed.

"I'll just go and get your files from Pettigrew's office."

I sat alone whilst he left me. When he returned I watched him curiously, his suave handsome profile as he turned away from me and perused through the files. I wondered if he had reached the information about my parentage and how he would react towards me. James Foster remained composed at all times and certainly showed no change of emotion at any time.

After quite a long period of time. He closed the file and looked at me directly. I felt ashamed and embarrassed. My eyes fixed firmly on the file that now lay closed on his table.

"Miss Sinclair what exactly are your instructions?"

"I have two requests." I briefly glanced up, catching his intent gaze.

"I need to arrange for the paperwork for the transfer of Edward Sinclair's estate to Albert Sinclair. I also need to arrange for my mother's estate in Somerset, which is being held in trust for me to be transferred to me when I turn eighteen in a few weeks.

"Yes Miss Sinclair. This seems quite straightforward."

He was now rereading the file. His eyes widened, he gasped then hurriedly tried to conceal his surprise.

"What is it?" I enquired concernedly.

"Miss Sinclair you stand to inherit a very sizeable estate. I think your fathers plan was to sell this property and give you a portion of this fund as an annual allowance till such time that you married, although according to these recent letters I think he was planning for you to be ordained in a convent in Paris."

"What to become a nun?"

"Yes I think so, was that not your wish?"

"Most certainly not!" I blurted.

James Foster smiled. A warm smile that etched itself on me. My anger instantly subsided and I could feel myself becoming less restrained in his company. So that was what my father had hoped for me. To send me away and lock me in a convent! Did he really think that I would stand for that! Thank goodness that I was now in control of my life. What a blessing that he was dead. I couldn't see him planning such a life for his precious Charlotte. So he wanted to get rid of me and take my money all in one swoop.

"How much money is it?"

James cleared his throat and leaned back in his chair.

"It is a very large amount."

"What a thousand pounds? Five thousand? Twenty thousand?"

"Miss Sinclair, your fathers' personal estate is around twenty thousand guineas but your late grandfather was an incredibly astute property and banking man. He also had old money that had been in his family for generations. Your worth Miss Sinclair is approximately four hundred thousand guineas."

I was stunned. Now I began to realise the greed and ambition of my father. He wanted my money. He wanted to ruin my life as much as he possibly could so that he could gain what was rightfully mine. I could not imagine such a vast amount of money. It seemed huge and beyond comprehension.

"Your grandfather was a very shrewd business man. He invested his wealth wisely and owns most of the bank buildings in London and across the south of England. He leased these properties to wealthy tenants and there is a stream of income that is adding to this account every week. The interest that you are earning is phenomenal by itself."

I looked up at James. My face was expressionless.

"Are you well Miss Sinclair? Can I get you some tea?"

"No, I am just a little overcome by this news. I had no idea."

I could feel my hands shaking on my lap. I had been living in a dilapidated old mansion for all my life and I was really an heiress. The staff must have been paid out of a bottomless fund and all this would have been removed from me without my slightest idea as to its value.

"Who pays the staff in Somerset?" I wondered

"There is an account that was managed by your father; he was to ensure that you were brought up as comfortably as possible. Your grandfather had unfortunately died suddenly and as he was your guardian, your father took control of the estate and was to manage it till you came of age. If anything happened to you or if you gave up your status by ordaining yourself into a convent for example then all wealth could be reverted to your next of kin who was your father. I think this was his intention."

"Oh"

"There will be paperwork that I need to draw up in order for your inheritance to come to you. I would advise that you leave all of the investments in place since they are all sound and profitable.

201

Is there anything else that you wish me to do for you? Can I help you find a carriage? Where are you staying?"

"This is a little awkward." I stumbled. "I am staying with my fathers' family the Sinclair's in Inverness Gardens."

"Do they know of your circumstances?"

"Oh no! God forbid! They think that I am Edward Sinclair's niece from Northampton. No, they have no idea about who I really am and I would appreciate your discretion in this matter." I shot James a defiant look. A defensive look that I had become adept at.

"Of course Miss Sinclair, our clients confidentiality is respected at all times. You do seem however a little overcome by the entirety of what you have learnt today and I would like to escort you to a carriage that can take you home."

I actually agreed that I needed to digest all of this information but at the same time I had come here for a purpose and wished to conclude all business that needed dealing with.

"Thank you for your concern Mr Foster but I really do need to get all these papers signed as well as bringing Albert's papers home for his signature."

"That is not a problem Miss Sinclair I can get the paperwork together and deliver it myself in a couple of days or whenever it is convenient for you. I think that you need some time to decide what you wish to do with this new wealth, as it will only be a few weeks till your birthday. I suggest Thursday afternoon how is that for you?"

Thursday afternoon was fine. In fact any time that this handsome articulate young man wanted to come and see me would be fine. James Foster was unlike any other gentleman that I had met. He was quite intelligent and exuded an authority about him that really was quite an attractive feature. "Alice Foster" I wondered in my head. Hmm it had quite a nice ring to it.

"So is Thursday convenient?" He asked again.

"Oh yes but perhaps come late in the day when Albert is home and then he can sign the papers there and then."

"Of course Miss Sinclair. Between now and then I will reread these files and make sure that everything is taken into account and will all be dealt with efficiently."

I rose from my seat. My legs felt a little weak and shaky. James came around from his side of the desk and took my arm. I blushed profusely and stepped back a pace. He led me outside the building and we hailed down a carriage. He gave them the address and serenely waited for the carriage to pull away before turning back to his offices.

Alone in the carriage I felt like the queen. I had only stumbled upon this fortuitous news. What if my father hadn't died? Could he have legally stolen all this from me? Perhaps all this money could overlook my illegitimate status? How many rich Fitz's were there out there with coins jingling in their pockets and no shame in their name?

Realistically I didn't need the Sinclair's anymore. I could rent my own apartments and build my own life. However maybe that wasn't the way to earn respectability. Maybe I needed the support cushion of their name to open the doors of society for me. I knew that they were becoming irritated with me but perhaps I could tease this out just a little till I could find a suitable husband.

The carriage trotted along. My mind cantering with it. I didn't want a husband that would dominate me and take what was mine. I didn't want a male ego father substitute who would walk all over me. Where was the guarantee? Perhaps I could hide the extent of my wealth. There was one person that loved me totally and had no financial aspirations. There was only one person that had ever loved me. Perhaps I should go home and see how he was. The windswept straw hair those blue cornflower eyes, those

strong arms that longed for me. I had made a promise to him, then just turned my back, seduced by all the glamour of London. Maybe I should stop all this pretence and just go home.
The carriage came to a halt. The grand house on Inverness Gardens stood proud in the spring sunshine. Gentlemen tipped their hats, ladies curtsied. This was a whole different world and now I had to choose.

Chapter 32

We were all assembled around the table for dinner that evening.
The mood was buoyant and slightly more uplifting than it had
been in previous weeks. The younger children were laughing for
a change and telling each other silly jokes. Even Lady Sinclair
who always looked so grand and regal at the head of the table
was smiling and throwing back her head in laughter at the
children's antics.

"It's so lovely that we are all being normal again mama"
Exclaimed Charlotte.

"It seems that we have been sad for so long and nothing happy
has happened in this house"

"Yes my dear you are quite right. I think that we had all
forgotten to smile. Perhaps this is the turning point and things are
going to get better now for us all."

"Mama?" Began Jane.

"We used to go on picnics down by the river. Might we do that
again sometime, it used to be so much fun!"

"Oh yes mama! Please mama! We haven't been for ages! Could
we go soon?"

Lady Sinclair's sad eyes softened. She gazed around the table at
her children and her pride was so overwhelming it was almost
palpable.

"Yes!" She said with gusto.

"Yes we shall go. We'll go on Saturday and have a lovely
picnic. I'll get cook to bake all those wonderful treats that she
used to make and we'll have a lovely day all together."

"And can we give the broken biscuits and left over sandwiches
to the ducks?" Added Emily.

"Yes, oh what fun!"

Even I was squealing with excitement at the thought. I had never really been on a picnic and so was eagerly anticipating the thought of Saturday. So this is what families did at weekends. I so wanted to be part of this family but I knew that my days here would soon come to an end. This charade that I had played would soon be over and I would have to leave this cosy little cocoon forever. I wanted to stay. I wanted to be loved. I wanted Lady Sinclair to brush my hair and tell me stories of when I was little like she did with her daughters. I so wanted to stay but the risk of being exposed would always be a fear looming over my head so sometime soon it would be time to go.

"What happened at the lawyers?"

Albert interrupted my thoughts.

"Oh it was bizarre. I had to see old Mr Pettigrew who is quite insane and couldn't fathom what I was there for. Eventually I saw another chap young Mr Foster who was quite charming and helpful and seemed to have his head screwed on his shoulders. He's coming over on Thursday with the papers for you to sign Albert."

Charlotte's ears picked up.

"How young and charming was he?"

I could feel the rivalry in the heavy tones of her voice. She was almost annoyed that I had made the acquaintance of some eligible bachelor before her. I played to her curiosity and in an equally syrupy voice replied.

"Oh he was most, exceptionally charming and most perfect in his appearance and demeanour."

It was now Albert who turned to me his eyes blazing with scorn. I had momentarily forgotten his affection towards me and realised that I was rubbing very coarse salt into his open wounds. We had never fully resolved the situation between us when I had returned to London when he had once again tried to propose to me.

However I believed that I had given him enough negative signals to make him comprehend for once and all that I had no intentions towards him.

"Oh not really Albert. He was an ugly frightful bore you know? Tell me any lawyer that isn't completely lacking in personality?" Albert nodded and faked a laugh.

"So he's coming over on Thursday is he?" Questioned Charlotte.

"We'll see then for ourselves wont we?"
Charlotte looked down to her plate her dark eyelashes covering those mischievous eyes and continued to eat. She had a sly grin on her face and I knew that come Thursday I would be in big trouble when the dashing and gallant Mr Foster came to call.

"Alice you will help me with the preparations for the picnic. First thing tomorrow morning we will make lists of things to do and things we want cook to prepare." Asked Lady Sinclair.

"Don't forget treacle pudding!" Added Archie.

That night I slept very little. My mind was plagued with all kinds of thoughts and just when I thought I had fallen asleep and was dreaming I realised that I was actually wide awake.
Eventually I feel asleep and dreamt that I was a princess who had just inherited a vast kingdom and was preparing a great feast for my subjects on the lawns next to the river. There was everything delicious that you could imagine including treacle pudding. Then a figure approached, I couldn't quite make out who it was. Was it Albert? Was it William? Was it Tom or Mr Foster? No it was…could it be? My father!
I woke in a sweat.

The next morning I found Lady Eleanor in the kitchen. She was already talking to cook about what to put in the hamper. Cold meats, cheeses, fresh buns, desserts and cakes.

"This sounds so mouth watering I wish we could go now!" I exclaimed

"Yes it is exciting, we used to do this all the time and it was so much fun. The children just adore it. It's just all day fun and laughter. Edward so loved our picnics. We will miss him but I'm sure he would want the children to be happy again."

Lady Eleanor was becoming more of herself again since the death of her husband. She seemed to have lost the burden and that heaviness that she had carried around with her for so long. Today she was wearing a floral button up blouse and a black skirt instead of her mourning clothes that were very solemn and completely black. Her hair was up in a bun but she had left a few wisps at the side that were curled around her face. She actually looked much younger than she had done and I knew that she was now on that path back to her old self.

There was so much to do and as usual Lady Eleanor relied on me and gave me many responsibilities concerning all matters in the house. Before I knew it, it was Thursday and the doorbell was being rung. We were in the garden with Lady Eleanor and the girls. The younger children were playing hide and seek and scurrying around the hedges and bushes.

"There's a Mr Foster here to see Miss Alice and Master Albert." Announced the maid.

Charlotte looked up from her book and raised an eyebrow to me.

"Thank you Martha" Begun Lady Eleanor.

"Please show him through to the garden and then you can bring tea and serve it out here."

"Certainly madam" she bobbed a curtsey and left.

Momentarily she returned with a dapper suited Mr Foster. He seemed slightly taller than I remembered but with the same deep brown eyes and the wisp of brown hair that hung over his right eye. He smiled broadly when he saw me. Came over and graciously kissed my hand. I introduced the rest of the family and he bowed his head to each in turn. When I introduced Charlotte she sprung from her seat and offered him her hand.

"Little vixen" I thought, but then inclined my head and returned the coy smile that she offered to me.

"Mr Foster, we were so looking forward to your call today." She began.

"You are nothing like what we expected!"

"Oh and what did you expect?" He questioned.

"Well," Charlotte hesitated.

I could bear no more and leapt from my chair.

"Please Mr Foster wont you sit down, look here comes Martha with the tea. How do you take your tea Mr Foster?"

Charlotte could tell the nervousness and tension in my voice. She sat down opposite Mr Foster leaving the seat beside him free for me.

"Hmm good tactics" I thought. "Then he can look at you more clearly."

In fact now that I was looking at Charlotte I could see that she had definitely made an effort. Goodness, how tight had she pulled those corsets round her waist? She had obviously spent the whole morning curling her hair and pinching her cheeks so that they glowed radiantly. The trouble that she would go to steal my Mr Foster. Surely he though could see right through her. He wouldn't fall for all that false charm would he?

"So Mr Foster how long have you been practicing law?"

"Oh not too long Miss Charlotte about five years"

"And do you enjoy your work or do you find that your profession is full of frightful bores lacking in personality?" James Foster laughed.

"What ever made you have that impression of lawyers Miss Charlotte?"

"I think Mr Foster is a very busy man and does not have the time for all this title tattle." I snatched his tea that he was just about to take his first sip of and replaced it on the table.

"Let's go into the study Albert and we can conclude all the work in there."

Albert and Mr Foster both rose obediently a little shocked by the authoritative tones in my voice.

"It's been such a pleasure Mr Foster." Charlotte fluttered her lashes.

"Will we see you again?"

"It would be delightful to be in your charming company again."

"Well in that case what are you doing Saturday?"

James Foster looked a little shocked. I was frowning so hard I thought my eyes might converge together!

"We are having a picnic in Richmond by the river. We would love it if you could join us. Wouldn't we mama?"

Lady Sinclair had no choice but to join this façade and had to agree with her overly flirtatious daughter.

"Yes Mr Foster we would be delighted if you could join us and then you would have plenty of time to discuss all your legal matters with Albert and Alice."

"Well thank you. This was quite unexpected, but I wouldn't like to impose on a family outing."

"Good" I thought.

"No" Interjected Charlotte.

"You won't be imposing! We insist you accept!"

"Well in that case thank you so much I will definitely be there."

He went over to Charlotte kissed her hand and said his goodbyes.
Oh no he was smitten, it was fifteen love to Charlotte.
As we turned to walk inside I heard Lady Sinclair rebuking
Charlotte for her blatant lack of subtlety.

"It is not becoming for a young lady to have to try quite so hard
Charlotte do you have no shame?"
I could feel Charlotte's eyes boring into my back as we walked
away from the garden and into the house.
Albert and I stood in the study.

"Your *cousin* is very endearing."

"Is she?" I replied

"Wonder why she thought all lawyers were boring? Where
could she have got that notion?"
Albert and I exchanged glances but neither of us said anything.

"Well it seems that we have plenty of time now to do
everything on Saturday so if you like we can sign all the
paperwork now and then on Saturday I can talk you through the
procedures that will take place next. Would that be acceptable?"
I nodded defeated. I had been looking forward to my first picnic
so much but as usual Charlotte had to stick her spanner in the
spokes and change all the arrangements.
I didn't stand a chance now with James Foster and felt quite
despondent as he left that afternoon.

"See you Saturday then."
He walked away then turned winked and smiled a warm starry
smile that I had no choice but to respond to with an equally starry
smile.

"See *you* Saturday then.
I closed the front door. My heart was leaping. Maybe Saturday
wouldn't be too bad after all.

Chapter 33

The day began with frostiness on the ground and a cool stillness in the air. At first I thought that we would have to bundle up warmly for our picnic but the skies seemed to be cloudless and I decided to wait a while before dressing just to see what the weather would bring.

By nine the sun was rising in the sky and its rays bathed the garden with a golden orange glow. The air smelt sweet with honeysuckle and sweet pea. Dogs barked in the distance and the smooth roll of carriages in the street was already in the rhythm of normal weekend life.

I was reminded of how different it had been so far away in the countryside where the lone cuckoo would echo its song across vast fields and the hay would gently sway in the summer breezes. Sometimes I did feel quite homesick. Not for people but for the land and the church bells that rung out every Sunday for mass and silly insignificant things like the creak of the staircase in the middle of the night and the swish of the old grandfather clock as the pendulum swung back and forth.

I was feeling a sense of in trepidation mixed with uncertainty and I didn't know why. I had been sleeping badly this last week and my nights had been plagued with strange unsettling dreams. I felt weary, but the rising heat of the day lifted my morale slightly and I knew that I would have to face my insecurities and tackle the day ahead.

Outside I could hear the servants packing the carriages their voices low, rising above was cook squeaking voice telling the boys not to pack the heavy items on top of the breads and pastries.

Within the house there was bustle. Children running down corridors, heavy footsteps as they dragged down their games and balls.

"Come on Alice!"

Archie was breathless.

"We're getting ready to set off. You'd better hurry up or we'll go without you!"

"Is anyone else here?" I questioned.

"No, like whom?"

"Like, err Mr Foster maybe?"

"Nah don't think he's coming."

Archie put his hand in mine and began lunging me towards the door. I was feeling a little sense of relief that Mr Foster wasn't here but not convinced by Archie's complete brushing off of the fact that he was not coming at all. Would he really turn up? But then, I suppose it would be rude to just not show.

"Archie don't drag me down the stairs so quickly I'll fall!"

It was quite funny in a way to be pulled down stairs by such an overenthusiastic child. I liked Archie he was fun and full of life. There was a natural quality about him, an innocence that I remembered in myself when I was about his age. No pretexts, no pretence things were said as they were. I liked that. What a shame that things all turn into a charade as we get older. The other thing that I liked about Archie was that he treated me like a sister, something that was quite unique to me and so unlike everyone else to whom I was merely a cousin. Except Albert of course, but that was another matter completely.

"You will promise to play with me wont you Alice? The other girls ignore me sometimes because I'm just a boy but you're more fun than them!"

"Am I?"

"Oh yes you're the best Alice."

By the time I had reached the bottom step I had quite a gleeful smile across my face.

"Good morning Alice and aren't you looking chuffed about something this morning."

"Thank you Charlotte and good morning to you too."

"Well you can wipe that smile off your face because he isn't here yet."

I had a momentary loss of memory.

"Sorry, who?"

"Don't play games you know perfectly well who!"

"Oh yes" My memory restored.

"Oh never mind then and you appear to have gone to so much trouble dear Charlotte."

I retracted my claws and stepped towards the door where Lady Eleanor was tutting at our behaviour.

"We are all going to have a lovely day, so please everyone no fighting and lets all just be really pleasant to each other. And no teasing the little ones!"

"Yes mama"

"Yes Lady Eleanor."

There were two carriages. Lady Eleanor and the girls in one and the boys and the servants above in the other. Charlotte was frantically scanning the streets and looking out for our missing guest, as she stepped aboard.

A carriage came screeching around the corner. Mr Foster leapt from it and paid his fare. He ran alongside our carriage his tails flapping in the wind.

"Lady Eleanor my sincere apologies for being so late I do hope that I haven't held you up."

"Oh how lovely that you could join us Mr Foster we were beginning to think that you wouldn't make it."

214

"I nearly didn't. My brother called upon me late last night and we talked till quite late. But I shan't detain you any longer." James Foster scanned the carriage and nodded to us all. His eyes seemed to rest and linger on Charlotte for just a few seconds longer than I felt comfortable with. He seemed to have a radiance about him that grew on me each time I met him. It was something in his eyes, his smile.

"Mr Foster would you get in the other carriage with the boys there is much more room in there. You can tell us all about your brother when we arrive."

Lady Eleanor then closed the carriage door leaving James Foster to step behind the carriage and out of eyeshot into the carriage behind.

So he did come. In some way I was pleased and then when I looked over at Charlotte and her over laced corsets I felt suddenly resentful that she was being so determined to poach him from me. However there was a saving grace of sorts that we were sure to explore in far more depth later that day and that was the situation of the brother who hopefully would be an identical twin brother and then we could have one each! Oh if only life's problems could be sorted so easily. I was still struggling to come to terms with the multitude of problems that I had to face. I had no one to talk to and that was the scariest part. I had looked over some of the paperwork and realised that most of the investments that my father had made were sound and would provide me with an income that was more than generous for the rest of my life. There was no need to make any changes to anything that was in place at the moment. It would all have to remain secret though. If word got out I'm sure that the street would be filled with hundreds of eligible suitors desperately trying to prise my wealth from me. I would have to be suspicious of everybody and that would have to include James Foster himself. I knew that he was bound by some sort of confidentiality but how far did that really extend? How many tankards of ale would it take for him to reveal my secrets? After about an hour or so the carriage began to roll quickly down the steep hills towards the river. I could feel the horses stumbling and resisting the weight against the muddy banks.

"Look we are here girls!"

I looked out. The river glistened like it was filled with fallen stars and the sun danced in mini rainbows as it ebbed to and forth. Swans glided along in pairs and ducks squawked loudly as they flapped their wings on the verges.

I stepped from the carriage. The heat of the sun caressed my face like a warm hand. I lifted my palm and shaded my eyes from its glare as I looked over the beautiful scenery before me.

"I've brought the easels and canvas" Albert was behind me almost reading my thoughts.

"It's breathtaking isn't it?"

"It is perfectly lovely Albert."

"Just like you sweet Alice."

I hesitated before responding. That long overdue talk with Albert I felt was now imminent.

"Albert?"

"Yes"

"May we walk and talk a little?"

"Oh yes I would love to stroll with you. There are some lovely little inlets down the river. I could show you if you like?"

I smiled and nodded. Lady Eleanor was organising the servants and arranging where we were to set up the picnic. The younger children were playing Piggy in the Middle with Archie already cast in the role of "piggy". Charlotte was having problems opening her parasol and Mr Foster was gallantly coming to her rescue.

Albert turned to his mother.

"Is it all right if Alice and I go for a little stroll mama?"

"Yes no problem we shan't have lunch for at least another hour. Make sure that you are back by then."

"Of course mama."

We set off. I was rehearsing the words in my mind but having problems trying to verbalise them in a caring considerate and unintimidating way. I knew that this conversation had to be had though so I drew a deep breath and began.

"Albert you are a very dear cousin to me."

Albert's eyes were smiling and he seemed very reassured by what I had began to say leaving me to feel that a slightly more brutal approach was needed.

"…And that is all that you are to me and all that you ever will be."

He looked dejected.

"But I know how deep your feelings run for me and I am afraid that I could never return those feelings in the same way."

A tear began to well in his eye.

"Albert the truth of the matter is simply, well, I'm just not good enough for you and you deserve the very best. Which I am certainly not."

He said nothing. He just stood looking like an abandoned puppy.

"Albert one day you will find someone who will make a very fitting wife only it won't be me."

Still nothing.

"I am so sorry."

He took my hand in his and looked me straight in the eye.

"Thank goodness Alice. I thought that you had an interest in me and I was struggling to find a kind way to tell you that I did not. Well not any more. Not since William introduced me to his cousin Clara who is complete sweetness."

Now it was me who was speechless. My mouth fell open like a panting dog but without the panting!

"Oh" I managed.

"You are right Alice we will be dear cousins though and I am so pleased that I do not have to pretend anymore."

I smiled. He smiled. Then before we knew it we were laughing like small children at the irony of the whole situation.

"Come on Albert let's get back. We've been ages and I'm starving."

I linked my arm through his and we started to retrace our footsteps.

"So what's this Clara like then? You must tell me all about her…"

Chapter 34

By the time Albert and I had returned to the party, we were completely at ease with one another and all tensions between us had been dissipated. It was quite a relief for me to feel so liberated from this noose of trying not to hurt Albert. It was important that he would never know the truth of my dark secret about my parentage. I would certainly have been ousted and expelled from this society were anything even remotely resembling scandal, exposed. It would have finished me off forever. I felt now that Albert and I could be friends and I wanted that more than anything.

Mr Foster was sitting alone next to the river. I wondered if he had already had the full flirtatious interrogation from Charlotte in my absence. He was on a rug leaning back against a tree trunk. In his right hand he held small leather bound book. Charlotte, Emily and Jane were helping their mother arrange the food. Archie was tossing pebbles into the river and in so doing upsetting the ducks and geese who squawked loudly flapping their wings and trying to protect their young.

"That looks interesting."I peered over James' shoulder to see what he was reading.

"Yes it's a book of sonnets."

"Sonnets? That doesn't seem very you, if you don't mind me saying so."

James Foster gave me that mysterious look. The one that unsettled me and made me look away from the intensity of his eyes.

"And why shouldn't I read sonnets? I find all kinds of poetry quite alluring."

"Really?" I smiled

"I think we are about to have lunch. Everyone seems to be assembling over with Lady Eleanor wont you come and join us. You can tell me all about your favourite sonnets."

"I would love to Alice. Thank you."

He got up and we walked over to the others. James was still reading but now out loud.

"But thou contracted to thine own bright eyes
Feedest thy lights flame with self-substantial fuel
Making a famine where abundance lies
Thyself thy foe, to thy sweet self too cruel."

I turned to him. I knew he was reciting a quote but somehow it sounded like he was talking about me. Reading my soul. Seeing something that I was trying so hard to never reveal. I said nothing. There was no reply and I knew no equally fitting verse to respond with.

We took our places on the rug beside the rest of the family. Plates were laid and bowls were passed around from which we heaped generous helpings of vegetables, pastries and cheeses. Cook was carving cold meats and laying them on a plate from which everyone was reaching and taking food. Her fresh chutneys complemented the meats and cheeses and the breads were fresh and crusty. We drank cider and laughed. Lady Eleanor laughed too, but in a silent moment I noticed a lone tear trickling down her cheek and realised that her happiness was still tinged with the slightest hint of sadness.

However much I hated my father he was still her husband and I assumed that she had had to put up with a lot over the years. She must miss him in her own way. I missed him too. I dreamt about him more and more frequently lately. Strange dreams where he asked me for my forgiveness. Dreams that my mind conjured to

220

soothe my anger towards him. Dreams that would now never come true.

Charlotte was lying on her back. Picking the petals off a dandelion. She rolled over towards James Foster.

"So are you going to tell us all about your family?"

"Oh you mean my brother? Yes he is so scatterbrained and I do once again apologise for my tardiness this morning!"

"So what does your brother do?" I interrupted

"He's training to be an accountant. He works for a company in the city. He loves numbers, always has, that's his forte he's going to be a great man one day."

"And is he like you? In appearance I mean." Enquired Charlotte.

"No he's more like his mother I suppose."

"His mother? Don't you share the same mother?" Charlotte was now sitting, her curiosity seeping at the seams.

"No my mother died when I was quite young and my father remarried so my brother is actually a half brother." James finished his sentence with his eyes cast over towards me. It was as if he was trying to tell me that he knew what it was like to have family that wasn't quite whole.

"Oh!" Charlotte was practically leaning into his lap.

"How absolutely fascinating Mr Foster. How romantic to have half brothers and sisters. Do you have any other siblings?

"No. My step mother died after my brother was born and then my father didn't marry again. It didn't seem to agree with the health of his wives!"

We laughed.

"But in answer to your question Miss Charlotte my brother is fair haired, with a touch of auburn in his locks and his eyes are a deep corn blue."

My heart missed a beat. It almost sounded like a description of Tom so far away in Somerset. So cruelly abandoned by me and discarded from my thoughts.

James and Charlotte remained locked in conversation. The rest of the children had started roaming from the picnic area. Albert was teaching Archie to fish in the river. The girls were skipping.

I got up and walked away. The thoughts of Tom were now creeping into my head. I felt a sadness that I had not experienced for a long time. A yearning for him. For his touch. The image that I had in my head was of his poor beaten body lying in the dirt, pain oozing from his wounds. I wondered why I had this cruel streak within me that allowed me to be able to just walk away and shut people out of my life. Maybe it was because I had been abandoned and shut out of the lives of the very people that should have cared about me.

A tear escaped from my eye. I quickly brushed it away before anyone saw. I was feeling very fragmented. I felt that I had been torn in half from the Alice that had grown up so far away to the Alice that I now was. What would fate bring for me next? I didn't know if I could cope with being an heiress living a life so far removed from my comfort zone. I felt that I was an actress on a stage playing a tragic heroine in a story that had no hope of ever having a happy ending.

Would it be easier to just go home and live the way I was destined to be. Something inside me missed Tom so terribly. I knew that I could trust him with all my heart and feel safe with him. The people around me here were such hard work and I felt on guard with them the whole time. It was funny that all my life I had craved to be with a family and now that I was, I realised that having peace and quiet was far more favourable. I was still slightly jealous though of the girls' relationship with their mother. That was what I wanted. Someone that cared for me unconditionally.......but maybe that could be Tom too. Here I was on a beautiful summer's day, surrounded by people and I was feeling such melancholy. Lonely but not alone.

I wandered back to the group.

Lady Eleanor looked up, her expression was one of concern.

"Where is Archie?"

"Wasn't he fishing with Albert?

"No he got bored with that and came running after you. Haven't you seen him?"

"No."

Lady Eleanor got up and started calling out to the other children. Her voice at first calm seemed to rise with urgency and panic.

"Don't worry mama I'm sure that we will find him." Jane held her mother's hand.

"But he's such an inquisitive child always running off to do things that he shouldn't be doing. He said he was going to find Alice."

I suddenly felt responsible. Maybe I shouldn't have wandered off like that, consumed in my own little world.

Charlotte and James now came closer, as did Albert.

"Let's all spread out and call him he must be somewhere. Probably terrorizing some swans and cygnets, trying to pluck out their feathers or something!"

We ran. We called. Nothing.

The servants that had been having their own little picnic a little distance from our own were now also participating in the search. Long minutes passed. There was still no sign.

I felt sick. Beads of perspiration were dampening my back. Where was little Archie? Lady Eleanor was now becoming frantic, her eyes were startled, her expression vacant and pleading.

"Mama!Mama!"

Emily was standing at the banks of the river. She seemed frozen. We all ran over and to our horror there was Archie lying face down in the water. He was motionless.

Albert and James leapt into the river. We all scrambled to the edge our skirts and petticoats trailing in the mud. Albert and James waded into the river and pulled at his collar. He floated towards them with the weightlessness of a feather. They turned him over onto his back. His eyes were closed and he looked as if he was sleeping. They brought him to the side and gently lifted his body his clothes now heavy, saturated with water, onto dry land.

"Archie! Oh God, no! No!" Lady Eleanor took her wet son in her arms and cradled him.

"Wake up my baby please wake up!"

There was no movement from Archie. His face was sallow and pale, his lips blue. His eyes remained closed.

The girls were all crying and clinging together.

Horror shrouded Lady Eleanor's face. Her lifeless child, fading from her.

Somehow a crowd had gathered around us. People from all over the park that had joined to help us in the search for him now stood, caps in hand peering at the tiny drenched body laid on the green grass verge.

"We need to find a doctor. Someone help please!"

Through the crowd a voice called out to be let through.

I stepped back. A shiver ran down my spine. I knew that voice. I knew that hair, those eyes.

He rushed forward. Grabbed Archie from Lady Eleanor and began pushing on his chest and breathing into his mouth.

"What are you doing?" Lady Eleanor demanded.

"Get off my son! What are you doing to him?"

Archie coughed. Then rolled to his side and threw up some water.
He coughed again, then began to cry. The colour was now
flooding back to his cheeks. His eyes seemed startled
   "Oh, my baby! Thank you sweet God!
Her tears rolled into the musky wetness of Archie's hair.
The girls hugged their brother. Albert hugged me and James
Foster stood looking quite perplexed. Cook clean fainted into the
arms of the menservants.
The kind stranger stood and without fuss wriggled free of the
crowd that were assembling around the poor child. Our eyes
locked for a very brief second. He nodded acknowledgment to me
and as mysteriously as he had come, he was gone.
I looked for him above the heads. I thought to go after him, then
decided that indeed I would. Stupidly I wasted precious seconds
and when eventually I did go scrambling through the throngs of
people he had disappeared. For a moment I wondered if it had all
been an illusion. My imagination just getting carried away with
me. Could it really have been him? Why was he here in London?
Why did he just disappear?

Chapter 35

Archie was now confined to his bed following Saturday's
disastrous picnic. Everyone was making a big fuss of him and
Archie was lapping up all the attention most gratefully.
"I swear Archie that I will never tease you again."
Jane and Emily were sitting at the foot of their brother's bed.
"Yes and I swear that I will always be the perfect sister." Emily
added
"But I swear I will always share all my sweets with you."
"And my puddings and I won't pull your hair or scribble on
your homework."
"I will be the best sister that you can ever imagine possible!"
Jane announced triumphantly.
Emily threw her a scalded look.
"So will I!"
"You won't. You always make promises and break them!"
"I do not! How dare you! What about the time when you
promised not to finish the last piece of cooks chocolate pie and
you did!"
"I never!"
"I know it was you!" Emily shoved her sister so hard that Jane
fell off the bed and into a heap on the floor.
Jane stood with that glare in her eyes like a cat about to pounce
on a mouse. She then leapt at her sister with such force that Emily
now fell on top of Archie's legs. The two girls rolled, pulling at
each other's hair and screaming at each other as they did so!
I entered the room alerted by all the yelling.
"What is going on in here?" I demanded looking at the two
bedraggled girls with their hair all messed and pulled from their
plaits.

"It's her!" An accusing finger was thrust into Emily's face.

"It's not me it's her!" An equally angry finger just missed the bridge of Jane's nose.

"Enough!" I screamed above the rising crescendo.

"Archie you are witness. What's going on?"

He pulled the covers from over his face where he had been hiding from his sisters and more so from the fact that it had been he who had eaten all the chocolate pie.

"Well, I suppose, they were fighting about who was going to be the perfect sister."

"Really? And in your opinion who is the perfect sister?" I asked flippantly

"You are." Came the simple but poignant reply.

"Oh Archie." I was overwhelmed. I went over and planted a kiss on his forehead. I then turned to the two girls who were sheepishly staring at the floor and ordered them out.

"Your brother nearly died a few days ago! You should be ashamed of yourselves conducting yourselves like street women! I suggest that you go to your rooms where you can reflect on your behaviour. Then later when you are truly sorry you can come back and apologise to Archie.

"Yes Alice."

"Sorry Alice and sorry Archie"

Archie turned in his bed and let out a convincing moan.

"I am so terribly weak." He began

"I think I saw the angels coming for me."

Archie lay arms outstretched, eyes half closed, as the girls left the room.

As soon as the door was closed he sat bolt upright and smiled a huge grin.

"You little cheater." I sniggered

"You love all this don't you?"

227

He nodded enthusiastically.

"Do you really think I would have died if that kind man hadn't saved me?"

"I don't know Archie. It was very frightening for everyone. You gave us a big shock."

Did anyone find out what his name was? I mean the man that saved me?"

I didn't know what to say. I had gone over the scene time and time again in my mind and now I wasn't sure. Maybe I had imagined that it was him? Perhaps it was someone similar? I doubted so much that now I believed that it couldn't have been him.

"No Archie we didn't ask his name. He came and went so quickly that no one thought of it."

Lady Sinclair opened the door. Archie threw himself back on the pillows and closed his eyes again.

"Oh my poor darling, are you still unwell?"

"Yes mama" Archie replied in a very subdued croaky voice.

"Well you shall stay right there and don't worry about your lessons until you are well again."

Only I saw the grin that momentarily passed his lips.

When Lady Sinclair left, Archie sat up and said.

"You won't tell will you?"

I knew what it was like to be confined to bed and the advantages that it could bring. I squeezed Archie's hand.

"Don't worry little soldier. It'll be our secret."

James Foster had called the previous day to see how Archie was doing. He had been very concerned and a little dazed by the whole incident. He had left the park in a cab on Saturday his clothes completely soaked from his attempts to pull Archie from the river.

As usual I had been the one to console Lady Sinclair. She had been in a terrible state of shock and quite understandably following her recent bereavement. She had kept muttering about how she couldn't have coped with two funerals in two months. No one could have. How can anyone bury a ten year old boy? I did try to explain that thankfully it wasn't even a consideration as now Archie was well on the mend and would be up and about in no time.

At least that was when he decided that it was boring just lying in bed all day. Archie had trusted me with his secret and he had also called me his perfect sister. What a wonderful boy he was! I knew that he had called me sister but I'm sure that he meant it in a cousinly way!

Since Saturday I had been questioning my mind, convinced that it had been playing tricks upon me. My doubts had become so real that I had almost convinced myself that it could not possibly have been Tom. It was some kindly stranger that just happened to be the same height, the same build, have the same voice and when he looked at me for that brief moment, the same eyes. But no, not him. No not possibly. So why did I feel this sense that eyes were following me? Why did I sometimes turn sharply because I felt someone's gaze on my shoulder but when I looked behind me no one was there?

I went over to the window pulled up the sash and looked out onto the street. A grocer's boy was delivering to the next door house. People were strolling along but there was no one that looked out of place. No figure lurking in a shadow waiting to wave to me and reveal himself. I remembered that time that seemed so long ago when I was sitting in the rose garden back home and Tom was trying so hard to talk to me through the bushes. Now here I was and in a way I was desperately hoping that he would appear.

And if he did? Then what? Would I run to him? I was in a strange dilemma. Wanting but not wanting.

I had not yet decided what I was to do with myself. My time here with the Sinclair's was coming to an end and I had to definitely consider what I would do next. Lady Sinclair had been very temperamental with me on and off over the last few months. One minute she needed me by her side to help her with all kinds of organisation and administration and the next she seemed to tire of me and turn positively nasty as if she despised my very presence. At times like those I wondered if she had any inkling of my true identity. Everyone had commented on how alike Charlotte and I were and how we were more like sisters than cousins. Lady Eleanor must have noticed or had her suspicions. Could she really be so blinkered about it?

It was a lovely afternoon and I decided to stroll into town. The walk was very pleasant but the people were so different to country folk. People walked briskly past each other with only the occasional person stopping to tilt their head and say good morning.

I walked down as far as the shops. It was a fair walk and the windows were filled with very elegant samples of gowns from Paris and Rome. I was half tempted to go in and be measured up for some new finery but decided that there would be plenty of time for that in the future. If I started this now there would be too many questions asked in the Sinclair household and I didn't want to have to explain where all the money came from.

I began to walk home. The sounds of hundreds of footsteps on the busy London pavements thinly reduced as I followed the leafy roads back to 14 Inverness gardens.

Then there were only two sets of feet pounding the pavements. I stopped momentarily. They stopped too. I instantly knew. I had

been anticipating this most of the week. I hastily spun around
before he could hide and there he was right behind me.

"Tom."

"Alice"

I wanted to cry. I could feel a mountain of emotion welling up
inside me. I wanted to run to him but couldn't. It had been nearly
three months. I had abandoned him for an awfully long time. Did
he feel resentment? Was he here to tell me that I was some selfish
London lady now and that he hated me?

His face hard and weathered beneath a light brown cap scanned
mine looking for some response to his unexplained appearance.
I began to shake. My knees beneath my petticoats and dress now
quivering so hard that I feared he would see and laugh at me.
His mouth reluctantly turned up slightly and he smiled that warm
lovely smile that told me that I had nothing to worry about. He
opened his arms and I could feel myself almost in a dream like
state moving towards him and being enveloped in his embrace.
After what seemed like long minutes he loosened his hold and I
stepped back. He reached out his hand to me and we walked hand
in hand not speaking a single word.

There was so much to say yet the warmth radiating through our
hands and between each other spoke for us.

Eventually we found a bench and sat gazing and losing ourselves
in each other's eyes. I had never felt such an overwhelming
feeling for anyone. Yes I admired gentlemen like William and Mr
Foster but this tugging and twisting in my gut was unparalleled.
When Tom reached over, gently stroked the skin of my cheek
then leant over and kissed me, I could have quite happily fallen
off the edge of the world.

There were no doubts. I knew that I had been fighting this feeling
but now I had succumbed and I could never love another. Tom

was the part of my soul that had been missing from me. I now felt complete.

A conversation was inevitable but nearly an hour had passed without one.

"Tom, I don't know how to say this but I am so sorry that my father beat you and left you for dead"

Tom paused then voiced his thoughts.

"Then you left too."

A tear rolled down my cheek. I felt like I had lashed that whip.

"I am so sorry Tom. I had to go; I knew that Maud and Nurse Dunn would care for you. Did it take you very long to recover?"

"I suppose it did. So many days all rolled together and then weeks and months had passed. I had to get well Alice. I had to get well for you."

"Tom you are always there protecting me. Like that time when I ran away to London and then when you saved Archie."

"I didn't want to reveal myself to you. Not like that in such a large crowd but then the poor boy would have died so I had to do something."

"And we were all so grateful Tom. It would have been awful if you hadn't been there.

"But then Alice I was afraid."

"Of what?"

"Of you. You looked at me as if I was a stranger. You looked right through me and I thought that I would just go back because you didn't care for me anymore."

"I was in shock Tom! My little brother nearly died right there on the lawn. I was scared Tom and......well I didn't believe that it could really be you."

Tom looked at me anxiously.

"Are you coming home Alice?"

"I don't know. There are still some things that need to be sorted out here."

"There are things that need to be sorted out everywhere. There are things that you need to be told Alice and I don't know how to tell you."

I felt very cold despite the sun blazing down upon me.

"What things?"

"Well there are things like gossip in the village and stories that get passed from so many lips to ears that on the way the stories change and are nothing like what they began to be."

"Is there something that you've heard Tom?"

"Yes"

I could feel a shiver run down my spine. Why was I feeling so frightened?

"What is it? Tom tell me!"

"I don't know how."

"Is it silly rumours that Mrs Knight has spun around? Where did you get this information?

"From your father. It came out in anger as he was beating me. I think he meant to kill me and that his words would never come to light."

"What!"

"Well when I was half out of my mind and dying in that barn I tried to tell Maud to tell you"

"Yes that's right you were mumbling something about the other, the other."

Tom hesitated.

"Alice it wasn't "other" that I was trying to say."

"Well what was it then?"

"It was "mother"......... I was trying to tell you the truth about your mother and that she is still alive…"

Chapter 36

Free falling from a great cliff, waiting to hit the ground, wind fleeting past your ears, stomach turning, feeling of complete helplessness. That's how I was at this moment.

Tom held me. If he hadn't I would have fallen like a sack to the ground. Why was my life such a lie? Maybe there was some mistake about what he was saying. Could my mother be alive? Who was she? Did I know her?

I was bursting with questions and when I finally regained my composure and felt that I wasn't completely insane those questions spilled out of me.

"Where is she? Who is she? What else do you know?"

"Calm down sweet Alice. I know this is all a big shock to you."

"What do you know?" I could feel my frustration turning to anger.

"You have known this information and have waited till now to tell me! This is outrageous! How would you feel if you found that you were a bastard and then the mother that you believed dead was still alive and didn't have a care for you?"

"I'm sorry Alice."

"Sorry? What do you care? Who is this so called mother anyway? She is no mother if she could abandon me!"

"Alice, you cannot judge you don't know all the facts and circumstances."

"I can judge and I will! I have a mother who wants nothing to do with me so likewise I want nothing to do with her!"

"Alice you don't mean that!"

My lip began to quiver. Of course I didn't mean it but I was so raw and bruised that I couldn't comprehend it. I began to cry. I cried for all those years longing for my mother. Praying that she was watching me from heaven and loving me the way a mother loves her daughter, the way Lady Eleanor loves her daughters.

"Alice can I take you home?"

I looked at him remorsefully.

"I'm sorry Tom for snapping at you like that."

"I did try to tell you as soon as I was able to travel and come back to London."

"I know."

"So do you want me to walk you home?"

"No. Well not yet. I think I want to know more."

"Are you sure Alice? Look what's happened already."

"Yes but I'll be fine. I will. I promise."

I gave Tom a smile to try to reassure him that I wouldn't react in the same way again. I needed to know everything that there was. How could I not? I would have to restrain myself if I wanted to hear more.

Tom swallowed and uncomfortably shifted his gaze. He had removed his cap and his fair hair hung loose and wavy over his neck.

"I don't recall everything Alice. You must remember that your father was lashing that whip and I was passing in and out of consciousness at some points. He was ranting like some lunatic and some things were just unclear and I didn't understand."

"So what do you remember?" I whispered, holding my breath.

"He told me that you would be sent away for your own good just as your mother had been. That it was for your own sake that you knew nothing about that sorry state of a woman or where she was. He then said that you had been such a burden to him and to his career."

I nodded
"Is that all?"
"There was one thing."
"What?"
"I think. I think Lady Sinclair knows where your mother is!"
"Lady Sinclair?" I repeated incredulously.
"Yes!"
"But how? Why?"
"I don't know. I think…well...I suppose that you'll have to ask her."
"I couldn't!"
"Well then I know no more and you will never find out."
"Oh Tom!"
I took a deep breath then let out an equally deep sigh.
"I can't. I cannot possibly speak of this to Lady Eleanor. Not ever."
"Well that is your decision Alice. No one says that you have to say anything today or even tomorrow. I think you should think very carefully about this before you say anything to anyone."
I dried my tears and took Toms hand, which I held in my own small frail hand. He gently stroked it and kissed it till I felt all the sadness and confusion subside within me.
"I think I should go now."
"Yes of course, let me walk with you."
When we reached the end of my street. We said our goodbyes and arranged to meet in the park at the same time the next day. I promised that I would not do anything rash and hasty; a promise that I might struggle to keep.
I went back into the house that was my home for the time being. I went straight to Archie's room. Archie was my friend as well as my dear brother and I needed to be near someone that had no animosity or secrets from me.

"Hello Alice!" Archie sat up and gave me the hugest smile. I sat beside him on the bed and he threw his arms around me.

"Your eyes are sad, have you been crying?"

"No!" I replied defensively.

I was amazed at how perceptive this little child was. I wondered just how well he could see through people.

The door opened and Lady Eleanor came in.

"Good afternoon my darling and hello Alice. We didn't see you all afternoon where were you?"

"Oh I didn't think anyone would notice my disappearance." I replied nervously.

"I went out for some air. I walked for miles, I just forgot the time."

Lady Sinclair arched her eyebrow and peered at me curiously.

"Are you well Alice? You seem a little out of sorts."

Apparently my state of mind was more apparent than I thought.

"I have been feeling a little unwell. I think it's all the excitement this week with little Archie here and all of us being so worried about him."

"Well if you are unwell Alice it's not the best idea to be near Archie is it? We don't want him getting an infection from you on top of what he has already. Do we?"

Archie realizing that I may be restricted from coming to visit him sat up from his sprawled state of stupor.

"Mama I really am so much better. Please don't stop Alice coming to see me. Without her feeding me and reading to me and helping me to recover I would not be as well as I am now. Please don't send her away mama."

Lady Sinclair was not amused.

"Archie I do believe that you have been lying to us! I have been in your room for ten minutes during which time you have lain there groaning and suffering, then you have the audacity to sit up

237

and speak to me completely coherently and without any sign of malaise!"

Archie who had forgotten just how convincing his acting could be and how well he had played his previous role, now looked sheepishly down into his blankets.

"Tomorrow Archie you will get dressed and come down for your lessons and you will have extra work to do to make up for all the days of pretence! I am most displeased!"

She then turned to me, her face crumpled with anger her eyes narrowed and suspicious.

"Did you know of this façade?"

"No of course not. With respect Lady Eleanor you know how young children suddenly recover from illnesses. Archie has definitely had a fever and I myself have been administering his physic three times a day. I am sure that has helped Archie. Please don't rebuke him. He would never feign something so serious. Remember he nearly died last Saturday."

Lady Eleanor stood silent digesting my words.

"Hmm" She muttered and with a grand swish of her skirts left the room.

I turned to Archie and dropped my jaw.

"That was close Alice. Thank you for sticking up for me like that."

"Yes Archie but you must remember that if you are going to start a lie than you must see it through or you will be exposed as a liar and cheat!"

I left his room and slowly walked back to my own. I wanted to be alone. My words to Archie echoed in my mind. How appropriate they were to me. I too had to see things through even though they were so disturbing.

The day was like a blur in my mind. The thought of seeing Tom had filled me with excitement and longing and yet the news that he had brought me created tension, confusion and hurt. I wanted to run away from myself but I desperately needed time to think this all through. I opened my bedroom door. Charlotte was sitting on my bed.

"Oh no!" I thought, but smiled courteously anyway. I would have to get rid of her quickly I just could not face this now.

"Hello Charlotte."

"Good afternoon Alice."

"Is there something that I can help you with?" I asked with some slight irritation in my voice.

"Alice I just thought that it would be nice to catch up and spend some time with each other. We haven't really spoken much lately and I thought it would be nice to get to know you a little better."

"Yes that would be nice." I replied politely but really I was thinking this is just not the time.

What could I say to get rid of her?

Charlotte I need some time on my own because I've just found out that my dead mother is really alive? Didn't think that would go down that well, although Charlotte would have been all over me to find out all the gossip and intrigue about this stranger that was living amongst them. I had no choice but to entertain her. Charlotte smiled in her coy way, which meant she was going to ask me something or challenge me in some way.

"Alice..." She began

"I was wondering if you could have a few words with Mr Foster."

"Why Charlotte?" I said directly.

"Well I asked him if he would like to escort me to the theatre one day because there is a wonderful play that I had heard so much about and he replied that it would not be proper on account of the fact that he was considering courting another."

"Really?"

"Yes and when I asked him who this other was, he merely replied that it wasn't of my concern which I thought was terribly rude!"

"Well quite honestly Charlotte it is a little forward and not becoming for a young lady to be so direct with a gentleman. I don't think your mother would approve."

"Oh yes mother would absolutely die if she knew. She keeps telling me off about it already but I just can't help it. What am I to do? I try to flatter them and say all those things that they would like to hear as encouragement from me but for all my subtlety they still don't seem to hook to the bait, so, well I suppose I just come out with it."

"Yes you do!"

"Is that so bad?"

"Yes."

"So what should I do?

"Perhaps you are just trying too hard. Anyway you have hundreds of admirers so there's bound to be one that slips through your net."

"But it's the one that slips through the net that I want. Can't you speak to him and find out who this other girl is and so we can get rid of her."

"Charlotte!"

"I don't mean kill her or anything but perhaps just spread a few harmless rumours that would throw him off her scent."

"No. Sorry Charlotte. I won't be party to anything as sordid as that!"

Charlotte protruded her bottom lip and adopted a sulky face. I realised how young she really was and how basic her problems were compared to mine. From being irritated with her I now found her quite a distraction to my predicament and positively amusing. I felt smugness about James Foster not having any intentions towards her and had my opinions as to whom he really was hoping to impress.

Charlotte stayed in my room for the rest of the afternoon till it was time to go down for dinner. She knew that I was resolved in my conviction towards her flirtatious behaviour but she was unperturbed and still had the opinion that she would strive to get what she wanted as she cared little for her pride.

Many thoughts crossed my mind throughout the evening but I knew that the next day I would ask Tom if he could help me with one of the hardest decisions I would ever have to make.

Chapter 37

Lady Eleanor blows hot and cold with me. Sometimes I am
fearful of her and sometimes I think that she does care about me
and I am safe here. Now I'm not, I am afraid. I watch her like a
hawk sizing up its prey. It's strange because as I am watching her
I feel that she is watching me, both of us treading on uncertain
ground and nervous of each other's reactions. I am guessing
though. I am assuming that Lady Eleanor knows who I am. But if
she did, would she not throw me out in an instant. Would she
allow me to stay here and taint her precious family?

I am desperate to ask her all those questions that flooded through
my brain last night and prevented me from sleeping. Does she
really know the answers? Tom did say that he was hallucinating
and possibly could have got it wrong. If I were to say something
and she does in sincerity not know anything then would I just be
exposing myself for no reason and allowing myself to fall into a
pit?
My heart beats heavily. I feel on edge and nervous at the slightest
thing. I know that this will not change till I know the truth. I must
know the truth. It is my right to know.
I have no choice but to find a moment when I can ask. It will
have to be when I have done some task or favour for Lady
Eleanor and she is happy with me. She can sense my jumpiness
and I know that she pries for reasons in the same way as I would.
I must try to calm myself.
I sit on the park bench twirling my parasol over my shoulder. I
am waiting for Tom hoping that he will give me answers and
soothe my irritable temperament.

I see him approaching. He looks quite the gentleman. He is staying at a lodging house not too far away and has borrowed some clothes from a trunk of my fathers that was left in Somerset. I told him that I didn't mind and it was the least my father could do for him.

He looks up and is amazed to see me. I am early. Very early. I was too irritated to stay in the house, so came here so I could think, not that it's helped. My mind is so jumbled.

"My love."

Tom is by my side and he kisses my hand. His soft lips leave my hand unwillingly and I see that look of longing in his eyes.

"Tom, I am so troubled."

"I can see my dearest. Your eyes are red and you look tired even though it is still only morning."

"I couldn't sleep. I am so exhausted. So confused."

"My dear lets walk a little and find a more secluded spot."

I understand what he is saying and we walk together deeper into the park till we find a little clearing.

"Let's sit on the grass." I suggest.

"But what about your dress?"

"I care little for my dress on a day like today."

Before Tom can object any further I sit down and beckon to the space beside me where Tom sits cross legged. Quite without thought I lay across his lap and close my eyes as the sun squints through the trees and dazzles me.

"You are so beautiful Alice."

"So are you Tom."

He laughs and I laugh too.

We have been together for only a few minutes and already all the frustration and irritation is rising and floating away from my body like breath on a winter's morning. I am feeling a sense of liberation that only Tom can give me. I reach up and stroke his face. In response he leans down to me and covers my face with kisses. My whole body is warm and smiling. I feel so much love and wonderful peace.

"How do you do it?"

"Do what?" He asks inquisitively.

"Make it all go away."

"You're speaking riddles again. Make what all go away?"

"Sadness." I say simply.

Tom lies down beside me and I feel pieces of twigs and grass between the fallen strands of my hair. He takes me in his arms and holds me close. I feel so peaceful, so relaxed and I begin to slowly drift. Next thing I know I am waking.

"How long have I been asleep?"

"Two hours maybe three"

"No!"

"You looked so tranquil, I could not wake you. I watched you sleep, watched each breathe."

"Tom!"

"Yes my sweet."

I feel like I have been drugged. In my sleepy haze I'm carefree; I uncurl like a waking kitten and stretch.

"We must talk about this situation that I have to deal with."

I realise that my mind is so much clearer the sleep having been badly needed. I am now fresher in my thoughts and the rocky mountain that faced me before is now only a daisy covered little hill.

"I want to come home Tom, but at the same time I like London and all the excitement that it offers."

"But are the decisions that you need to make dependant on where you will live?"

"You mean where we will live?"

"Alice I can only dream. I am low class and though I can learn quickly I know that I cannot expect more from you, now that you are a lady. You've lived in this fancy house and become accustomed to fine things so much so that you forgot me…or so I thought."

I could tell that he was fishing. Trying to get some reassurance that I did care for him and that all those months that I had abandoned him was due to some other reason than my absolute indifference.

"Tom I never forgot you! You cannot be forgotten! I was not brought up as a lady or a servant. I was just raised by people that had no regard for station. Yes I was due respect but I never got it and in a way that is an advantage to me now as I feel in no way superior or inferior to anybody. I wish that my life was not so complicated but that is the hand that I have been dealt, so I will take it and play it with as much wisdom as I can."

Tom looked at me brimming.

"I am so proud of you. You get knocked over, yet time and time again you just rise above it and keep coming back."

"Look who's talking!" I laughed.

"If anyone's been knocked over and still came back it was you."

Yes I was a fighter. It was my gutsy nature. I was not like other girls but then I had not really had role models to follow and learn from. My teachers had been the heroines in the books that I had been left to read from a young age. They were my company. They were my only real friends.

"So your decision?"

"Yes." I paused

"I cannot stay with the Sinclair's but Somerset seems so far away and so dead. Don't get me wrong I really love my house but

245

nothing ever happens in the village and now that I have discovered this place I want to be a part of it."

"So what will you do?"

"I am very lucky Tom. I am fortunate enough to have the funds to make whatever choices I wish."

I wanted to tell Tom about the £400,000 pounds that I had inherited from my grandfather's estate. I trusted Tom but I knew that a figure like that would be too daunting for him to accept. He would know in time and I would make a gentleman out of him yet. We were both young and bursting with energy for life. Both able to have that strength of mind to take on anything new and ultimately succeed.

Tom didn't ask any questions. I had said there were funds and he accepted that it was all the information that he needed.

"So now what?"

"I think Tom that I need to fill all the blank spaces in my life and then we can decide where we will go and what we will do."

"I'll be right behind you Alice. You know that I will help you." Of course he would. He was here now. I knew that he would always be my rock. I wasn't scared with Tom by my side.

"I need to go now."

I got up and brushed the foliage from my clothes.

"I am going to speak to Lady Sinclair. I have no choice and I think I feel brave enough to do it. Shall I meet you here tomorrow?

Tom took my hand then drew me towards him and kissed me on the lips.

"Till tomorrow my angel."

He pressed a crumpled piece of paper into my hand.

"This is the address of the lodging house where I am staying. If you need me at any time come and find me. Good luck Alice. I am with you always."

I watched as he walked away from me and disappeared out of sight. I turned to walk home willing myself all the way to be strong and do what I had to do.

As I walked up the steps, the door to the house was half ajar. Sarah the housemaid was on the porch cleaning the windows and scrubbing the hallway.

"My lady was looking for you."

"Thank you Sarah. Do you know where she is?"

"She's in the study and she's not looking too happy. I'd better hurry up if I were you."

I wondered about Sarah's attitude. She didn't speak to anyone else in the house the way that she spoke to me, but still I didn't say anything to her, what was the point? I didn't want tongues wagging below stairs making up all kinds of stories and rumours about me.

I went to find Lady Eleanor a little concerned as to what she wanted with me. I found her in the study sitting at the desk a thousand papers strewn all over in random heaps. She was looking most perplexed.

"Oh at last!" She sighed as I walked through the door.

"I cannot understand a thing and there is always someone knocking on the door wanting payment for something or other and I don't know whether it its right or wrong. Alice you understand all these papers you must help me to get all this in order."

I perused the table and scanned the array of bills and documents. I knew exactly how to file everything and what was to be done. Lady Eleanor stood up and walked around me.

"What's this?" She tutted and her fingers threaded out a few blades of straw coloured grass from my hair.

"Alice, a young lady must really look presentable and proper at all times."

247

"Yes Lady Eleanor of course."
I sat down and began working. Lady Eleanor left me after several minutes and when she returned a couple of hours later there were five neat piles on the table.
"Where are all the papers?"
"They are right here. They are in separate sections of bills to be paid, invoices, bank statements receipts and miscellaneous documents. Would you like me to deal with the ones that need bank orders?"
"Yes Alice. Most definitely. You are so clever. I don't know how you are able to just sit down and do what you do."
I smiled but said nothing. My heart was ready to leap out of my chest. This was the moment that I had been waiting for to ask the question that had been troubling me all day. I opened my mouth to speak but the words seemed locked in my throat. I tried again but this time Lady Eleanor saw me and turned to me with a slight inquisitive arch above her left brow.
"Yes Alice?"
"Lady Sinclair." I stuttered.
"I have something that I would like to ask you…"

Chapter 38

"What is it that you need to know Alice?"
I looked up at Lady Eleanor trying hard to stop my bottom lip
from quivering. This was it, the moment I had dreaded and I
didn't want to lose my nerve.
"Lady Eleanor, I have reason to believe that you knew of
someone who was distantly related to me. Her name was Isobel
Lavelle."
She stopped abruptly and her face went an ashen shade. She
turned so she was no longer facing me and walked towards the
window.
"The daughter of Sir George Lavelle?"
"Yes I believe so." That was my grandfather's name.
"I haven't heard that name for a very long time, how do you
know of this person?"
I had to think quickly. I hadn't pre empted all these questions and
felt myself beginning to fluster.
"I think that she was a friend or distant cousin of my mother."
"But your mother, my dear is the sister of my late husband and
any relative of hers would be a relative of his too."
I had slipped up. She couldn't know who I really was or she
wouldn't have said that would she?
"Well maybe she wasn't a relative but just an acquaintance."
"And why do you wish to know about her?"
"I heard about her many years ago and that there was some
great mystery that surrounded her death. I just wondered if you
knew anything about her?"
"Her death?"
Lady Sinclair slumped into a chair. Her eyes began to water and
tears began to fall. Instinctively I rushed to her side.

"Lady Eleanor I didn't mean to distress you."

"I'm sorry Alice it's just that I haven't heard of her for such a long time, maybe eighteen or nineteen years. I didn't know that she was dead."

"Well possibly she isn't. All I have heard is hearsay; gossip, rumours and I could very well be mistaken. Did you know her well?"

I gave Lady Sinclair my handkerchief and she wiped away her tears.

"Isobel and I were the best of friends, almost sisters. She was an only child as was I. Our fathers worked together and our families were close."

I could feel my hands shaking but I sat myself down beside Lady Eleanor on the window seat.

"So what happened?"

"I married Edward and then, well I think Isobel was jealous of my happiness and she coveted whatever was mine. There was a big fight and Isobel was sent away."

"Sent where?" I was stifling my sobs.

"Away! Away from me, away from Edward and away from her……."

She looked up at me tears were now streaming.

"Away from her baby."

"Her baby" I repeated softly

"Yes. She had a child. The baby was supposed to be sent to the poorhouse but Isobel wouldn't have it. She said that she would rather die than let her baby be beaten and starved in a place like that. So she left the baby with her father and she was sent away instead."

I was choking back the tears. I could not contain myself. Lady Eleanor was equally distressed but didn't notice my reaction.

"But why couldn't she stay? Why couldn't they both stay?"

"Because of the disgrace and the shame. It wasn't possible."

"But Lady Eleanor she was your friend. Why did you not try to help her?"

There was a pause. Then the tone in her voice changed.

"Because she was a traitor! She betrayed me and I hated her. I wanted rid of her and I was the one that insisted that she go!"

I swallowed hard. Wiped the tears before they were seen.

"Why did you hate her so much?"

"Because she was a thief. She stole from me my most precious thing!"

"What?"

"Trust."

We sat in silence for several long minutes. Lady Eleanor couldn't bring herself to say what that trust was but I already knew the answer so didn't press her any further.

"Do you know what became of the baby?

"That ragged thing! No! Edward said that he would take care of it and the matter was never to be spoken of again. So it wasn't. I never dared to ask. Our families fell out and never again spoke. Over the years I pushed it further and further from my mind."

"I'm sorry that I have reminded you of this." I whispered.

"You didn't remind me. I have never forgotten. It lingered in there like a moth flitting around in a dark cupboard. I was never rid of it. As my children grew up I claimed my revenge on her. The love between mother and child is a very special thing Alice as you must know and I knew that Isobel would be denied that because of what she stole from me. It was her punishment. It was what she deserved!"

I was now seething at this woman's cruelty and venom. How dare she deny me my mother. How dare she be the one responsible for my sad and lonely motherless life. Though behind my eyes there was rage beyond rage, the rest of my face masked me and I continued.

"But what about the baby, surely the baby was punished too?"

"That baby did well! It was saved from being thrown in the poorhouse! Whatever its life, it did better than that."

I reflected for a moment and for once could see her point.

"But surely every child needs its mother?"

"Yes and that reminds me I must go and look in on Archie. Alice I don't want to continue this conversation. It is the past and of no concern to you. I trust that you will not mention this to Charlotte or Albert they are not to know of such things."

"Yes Lady Eleanor. I would not speak of this anyway. But if I can ask you just one more thing?"

"Yes alright but quickly." She replied quite flustered.

"Where was Isobel sent?"

"I have no idea. All I know is that Edward spoke to the priest at St Bernard's and the next thing she was gone."

Lady Eleanor closed the door behind her. I was left alone. I felt very cold. I looked over my shoulder. I felt like I was being watched but no one was in this space with me. Lady Eleanor hated my mother so much that she would deny her, her own child. I was brought up to believe my mother was dead yet every time I had asked to visit her grave I was fobbed off with all manner of tales about children not being allowed to go to a cemetery.

I sighed. It was a relief to at last know that my mother had loved me. That she had sacrificed her own life to give me mine. Lady Eleanor was right; I could have ended up in a workhouse, parentless and even more alone. At least I had been spared that. I was sure that Lady Eleanor didn't know who I was. She had shown no indication at all in fact she had referred to my mother as Edwards's sister. Maybe she didn't know that Isobel's child had been a girl, had no clue to suspect it could be me.

I was desperate to tell Tom. I was angry with Lady Eleanor and needed to talk to someone about it. At dinner that night I chatted away with Charlotte about her latest fancy and tried desperately hard to stop my mind from wondering back to that stumbling block that kept presenting itself.

In the dark shadows of night I was making plans in my mind. I would have to go to St Bernard's and see the priest that was the next logical step in the plan. Where would that lead? Would that take me to my mother? Or another slammed door?

I couldn't sleep. I tried but my buzzing mind prevented me. At six am by the time the delivery men were rolling their carts in the street I was up and dressed. I uncrumpled the little note that Tom had slipped in my pocket and decided that I could not wait any longer to tell him my news. I crept down the stairs and as I closed the front door behind me saw Sarah the maid's eyes staring at me between the banisters.

"Damn" I muttered to myself. That would probably fuel the gossip below stairs.

I knew the place where Tom was staying. I walked there at a fast pace which gradually turned into a slow run. Faces on the streets were increasing as the hour waxed. I turned and looked up and the lodging house where Tom was staying.

I knocked on the door. A stern faced rounded woman came to the door. She looked me up and down.

"Yes?"

"I've come to see Mr Tom Sullivan"

"And who shall I say is calling"

"Miss Alice Sullivan his sister."

"Hmm, I don't agree with young ladies seeing gentlemen after hours but I suppose it is daylight and you are his sister aren't you? So all right then. He's in room nineteen. Up the stairs and along the corridor"

"Thank you so much" I lifted my skirts and practically sprinted up the stairs.

I knocked gently on his door. I heard a grunt from within. I tried the handle the door was unlocked. I tiptoed in. Tom sat up in his bed.

"How did you get in here?"

"And good morning to you too."

"Sorry Alice good morning"

"I told the landlady that I was your sister and she let me in without batting an eyelid"

"Clever girl" He laughed

"I've so much to tell you. I couldn't wait couldn't sleep. We have to go to the church and see the priest!"

"Alice slow down." Tom was getting out of bed and putting on his breeches.

"All right, start at the beginning."

I relayed the events of the previous day at such a speed that I was almost out of breath by the time I was finished.

Tom put his arms around me and sat me on the edge of his bed.

"Alice my love. I don't want to dampen your excitement but you must prepare yourself for answers that you may not want to hear. Even if we go to the priest he may not know anything.

"Yes but I don't want to think of that. My mother gave me away so that I would have a life. Where is she? What became of her? I must find her! I have money now that will solve all the problems of years ago. I want to give her back her life."

"If she is still alive," Tom added.

"Don't say that! I've come so far she can't be dead! God wouldn't be so cruel."

Tom held me. I didn't want to think negative thoughts. I wouldn't listen to Tom. Now I was angry with him and pulled away from his embrace.

"Fine I shall go to the church on my own. If you don't want to come I shall see this through alone. I have always done everything alone my whole life so this will be nothing new." I got up and grabbed my bag.

"Alice sit down!" Tom exclaimed.

He had never raised his voice to me and in shock I sat down obediently.

"I never said that she was dead I just said that you must be prepared in case she is. You have had so many disappointments and I want you to be strong in case this is one more. I don't want it to be. I want you to find your mother, if I did not I wouldn't have tried so hard to get to you with this information. We will find her together and whether the news is good or bad I shall be there for you. Do you understand?"

I nodded sheepishly. In a way I was quite pleased at Tom's reaction. I admired strong people that were unafraid to speak their minds.

A loud banging on the door interrupted him.

"Keep your voices down in there! You're waking up the whole street!"

"Sorry" Tom called back.

"Thank you Tom. I love you."

His face turned from a scowl to a huge broad grin.

"You silly little girl. I didn't mean to shout but sometimes you are on this high horse of yours and you refuse to see anything from any other angle."

"I know," I admitted.

Tom took my hand.

"Come on, I think we need to go to early morning mass.

Chapter 39

We walked down the dusty London streets. Smog was rising and when you breathed heavily you could feel the weight of the air as it settled on your chest. In the distance peering above the clouds and smoke we could just make out a huge steeple ahead of us.

"You ready for this?"
"I'm not going back now." I replied
We ascended the steps of the old church. The walls were grey and pigeons cooed in every nook and crevice. Tom opened the heavy iron door. I had not really been in many churches. As a child Mrs Knight had taken me a couple of times to the village church at Christmas. It had not meant anything to me. I had not been brought up to feel any great religious conviction.
We walked into the church. The coolness of the stone floors and walls seemed to enclose me. I pulled my shawl around my shoulders and wrapped it over my neck. The altar at the far end reminded me of sacrifices and death filling me with a sense of fear and foreboding. Tom took off his cap and held it in his hand. I watched him. He obviously had great respect for this establishment and showed a reverence towards his surroundings. It was deadly quiet in the church. The tombs that lined the side walls reverberated to the sounds of our heels as they hit the paved floor. It felt eerie and uncomfortable.
"Don't worry!" Tom felt my apprehension.
"It feels like it's full of ghosts in here."
"Hello!" A voice came from behind us.
Instinctively I jumped and shrieked.
"Oh sorry to frighten you child" Came a gentle Irish lilting voice.

"I'm the priest; I'm father O' Malley" He reached out and shook our hands.

"Have you come here to pray?"

Tom squeezed my hand tightly. I looked at the ageing priest before me He was easily in his sixties with greying hair around a very bald patch. He was short and quite stout. His eyes were deeply set and he had a round clean shaven face with smiling eyes.

"No we haven't come here to pray." Tom replied.

The jovial face dropped and Tom realised that he had been a little abrupt.

"No sorry father we have come here to talk to you."

"We have something very important to ask you."

His expression changed again and he produced a very coy grin

"Oh I see!" He exclaimed

"Well we will have to see what I can do for you then wont I? He said giving Tom a wink.

Tom and I darted blank looks at each other.

"Follow me children come to the vestry where I keep my diary and let me see what I can do for you."

We followed him obediently not daring to contradict him. We entered the vestry, which smelt of stale musky clothes and moth balls.

"So what date did you have in mind children?"

"But father I'm not sure that you understand we need to speak to you as soon as possible about something very important."

"Very soon, very important?" He echoed.

"Well I suppose we had better find a date very soon then shall we? Will tomorrow do at eleven in the morning?"

"Yes that will be fine we'll be back then."

We practically ran out of the church.

"What was that all about?" I said breathlessly.

"Just a silly old man, don't worry about it Alice we'll get all of this resolved tomorrow when we come back.

"Oh I do hope so." I sighed.

"Come on let's try and find some breakfast I'm starving and we can plan what we are going to talk to him about tomorrow." Tom suggested.

We sat over our tea and oat biscuits. I felt irritated and unable to settle.

"Alice please calm yourself, there's not much that we can do until our appointment with the priest tomorrow."

"I know but why didn't we just ask him and find out what we need to know?"

"Patience Alice!"

"Yes but why do we have to make an appointment? What's the silly man doing all day that he can't give us the time now?"

"Alice you can wait another day. You've waited your whole life, what's another few hours? In any case I'm sure the priest is very busy and it's disrespectful to call him silly."

"Sorry Tom. It's just that I don't understand about churches and all this religion. It's never been a part of my life."

Tom looked down and almost shamefully asked.

"Did you never go to Sunday school? Did you never learn all the miracles and wonderful things done by our Lord?

I threw back my head and laughed.

"It's just stories! Yes I read some of them but in answer to your question, no I never really went to church except a couple of times for midnight mass and I was so tired and bored that I always fell asleep!"

"That's a shame"

"No it was a really good sleep." I joked.

"But no one bothered to take me after that. Christmas didn't really mean anything to me. It was a plate of cold meats and

258

mince pies left out for me whilst the staff either went home to their families or celebrated in the parlour whilst I was sent to my room. It was just another day. No miracles. No presents and no parents!"

I thought that Tom could understand that all my life I had not had the experiences that most children have and that was because of either the selfishness or indifference of the people around me. I now desperately wanted to make something turn out right and if that meant that I had an opportunity to find my mother and bring her home than I would stop at no less to make sure that happened.

"My mother used to stuff our socks with apples, sweet meats and pies. We used to love waking on Christmas morning, open our curtains and see the world as a white sheet. We may not have had the lavish gifts of the rich folk but we would sit around our fireside and sing carols and imagine that the footprints out in the snow were from Jesus own feet as he came to listen to us singing praise to him on the day of his birth."

I looked at Tom incredulously.

"Jesus probably never saw snow!"

"Don't be silly Alice, Christmas isn't Christmas without snow!"

"Jesus was from Bethlehem that is in Palestine. It's hot there, they don't have snow. It's like Africa they don't have snow there either!"

"So Jesus never had a white Christmas?"

"No!"

Sometimes Tom's lack of knowledge irritated me intensely. It was only books that separated his mind from my own. The thing that I did like though was his thirst for information. I was sure that he would be asking more questions soon as that was his nature to do so. This was in sharp contrast to my half sister Charlotte that had books and information at her fingertips but no

259

desire at all to stretch her mind with them. When I had tried to have rational conversations with her about important matters she had just yawned and was more preoccupied with curling her hair and tightening her bodice so that she could look even more radiant for the next available suitor. All that seemed such a waste of time to me. She looked the same with or without all the effort!

"So how do you know what the weather is like in Africa?"

"Books and newspapers." I replied.

"I used to follow the war in Sudan with a lot of interest........."

"Yes" Tom nodded remembering that there was a time that I worried about my father whom I believed to be posted in Sudan. We sat silently both thinking of the same lies that had been fed to me for so long.

"I think I should go."

Tom reached over and took my hand.

"I need to be doing something. I cannot just sit still. I will come for you tomorrow morning and we will go back to see the priest. There is nothing that can be done now any way."

Tom nodded silently. I got up but gestured to him to remain.

"Tomorrow quarter to eleven outside the church?

"Yes" and I left.

When I got home Sarah the maid gave me a look as if to say that she knew that I had sneaked off at the crack of dawn. I didn't care but when she approached me with a smug look on her face, I wondered what she was about to say.

"Forgotten something have we miss?"

"Sorry?"

"Were we in such a hurry to go out that we forgot that we should be somewhere else?"

Sarah's pertinence was so infuriating that I almost wanted to slap her.

"What? What is it?"

"Did we forget that Mr Foster would be coming around with some papers for you today?"
I had clean forgotten. Naturally my mind had been filled with more pressing issues.
"Thank you Sarah where is he?"
"In the drawing room of course and he's been waiting almost an hour."
I gave Sarah a look of indignation. What was the point of chastising her? I knew that servants usually knew of things that they should not and so it seemed more sensible for the time being to say nothing. I rushed to the drawing room and threw open the door.
"Mr Foster I am so sorry I am late."
He bowed his head.
"I was beginning to worry; no one knew where you had gone."
"I went to church." I replied without being unnerved.
"Oh" Mr Foster looked surprised.
"I'm sorry I didn't realise you were so religious."
"Does my piety amaze you?" I said cynically.
"No, no of course not Alice. I have always thought of you as being most devout."
There was no emotion in his face to tell whether he was being sarcastic or sincere. I thought it best to move swiftly onto another conversation.
"So why are you here today Mr Foster?"
"Had you forgotten Alice?"
I had. So I said nothing and just smiled.
"Tomorrow?
I smiled dumbly.
"Your eighteenth birthday when you come of age and inherit £400,000?"
"Oh that!" I exclaimed

"Yes that!" He repeated.

I felt embarrassed. He was right it was a pretty big thing to forget.

"If we get everything signed off today, then it will all automatically transfer to your name at midnight tonight and tomorrow I'm sure you will be celebrating in style."

"No hardly. The Sinclair's are unaware of my impending financial situation. I shall not be sharing this information with them for reasons that you and I only know. You do understand that do you not Mr Foster?"

James Foster seemed a little insulted by my condescending tone.

"Yes of course Miss Alice. However if I may be so bold I do think that it would be a shame not to celebrate such a momentous occasion. If you are not intending to celebrate then at least allow me to escort you to the theatre or out for dinner."

James Foster was a very eligible and well educated young man. However I wondered how much influence my imminent wealth had over his decision to escort me anywhere. I wasn't interested anyway and didn't trust anyone or their motives, except Tom of course. I never had any reason to doubt him. Even when I had told him that I had money he hadn't questioned or bombarded me with suggestions as to what the funds may be.

Tom had integrity about him uncommon in men of means. He had a love of nature and beings that surrounded him. He wasn't driven by greed, which unfortunately seemed to be the fault of most gentry.

I turned to James who was standing waiting earnestly for an answer. I didn't want to disappoint him but knew that I must.

"Dear James thank you so much for your kindness but I have an awful lot of things preoccupying my mind at the moment and feel that this is not the right time for me to be escorted anywhere."

James frowned.

"I mean it is terribly nice of you to want to take me out on my birthday but I really don't think that I should go."

Why was it so hard to reject someone? Why was he looking so sheepish? Why were those eyes so doleful?

"Well I insist," He began defiantly." Where else would you go on your coming of age? You have no other plans and it would be an awful shame to let this day just pass without ceremony. At least let me take you for a little light supper, perhaps tomorrow at eight?"

I struggled to smile but felt duty bound to do so.

"Wonderful!" His face creased into the widest grin." I shall collect you at eight."

James scooped up the signed papers and put them into his briefcase. He kissed my hand. Smiled with his eyes and was gone leaving me standing in the drawing room wondering why I hadn't been able to get myself out of this predicament.

Before I could think another thought Charlotte came bursting into the room.

"Alice! Sarah has just reminded me that it's your birthday tomorrow! How exciting! What shall we do?"

How did Sarah know it was my birthday unless she had overheard my conversation with James? If she knew that then what else had she heard? That girl was becoming a problem. Between the crack of the door to the hall I could see her polishing the banisters, she made me feel uneasy and exposed. I would have to do something about her.

"Alice this is so exciting!" Charlotte was enthusing.

My mind was certainly being cast in many distracting directions. I didn't know what to focus on first but Charlotte seemed to be the foremost contender and I knew that I would have to entertain her ideas otherwise she would never leave.

"Yes Charlotte, I'm going to be eighteen tomorrow what do you think we should do?"

Chapter 40

My first thought when I opened my eyes was that today August 31st 1892 I was eighteen and a wealthy heiress.

I blinked in the daylight. Today I was rich. Very rich. It felt quite satisfying, like discovering that you were a princess or someone grander than your wildest dreams. I smiled to myself like a little girl that had just been given her first puppy or kitten.

I wouldn't tell anyone about my wealth but I was resolved to the fact that I would take immense care of it and make sure that I had enough to live on for the rest of my life.

I thought about my mother. She had been the same age as me and in the same position of wealth although her status was a little more esteemed than mine. She had given it all up for me, for her baby, her child that she would never know. I didn't quite understand how anyone could do anything so altruistic, but she had, and she had done it for me and me alone. How easy it could have been just to discard me and still have her life.

I wondered whether she had any regrets, whether somewhere in the world she was waking up knowing that it was the day that eighteen years ago she had given birth to her daughter. I hoped that she was still alive and that our meeting with the priest would throw some light on her whereabouts.

There was a tap on the door and then laughter and squeals as the Sinclair children bounded in and leapt on my bed. Archie had his head on my lap and the girls were hugging me and presenting me with small wrapped gifts.

"Oh thank you so much everybody, this is wonderful!" I said overwhelmed by their excitement.

For nearly an hour they stayed jumping rolling laughing and singing. I had never experienced a birthday morning quite like this. It was a vast contrast to the birthdays I had in the past, waiting alone for the postman to bring a message from my father, the one which never came. This was fun and I was beginning to enjoy the novelty and attention.

"Is there any word or birthday wishes from your family?" Enquired Emily

"No" I shook my head." Not yet."

It seemed a good opportunity to announce my departure.

"But I shall of course be seeing them all soon. They miss me terribly and I must return in the very near future."

Archie's little face screwed into a contortion.

"But Alice you mustn't go! Not again! You will come back though, you won't stay away forever?"

I loved Archie. He was my favourite by far of all the children and the one that I knew I would miss so terribly when I did leave.

"I'm sorry Archie but I need to be with my family too. You wouldn't like to be away from your family would you?"

He looked around the room and then cheekily responded.

"Yes!"

Jane pushed him.

"Yes and we want you to go too!"

"No we don't!" Said Emily pulling her brother up.

"Remember the trouble we got into last time Jane? We've all got to be kind to each other remember?"

"Cake!" Piped Archie.

"Can we have cake for breakfast?"

"I don't see why not." I replied

"Yes if we are celebrating then that would be perfectly exquisite thing to have for breakfast lets go down to the kitchen and see if cook has any of that delicious chocolate cake left over."

Archie's eyes lit up. That was his favourite. The children didn't need to be asked twice and jumped off my bed and ran down to the kitchens.

Alone in my room I was left to choose what to wear. It was my birthday and I wanted to wear something special. There was one dress that I loved which was the first dress that the dressmaker had made for me this year after I had recovered from my illness. It was pale blue with an embroidered bodice and tiny lace ribbons along the sleeves. It was very delicate and so I had not worn it often for fear of spoiling it.

I looked at myself in the mirror as I brushed my long fair hair. I was changing and had done immensely in the last year from the child that I had been previously. So much had happened to me. I could not even recall the number of things, there were so many. I had been on the edge of life and death myself a few times but in the end I had survived and become stronger and more determined not to be crushed by those that wanted me pushed aside. I thought of my father with disdain, how he would have hated me by now.

I glanced at the clock in the hall as I went down the stairs. It was nearly nine. I would have to be away by ten fifteen if I wanted to get to the church to meet Tom. I went in to breakfast. Cook had laid a big runny chocolate cake in the centre of the table Lady Eleanor looked at it disapprovingly.

"I know that it's your birthday Alice but really we shouldn't be eating chocolate cake at this hour. I shall tell cook to take it away and save it for tea time."

"Oh no mama" Emily and Archie wailed together.

"Please mama." Archie began.

"Its Alice's last birthday with us she has to go home to her family because they miss her so and so she wont ever be able to have chocolate cake for breakfast ever, ever again so we absolutely must have it mama!"

"Mmm" Lady Sinclair weighed up the situation.

"Well I suppose if everyone just has the smallest piece."

"Thank you!" Came the communal reply.

"So Alice is Archie correct are you leaving us again?"

"Yes I believe it is time to go."

Lady Sinclair was staring at me and I felt most uncomfortable.

"Last time when you left Alice you didn't tell anyone that you were leaving you just went off with father and didn't say a word." Jane interjected.

I smiled sweetly.

"I apologise for that last retreat. I shall make my farewells properly this time."

Lady Sinclair's eyes were still fixated on me. The memory of that last departure was uneasy. I was sure that Lady Sinclair had seen me bundled into the carriage on that morning bleeding and bruised. Had it been Lady Sinclair? Or maybe one of the servants, Sarah perhaps?

"Yes that was the last time that we saw your father that was Edwards last day in this house." Lady Sinclair directed that fact to her children as if they dared not to forget it.

The look that was now coming from her direction was one of hatred. I felt loathed and blamed. Lady Sinclair raised a handkerchief to her eyes and dabbed away her tears. I wanted to leave right now and escape this situation.

The clock struck ten in the hall. I wanted to go right now. I needed Tom desperately I wanted to be with him, and more importantly I needed to find the information that I was desperate to know.

"May I have a word?" Albert was by my side.

268

I looked up at my brother. He was looking quite pale and thin. I hadn't really had much conversation with him over the last few weeks. Not since the picnic when he had told me all about William's sister that he was head over heels in love with.

"Yes of course but it will have to be quick." I was wary of the minutes ticking by.

"Let's go to the garden it's so beautiful at this time of year." We went outside down the little paved steps that led from the drawing room at the back of the house. The fruit trees were heavy with small budding fruit and the sweet smells from the rose garden bathed the morning air.

"I would like to wish you a very happy birthday Alice."

"Why thank you Albert. It means so much to me to have all my family around me. I am so grateful to all of you for your kindness."

"Alice you know that you will always be very special to us and I am perturbed by the fact that you are going away and that we may never see you again."

"Albert, I am not leaving the planet of course we will see each other again. Now I really must go otherwise I will be late for something."

"But Alice I really would like to discuss something further with you."

"Yes Albert?"

"Well I am at a loss as to where to start."

"Perhaps we should have this conversation later then......" Albert grabbed my sleeve.

"No I really must speak with you now it is something that's tearing me apart."

"Oh Albert I am so sorry. But what do you want me to do?"

"I just want you to help me understand what I am to do with Clara, she doesn't seem to be returning my affections towards her and I am being left to feel most forlorn."

"Well that's a shame Albert and I really do sympathise but this will have to wait till later when I have thoroughly thought through what is the very best advice to give to you that will make her come running to be with you."

"Do you think that you could do that for me?"

"Yes Albert it will be no problem but I really must go now." I could hear the clock inside chime the half-hour and so I was already late.

"But Alice I will die of a broken heart if I don't win her affections."

"Albert you won't! Any way if she doesn't feel the same then there will be someone else!"

"Oh Alice how can you say that?"

"Albert I have to go."

"I thought you cared."

"I do, but I have to go."

"Oh all right be like that!"

"Thank you, goodbye."

I grabbed my skirt and turned to run from the garden and into the street.

"Miss Alice."

I stopped in my tracks.

"Yes?"

Sarah the maid looked at me in that strange mischievous way that I just could not fathom.

"Well miss…"

I could feel my irritation rising through my toes and up through my body.

"Well I just wanted to wish you a happy birthday miss."

I observed her curiously. What was she up to or was she just trying to be nice?"

"Thank you Sarah."

Now I was really going.

"Are you still here Alice? I thought you were in such a hurry?"

"I am Albert! Goodbye!"

Before anyone could say anything I was gone. I went across the grass over the rockery and down by the side of the house till it came out in the road and then I was away as fast as I could tearing down the street like a hare.

I arrived at the church. The street was busy with people moving in all directions. I couldn't see Tom. I looked in the cemetery beside the church. Nothing. I ran around the whole building but he was nowhere. I didn't want to go in alone.

What was I to do? I was annoyed that I was so late. Angry that I had not shaken off my obstacles sooner.

"Oh there you are!" I turned to see Tom's anxious face.

"I went down the street to try to find you I was getting worried, thought that you might not turn up."

"I'm here now. I'm sorry it wasn't so easy to get away."

Tom pulled out a posy from behind his back.

"Happy Birthday darling"

I jumped into Tom's arms, oblivious to the passers by.

"Thank you so much what beautiful flowers."

"For a beautiful girl or should I say young woman, I mean you are eighteen now."

I smiled bashfully. Yes I was all grown up and ready to face the world.

Tom took my hand and led me towards the heavy iron doors of the church.

"Come on, let's get this out of the way and then we'll go out and celebrate the rest of the day together."

I nodded. I had been dreading this moment but now anticipated it with fervour. Tom pulled the latch and we walked in, not quite knowing how this moment was going to change my life.

Chapter 41

The priest was waiting for us when we entered the church. He greeted us with a broad smile and made me feel less on edge than I had been the day before, when the church had felt very cold and unwelcoming. It was later in the day than when we had been there the day previously and the sun now flooded in through the stained glass windows, bathing the pews and aisles in an orange glow. Even the windows themselves seemed alive in colour and images. I stared at one of them. It was of a ladder stretching up into the clouds, cherubs stood on every rung. It conveyed warmth and I suddenly wasn't afraid of being here. It felt inviting and the priest that was beckoning us to follow him seemed unintimidating.

We walked through to the back of the church and along to the priests small living quarters that adjoined the church. We then went through a small dimly lit passage. We took a seat in his small parlour. There was an awkward silence for a few seconds then he began.

"So my children, what is it that you are so desperate to speak to an old priest about?"

Tom looked over to me. This however was my problem and it was down to me to speak and tell my story.

"Father how long have you been with this parish?

The old man laughed his face crinkling like a paper bag.

"Oh child I have been here so long that I think there were still dinosaurs roaming the streets."

I smiled. Wonderful I thought. Then this is the right man and he should know something about my mother and her whereabouts.

"Could you remember something that happened about eighteen years back?"

He paused and shrugged his shoulders.

"That's a long time ago. My memory isn't what it used to be. Maybe I will, maybe I won't you'll have to try me, so what is it that's troubling you?

"Well I don't really know where to start. It concerns a lady called Isobel Lavelle, she was having a baby, she was unmarried. She may have come to see you or you may have seen someone called Edward Sinclair who would have come on her behalf." His forehead frowned and he put his hand to his head and contemplated for several moments.

"Those names ring bells but I will have to check in the record books. Why do you need to know about this person?" I almost felt ashamed. I felt small and embarrassed to declare my illegitimacy.

"I believe that Isobel Lavelle was my mother."

"Oh" he said

"I understand, now I see. This will help me locate her whereabouts, unwed girls were always sent to several places. It shouldn't be too difficult to find which she was sent to."

"Thank you"

"But you must consider the fact that this was a very long time ago and Isobel would have been sent away for her own good to start a new life. She won't want someone turning up years later making her relive old memories that are better left alone and forgotten. I don't think I should be giving you this information." Tom who had been sitting quietly all along now spoke up.

"We understand your concerns but Alice has had a very troubled life not knowing whether her mother was alive or dead and never knowing the truth of anything. She has struggled on a daily basis to find answers and you father, are her last hope. We are depending on you to help us and be honest with us when everyone else has just lied. You will be honest with us father wont you?"

I wanted to pat Tom on the back. He was amazing. The priest was now in a difficult position to reject helping us.

"Well all right, yes I suppose that you are right young man, the Lord says thou shalt not lie and I suppose this young lady has had her fair share of untruths."

I smiled a relieved smile. We got up and walked back to the vestry beside the main church. There on the shelves at the back were volumes of large record books. The priest pulled out a stool and climbed up to the top shelf. He began bringing down books thick with dust from yesteryears. We all coughed as the mist of grey dust choked the air. Tom then helped him down.

"Should be here, we should find something amongst all this lot. We'll have your answers here somewhere" he repeated.

He brushed off the dust and began opening the heavy leather bound pages. He tutted, shook his head and reached from one book to another.

"Ah" He announced at last.

"April 1874, there seems to be something here"

I thought that that would probably be right as it was just before I had been born.

"What have you found?"

"Well…" He began slowly still perusing the words on the page.

"It appears that an Edward Sinclair came to see us to arrange for his ward to be ordained into the church. Yes this young woman that he brought was sent to Kinsale in County Cork to work at St Theresa's convent there.

"Is that where she is now?" I asked, the words breathlessly escaping from my dry dusty throat.

He shook his head.

"I don't know, this was all a long time ago, who knows what may have happened to her over all these years."

I knew that he was right but I yearned for that glimmer of hope that she would be waiting somewhere for me.

"You'll have to write to St Theresa's and find out if they have any more news for you"

We nodded our appreciation. Shook his hand and left the heavy iron door thudding behind us.

"So when will you write?" Tom asked.

I gave him one of my looks and laughed.

"Seriously Tom! I thought you knew me better than that!

"Sorry?"

"Do you really think that I'm going to write and wait several weeks or even months for a letter, I think not? I will find out about carriages to the docks and then boats over to Ireland. I'm going to find my mother."

"But Alice that is a very difficult journey. It will be fraught with many hazards."

"So I take it that you're not coming?"

"No of course I'm coming but this may lead us nowhere, she may not even be there anymore!"

"So what do I have to lose? Tom you can be most infuriating sometimes. You know this is the most important thing in my life. I hate it when you try so to discourage me!"

I walked several paces ahead of Tom.

"Alice wait I'm sorry. I'm just trying to be realistic, you've had so many disappointments you must be prepared."

I snarled, said nothing and kept walking.

"I'm going to the tram station; I'm going to find out about how to get to Cork!"

"Just wait."

"No!"

"Don't you want me to come with you?"

"No!"

Tom looked amazed and sad all at once.

"But it's your birthday Alice; please could we just enjoy a lovely day together?"

I wasn't feeling like doing anything lovely. I was feeling very tense and just wanted to do what I was feeling compelled to do. I was a bubbling pot and now was ready to explode. Tom was irritating me and he knew it. He politely tipped his hat and stepped back. He then came forward kissed my hand and bade me farewell. I watched him as he retreated down the street alone and for a split second felt like running after him, but I didn't.

I marched on defiantly like some warrior off on a mission. I went to the information office and found out that I would need a ticket from Holyhead that would take me across to Cork. The next stage coach was tomorrow evening and defiantly I booked my place on it. I didn't care if Tom came or not. He could always get a ticket and ride above the carriage. I had given him enough allowance to cover all his living expenses and lodging costs so he would be well capable of following if he wished.

I walked through the park and sat myself down on a bench. I breathed deeply inhaling the last sweet airs of summertime. Nobody was able to understand this need inside of me. Nobody with a mother could feel the burning loss of one without. Tom didn't understand. I knew there was someone out there of whom I was a part. Someone who shared my expressions, my features, my personality. She had been stolen from me and now I could do no less than fight to get her back.

Chapter 42

It was early afternoon on my birthday when I arrived back at the Sinclair's house. Sarah was just leaving and had her bonnet ribbons flowing open over her shoulders. She seemed a little startled to see me as she hurried off. I ascended up the stone steps trying to shake off that gnawing feeling that always bothered me whenever I saw her.

Nobody was around and I went to the kitchens to see what was left over from lunch. I wasn't exactly hungry but I did feel so nervous and anxious that I might possible faint if I didn't eat anything. I grabbed a couple of biscuits then went back to my room to pack.

I took all my clothes from the cupboards and lay them on my bed. I thought for a moment as I looked at my small bag and wondered how on earth they would all fit in there. I realised that I would have to travel light. There was no way that I could trundle this heavy bag all the way to Ireland single handed. Anyway there was no need for all these clothes. What I was wearing plus two other travelling dresses would be ample enough as well as manageable.

I pulled the ticket that I had just bought from my pocket and slumped into a chair.

"Is this going to bring me to you?" I whispered out loud.

My mind was bombarded with a multitude of things. I had imagined that I would find my mother waiting for me in a convent and I would bring her back to Somerset .I would employ builders to completely renovate the place and gardeners would work flat out on the gardens to restore it to the home that she had once known. We would then all live happily ever after. Sitting here I wondered how much of my fairy tale would actually come true? Perhaps she liked her life in Ireland and didn't want to leave? Maybe she had left the convent and I wouldn't be able to find her. Maybe she did want to forget me and her troubled past? My cheek felt hot with tears. Maybe Tom was right and I should prepare myself for disaster. Even the priest had warned me to leave well alone. Tears were falling on my ticket and smudging the ink. I quickly pulled out my handkerchief and dabbed away the wetness.

What was I to do? Why was I now feeling so scared and apprehensive? Is this what girls were supposed to feel on their eighteenth birthdays? I didn't think so! Why was my life so fraught with torment? It wasn't fair I just wanted what everyone else had and I didn't see why I had to struggle so to get it!

I lay on my bed and let my mind meander down roads my conscious mind would never wander. I tossed and turned fighting enemies I never knew existed until I was awoken by a sharp nudge in my ribs.

"Alice! Chocolate cake!"

"What?" I rubbed my eyes and looked at Archie standing beside my bed.

"You know, mama told cook to put it away till tea time and now its tea time so come on it wouldn't be right to eat it without you."

"No its fine Archie please go ahead, I'm just feeling a little tired."

"Nonsense!" His little arm clamped around mine and he began pulling with all his strength, which actually surprised me as I began to slide off the bed.

"All right fine I'll come but only because its you!"

We went down to the dining room. There displayed in the middle of the table was the chocolate cake minus a few pieces that had been eaten at breakfast time.

"Well where is everyone Archie?"

"They're not coming!"

"I thought you said this was a party?"

"It is a private party."

"Oh"

Archie shuffled his feet a little eyes fixed on the floor.

"I didn't want everyone else. You are going away and I wanted it to be just me and you."

I lifted Archie's chin and tried to look into his eyes but he turned away and refused to return my gaze. I saw a tear welling in his eye and instinctively pulled him close to me and hugged him.

"Please don't go away Alice."

"But I have to."

"Why? What's so important that you have to go?"

"Oh Archie I wish I could tell you but it's very complicated." There was a silence.

"I'll write to you if you like?" I suggested.

His face lit up.

"I've never received a letter. Would you really?"

"Yes absolutely. Now come on cheer up and let's have some cake."

We sat down and I pulled two plates towards me and began cutting.

"Can we play chase in the garden next?"

"I think I'm a little old for that now Archie."

"Please" he said pulling out his bottom lip and adopting a glum expression.

"Yes why not." I replied kindly.

For the next two hours Archie and I ran and fell, giggled and squealed and climbed trees. It took my mind off my troubles and cleared my head better than any therapy could.

"Miss Alice" The cook was calling me as I was up the tree trying to reach a bird's nest for Archie.

I looked down and to my horror there was James Foster. I was aware of my bedraggled hair and messed up clothes.

"Good day Alice" He called up.

"I didn't expect to find you up a tree!" He chuckled." Did you forget that I was taking you out for supper to celebrate your birthday?"

A wave of recollection came over me now, yes I had completely forgotten. It's not even that it had slipped to the back of my mind, it had gone completely. I wasn't sure if I wanted to go, but I could hardly feign illness when I was here bursting with energy and half way up a tree!

In my mind I was thinking that really I should go and find Tom and apologise for the way I had treated him this morning. I had been unfairly brutal to him and as usual he had just taken it from me without argument.

"Yes I am coming."

He leaned over his hand to help me as I stepped down a branch then before I knew it I had leaned back into his arms and he was carrying me out of the tree.

His arms were strong. His eyes warm and intense. I blushed profusely ashamed to acknowledge that I actually liked this feeling and being in his arms.

He put me down on the grass.

"So shall I wait here for you?"

"Yes, I mean no! Won't you wait in the house in the drawing room?"

I scurried up the stairs and to my room where I quickly changed brushed my hair and was downstairs within five minutes.

"Oh my gosh!" Exclaimed Mr Foster.

"Is something wrong?" I enquired.

"I've never known a young lady to transform quite so quickly from a caterpillar to a butterfly."

"Well how long should it take?"

"I don't know but perhaps you could explain that answer to all the young ladies that seem to take hours and hours to do what you've done in moments!"

I smiled bashfully. I also didn't know why it took ages for some girls to get ready. I knew that Charlotte fell into that category. She would spend all day teasing her hair and trying on every outfit in her wardrobe at least ten times till she was happy with her appearance.

Mr Foster offered his arm and we strolled out into the evening. He hailed a cab and we clip clopped all the way to the city where we stopped outside a little establishment that seemed to be filled with very expensive looking ladies and gentlemen. Tiny lanterns adorned the windows and made the light dance as it reflected on the glass.

"This looks very exclusive!" I commented.

"This is the new Ritz! James retorted.

He helped me from the carriage and together we walked into the restaurant.

Elegant ladies in mink stoles sat at tables with gentlemen in the finest attire. They sipped wines and champagne from perfect crystal glasses and the cutlery all shone in real silver.

"This place must be terribly expensive I whispered in James ear."

"Yes and don't worry yourself because I'm paying."

"Thank you but I mean that it isn't necessary for you to spend quite so much money on me."

James laughed.

"But you are worth it! Anyway I earn fortunes working as a solicitor and never spend my money so it's a pleasure to be able to on someone as charming as you."

The waiter showed us to our table and I felt very guilty about wasting poor James money. We were only here because James thought there was some prospect of courting me. I felt most uncomfortable with the thought of deceiving him. I was leaving tomorrow and probably wouldn't ever see James again, so at least I wouldn't be prolonging the lie. By the next time he would ask of me I would probably be well on my way to Ireland and too far away to worry about the reaction that had been caused by my hasty departure.

Despite my self-protestations the evening was remarkably wonderful. After the first glass of champagne I actually allowed myself to relax enough so that I could enjoy myself and with every subsequent sip of wine I found James even more alluring, funny and witty.

"So would you like to come to the theatre with me at the weekend?"

What do I say? Sorry but I'm going to Ireland and will never see you again? James was so perfectly adorable, well educated and in everyone else's mind a perfect match for someone like me and he had the advantage of knowing about my dubious parentage, which didn't bother him. If Tom hadn't been in the frame then I would probably have been very interested even though I wasn't sure how much I trusted James motives. However Tom *was* in the frame and very much so. He was the man that I loved and that I wanted to spend the rest of my life with. In fact the more I sat here with James the guiltier I felt that I had been so mean to Tom and not even bought him a ticket to accompany me.

The restaurant began to empty and the waiter brought my coat. James paid and we went to our carriage that had been waiting for us. On the way back I felt it was only right to say something.

"James, I will have to go away for a while on family business. That is why I will not be able to accept your theatre invitation at the weekend."

"Oh but how will I survive without your wonderful company and endearing smile?"

"James stop flattering me. You will survive just fine."

"When will you return?"

"I don't know."

"You will return wont you?"

I looked at him trying to be direct but compassionate too. He really was growing on me and I considered that I may have been a little hasty to judge him previously.

"James I will contact you on my return."

"Is there something that you would like me to do for you? Is there anything of this family business that you need help with or any assistance?"

I shook my head as the horse stopped outside my house.

"Thank you for a lovely evening James. I'm sorry that this will be the end of things between us but you have been perfectly charming and I have really appreciated your discretion with so many more personal things."

James nodded acknowledgement.

"You make this sound so final. I hope it won't be. You will come back wont you?"

He was so emphatic that I felt almost compelled to say yes, but I couldn't, so I just shrugged my shoulders like some little schoolgirl.

James stayed in the carriage, I watched it turn the corner as I stood on the steps of the Sinclair house.

When it was out of sight. I began to run. I ran so fast that my shoes began to rub and I could feel them blistering. I knew that it wasn't safe to be out on the streets alone at this time of night but I didn't care, I just wanted to get to Tom to apologise for my arrogant and unacceptable behaviour and to tell him that I loved him. Maybe he had forgotten how I felt. It had been a while since I had said those words and now I felt so sorry and so drawn to him. It was very, late he was sure to be in his little lodging house. Breathlessly I stopped outside. I could see the little window of his room and the orange glow of a candle flickered in the night. Good, I thought he would still be awake and I could tell him all about our plans for tomorrow when we set off for Holyhead.

I opened the latch of the back door. Luckily it was still open. I began to creep up the stairs shifting the weight carefully from one foot to the other so as not to make any noise.

"Evening miss and where do you think you're going?"

I had been caught! The rotund landlady was standing behind me wearing a long nightshirt, her hair in a long grey plait.

"I am so sorry to disturb you," I whispered.

"I just need to give a message to my brother. I shall not be long and I won't bother anyone."

She looked me up and down breathing heavily with a chesty sigh.

"Brother?"

"Yes."

I had used this excuse to get into his rooms previously and it had worked but now I was being scrutinised by the frosty eyes of the landlady.

"Big family?"

"Yes I suppose." I replied curiously.

"Well I suppose you'd better be quick then."

"Thank you" I said with relief.

"And you'd better tell your other sister it's time to go too."

"Other sister?"

"Yes the other young lass she's been in there for a while, says she's his sister too."

I leapt up the stairs forgetting that I had promised to be really quiet. Tom hadn't mentioned anything about Maud coming down to London. I hadn't seen Maud since I had left Somerset it had been ages and I really missed her, she had been my first friend after my illness and I owed a lot of gratitude to her for caring for Tom in my absence.

I was quite thrilled to be seeing her again.

I reached Toms room, number nineteen and slowly turned the handle.

Chapter 43

Utter despair, like cruel scalding pain pouring over me, a wound so deep that the bullet travels, never stopping.
I am lost, so lost. I cannot cry. I'm numb. How can you know someone so well yet be so deceived?
My mind is fogged. I try to recall what happened? What is this red stickiness in my hands?

I am sitting in a chair. I feel like my blood is chilled as it runs through my veins. My head feels very light. I lean forward and vomit violently. My ribs ache, my heart thumps in my chest like it's trying to escape. My hands are trembling as I put them to my face and wipe away bile from my lips.
"What have you done?" A voice echoes in my ears.
"I don't know." I reply to the silence in the room.
I feel a blanket wrap around my shoulders. I am grateful for its warmth although it gives me no comfort. I want to close my eyes and never have to open them again.

I don't know how long has passed. I have been sitting here forever. Fragments are flashing in my mind, I try to block them, but they keep coming. It's like scenes in the theatre. My head aches and I am not sure if I am just having a terrible nightmare, although it feels like something far worse.

I open my eyes. Tom is sitting on the edge of the bed his face buried in his hands. He's crying.
Did I see him with her? Was it real? I pulled her by her hair. I dragged her screaming. She was so light as I slammed her head to the bedpost, till she screamed no more and slumped to the floor.

Tom was yelling. I slapped him so hard around the face that my hand stung. He didn't retaliate. He hung his head in shame. I hit him again. My rage had filled me with the strength of a warrior.

"You bastard!"

He sat beaten. Then went to the limp body heaped on the floor. She didn't move. He called her name then lifted her like a rag doll, her eyes closed, her face covered with streaks of blood that poured from her head.

"She's not breathing!"

"Good!" I retorted.

"Alice we must call a doctor!"

I just stared. We both knew she was dead.

The landlady was standing in the open doorway her face white with horror.

"I've called the police!"

I am standing, I feel dizzy. I need air. The room reeks with blood and vomit. I hear a whistle blowing in the street and footsteps rushing to the lodging house. I have to escape. I cannot stay here. I get up and run to the door pushing the landlady out of the way. I run down the stairs as the policemen come charging up.

"Where do you think you are going young lady?" A rough fist grabs hold of my arm and drags me back to the room.

"Not a pretty sight constable!"

"Lovers tiff gone wrong!"

The two policemen glare at me.

"So what's happened here?" They direct their question at Tom. Tom hangs his head says nothing, they turn to me. I look at Tom with contempt. Blackness and anger overwhelming me.

"It was him sir!" I stretch out my hand and point my finger straight at Tom.

"He killed her!"

Tom's eyes show fear but he still says nothing. He turns to put his shirt on. His back is criss crossed with scars. Scars he suffered for me. For a second I feel sorry, sad and bewildered then I realise that now I have scars too, except mine are internal, invisible. My scars salted with betrayal but only I know that they are there. Only I feel their cut and their lancing pain.

"Is this correct lad?" The policeman asks.

Tom says nothing. He looks over to me as a tear falls from the corner of his eye and he nods to the policeman.

"You'll hang for this boy"

We leave the room.

"You'll have to come with us too." The policeman tells me.

"We need to take a statement from you."

"I have a lawyer" I manage to say with my shaky voice.

"Well you'd better give us his address and we'll get him for you."

I open my bag, take out the address and give it to the policeman who passes it to another young constable waiting in the stairway. We depart. All the other lodgers have come out of their rooms and are watching us as we leave and are escorted away.

The police station is damp. A little oil heater sits in the corner of the room, it is lit and its fumes fill the room long before its heat warms us.

"We need to know everything that happened."

My mind is a blank sheet again. Tom still says nothing. My eyes are fixed on the floor but when they do for a split second look up they meet Toms. He mouths the words "why". I look away and don't respond.

"Your lawyer is here Miss Sinclair."

I am taken from the room. I know Tom is watching every move but I cannot look at him. I am thinking of his scarred back.

James is pacing as I walk into the next room. The door closes and we are left alone.

"What the hell is going on?" He demands at the top of his voice.

I recoil. I don't want him here. He is frightening me. I am very confused, a few hours ago I was with this man for what I thought was the very last time and yearning to be with Tom. Now we are here in a police station and I am a murderess. How I wish I could turn back that clock. How I wish I had not ran to see Tom. I wanted to wake up from this nightmare and find myself at home in my own bed.

"Well Alice? Two hours ago we were enjoying a lovely evening how have you got yourself involved in this mess?"

I shrug. James is becoming more and more impatient. He comes around the table and holds me by the shoulders his eyes scanning me for a clue to solve this mystery.

He softens.

"Alice are you hurt? Did he touch you?"

I shake my head.

"Why were you there? It's not safe for a lady to be in a neighbourhood like that late at night and unescorted. Why were you there?"

From the muted voice within my throat I find some sound and croak out.

"You must protect me James."

"Yes of course I will. But why do you need protecting what have you done?"

"Nothing!" I say quickly.

"She fell against the bed post. He pushed her. He murdered her! It was him!"

"Alice slow down. Did she fall or was she pushed? Was it an accident?"

"Yes, I mean no!"

He frowned at me.

"Wait here! Let me go and see what the boy has to say."

He leaves the room. The room is stark. Grey walls that line a grey floor. A table and three brown chairs.

I ask myself why. She had always been around, eyeing me like a stalking beast waiting for her opportunity to pounce and steal what was mine. I had known that he had befriended her when he had first come down to London and found me at the Sinclair's house, but this! This betrayal! No, I could not understand it. Were men really so weak? How could he? And her, that evil little bitch that thought she was better than me! I couldn't bring myself to say her name not even in my mind.

Door reopens.

"He won't talk, won't say what happened he's only said one thing…"

He looks at me suspiciously. I'm wondering what he has said, whether or not he has incriminated me.

"He says that he is responsible for everything. I don't understand Alice what is going on? If he has murdered this girl then what is it to do with you? Why were you there?"

I cannot think so the first word that comes into my brain is blackmail.

"They were blackmailing me?"

"What!"

"Yes they were going to expose me and I had to pay them off but then they argued and he hit her."

"Is this the truth?" James was looking at me very incredulously.

"Why did you not tell me any of this before hand? Why did you say nothing tonight?"

"I'm sorry James. I didn't want to involve you, I thought I could handle this."

I shrug my shoulders.

James taps his fingers on the table almost as if he was trying to find the missing piece of a jigsaw.

"James you must keep my name out of this. Tell them this has nothing to do with me. I want to go home. Please James make this go away!"

"You don't need to tell me that. That is my job!"

"I'm sorry James I am just very tired and very distressed. I have seen a young girl killed right in front of me and now I just want to get home. This is all too much for me. I'm sorry if I have insulted your professionalism. I am just so very tired."

"I know. It is very late. Let me see what I can do. Give me a few minutes."

He left the room again but this time came back quickly.

"Let's go!"

"Am I free to go?"

"Yes, let's get you home. I've sorted things out as much as I can. You will have to make a statement tomorrow but I will sort that out. I have connections and I can keep your name out of this. Now let's take you home."

We left together and said not a word all the way back to the Sinclair's house.

"You're not going to run off again are you?" James joked.

I shook my head solemnly. Thanked him and alighted from the carriage. I opened the front door and made my way up the stairs to my room. I lit my candle and was horrified to see my bloodstained face in the reflection in the mirror. Was this the face of a murderer? Could I let Tom take the blame? Could I murder again by letting him hang?

My head was about to explode. My search for my mother would have to wait. I wouldn't be able to go anywhere till this was sorted out. I hated Tom. I couldn't fathom how he could do that to me. It served him right that he should take the blame for this. As for Sarah, well that scheming little cow had what she deserved. They both had what they deserved.

It was almost daylight by the time I fell asleep on my eighteenth birthday.

Chapter 44

Who am I? An adult, an heiress a murderess? I long for the
tranquillity of Somerset, was it really so long ago that I had been
that simple girl?
James had told me to stay in and wait for him to come with news
of what was going on. I stayed in my room. I read. I didn't want
to go out or see anyone.
By noon he had still not come. By lunchtime there was a knock
on the front door and the police had arrived to break the news
about Sarah. There were gasps and shrieks from cook and lots of
tongues were wagging within the house. By the time the news
had filtered up the stairs and to me via Charlotte the story was
completely distorted.
   "Charlotte please go away I am sleeping and don't feel very
well today." I pleaded.
   "But Alice this is terribly sensational I must tell you!"
   "All right if you insist." I sighed.
She sat on the end of the bed and began churning out all the lurid
details.
   "...And poor Sarah was bludgeoned to death with an axe that
broke her skull...and John the footman is so terribly upset
because he and Sarah were planning to get married in the autumn
and this terrible murderer must have dragged her off the streets
and into his rooms where he brutally attacked her before
murdering her! Isn't it just awful?"
   "Hmm.I didn't know Sarah was getting married?"
   "Yes they've been childhood sweethearts. Isn't it sad, totally
besotted with each other? Can you imagine the mind of a
murderer taking someone's life? Choking the breath out of their
lungs and watching them die? I hope that murderer swings for
this then we can all sleep more soundly in our beds."

I pictured Tom in my mind swinging from the gallows. Served him right.

Slowly in my mind I was beginning to shift the blame from myself. It somehow seemed such a long time ago and it couldn't possibly have been me, could it?

"Have the police gone?"

"Yes they've just left."

"Did they say anything else? Anyone else that was on the scene?"

"No, why do you think there was an accomplice?"

"No, just wondering that's all."

"It's terribly frightening all this, imagine a real murder and here under our very noses!"

"Yes Charlotte that is quite enough now please let me get some rest."

"Why are you so tired anyway? Did you have a late night with your gentleman friend last night?" Charlotte asked coyly.

"Yes it was quite late." In my mind I remembered my two endings to the evening.

"So, when are you seeing him again? Is it serious? Are you in love?"

"Charlotte!" I said disapprovingly.

The door chimed. Charlotte leapt from my bed and ran out into the hall to see who had arrived then returned.

"It's for you and talk of the devil! Thought he would be at work at a time like this, he's obviously very keen!"

Thank goodness, I thought. I was very nervous and eagerly anticipating what James would have to tell me.

We came down the stairs and I beckoned to James to come out to the garden. I thought it would be better to sit in the summer house at the back of the garden and away from all the ears that might eavesdrop on our conversation.

"So?" I asked eagerly when we were seated.

James shook his head.

"I am very confused Alice. We've been interviewing the boy Tom all morning and the girl appears to be his sister."

I gasped.

"He says that it was all some terrible accident and there was no murder at all. Just some gross misunderstanding. He denied that he knows you but when we pressed him he told us that he was from Somerset and was previously employed at Sparrows Hawk Manor where his other sister is currently employed, I believe this is your home in Somerset. His sister, Sarah worked in this house has been in service here since approximately the same time as your arrival here. I cannot understand why he would murder his sister but I also don't know why you thought you were being blackmailed. When we suggested it to him he was visibly shocked and upset and you know Alice, I believe him."

"How could she be his sister?"

I was asking this question of myself more than I was asking it of him.

"Why not? Families from the country send their children to be in service. It's a good life for them especially in the homes of the gentry."

Now I was the one who was confused. It was falling into place though; Sarah was his spy and his informant on my whereabouts and state of health. That was how he was able to know how I was and when we went to the picnic how he knew where we were. Why hadn't he told me? Why had he led me to believe that she was a threat to me?

"Can I see Tom?"

"No!"

"But why?"

"Alice, this has gone really too far. I believe that he is protecting you and that there is an explanation to all this but I cannot help you if you flatly refuse to co operate and help yourself!"

"What do you mean?"

"Alice stop playing games! A girl has died! Just tell me what has really happened and why you were there last night?"

I couldn't tell him. Not without incriminating myself and having to possibly face the gallows. It was very hard to sit here and think on my feet.

"James I will tell you everything if you promise that you will protect me and not judge me?"

He eyed me like one eyeing a stranger that you've just met. This was an Alice that he did not know. He must have felt shocked with me and my ungenerous attitude.

I would tell him the truth but only the bits I felt relevant.

"Well where should I begin?"

"Just start Alice, but please just be truthful."

I began to tell the story of how I had discovered the truth about my father and how till that time I had been completely in the dark about my true parentage. Tom had given me information and being the type of person that could not simply sit and do nothing had decided to go off to London and discover my own truth. I had pretended to the Sinclair's that I was a cousin and with the help of Tom had then found out that the mother whom I believed dead was really alive and had been sent away. I had been at the lodging house the previous evening simply to find some more information from Tom.

"Yes Alice very nice story but how does Sarah end up dead on the floor?"

"She slipped and fell."

James looked at me coldly. He knew that there was some truth in what I was telling him but that also there were bits that I was not telling him. But I could not. How was I supposed to say that till yesterday I loved Tom and thought that his relationship with Sarah was a betrayal of me and that I had got it wrong and killed her mistakenly in an act of passion! It was ridiculous. Even as I thought it, I could not comprehend that it made any sense, so I could not possibly relay it.

"So this is all you will say?"

"Yes"

"So you will defend the boy that you told the policeman was a killer?"

"I was in shock! I didn't know what I was saying."

"And you are clear minded now?"

"Yes"

"And will you make a statement to that effect?"

"Yes but I must see Tom, please James."

James disapproved. Of that he made no concealment. However I was insistent and he knew that if he gave in to me he might be able to get more from me eventually.

"Alice, fortunately I know people and I think it may be better to say nothing. I can tell people to forget that you were ever there and they never saw you. Do you understand me?"

"You mean bribe them?"

"We don't use words like that."

"So I won't have to give a statement?"

"No, I think that it's the best way forward. Anyway I'm not sure with you Alice, your story changes from minute to minute and that will only create suspicion and ultimately make things worse."

"Oh"

"I'm not convinced with you and so a judge certainly won't be either. We just won't move in that direction. I've decided that is for the best."

"You've already sorted this haven't you?"

"How do you know?"

"Well when the police came this morning they didn't mention anything about anyone else being on the scene."

He nodded.

"Alice you asked me to help you and I have. Don't even think about changing stories at this stage. In fact don't do anything or the only person that will end up swinging will be you. Are we clear on this?"

I looked deep into his eyes. I could see sadness and confusion but also understood the great efforts that he had made to try to protect me. I had no choice but to acquiesce.

"Don't go out. Do not get yourself involved in any trouble and please do not do anything silly. If you do, I cannot be responsible for you and I won't be able to help you. Stay very discreet until this has all blown over."

He got up from the stone seat and bade me farewell then turned to walk away.

"Will I see you again soon?" I called out and then almost immediately regretted saying it.

He shook his head, coldness and indifference in his eyes.

"I shall make contact with you when I think necessary." And he was gone.

I felt very stupid as if I had been chided like a small child. James was clearly not interested in me anymore, I think he hated me. What was I to do? I could not believe that I could have done what I did and now what would happen to Tom? How could I live with that too?

I went back to the house. Luncheon was being cleared in the conservatory. I sat and picked at some food. The conversation around the table was purely about Sarah and the speculation and theories being thrown around the table were really quite comical. So Tom wasn't unfaithful to me. I had doubted him and let my unforgiving mind attack him too. Tom that had always been there for me; my strength when I needed support. Now everything was being destroyed by me. It was as if I had no control, no faith to believe that the people that said they loved me really did. Sarah shouldn't have died, I didn't push her that hard, she was just weak, that's all, it was an accident. Maybe if Tom had told me and Sarah hadn't been so cocky with me then none of this would have happened so in a way it wasn't my fault. I could go and tell the police everything, tell them that she fell and that Tom was innocent but then James had said no, not under any circumstances. I was burning to speak to Tom. What was he thinking of me? Alone in his cell in the police station with only a small barred window for light. I had seen him sitting there when we had left the other night. I wondered whether they had beaten him, tortured him?

Scars on scars all from me.

His last word to me was *why*. Now I was the one that was wondering why. That little barred window must open onto the road somewhere. That's what I had to do! I ran to my room and grabbed a light shawl and draped it around my head and shoulders. I began walking to the station my pace quickening all the time till I could feel that my feet hardly stayed on the pavement at all. My heart was beating anxiously as I turned into the station road and skimmed around the piles of rubbish and rat infested bins to the back of the building. There below me where about five tiny barred windows just about at street level. One of them must be Tom's cell. I desperately tried to remember which

300

one. We had passed three rooms as we left, so he must be in the one before last. I crept over and had to crouch down to see within. It was very dark and poky. I was almost prone on the ground trying to peer through but I could see a shadow within lying on the floor.

"Tom?" I whispered.

Nothing.

"Tom? I said slightly louder.

The body stirred and began to roll over. He sat up on the floor and turned towards the window.

"Tom is that you?" I said in a low husky voice.

He stood. Then limped over towards me. I wasn't sure. The face that I saw was swollen and the eyes looked black and puffy.

"Oh my God!" I recoiled

Tom had been beaten and badly too. I couldn't face him. I felt guilt remorse and shame all rolled into one very bad person.....
Me.

I got up ready to run away, to hide from my shame but then I heard a thin voice call to me and I knew I had to stay.

Chapter 45

The voice behind me was apprehensive yet held the same tones that I recognised so well. I turned and crouched down besides the dirty opening. The face that I saw within was one that frightened me.

"Alice?"

I breathed heavily forcing myself not to cry, my teeth clamping over my bottom lip.

"I'm sorry Alice."

"What?"

"I'm sorry for putting you through all of this."

"Tom? I should be apologising to you. I have done something terrible and then blamed you when I should have been protecting you."

"No, it's all right. I know. They beat you too and you said things that you didn't mean."

"Tom what are you talking about? You are not lucid!"

I clutched the dirty bars and gaped at the pathetic creature before me. What had they done to him? He had been beaten to a pulp and wasn't sure what was real or imaginary. It was sad. I felt so bad for him. It didn't seem the right moment to remind him that I had murdered his sister. He had always protected me, now I had to do whatever was in my power to help him too.

"Are you being fed?"

He laughed a feeble laugh.

"I don't want any food. I don't want anything I just want to get out of here and help you."

"Help me what?"

"Find your mother."

"Tom! Listen to me. I need to help you now. My mother can wait. She's waited for eighteen years and I'm sure it can wait a little bit longer."

"Are you in another cell?"

"No Tom I'm outside."

"How did you get out? Did you escape? How can I escape?" Tom wasn't making sense. It upset me to see him so disorientated like this.

"I didn't escape they let me go. I'm going now but I'll be back later. I'm going to get you some food."

"And a blanket...please."

"Yes of course."

"Ask Sarah she'll get you the things from the kitchen."

"What!" I said startled.

"She'll help you, she watches you for me to make sure that you are safe."

I swallowed hard and left. Tears were welling up in my eyes. I felt dreadful. I was damned. When Tom came to his senses he would hate me too. I wondered how badly he had been beaten, why was he acting so weirdly? Did he not understand what had happened and what was going to happen to him? He had no concept of the terrible crime that had been committed or more so who had done it.

I went home and fetched a basket went to the kitchen and began emptying practically the contents of the larder into it. I then pulled a blanket from my bed and folded it neatly laying it on top of the basket before slinking through side streets and passages until I was back at the police station. I called to the window and Tom came. I squeezed the food and blanket through the small bars until he had everything. As the last item went through he took my hand and held it firmly.

"Thank you so much."

He had a wedge of bread in his other hand and was eating it with fervent eagerness.

"I am so hungry." He tried to justify.

"I know you are my love."

The blanket was already around his shoulders. I wondered how long it would be till his sanity returned and till he would turn on me and despise me. I left with the promise that I would come every day and bring him food.

I was torn. I wouldn't let him hang. I had promised James that I would not do anything foolish and I would try not to, after all I could be the one swinging instead and that wouldn't do. I had to come up with some other plan. I needed Lady Sinclair's help. I thought that I had possibly exhausted James contacts but Lady Sinclair would have a lot of friends in parliament and court and she was sure to know the judge that would preside over Tom's case.

So how could I plead to Lady Eleanor? I would have to expose myself. If that was the only course of action than so be it. I had wealth of my own it would be compensation for the loss of status that I would endure.

"So you are still here? I knew you wouldn't leave! Hooray hooray!"

Archie was waiting near the front door his little face all aglow.

"No not yet Archie it's all been delayed a little but I will be going soon."

"Are you not going because there is a murderer somewhere? I wouldn't want to go anywhere either."

"No that's not why. Anyway if you go out with someone you will be safe. Is your mama about?"

"Yes she's in her room."

I will see you later then Archie, perhaps you would like to go out and feed the ducks in the park?"

"Oh yes! I would love that!"

I went up the staircase. Why did I feel like an actress playing so many different roles? I knocked on Lady Eleanor's door.

"Yes come in."

I went in. She was sitting at her dressing mirror brushing her hair. When she saw me she offered me the brush and I stood behind her and began to brush her silky long brown tresses. The last time that I had done this was just after my father had died and she had been in mourning and refused to come out of her room.

"Are you well Lady Eleanor?" I began to break the silence jarring the atmosphere.

"Not really."

Her candid response startled me somewhat.

"I'm sorry to hear that. Can I be of any assistance to you in any way?"

"No!"

Lady Eleanor was in one of those moods that unsettled me. When she was like this I was never sure whether she hated me and was about to come out with some terrible accusation. I always assumed the worst but then that was probably because the worst, was the level that I expected from anyone when it was in reference to me.

I carefully separated the fine silky strands of her hair through my fingers and teased it into small curls that I pinned around her head. The silence was unbearable. I could feel her eyes watching my every move and now was definitely not the right time to go confessing all. I couldn't ask her what was the problem but something was definitely on her mind.

"What will the neighbours think?" She finally blurted out.

"About what?"

"About police coming to our house in the middle of the afternoon! About my servants being murdered! What else would they have to wonder about? I saw the curtains flickering and I could see eyes watching. This is not good. I am not happy with this situation."

I felt a weight lifting from my shoulders. Well it wasn't me directly. Or not that she knew.

"Lady Eleanor please don't fret. There is nothing that can be done to change the situation. It will pass and everyone will forget."

"But there's going to be a court case in the next week and then they'll be the execution that won't be so pleasant."

I recoiled. There would not be an execution. I wouldn't let there be.

"But what if it was an accident and he is innocent?"

"What do you know of this Alice? Why do you think that he is innocent?"

"James told me, James Foster. I think he is involved in representing the boy."

"Well good luck to him" she chuckled.

"I know all the judges in this parish and none of them take lightly to young girls being murdered."

"Yes but surely if it were an accident, that's got to be different?"

"But who's going to prove it? Not Sarah, she's not here to defend herself. Likely he will get the death penalty."

"But he's innocent."

"You seem very sure, what's James been telling you?"

"Nothing other than the boy says it's an accident."

"Well we'll just have to wait and see wont we, we'll find out when the trial is and we can go along and watch, it'll give us something to do."

At that she got up and left the room. Archie was standing just outside the door.

"Are you ready to play now Alice?"
I didn't want to play. I had to play though because I had promised. My mind was preoccupied though with what I could do. I needed to get to see James and find out about when the dates were for Tom's trial and if money was needed for his defence. Surely an expensive barrister was better than none and I had plenty of money for the best.

The next day I went to James office. He seemed surprised to see me.
"Won't you sit down Alice?"
I obeyed.
"And what brings you here again?"
"I would like to pay for Toms defence."
"Really?" He said raising an eyebrow.
"And why would you want to waste your money on someone as trivial as that?"
"James it is my money and I can waste it on whatever or whomever I please." I retorted arrogantly.
How dare he question me so coldly, what did it matter to him as long as he was paid.
James stared at me with daggered eyes so piercing that I had to turn away.
"I do not appreciate your judgement Mr Foster, I find it most disdainful."
"Miss Sinclair you are a very strange and unconventional girl."
"And you can keep your comments to yourself!" I responded acerbically.
"Perhaps all this inheritance is ill proportioned?"
I was smouldering inside.
"Perhaps you could explain your comments?"
James turned to me and sniggered.

"You are just a very naïve little country girl after all aren't you?"

That was it; my blood had just boiled over. I marched up to him and slapped him hard around his face. His startled expression was a very pretty and satisfying sight.

"Oh!" He muttered in shock and put his hand to his crimson smarting cheek.

My hand was burning but I didn't care. I picked up my parasol and gloves and marched out the door without turning back. I found my way out of the building and once out in the fresh air burst into tears on the corner of the street.

How dare he! I angrily kicked at a pebble on the ground much to the amazement of the passersby. I began to take great strides, breathing deeply and angrily. I stopped at the bakers and bought several cakes and pasties then went directly to the police station. I was still sobbing when I leaned down to the little grill and called Toms name and gave him the food. This time after he took it he clenched my hand interlocked his fingers with mine and kissed each finger.

"Thank you sweet angel Alice."

I shook my head and dabbed my tears. I was no angel. What was I? How was I going to save him? What could I do or say to make this all right? How was I going to get him a barrister?

"Why are you crying Alice? Don't be sad everything will be just fine."

"Tom did they hurt you?"

"No nothing could hurt me. I've suffered much worse as you know and lived to tell the tale."

Tom turned and as he did so I noticed that there was dried blood all over his head. They must have hit him so badly that he had forgotten what happened and the terrible danger that he was in. I got up to leave.

"Thank you for the pasties, I would starve without you, thank you my sweet."

"Don't worry Tom. I will sort this out, I promise."

With the sting of tears in my dry red eyes I left. With only hopelessness and despair to escort me home.

Chapter 46

The date was set for Wednesday, only two days later. I had to contain my frantic feelings of complete inadequacy and terror of the forthcoming time.

What was I to do? I had attempted to see several lawyers but with the imminent case, no one else was prepared to take it on, especially with the facts so badly stacked against Tom. I felt helpless. It was all in James hands and he was in no mind to help Tom or me.

By Tuesday evening, when I thought that I would be going to court and sitting anonymously at the back, I discovered that Lady Sinclair and the rest of the household were intent on attending and *watching the scoundrel found guilty*. I had no choice but to pretend that was the reason why I was going along too.

Wednesday morning, I dressed soberly and got into the carriage with Lady Sinclair, Charlotte and Albert. The carriage trotted through town and up The Strand to the law courts where we alighted and were led to our court.

The room was brown, warm in a cold sort of way and reminded me of the inside of a library but without books. To the left were two rows where the jury where sitting patiently. There were not many spectators in the gallery and to the front right, were the court officials. Immediately before the judge there were two desks. At one sat a red faced round barrister heaving a great wad of files into the hands of his clerk. The other desk was empty. There was a buzz from the side door and Tom was led in with two policemen and James Foster. Tom had been cleaned up somewhat and wore a frayed jacket. His eyes were glazed and he seemed a bit dazzled by the bright lights of the court.

Boos echoed from the gallery. I turned angrily to glare at the perpetrators. They in turn continued, oblivious to my very presence.

We all stood as the judge entered, then we sat as beckoned by the court clerk.

I could feel my heart pounding. I felt like I was the one standing there in the dock. But for the grace of God I would have been. I could see James turn and scan the court. I looked away so as not to look at him but after several seconds when I felt the coast was clear I looked up. His eyes were clearly focused on mine. His face was expressionless, I felt that I had no choice but to smile courteously and then quickly look away.

The case began. Truths and untruths hurled from mouth to mouths with venom and subjection. It was a farce. Here was a young boy fighting for his life and every word he uttered was shot down by a clever wit tongued prosecuting barrister. James was doing his best but there was no contest and poor Tom would be the ultimate loser in this battle of words.

The prosecuting barrister came to the stand and glared over at Tom for a terrifying few minutes. Tom looked scared and I felt totally helpless that he had to suffer that intimidating episode.

"So you murdered this young girl and cruelly extracted the life force from her!" Spat the prosecutor.

"No" Answered Tom simply.

"You found a heavy object and smashed her poor skull till she did not breathe and was laying in a pool of her own blood!"

"No" Tom s voice was quivering, he was becoming visibly frightened.

"Brute" I muttered under my breath. I was grinding my teeth together trying to remain calm in this circus of officials determined to convict Tom.

He continued like a fierce dog, growling and biting, spitting venom, trying to break poor Tom. Tom somehow remained calm and however much goaded by the prosecution, still maintained short and calm answers. For all his faults James was trying to object to a lot of what the prosecution was suggesting but the judge seemed to be siding with the prosecution and overruling all objections.

The day was long and gruesome. Tom appeared to be in some kind of stupor and that was definitely not helping his cause. He had obviously been instructed by James to not mention me or anything that would place me at the scene or incriminate me in this murder. He was doing an excellent job and with every word was digging a deeper and deeper grave for himself. I tried to remain objective like some outsider but in my heart I could not lie to myself. What was I to do? I could go to James and give myself up. But I couldn't and I wouldn't. If I really loved Tom could I sit here and let him die for me? I was in torment; I would have to try harder with Lady Sinclair, do anything that a desperate person would, in order to help.

By late afternoon we were all becoming quite tired. Albert had left to go to meet some university friends. Charlotte and Lady Sinclair were trying to stifle their yawns and appear composed even though they were wilting rapidly.

"Lady Eleanor?"

"Huh, oh yes?" I think she had momentarily nodded off.

"I think the boy in the witness stand reminds me very much of someone would you not agree?"

"Lady Sinclair scrunched up her nose and squinted. She looked out beyond the crowd and straight at Tom. Her heavy brocade skirts noisily swishing as she adjusted to get a clearer view.

"I can't be too sure but yes there is something uncannily familiar about him, I can't put my finger on it though."

"Perhaps we should try to get a bit closer to see him?"

"I don't think so Alice! Why does it matter? Even if we got closer what would that achieve, that we know a murderer?"

"But perhaps he's not a murderer maybe he is innocent?"

Lady Sinclair patted my hand.

"Alice you must not worry so much about this court case. It doesn't matter. My friend Justice Gordon will probably find him guilty and by this time next week we'll all have forgotten about this."

"But Lady Eleanor what if we found out that this boy was innocent and that we were indebted to him in some way?"

"Alice you are very curious, what are you talking about?"

"Well I believe that the boy down there is none other than the boy that saved Archie from being drowned! I believe that he is that guardian angel that we have been searching for and that he now desperately needs our help. James Foster told me that he had been terribly beaten in prison and that was how they managed to get a confession out of him. Look at him Lady Eleanor he seems so helpless and timid he could not possibly be a murderer."

By this stage Lady Sinclair had sat far forward and was peering frantically at the boy.

"Court is now adjourned until ten tomorrow morning please rise for Judge Gordon" Announced the clerk.

"Quick!" Lady Sinclair grabbed my wrist and we ran out of the gallery doors and towards the front of the court. Charlotte was left behind in amazement at our sudden departure.

We turned the corner and rushed in to the front of the court where the constable was handcuffing Tom to take him back to the cells and transport him back to the police station where he was being held.

We stopped in front of them. James stood immediately before us baffled as to what we were doing here. Tom looking weary and expressionless seemed to lighten as he saw me.

"Yes Alice I do believe that you are right!" Lady Eleanor exclaimed. "I think this is the boy!"

James shot forward and whispered harshly in my ear.

"What is going on Alice? Are you insane? Why have you brought Lady Sinclair here? I told you to stay quiet and leave me to do my job, why are you always so disobedient?

"I must speak to Lord Gordon" Announced Lady Sinclair.

"Lady Sinclair" James approached.

"Please would you step into my office I think we need to discuss this since I am representing the defendant?"

"But this is absolutely critical that I speak to the judge where he is?"

"No Lady Sinclair you will speak to me first and then we can talk to the judge."

He ushered us into a stark little room at the back of the court. As the rest of the people dissipated away into small chambers or simply out into the vast corridors and into the street.

"Wait here!" He instructed angrily.

"Alice I think I would like to speak to you first."

He closed the door on Lady Sinclair and James and I stood in a narrow hallway beyond the court.

"What the hell are you playing at?" He shouted angrily.

"I'm sorry James but I had…"

"You had to what? Jeopardise your life! You are just a stupid girl!"

"But there was an opportunity to…."

"To what?"

"Please James if you just let me speak."

314

His face was red with rage his eyes darting with frustration and anger.

"Everything is going to plan Alice I don't need your interference."

"What plan? It looks like there is no plan. Tom looks hopeless up on the witness stand. He is being mashed by that pompous prosecutor and he is saying nothing that will help him get off."

"Exactly and that how I want it."

"But why James? If it continues like this he will be hung by the end of the week. Do you not care at all?"

"Alice I am doing all this for you. It's you or him! If he implicated you than it would be a much sadder story, you would be up there on the stand and it would not be nice, let me tell you. Just let him go and you will be free."

"So you won't even try to defend him?"

"There is no defence. We cannot call witnesses as they will all testify to the presence of a certain young lady at the scene. You really don't want that Alice. I am doing the very best that I can for you."

"Why? Why are you doing all this for me?"
James swallowed and looked at me in that deep twinkling way that I remembered from not so long ago.

"If I have to tell you why, then you really are less intelligent than I gave you credit for."

"Oh" I replied, not sure that I really understood what he meant.

"However James there has been a change of plan and that is where Lady Sinclair comes into it."

"Really? Enlighten me."

"Well I'm sure you remember the picnic in the summer when Archie fell into the river."

"Yes"

"Well the boy that saved Archie was none other than Tom and Lady Sinclair has recognised him and wants to come forward and tell the judge that she knows that this boy who saved her child's life could never be a heartless murderer."

"Well you really are a very clever girl after all Alice. A character witness with as much esteem as Lady Sinclair and one who just happens to be a personal friend of the judge would certainly help things out a bit. I was beginning to think that there was no other outcome for this but maybe there is."

"So Lady Sinclair can go to see the judge?"

"No it doesn't quite work like that. I would have to put her up as a witness and she would have to swear that he is of good character. The judge would then have to make his own assumptions."

"Shall we go back and speak to Lady Sinclair then?"

James looked at me for a few moments. He said nothing, yet so much. His feelings running a lot deeper than all this trouble that I had caused. We both understood each other in those silent moments.

"Yes let's go back and explain the procedure to her."

We went back to the interview room where Lady Eleanor was looking quite flustered and disturbed at having been left alone.

"I'm sorry Lady Sinclair but there were some issues that I needed to discuss with Alice before we spoke. How can I help you?"

Lady Sinclair told James the story about how she recognised the boy and that she wanted to help because she was deeply indebted to this person for saving the life of her younger son so soon after the death of her beloved husband. She took out a handkerchief and wept and James explained that the only way for her to help would be to testify the next day in court. He was sure that it would make a difference to the outcome of the case.

Lady Sinclair thanked James who then escorted us out through the back door till we were back outside and out into the street. Once outside we found a very disgruntled Charlotte.

"And where do you think you two ran off to without telling me? I've been standing here alone being accosted by all sorts of strange fellows."

"We had far more urgent things to do, so I'm sorry but I didn't have time to discuss this with you first Charlotte!"

Charlotte scowled.

We hailed a cab and all jumped in.

"I am so tired I cannot wait to get home." Declared Charlotte indignantly.

"Well you will just have to wait for a little longer than my dear. Bartholomew Place please driver."

"Sorry mother where are we going?"

"I just need to stop off and see an old friend first before we go back. This is very important."

"Who mother?"

"Lord Gordon."

"The judge? Replied Charlotte.

"But Lady Eleanor, James said that was not procedure." I reminded her.

"Well I'm not bothered what James says am I?"

"Will somebody please tell me what is going on?" Asked an increasingly irate Charlotte.

"Yes Alice will tell you everything." Declared Lady Eleanor, as she alighted from the carriage at the requested address.

"Wait in the carriage, I won't be long."

It seemed like ages that Lady Eleanor was gone and I wondered whether she had just simply forgotten about us. I told Charlotte that I had thought that her mother had recognised the boy on trial and that we had gone to have a closer inspection as soon as the trial had concluded for the day and yes, in fact I had had to agree with Lady Sinclair, that the boy was indeed the same one that had saved Archie.

"Actually come to think of it, I had thought there was something familiar about him too but I hadn't realised that he was the saviour!" Added Charlotte.

Eventually Lady Sinclair and Justice Gordon emerged from the house laughing and smiling. The judge took Lady Sinclair's hand and kissed it ever so slowly, to the impatience of the young ladies waiting to get home.

The footman opened the door for her and she stepped up into the carriage her face all aglow, cheeks quite flushed and red.

"The judge is such a charming fellow and so clever. It's such a shame about his poor wife who died last year she was such a lovely lady."

Charlotte and I exchanged looks and then she began to giggle.

"And what is so amusing about Lady Gordon's death?"

"No nothing mama. We are very sorry to hear of it." Replied Charlotte trying desperately to stifle her smiles.

"So Lady Eleanor what did the judge have to say?"

"Oh that it has been such a difficult year for him being alone and widowed...."

"No. I mean in respect to the court case, is there anything that he can do to help?"

"Oh that, oh yes, of course he will help."

Once again Charlotte burst into laughter and was only able to contain it by looking out of the window all the way home. When we did eventually arrive, we ran upstairs to Charlotte's room where she fell on the bed in absolute peals of laughter so loud

that the younger girls burst in and demanded to know what was
going on.

"It's not information that we care to divulge to such young,
innocent ears." Declared Charlotte.

"I will inform you when you are older."

"Oh that must mean that Charlotte's besotted with some young
gentleman again!" Emily conceded.

"No not me!" Retaliated Charlotte.

"Alice then?"

"No not Alice"

"Then who?"

"Never you mind." And with that the younger girls were
pushed out of the door which was promptly closed.
Charlotte slumped down on her bed.

"Actually it's quite shameful. I've never seen mother flirt it's
quite disgusting."

"Well she did seem happy I don't think she stopped smiling all
the way home. Anyway she was there on behalf of Tom not
herself so it's not that bad. Hopefully she impressed the judge
enough to save the boy."

"Hmm I suppose it did achieve its mission but it's still not right
of mother."

"Well there's only one way to find out just how successful she
was and I suppose we will find that out tomorrow…wont we?"

Chapter 47

We stepped into court the next morning. I was feeling unusually optimistic. James caught my eye and I gave him a polite grin to which he responded with a nod. Albert had given the day a miss. Charlotte sat to my immediate left with her mother beside her both looking glorious in their autumn finery.

Lady Sinclair smiled when Justice Gordon looked her way and acknowledged her. She seemed to be quite comfortable with all the attention she was getting from the people in court admiring her, sitting so regal in the front of the gallery.

The noise and hum from the spectators in court was escalating. There was a lot of excitement when a murder case was coming to a conclusion. All seats were filled and the standing room in the gallery was heaving with sweaty commoners just out for a bit of entertainment.

"These people don't even know Tom but they're here to see him hang." I said to myself.

Tom was led in and the crowd now whipping themselves up into a frenzy, began to boo. I snarled at them and angrily shook my head. Something inside me was so overwhelmed that I thought I might cry. I never cried so why now was I feeling such a compulsion to do so? Was it just the thought that this horrible ordeal was almost at a close, or was it something else?

The clerk rose and hit his anvil like an auctioneer.

"Silence in court for Justice Gordon!"

The prosecution was looking comfortably smug.

"Mr Foster" Began the judge

"I believe that you have a witness that you would like to call to the stand."

The prosecutors face dropped and he shrugged his shoulders at his co counsel.

"Yes your honour, I would like to call Lady Eleanor Sinclair to the stand."

Lady Eleanor stood graceful as a swan and glided down to the front of the court where a bible was thrust into her hand.

"Do you swear to tell the whole truth and nothing but the truth so help you God?"

"I do"

"Very well Lady Sinclair. I do believe that the defendant is known to you in some capacity. Could you please relate to the court how it is that you know this person?"

Lady Sinclair looked around nervously. The enormity of having so many faces peering at her had given her stage fright.

"It's all right Lady Eleanor." The judge leaned over his desk to whisper.

"You will be just fine." Their eyes met and she then redirected her focus straight at James and began to answer.

"Yes I do know the defendant. It was earlier this year in the summer when we went on a picnic with my family. It was the first time that we had ventured out since the death of my husband earlier this year when he died of a heart attack"

"I am very sorry for your loss Lady Sinclair. Please do go on."

"Well after we had all eaten our lunch my younger son Archie wondered off and no one could find him anywhere. There was great panic until we did eventually find him."

"And where was that?"

"He was floating face down in the river Thames!"

There was a huge gasp from the crowd. Lady Sinclair quite overcome with being up in the witness box began fumbling with her bag until she found a handkerchief with which to dab away her tears.

"I understand that this is quite an emotional moment for you but could you carry on please?"

"Yes of course."

"So when your son was pulled from the river was he breathing?"

"No he was quite pale and his lips were blue. I held him in my arms and he made no movement. I was sure that he was dead." She whispered.

"And what did you do?"

"I called for help and suddenly from the crowds this young lad appeared. He took Archie from me and began breathing into his mouth and pushing on his chest."

"And?"

"And then Archie began to cough and splutter and he was breathing again."

"So it was like a miracle?"

"Oh yes it was the most wonderful moment. I could not believe that God had given me back my child, I was so thankful."

"And Lady Sinclair do you see that lad who saved your child here in court?"

"I do."

"And could you point him out to us?"

Lady Sinclair raised her hand, protruded her index finger and pointed straight at Tom.

There was a simultaneous gasping from the crowd.

"And do you believe that this boy who saved your son and almost certainly brought him back from the dead could be a brutal cold blooded killer?"

"Most definitely not!"

"Is there anything else that you would like to add?"

"Yes, this boy was the brother of Sarah the girl that died. She was in my employ and therefore the boy was often around at the house to see his sister. I noticed him out of the window and in the courtyard. He was always of impeccable manners and warm and friendly towards his sister. There was no ill feeling between them and I believe that the injuries that caused the girls death were due to a fall and not due to the hand of Tom."

The prosecutor jumped up.

"I don't think Lady Sinclair is an expert in how the girl died!"

"Sit down sir! Roared the judge.

"Lady Sinclair is entitled to give her opinion as a character witness!"

The judge turned to Lady Eleanor.

"Thank you so much for your testimony here today. It is very much appreciated and very helpful to know that there are people of esteemed character prepared to give testimony under such difficult circumstances. You have been a most excellent witness here. Thank you, you may step down."

Lady Sinclair walked back to her seat all eyes upon her.

"Well done mama you were superb!" Congratulated Charlotte.

"Well that was pretty nerve racking, I don't think that I would like to do that again."

"I didn't know that you'd observed him previously at the house with Sarah?" I commented

"Hmm yes. Well let's not talk about that shall we!"

I smiled secretly to myself. I hadn't banked on that added gem and they all helped enormously at the moment.

The court was hushed into silence and the prosecution and then the defence were invited to give their closing statements.

The judge listened attentively to both sides and then gave his own summation.

"Gentlemen of the jury, you have heard from both sides and I urge you now to make your own conclusions as to whether this boy is guilty of the crime for which he stands here accused today.

I would heavily weigh the matter upon you of the testimony heard today by the very distinguished Lady Eleanor Sinclair of how the defendant was known to her, and that she has given him an excellent personal reference. Anyone disagreeing with her will be almost calling her a liar and that would be a most shameful thing to do. I ask you now to deliberate amongst yourselves and to bear in mind that there was no evidence to assume that this was not just a terrible accident."

The prosecutor jumped to his feet.

"But your honour he has given a confession."

"Sit down fool! Many a confession has been received by a drunk or beaten man!"

Then turning to Tom

"Were you beaten boy?"

Tom shakily looked around the court at his tormentors.

"Answer boy!"

"Yes" Mouthed Tom anxiously.

"Well there you go then, a forced confession means nothing."

The prosecution sat down seething at the complete change in the judge with whom he had only had dinner two days previously and had been laughing at the simplicity of this case. Now here he was making an absolute jackass out of him.

The jury were led from the court and we were told to wait in the vicinity till they returned with their verdict.

We went over to see James.

"Well what do you think?"

"Well Lady Sinclair you certainly saved the day. I told you that giving a character reference was all that was necessary, seeing the judge would not have helped anymore."

No one dared to tell James any different but it was most apparent that seeing the judge had made an enormous difference.

"His direction to the jury seemed very encouraging."

324

"Encouraging! He almost challenged them to call Lady Sinclair a liar if they declared Tom anything but innocent. I never like to predict an outcome, I prefer to be restrained but we shall see just how Justice Gordon may have swayed this."

"Ladies and gentlemen the jury are returning please take your seats immediately."

"Oh!" Exclaimed James "that's either very good or very bad. It's too quick."

"Good luck James." I whispered as we walked away and back to our seats.

The jury were led back in. Then Tom, then the judge. The court was deathly silent. In the next few moments we would find out whether Tom was to be hung or not. I couldn't breathe. The top button of my blouse seemed to be choking me uncomfortably. I could feel beads of sweat forming on the back of my neck.

The judge spoke. I held my breath.

"Has the jury reached a verdict?"

"We have your honour" Replied the foreman.

"And what say you?"

"We the jury find the defendant Tom Sullivan...We find the defendant..."

By now had my eyes closed so tightly and I was willing the words into his mouth, subsequently I completely missed what his response was.

"What? What?" I shouted above the roars of the crowds.

"He's innocent. He's free!" Charlotte exclaimed as she hugged me.

We went outside and into the street. My legs were feeling like jelly. I wanted to jump for joy but I didn't think that I could. I was then filled with an absolute compulsion to go and see Tom and wrap my arms around him and tell him that I loved him and was always here for him.

I made my way around to the back of the court. It was bedlam people pushing and shoving trying to get a glimpse of the defendant.

James saw me and weaved his way through the crowd till he had linked his arm through mine and we filtered into a quiet area.

"Well that's a great relief!" He sighed.

"Yes well done James, you were amazing!"

"Thank you Alice that means a lot to me. Perhaps we did get a little off track lately. I would like to maybe see if we could go back to the point that we were at before we had all of our differences of opinion."

I looked up at James. Sometimes that hard exterior just melted away and he seemed almost boyish in his demeanour. It appealed to me, as that side of him was far more approachable.

"Of course James, it would be lovely." I said simply.

"Well good day Alice I will call on you soon."

"James" I began nervously, wary as not to annoy him now that our differences had be reconciled.

"Would it be possible to speak to Tom?"

"Why Alice?"

"I just want to make sure that all is well with him."

James knew better than to question me too laboriously and I supposed that he was as cautious as I was about revisiting that uncomfortable place that we had both been at before.

"He's at the back of the court off the judges chambers. He will be released once all the crowds have dispersed. That's for his own safety of course. I'll take you to him. Follow me"

Once again we pressed our way into the crowd and back into the court then up a winding little staircase that led to a dark corridor. Eventually we reached a heavy oak door which James reached to open. He then stopped and turned to me.

"I think I had better leave you alone at this point. I'll be back in a half hour when the coast is clear to escort Tom outside."

"Thank you." And I tipped up on my toes and planted a kiss on his cheek.

I watched James walk alone back up the corridor with his hand to his cheek in amazement. When he was finally out of sight I slowly opened the door.

Tom was sitting on a high back chair near the window facing the road. He was watching the throngs of people mingling below. He turned to face me, his face was expressionless.

I ran towards him and threw my arms around him.

"Thank god Tom, you're free!"

Tom stood rigid, his body cold, unwelcoming to my embrace.

"Tom?" I reached to stroke his cheek.

He stepped back. His eyes staring at me like I was his enemy.

"What is it my darling?" My voice was quivering.

For several moments there was an unnerving silence in the room then Tom spoke.

"Get out! Leave you wicked vixen!"

I gasped, shocked.

"What is it Tom?"

His eyes were drilling into me.

"I saw you. I watched what you did. You murdered my sister with your evil little hands. You are a witch! Conniving and all bad. You are your father's daughter and I believed you. Fell for your motherless ploy, unaware of the poison within you. Never come near me again!"

I was speechless as I watched Tom's cheeks flush crimson with anger.

"Get out!" He screamed.

I stood motionless, dumbfounded.

He raged towards me, grabbed me tightly by the arms opened the door and threw me from the room. The door then slammed hard behind him.

I sat on the stone floor alone, my heart thumping.

On the other side of the door was my life, my future, the only person that had ever been true to me and really loved me. I had destroyed that.

I got up and spread my arms over the door.

"Tom, please, I am so sorry." The tears were escaping in streams.

He couldn't hear me, not through this heavy oak door. I felt a great finality. I banged on the door again.

"Please Tom."

Eventually I walked away with a heaviness so great, that knew I would carry with me for the rest of my life.

Chapter 48

I managed to regain my composure by the time I re-emerged
outside and met up with Lady Sinclair and Charlotte. I had no
intention of going home with them as I very much needed to be
alone and come to terms with everything that had happened.
I hastily made excuses about needing fresh air and bade them
farewell as they got into the carriage.
My head was exploding. I kept repeating to myself my
conversation with Tom and wondering how I could make right
what was so helplessly wrong. I had been in so many scrapes and
situations and now I felt like I was trapped in a box from which I
could not escape. I paused for a moment and sat down on a stone
pillar on the roadside. I hadn't realised, but I had walked all the
way down the Strand from the law courts and was now almost at
The Embankment. The streets were dusty and horses trotted by,
their heads low and blinkered as they pulled their carriages. I
turned and looked up the hill and wondered if they had released
Tom yet and if he would be coming down this road and past me.
Should I run back? Should I try to plead with him once again?
I wondered when his memory had returned. Had he been sitting
there in the witness box eyeing me with contempt this whole
time? If he had remembered, why had he not spoken up and
accused me? Was he just obeying James advice or did he really
care for me?
I felt most irritable and over energised. I continued to walk at a
brisk pace down to the river. There was a wind rising over the
Thames that cooled my burning cheeks in a very sobering way. A
lone gull squawked over head and circled a trawler pulling
downstream. There were a few small boats tied to the jetties
bobbing up and down in the wake of a larger boat.

My mind refused to clear despite the myriad of distractions around me. Bicycles whizzed past, children ran and squealed, pedlars called out to passersby to sell their wares.
I walked amongst them, brushing shoulders and loosely dripping tears of self pity.
I tiptoed right up to the edge of the bank and stood with my toes curling over the paved slabs. I stared down into the dark water watching, motionless.

"Miss you'd best step back, you'll be falling in if you're not careful!"

"Miss d'you hear me?"
I looked across startled and roused from my aberration.
A boatman sat in his rowing boat looking up at me.

"D'you need a ride miss? Across the river or up west?"

"Yes" I nodded, and walked a little way down the bank to some steps that led down to where I could climb into his rowing boat.

"Was worried miss thought you might fall.....or jump?"
I hoisted my skirts in one hand so as not to get them damp and the boat boy offered his hand to me as I stepped onto the rocky little boat.
I sat down on the wooden seat.

"Where to miss?"

"I didn't know." I shrugged my shoulders.

"Anywhere I suppose."

"Like a little tour of London? Houses of Parliament? St Paul's?"

"Yes thank you that would be lovely."
He was nonplussed, but nonetheless bothered as long as he got his tuppunce for the fare.
He dipped the long oars into the river as he inhaled deeply. It made a deep plunk sound as it hit the water then sashayed along and glided up river.

He exhaled as he stretched back, one eye watching me ever so suspiciously and assuming that I didn't realise what he was doing. The breeze over the river was quite chilling and I could feel the heat and stinging in my eyes subsiding as we gained pace and reached a less busy waterway. The late autumn sun was dancing on the waves and glinting shimmering rays into my eyes. I squinted and raised my hand over my forehead.

"So what's a young lady like you doing all alone up on the banks?"

I ignored him and gave him a false smile indicating that I did not wish to engage in any kind of conversation.

"We sees all types down here, rivers a funny place. Sometimes they goes up there to the great bridges and jumps off. We have to pull them out. Not much fun that isn't. Don't think about us do they? Just concerned with jumping in, don't give a thought for us poor sods whose have to drag their bodies all heavy with water back to the sides. And no thanks we don't get for doing it neither!"

I smiled at his complete lack of articulation and grammar.

"All rights for you to laugh it's no pretty sight! When I saw you I thought you might be one of them ones who goes jumping in." Funny, I had never even contemplated doing anything like that. I had struggled so much in my life that every fight made me feel that I was coming closer to achieving my goals and I still had so much that I wanted to do.

So would I have to do everything alone now? How could I win back Tom? He had just eased his way into my life as my protector. Even now when he had stood on the brink of being accused of murder he said nothing to incriminate me. Still my protector, my rock. Why could I not have been kinder to him? Why was I so jealous of my own shadow?

A flock of geese landed, skidded on the water and settled on the undulating current. Dockers carrying bales on their shoulders shouted out to one another, their voices amplified and carried by the wind.

"It's getting chilly now can we head back to Westminster."

"Oh so you have got a tongue." He said sarcastically.

His right arm pulled the oar at a forty five degree angle into the water, he pulled it continuously till the boat had turned around and we were facing the other way. It was getting late and I wanted to get back before Lady Sinclair got worried about me. I felt now that I could face everyone without being afraid to cry and show emotions that neither I nor anyone at the Sinclair household had seen before. Much of my despair had turned to anger. How dare Tom call me my father's daughter! He was a man that I despised, someone that wanted to disinherit and get rid of me. And, I was not evil. I was a survivor and that's all I had been guilty of.

I was sure that in time Tom would see sense, how could he not, it was just a momentary burst from him that he was probably right now regretting.

The boat pulled into a little enclosure and I paid the boat boy two pennies. He nodded in appreciation and reaffixed his grey little cap upon his head so that it covered his ears and kept out the wind that was gradually rising and rocking all the boats precariously.

I hailed a pony trap and made my way back to Inverness Gardens.

"So you are back young lady?"

Lady Sinclair was waiting by the front door.

"I've just seen off James Foster. I think he was waiting for you to return."

"Oh dear I'm sorry." I said apologetically.

"But don't worry my dear I had a nice long chat with him and we've sorted things out."

Lady Sinclair had a way of saying things in riddles and this was one that I could not quite follow.

"I'm sorry Lady Eleanor but what exactly did you sort out with him?"

"Why exactly what we discussed the other day."

"I beg your pardon."

"Oh Alice you are so slow sometimes!"

I was trying to remain composed but I really had no idea what she was talking about.

"The other day when you asked me what I would give if we found the lad that saved Archie."

"Oh yes Lady Eleanor of course. Well now you have been able to give him what he gave to you, his life in exchange for saving Archie's."

"Well that too."

I eyed her apprehensively.

"So what else did he deserve?"

"Alice you are most uncharitable! I gave him a substantial reward for all his unconditional efforts."

"How substantial?" I was getting irritated now. I didn't want Tom having any substantial reward.

"I gave him one hundred and fifty pounds!"

"What!" I almost shrieked.

"You can't give a common lad that sort of money, why that is outrageous. Have you lost leave of your senses?"

"Alice!" Lady Sinclair gave me a most displeased look at being called a fool.

"How dare you girl! This was done mainly on your recommendation I'll have you remember. It was you that said there was no price high enough to pay for saving Archie's life."

"I never said that."

"Do not contradict me. Anyway my financial decisions are nothing of your concern. I thought that you would be pleased with my generosity seeing as how fond you are of your young cousin Archie."

"Yes of course Lady Eleanor, I apologise for my insolence."

"Hmm"

Lady Sinclair tutted and walked away just as cook walked in.

"Mr Foster has returned my lady"

"Well I suppose it's you that he'll want to see." And with that she walked out her head aloof still disgusted with my outburst. James tapped lightly on the door then let himself in.

I welcomed him with a warm smile and he took my hand gently and kissed it. We went to sit on the window seat facing the garden.

"It's been quite a day" he began

"Oh yes" I agreed.

"I was a little shocked when I came over earlier this afternoon and had a brief meeting with Lady Sinclair." James continued.

"Yes I know she's told me all about it, and I agree it is a bit shocking."

"Did she tell you everything?" James enquired, his lip quivering slightly and his eyebrow arching as he formed his question.

"Well what else is there?" I replied intrigued.

"Well you must know about the money."

I nodded.

"She wanted to give him three hundred pounds but I told her that was a ridiculous sum for a boy like that. Finally she agreed after much persuasion to drop it to one hundred and fifty."

"Is she out of her mind?" I scowled.

James laughed.

"Well it's certainly an interesting family! After we agreed on the amount she then insisted that she wanted him to receive a job and work for her here in the house on a very substantial yearly income. She said that she wanted to make sure that he was adequately provided for."

"And I hope you did a good job of talking her out of that?"

"No, she wouldn't hear of it and said that I had to make the offer to him. I've just been to the inn where he is staying and broken the news to him."

"Oh" I tried to hide my surprise.

"He has accepted the cash as one might have expected, but he has flatly refused the job and has asked me to deliver a message to you personally."

My heart was fluttering like a bird.

"What did he say?"

"Alice, I don't really know what has gone on before and quite honestly I do not want to be told. However he has asked me to tell you in no uncertain terms that he will be leaving London for good and wishes never to see you again…"

I gasped and tried to hold my breath so my eyes wouldn't well with tears.

"Is that all that he said?"

"He was very angry Alice, he's been beaten and caged like an animal, he's lost his sister and he feels betrayed. Yes, he said other words but none which I would be prepared to repeat to a lady."

"Where is he now?"

"I cannot tell you."

"Please James."

He shook his head looked me directly in the eye and said.

"No Alice it's all over now."

Chapter 49

Several days had passed and still there had been no word from Tom. I had totally dismissed from my mind the possibility that he would reject me, and refused to believe that he would not come crawling back apologising for his haughty attitude.
I learnt from James that he had received his reward money and had gone away. I was not to be told where he had gone and I didn't want to make a fool of myself by continuously asking where he was. He knew where to find me, and when he was good and ready I was sure he would be there, whether I would was a completely different matter.
I had plenty of time to contemplate my thoughts and now knew that there was only one direction for me to take. I had carefully hidden inside one of my favourite books the address that the priest had given me and even though my mind had been over occupied in the last few weeks, I did still think about whether my mother was alive and if I could be brave enough to go off and find her.
I had always anticipated being accompanied on my journey but now it seemed that I would have to go alone.
I sat on my bed and opened the book. There, was the smoothed out paper with the Irish address neatly written in black ink. My fingers touched the words skimming over the paper and I knew that I would never really know myself until I found my mother.
I would have to get ferry tickets and plan this trip quite carefully. No more running away in the middle of the night like a thief. I would tell the Sinclair's that I was going home and in a way that was no lie because I felt that was where I really was going.
There was one other thing that I had to do and that was to speak to James. I had actually become quite fond of him and respected the way that he rarely succumbed to his sarcastic comments of

previous. He knew a great deal about me and had not betrayed any of my confidences, I therefore felt that I could trust him and maybe was ready to tell him just a little more.

"James?" I said as I sipped my tea in the little tea rooms that he had taken me to in the West End.

"Yes my dear Alice?"

"I don't know quite how to say this, so I just will."

"Yes"

"Well we have been through quite err turbulent times over the last few months and at times I have behaved quite badly, yet still you wish to spend time with me and take me out courting." James crossed his left knee over his right and pulled down his brown waistcoat. He eyed me with a slight frown over his brow that gave me no indication of whether his thoughts were good or bad.

"That is true Alice, you have been quite deplorable. However I find you a fascinating person whose qualities far outweigh all the negative attributes that you possess."

For a fleeting second I wondered whether my positive attributes were the four hundred thousand pounds that I had inherited?

"So what are these qualities that you admire so much?"
He smiled and kissed my hand.

"Alice it is like walking into the most beautiful fragrant garden and asking which flower smells sweeter than another. It is impossible to say."

"But what about the weeds in this garden? Do they not deter you?"

"No not at all." He chuckled.

"Weeds can be dug out and destroyed leaving just the prettiest blooms."

"Very eloquent." I congratulated.

"The truth Alice is that I find you quite unique. There is no one as intelligent, lovely and contained as you. You are furlongs ahead of all the other fillies and there is no doubt that you will win my race.

"You flatter me too much James" I blushed.

"Alice you must realise that all other girls are like Charlotte. Spoilt young women just concerned with their hair and clothes and incapable of having an intelligent conversation about important matters in the world."

"But James that is very modern, expecting a woman to be your equal. Surely that is why gentlemen have their clubs from which women are banned."

"It may be modern but I think it ridiculous that we have a queen on the throne that rules with more devotion and common sense than any previous male monarch. Even Elizabeth the first, was probably the best monarch before our present queen."

"I never knew that you were so in favour of women's rights?"

"Yes. Why should women not be given opportunities and be able to use their brains. You were well educated and well read and look how intelligent you turned out!"

"Well actually, I wasn't that well educated."

"Rubbish! You know about the world and places and peoples elsewhere, why I've even seen you reading in French!"

"It was all self taught. I spent a lot of my former years bed bound with no other pastime other than to read books that may have been a little too advanced and inappropriate for a young girl."

"Fascinating! I am just intrigued with you Alice I find you quiet extraordinary."

I looked up, he was gazing at me with absolute adoration. I had never felt so valued before. Even with Tom I had just been a girl.

He had never spun a web of words around me like this before and I liked it.

"Would you like some more tea?"

James broke the silence.

"No thank you I couldn't drink anymore."

"Another cake?"

"No, a girl has to look after her waistline but I suppose since I'm not like those shallow girls then yes, I will have another one."

And with that I reached to take one off the cake stand placed before us, oozing with a tempting selection of fresh cakes and pastries.

"James I have a dilemma that I need to tell you about and I hope that you will be able to understand and support me." I said very seriously.

"Yes of course." He sat up straight.

"As you know I was brought up in Somerset on my grandfather's estate that was left to me. I didn't know that I was illegitimate and that my father had another family. Recently I believed that I was an orphan after the death of my father."

"Yes do go on"

"Well it transpires that my mother and Lady Eleanor were best friends and when I was born my mother was banished and sent away from me."

"How intriguing."

"Well, I found all this out from the priest where my mother was sent."

"And is she still there?"

"I don't know, there's only one way to find out though."

"But Alice it will take months to write to these institutions and try to trace documents of people's whereabouts. As a solicitor I know how long all this litigation takes."

"I wasn't thinking of writing."

"Oh, what then?"

"I want to go. I want to find her."

"But you can't! You're just a young girl you cannot go traipsing off to some strange place."

"James you yourself said not only a few minutes ago how I was different. Well because I am, I will go. After all I came here all alone; I came to London to find the truth about my father now I have to do the same for my mother."

James seemed very contemplative as he looked at me not quite being able to make out just who or what I was. I could only smile and take his hand and reassure him that I was not mad but quite sane and courageous.

"I will have to consider this." He finally managed to stumble.

"Would you like me to take you home now?"

I reckoned that we had said and done enough for one day and that at least I had been open and honest with James. I felt that I owed him a bit more truth because we had rekindled our relationship with a completely new slate. I did feel so much better about this and being with James had actually helped my anger with Tom to subside.

We walked home. The days were getting shorter and it was getting dark by late afternoon. We hailed a cab and slowly trotted in silence all the way back to Inverness Gardens.

Outside the house James leapt from the carriage and helped me down. He looked at me with that thinking frown etched across his brow.

"Alice I will think very carefully about what we have talked about this afternoon. I would very much like to help you in your quest."

"Thank you James. Will I see you tomorrow?"

"Of course, but not till late as I have much work at the office to attend to."

"Till tomorrow then."

I stepped along the path and towards the front door.

Once I was back in my room I felt that I had to start to pack and begin sorting through my clothes. Ireland was a cold rainy place and I would have to take only the warmest of my clothes. I was excited. Something within me was bursting to leave and get on with my journey. I had been in London for too long and my departure was way overdue. Since recovering from my illness I seemed to have become very anxious to do whatever I had to do right there and then, even when that clearly was not the right move to make.

At dinner that evening I made my announcement.

"Leave? Again?"Repeated Archie

"Alice seems to be a bit of indecisive." Smirked Albert.

"But we like having you around you're like another big sister." Added Emily and Jane.

"Children." Began Lady Sinclair, Alice is not dying she will still be around, but she has her own home to return to. Besides we could go on a trip and visit her one day. Wouldn't that be nice? We've never been to your aunts' estate in Norfolk!"

I could feel the colour draining from my face. I sat quite still feeling nauseated at the thought of the Sinclair's turning up at a fictitious address.

"Hmm" I nodded speechless.

After dinner Charlotte stopped me in the hall.

"Are you sewing with us this evening?"

"No I thought I would read for a while."

"Oh."

"Is everything all right Charlotte?"

"Well, yes sort of."

We walked into the drawing room together and sat down. Then Charlotte began to sob.

"When you first came here Alice I hated you. Stealing my gentleman friends, my clothes and everything else that you did." I was marginally insulted but said nothing to exacerbate her distressed state.

"But then you became my very best friend as well as my cousin and I will feel your loss so deeply..."

"I will return."

"But will you?"

"Yes. Now don't you fret. I shall write too. We can write lovely long letters to each other."

After the words left my mouth I remembered that I could write to her but where would I receive letters?

I was touched by Charlotte, my sister, who didn't know that I was her sister. Maybe when all this was over I would return to London.

But for now the road ahead looked uncertain and I didn't know where this would really, all end.

Chapter 50

I handed my small valise up to the cab driver who rests it on top of the carriage. I then turn to the hoard of eager faces waiting to see me off. Archie is holding my hand tightly as he has done since breakfast this morning. He has definitely been the saddest and the hardest to say goodbye to.

The wind rustles and sheds a load of leaves that twirl like a russet cascade on to the road below. The horses stamp their feet scattering the foliage in frustration of having waited so long to begin the journey.

"Thank you so much for allowing me to be your guest and treating me like family for such a long time." I say to Lady Eleanor as I peck her cheek to say goodbye.

"Nonsense child you are family and we will miss you very much."

She replies dabbing a tear from her cheek with her handkerchief.

"Oh Alice" Charlotte has thrown her arms around my neck and is holding on so tightly I fear I will choke. Tears are rolling down her cheeks and dripping onto the back of my neck leaving my collar all damp.

"I shall miss you so much" She sobs.

Emily and Jane continue the chorus of wails as I hug them both. I then turn to Albert who gives me a nod.

I climb up the first step into the carriage. There's a gentle tug on my hand then a whisper.

"Can I come with you?"

"I'm sorry Archie, but I've got to go home." Why can't I come to your home? You've been to my home."

"One day maybe." I lie.

He says nothing but the bottom lip begins to slightly protrude and his eyes turn a watery blue shade. He rubs them furiously so no one will see him crying like a girl.

"Please don't go away forever like papa."

This time I take him in my arms and squeeze him so tight that he loses his battle with the tears which are escaping faster than he can stall them.

"I will be back don't worry."

Too distressed to linger I close the carriage door behind me. The driver lashes his whip and the horses begin to trot out of Inverness gardens and away from this life that I've known in London.

Everyone had been there and I supposed that maybe I was loved by my family after all, even though they were all unaware of the real bonds that connect us.

There was one face that was very apparently missing as I knew he would be.......James.

The previous day had been quite traumatic as I had explained to him that until I had established who I truly was I was in no position to belong to anyone else. It had not gone down well.

"I don't see what one has to do with another!"

"It just does. I need to establish my identity."

"But if you love me and want to be my wife why can't we do this thing together?"

"Because we just can't."

"So you don't love me?"

"I do, but I'm not ready to give you this commitment."

"Fine have it your way! You always do what you want anyway!"

At that he had stormed out.

I had hoped that he would turn up for my departure but he had not. In some ways I was relieved not to have had the confrontation at such an emotional time. In other ways I was confused because I felt that I would really miss him and just wanted to know that I had his support and approval for what I was about to do.

The horses' hooves fell silent and the heavy roll of the wheels screeched to a halt as we arrived at the coach station. The driver handed me down my bag and I went to find out from the ticket desk where I should wait for the Holyhead coach

"Bay eleven"

I came out and scanned the station looking up at the numbers. Only one other passenger was waiting at eleven. As I approached I realised that it was not a passenger at all.

"Hello Alice."

"Good day"

"I didn't want to say goodbye at the house. It was too impersonal."

"I understand."

"So you really are going?"

"Yes, are you angry with me?"

"I was. But I'm not now. I've realised that when you make your mind up to do something then it has to be done and no one or no situation will make you change your mind or be different. But that's just you Alice and I don't really want to change your spirit."

I smiled.

"Yes you do!" I teased.

James took me in his arms, his hand stroking my hair. He kissed my cheek as he released me.

"Please just come back and say "yes".

"I don't know how long I will be." I said seriously.

"I know."

"But I will write and let you know where I am and what is happening."

"I would like that very much."

A coach swung around the corner.

"Holyhead coach!"

"I have to go."

James reached for my bag and handed it to the driver. James held my hand and suddenly my chest felt tight and heavy.

"Goodbye Alice, I love you. Come back and marry me."

I smiled back a tear.

James leaned forward and kissed me softly on my lips.

"Coach is leaving, you coming or not miss?"

My head bent so as not to look at the man with my red swollen eyes I climbed aboard and took a seat.

As the coach pulled away I saw James blow me a kiss and wave. I felt totally wretched.

Chapter 51

It was dusk when I opened my eyes. I didn't realise that it was possible to sleep so long and almost felt embarrassed when I bumped into the landlady on the staircase whilst still wearing my night clothes.

"Will you be after feeling better my love? Would you like me to be bringing you up a nice bowl of soup?"

I understood the word soup, and by now I was ravenous even though this very morning when I had stepped off the boat, I had sworn that I would never eat again. I would have to get used to this Irish lilt, it was very difficult, especially when they spoke so quickly. I could only get one word in ten!

Immediately after I dressed there was a knock on the door and there stood the landlady a fairly tall woman with her hair neatly tied in a grey bun an apron around her waist. She was holding a tray with steaming soup and a fresh baked roll. It smelled divine; I welcomed her in and made room on the little table for the tray.

"So what'll be bringing a young lady like yourself to our green shores all alone then?" She offered without looking up.

"Well I need to find someone." I replied simply.

"This is a big country. And how were you hoping to do that then?

"I need to get to Kinsale and find a place called St Theresa's convent."

"Oh I see." She began faffing around and avoided looking at me.

"So you'll be one of those girls then?"

"Sorry?"

"How far along are you?"

"I beg your pardon?"

"Well girls only want St Theresa's for one thing. They go there drop off a little bundle and then leave. Suppose you're going to do the same?"

"No, I'm sorry I don't understand." I was quite unaware of what she meant, then the penny dropped and I gasped in amazement.

"Oh Mrs Murphy oh no! I'm not pregnant. No, I'm going there to find someone who disappeared an awfully long time ago." She looked me up and down and especially at my tightly fitted waist which showed no glimmer of expansion.

"So who are you after going to find? No one stays around there for very long."

"Err a relative." I replied bluntly, a little intimidated by all the direct questions that these country people loved to ask.

Mrs Murphy sensing that I didn't want to answer any more of her questions stood silent whilst I began to drink my soup.

"Do you know how I would get there Mrs Murphy?" I asked politely, scared that I may have offended her.

"Well there is a coach service from the next town and you would probably have to get a carriage there or walk, but with that heavy bag I think you'd be best with the carriage."

"Do you know how often they go from the next village?"

"Hmm, you'd be having to be going from Rosslare to Wexford then it might be a direct bus or you may have to change. It's a fair journey mind."

"I don't think that puts me off, as long as there are no boats, I'll be fine." I laughed.

That evening I went for a short walk around the town. It was good to be outside and feel the air on my face. I felt so much better than I had done this morning when I had arrived.

It was cold so I didn't stay out too long, just long enough to fill my lungs with the salty, fishy air.

I stepped back into Mrs Murphy's. There was a roaring fire in the corner and several guests were tucking into plates of stew. She saw me and pulled up another chair.

"Plate of Irish Stew for you dear?"

"What else do you have?"

"Nowt! Just Irish stew."

Well it smelt good and everyone else seemed to be enjoying it so I agreed to a plateful.

"Come and sit near Mr O'Leary dear" She moved my chair closer to the fire.

"He knows everything about transport and getting about; he'll help you get to where you're going.

By that time I had finished my stew, which was really rather good indeed. I had even cleaned my plate with great wedges of Irish soda bread, and had been informed as to the whole transport systems for the south east coast of Ireland. Mr O'Leary was one of those village know it alls who was only too willing to show off to someone new that he knew it all. It was superb. I now had a very robust plan and if I set off early the next morning I was due to be in Kinsale by mid day, the day after next.

I was up well before the cockerel sang his early morning call and had been the first to get on the stage coach to Wexford. The journey was relatively short as we travelled through fields of shivering sheep and cows.

From Wexford I changed coaches and we travelled south and along the coast, past small villages where people stopped and stared like they had never seen a horse and carriage. We arrived at our night stop in a place called Youghal. The inn was basic but lovely, warm and cosy and I slept well, eagerly anticipating our arrival the next day.

This time I needed the cockerel to wake me. I had to dress very warmly as the strong south wind was blowing quite fiercely and depleting all the trees of their foliage.

I watched every blade of grass and every hedge that we passed wondering if eighteen years ago my mother had travelled this very same route and if she had seen the things that I saw. It would have been very different for her knowing that she had been sent away forever to a new and sparse life so different from the one that she had been brought up to know. I wondered how scared she would have been. I wondered if she had also hated the Irish Sea. In no time we had arrived in Kinsale. The horses stopped outside the port where a few boats bobbed up and down in the wind. People were huddled up in their cloaks and shawls as they ran through the streets to get out of the rain that now began to pour down and resonate on the cobbled paving stones.

From the coach I could see an inn and decided to get my bag and make a run for it. Despite the fact that it was only about thirty yards I still managed to get soaked by the time I had walked over the threshold.

"Room for tonight please?" I asked

"Just one night then?" Came the reply.

"Well might be a few days, I'm not sure it depends if I find what I'm looking for."

The innkeeper raised a very bushy grey eyebrow.

"What you looking for then lassie?"

"A relative." I answered simply.

It then occurred to me that if I wanted to find my mother I would have to stop being so guarded and defensive and start asking questions around the town, otherwise all these years later no one was going to remember.

"Well actually I am looking for my aunt, her name was Isobel Lavelle and she came here about eighteen years ago to become a novice in the convent."

He shook his head.

"Can't say that name means anything and of course I wouldn't know any of the nuns names because they all get changed when they're ordained. You'd best go up there and speak to the reverend sister, she'll tell you a bit more I suppose."

"Is it far?"

"Nope ten minutes up at the top of the hill."

I paid for two days of lodgings and went to put my bag in my room. My room was at the top corner of the house so it had a window to the front and one to the back. To one side there was a little fireplace that was well stocked. I looked out of my window towards the sea which now seemed quite calm even though the tiny raindrops were making it glisten. From the back window I could see the convent high on the top of the hill. I wondered for a brief second if my mother could be there, if this really was the end of my journey.

The sun suddenly broke over a cloud and the rain stopped pelting down. There was no point waiting and deliberating any further. Ten minutes later I stood outside the convent.

It was a very big building, stone built and imposing like a dragon guarding the village. It seemed painfully silent as I stood outside wondering where I would find a bell to ring. Before I had time to ponder any further the door creaked open and standing alone in the enormous doorway was an old solitary nun.

"May I help you my dear?" The voice was soft and almost squeaky.

I stood tall and squeezed my hand tight till my nails dug into my palm. I was feeling terribly nervous.

"I would like to see the mother superior…please."

"Please come in. I'm afraid that the holy mother doesn't see the young girls that arrive here, we have other nuns that take care of them."

"Oh no, I'm not here for that reason." I quickly interrupted.

"I need some information about a girl that was here about eighteen years ago."

"Well do you dear? Well I'm sorry I don't think we will be able to help you with that!"

She turned to reopen the door that we had just entered.

"No please don't send me away. I have come from very far away and I desperately need to find out where this person is. You are my only hope!"

The old lady looked at me with an expressionless face.

"We are here to help those wayward girls who have lost their way in the world; we are not an information service. Good day."

The door was open behind me, but I wasn't leaving. I wondered why she was being so cruel and not even giving me a chance to ask about my mother.

"What's all this commotion?" Two more elderly nuns had now appeared on the scene.

"This young girl is here to ask questions about someone who was here many years ago. We haven't got time for this nonsense. I told her to leave but she won't!"

"You must go." Added one of the others.

"Please leave now!" And they began forcibly pushing me through the door.

"But I'm pregnant!" I declared.

They stopped in their tracks.

"Oh, did she say she was pregnant sister Margaret?"

"No!" The nun looked at me angrily with a sinister expression in her eyes.

"Well that's different then you'd better come in, you shameless sinner."

I breathed a sigh of relief. It was difficult to reason with these people but there must be someone within these walls that would be a little more tolerant and understanding. I would have to play along if this was the way they wanted it to be. There was no way that I was going to resign and just leave empty handed.

They bundled me up some stairs, through long corridors and up and down winding passageways until we reached a room where another girl was on her hands and knees cleaning.

"This is Constance; she will be sharing a room with you. She is nearly ready to have her baby and you will be able to take over her duties when she does. Constance show our new girl what to do. What did you say your name was girl?"

"I didn't, but its Alice."

"Good Alice we'll get you scrubbing like everyone else. There's always plenty of work to do, you have to repay our charity and pray for God's forgiveness for your terrible sins."

At that the door closed and I was left alone with the girl who looked no older than fourteen.

Constance got up and I could see that she was very heavily pregnant. She was red faced and sweating.

"Shouldn't you be lying down or something?"

"Oh no, I daren't." She replied in a perfect English accent.

I smiled." At last someone that I can understand!"

She laughed.

"How long have you been here?" I asked.

"Nearly four months, my step father sent me here. I'm *visiting an aunt*. But it's all right my visit is nearly over and I can go home soon."

"But what about your baby?"

"It'll be adopted."

"What about the father?"

She bit her lips and turned ashen.

"Constance?"

She shook her head.

"What is it?"

"Well that's why I don't want to go home; maybe I'll just run away somewhere."

"Why?"

"He said it I mustn't tell. I couldn't tell mama anyway. I never knew I would have a baby. He said it wouldn't happen. Then it did and I was sent away and punished! He should have been sent away and punished."

"Who?"

"You won't tell?" She pleaded.

"No."

"My step father. He came to my room every night for six months, then this happened. Told me it was normal between step fathers and children and it was our secret and I wasn't to tell. Didn't say that I was going to be sent here and whipped and turned into a scullery maid."

"You're whipped?"

"Yes, penance of Christ."

"Oh I'm so sorry." I sat down alarmed.

"How many girls are here?"

"Not many, about eight at the moment sometimes there are more."

"Constance I'm here because I need to find some information about someone that was here a long time ago. Do you know who I could speak to? Those witches that brought me in were despicable. Is there anyone who is kind that will listen to me?"

Constance shook her head.

"I'm sorry Alice, if you thought they were bad you should meet the rest. They seem to revel in punishing us wayward girls. There is no kindness or compassion in this place. If you can leave then go, they'll break you here and you'll be repenting for your sins for the rest of your life."

"Can I get out?"

"Yes you can climb out of the window."

Just then the door reopened and half a dozen nuns stood there glaring at me.

Chapter 52

I was trapped. Constance looked at me sadly as if she knew what imminent troubles lay ahead.

Six wrinkled, angry faces eyed me like a criminal. The fear and anxiety that I had felt in the court during Toms case was nothing compared to the terror that now overcame me.

They surrounded me like vultures, grabbed my arms and marched me from the room. I was powerless to resist and didn't dare to object, after all these were nuns, holy women of God. Surely any disrespect would be blasphemy.

I was taken down to the cellars at the very bottom of the convent. It reeked of stale muskiness and urine. A very limited amount of light came from a barred window at ground level.

"Take off your dress and put on this!" They handed me a torn, grey cloth smock.

"But........"I began.

A hand swiped across my face before I could say another word. Stunned I obeyed without question. They then shackled my hands into two ropes suspended from the ceiling.

"Why.......?

This time a wooden rosary cut across my cheek.

"Don't talk you whore!"

They began to beat me with rosaries, with birches, screaming the foulest obscenities as they did so.

"Let this be a penance for your terrible sins of the flesh!"

"This is what you get for fornication!"

"You are an evil sinner, whose soul shall be excommunicated!"

Each lash accompanied by searing words till it all became a haze and my body became limp and hung by my hands which were still tied to the ropes. I was aware of the sockets of my arms pulling and tugging. I thought they would tear from my body.

Then they cut me down and I fell to a heap on the floor.

"Get up!" They screeched

"Get up" they kicked.

Through bleary eyes I could make out two of the nuns coming towards me, I instinctively retracted but they dragged me by my arms and pulled me back up the stairs and through the building till I was back at the little room with Constance.

After the door slammed I was aware of a thin course blanket being pulled over my shoulders as I lay prone on my bed.

"There, there Alice, you'll be just fine. They do that to all the girls when they come. It makes some of us so bad that we lose our babies. Sometimes the girls don't come back either. They don't like us. Call us all the devils children, worst sinners ever created, an abomination before God."

"I cannot believe their cruelty. I never would have thought that anyone could behave like that, much less a nun!"

Constance looked wistfully straight ahead and into the palpable air that lingered with so much pain and sadness.

"You just get used to it and learn to behave the way they want, so that you don't get into trouble."

I was shocked. I hurt so badly and I hadn't even done anything wrong. The funniest part was that I had lied my way into this black pit. I had to escape. There was no possibility that I was going to stay. I was convinced that my mother could not be here. She would not inflict such pain on young girls when she herself knew of all the heartache that they endured without the beatings. It was enough to be abandoned and disgraced, torn from your families and friends.

"Constance will you help me escape?"

"They'll be watching you now. All the girls try to get away when they realise what this place is all about and when they catch you it's even worse! That really gets them cross!"

357

"Constance I have something to tell you. You aren't going to believe this, but I'm not pregnant."
She turned to me in disbelief.
"What? Why would you come here then?"
"I need to know that I can trust you."
"Yes of course Alice. What is it? Why are you here?"
"I was an illegitimate child and my mother was sent away and allegedly sent to this place. I've been trying to find her."
"Oh my God I can't believe what you are telling me! Your mother cannot be one of these nuns everyone here is evil and old and your mother would probably only be in her late thirties."
"Yes I thought that too."
"You're best going to the village and asking people there what they know, that's if she stayed here. Where else would she have gone? Was there any other family or somewhere she could have gone to stay?"
"I don't think so. She would have been all alone."
We went to sleep and I tried to fight back the tears of anger and frustration as I remembered the humiliation of being whipped with strings of rosary beads, which the girls here in the convent had been forced to make. It also brought back the very raw memory of Tom when he was beaten by my father in the barn and how he had suffered. It was almost as if I was being punished for all those bad things that I had caused either directly or indirectly in the past.
The next morning we were woken at about five by bells ringing.
"What's going on?"
"Its prayer time." Constance told me.
"Why so early, why do we have to pray?"
"Alice we have a lot of atoning to do or so they think. It's not something that we have a choice about. Come on hurry or you'll be in trouble again."

I pulled my aching and sore body out of my hard lumpy bed. As we rushed to dress I got a fleeting look at my face in the mirror. I was covered in bruises and my left eyelid had swelled so much that it almost closed my eye.

With no time to be horrified, Constance dragged me by the arm and we ran down the corridors until we reached the chapel. There kneeling amongst the pews sat rows of girls and in the front were the nuns.

"Is this everyone in the convent?" I whispered.

"Alice please don't talk. We can get into very big trouble if we are caught."

"Constance!" Boomed a very large voice.

"Oh no!" She froze and I could see tears welling in her eyes. When prayers were over, the sister with the booming voice came over.

"Constance you will come with me to the cellars to receive thirty lashes for disobedience. You will then sit at the penance table for your meals for the next two days where you will only receive cold water and stale bread!"

Constance glared at me and very slightly shook her head and I knew that meant say nothing or I would be joining her.

I scanned the church filled with empty broken girls and angry hollow nuns. There was no glimmer of warmth and certainly no love here. Not even the love of God.

I went back to my room unsure as to what I was supposed to be doing now. We all had chores but Constance was supposed to tell me what mine were. I would just have to wait till she returned. Twenty minutes later the door swung open and she was thrown back into the room. I picked her up; she was sweating profoundly and crying.

"I want to die. I cannot bear this. They can throw me in one of the unmarked graves out in the church yard. I cannot do this." She sobbed.

I put my arm around her and she sobbed over my shoulder. She felt very hot and heavy and even though I was sore and aching I still managed to ease her onto the bed. I went to get some water to clean the rosary wheals that were covering her back. I was horrified to see not only the damage they had just caused but the scars from previous beatings in every stage of repair.

"How often do they beat you?"

"As often as they want." Was her stark answer.

"What did you mean about the graves?" I questioned, curious about her strange comment.

She winced in pain.

"Sinners don't deserve graves. They have a mass grave for those that die here. Some girls die in childbirth as do babies and they all get buried out there. No headstone, nothing to remember that they ever existed. Doomed to purgatory as I will be soon."

"Constance don't say that you will be fine. You will go home soon."

"I'd rather die."

"Constance don't say that it's a sin!"

"Whose side are you on then?" She said sarcastically

I realised the absurdity of what I had said. I didn't believe in God. I had never been brought up to be fearful. I had gone with the Sinclair's to church every Sunday but that was a duty not a belief. Now here I was in God's house and felt that the doors were slammed shut on me and all these unfortunate girls that were here.

"Alice we had better start our chores or they'll be back. I have a plan though. If we scrub the floors in the dining room this morning we can do the kitchen floors this afternoon."

"Whys that a plan?"

"Kitchen gets deliveries on a Tuesday so the doors and gates will be open and you can slip out and escape."

"Oh Connie thank you, you are so clever and don't worry you'll be out of here too soon."

She didn't answer.

We went down to the scullery to get the buckets, cleaning rags and brushes to start our chores. We were both in a sorry state but Connie seemed very breathless and uncomfortable. Most of the time her face contorted and winced and I couldn't help but keep asking her if she was well.

"I'm used to being beaten, physically that is. It's just that I'm feeling quite sick today and a little strange."

"We finished our mornings work and went to the refectory for lunch. A thin broth and potatoes with bread was on the menu. I slipped my portion of bread inside my smock in order to give it to Connie later as she had been put on the penance table all alone with only some stale crusts to eat. I watched her, feeling so sorry for her. She was so young and had led such an unfortunate life yet she was accepting of her situation. I decided that I would have to come back for her after had found my mother.

"I saved you some bread." I whispered slipping it into her pocket as we went to get clean pails of water after lunch.

Connie was looking very pale.

We began scrubbing the floors. Suddenly her pail tipped over and she screamed.

"Connie!" I ran to her side.

"What is it?"

She was shaking and seemed consumed with pain.

"Is it the baby? Is it coming?"

"She looked up at me scared and fraught.

"Come on I'm taking you to the nuns, we need to get you help."

"No!" She shrieked.

"But what can I do? I need to get you help!"

"Yes but not the witches! I don't want them pawing me and touching me like I'm an animal!"

"Connie!"I began to cry as the area around her became awash with a mucousy red liquid.

"I must help you!"

"Just take me upstairs." We were both crying now. She clung to my hand and dug her fingernails so deep that I almost screamed out in pain at her next contraction.

We made it back to the room where she lay on the bed and began writhing in agony, saturating the sheets in sweat.

"Alice I'm going to die! I cannot take this pain!"

"I'm here don't worry, you won't die you will be fine. I'm going to help you." I reassured.

"Oh Alice" Her voice was quivering.

"I forgot. Go hurry please go the kitchen door will be open now. Go!"

I remembered my swollen face and the fact that I had to escape this dreadful place. I kissed Connie on the forehead and turned for the door. I then turned back and was horrified with myself for my blatant selfishness.

"No!" I rushed back to the bed.

"I'm not leaving you!"

Connie grabbed by another contraction looked at me incredulously. Once it had subsided she pushed me away.

"Go Alice or you won't be able to leave. You won't get another opportunity. Go!"

I shook my head. At that very moment Connie felt the urge to push and I lunged down to deliver her baby.

"Oh my gosh Connie its coming!"

She pushed again and this time a slithery blood stained baby fell into my arms. I wrapped a sheet around it and cradled it.

"It's a boy Connie it a lovely baby boy!"

At which point he began to wail and I placed him into Connie's arms.

The baby began to suckle and there was an overwhelming moment in that room when we were both exhausted but undeniably beaming at the wonderful bundle of life that Connie now held in her arms.

Even when the door opened after all the screaming, and the nuns came in, we couldn't help but feel very excited at this rare miracle that had just happened.

It wasn't until they took Connie and the baby away and the door closed on me with a heavy thud, that the reality hit me. I was now really trapped here.

Chapter 53

I have been so exhausted working in this dreadful convent that I have not had the time to devise how I am to escape. However once I regain some strength I have no doubt that I will. I know that my stubbornness and arrogance has unquestionably helped me to achieve my goals and however hopeless this one seems at the moment I am not daunted and know that I will soon be free. The days are so long and gruelling. We work like slaves from the first light of dawn till sundown when we have a very sparse supper and then too exhausted to care about our lumpy straw beds we just go to sleep.

I have seen Connie. I managed to spend some time with her when I slipped out of lunch early with most of my bread and vegetables hidden in my clothes. She was very grateful and completely ravenous. Her baby is so beautiful but poor Connie has been so sad and tearful at the thought of him being taken away from her. When she is feeding him she is in her own little private world with him. One that no one can intrude upon, not even me. She told me that she is trying to remember every breath that he takes, every gurgle that he makes so that she will always have that in her memory. He seems a very bonny baby and that will be good for him because then he may be chosen for a family and not have to stay in the orphanage forever. She says that she will come back for him one day and make sure he knows how much he is loved. It makes me wonder if my mother has the same love for me and is also waiting to be reunited.

The days that I have been here I have tried to scan every one of the nuns faces for any sign as to whether they could be my mother. I have attempted to find just one with any inkling of kindness that could even help me to discover any records or information dating back eighteen years, but it is all futile. The only definite information is that there are no records. Even the girls that have died here have not been recorded and the mass grave that Connie told me about has been confirmed by more than one person. I am convinced that my mother is not in this terrible place and my search will have to move on and further afield.

I have been most obedient at all times. I see the girls being punished for such minor things that it makes me nervous about doing anything that would take me down to those cellars again. I have only been here a few days but I am so humbled and changed as a result of it.

"Alice!"

I look up from the patch of floor that I have been scrubbing.

"Seems like you have yourself a visitor."

I am shocked. Who knows that I am here? I begin to stand.

"Get back down on your knees, finish this whole landing and staircase and then come down to the rectory."

I nod in agreement.

An hour later at record speed I finish my chores and head down to the rectory. I am bursting with anticipation and have gone through countless options in my mind. Could it be James? Has he followed me and has come to rescue me? Perhaps Tom, he was always there lurking in the background waiting like my guardian angel at times when I was in trouble. Or, perhaps the most bizarre solution, could it be my mother who heard that I was looking for her and has come to find me and claim me.

I knock on the rectory door eager to see the person waiting for me on the other side.

Sitting with the reverend mother is a grey haired man. He raises a bushy grey eyebrow and stares at me incredulously as if trying to recognise the girl behind all the bruises.

"Yes this is the girl, this is my niece and I have come to claim her." He announces a little anxiously.

He can see the relief in my eyes that someone has come, but what he does not see is the slight disappointment that he was not one of those that I anticipated.

"Well you had better go then." The Reverend Mother says flatly.

"And no telling tales or your friends back here may have to pay penance for you"

I understand what she is telling me and feel totally livid at the suggestion.

I walk out with the inn keeper anxious to know why he was minded to come and save me from this prison.

"Thank you so much!" I burst as soon as we have left the main door.

"Thought that there might be a problem. I mean you did say that you only wanted a room for two nights and then within five minutes you'd headed off for the convent leaving your bags and clothes and well I didn't mean to intrude but there was a great deal of money in your bag. So I reckoned that you must have come to some trouble when you didn't come back and there was only one place that I was sure that you had gone to."

"I cannot tell you how grateful I am and please don't apologise for going through my things, you must have thought that I had run off!"

We were back at the inn in no time.

"Shall I bring you up some hot water for a bath miss?"

"Yes and thank you so much for your kindness."

He handed me my small bag filled with my money.

"I didn't like to leave this just lying around."

I opened it and saw that nothing had been touched. I pulled out ten pounds.

"Thank you for your honesty too." I said as I handed him the note.

"Thank you miss, thank you so much. Miss would you like me to call the doctor for you?"

"No why?" I asked curiously.

He pointed to his face too embarrassed to say anything directly about the ghastly bruises covering my face.

"Oh."I put my hand to my cheek.

"He may be able to help, he's been in this town for a very long time."

"Thank you, but perhaps I could go to see him; I am feeling well in myself despite what may have happened to me."

I was scared to go into too much detail about the way that the girls were treated. It had been made clear to me by the Reverend Mother that if I said anything the girls would be punished and I couldn't do that to them.

I went up to my room; everything was exactly as I left it. I looked out of the little back window and could not believe that these last few days had been so eventful and bizarre. It seemed that I had only just been wondering what was within the convent walls and now almost miraculously I was back here saved by an inn keeper! In London my belongings and money would have been long gone and never recovered.

I had my bath and let myself sink into the warm water that soothed my aching body and helped ease my mind which was still amazed by all the events.

I rested and come down the stairs to be greeted by the inn keeper's wife who also offered her thanks for the money I had given them. She was a very delicate woman with one of those frames that seemed to be made of twigs.

"Was it very bad up there in the convent? We've heard the stories and it breaks my heart all those young girls with their babies and me and Mr Malley with none."

"Oh I'm sorry about that and no it wasn't so bad up there." I lied.

"It's all right Mr Malley told me what he heard the Reverend Mother tell you about telling tales. We all know it all right, but nobody likes to think about it, so we just pretend that it doesn't happen."

"But why do they have to be so wicked?" I blurted.

"It's just their way lovey. They think it's right to punish sinners. They think they have God's permission to act in the way that they do."

"But the girls they are punishing are being punished enough by their families by being sent here. It's not fair and the young men in question don't even get a word in their disfavour. That can't be right?"

"Women have always been second class and inferior, always have been always will be. It's just the way it is. You were born a girl and that was the beginning of the end."

I followed her into her parlour where she poured us two very big cups of sweet tea. We sat down and continued.

"But Mrs Malley it doesn't mean that we have to accept this. In London there are several movements calling themselves suffragettes and suffragists that are trying to change the way men think they can rule the roost. It's all about realising that we have a voice and should be heard."

"But who's listening to you dear? Its men and they all pretend to be deaf when it suits them!"

"I beg to differ. This is a modern world and new changes are happening. It just needs a few strong women to stand together and fight for what they believe in. Then girls like Constance up at

368

the convent won't be forced to give away their beautiful babies to orphanages"

"So who is Constance?"

"She's my friend, well sort of, I mean I only knew her for a few days but she was badly beaten for talking during mass and then she had the most beautiful baby boy with loads of dark hair and the biggest blue eyes. She's going to have to leave him in the orphanage and its going to break her heart to know that he won't grow up with the love of a mother."

Mrs Malley smiled at me and finished her tea.

"It's nice to have such a bright girl here. Mr Malley said that you are looking for your mother, I assume that you didn't find her in the convent?"

"No. Her name was Isobel Lavelle. Do you have any memory of someone round these parts with that name about eighteen years ago?"

She shook her head and looked at me almost apologetically.

"I wish I could help you but I can't. I'm fairly new to these parts have only been here for about ten years since I came down here to get married to Mr Malley"

"Oh."

"Never had any little ones just wasn't blessed with any."

"I'm sorry."

Her expression had changed to a most mournful one and I thought it best to change the subject even though an idea was brewing in my mind that I would try to approach later with her, when the timing was right.

"Could you tell me how I get to the doctors? Mr Malley thought he might be able to help me?"

"Yes of course Dr Dolan will know everyone and he should be a good contact for you in your search. It's the last house at the end of the village lane opposite the lake."

Not being one to waste any time I eagerly set off and wandered down the very green leafy road. It was cold and had been raining. I was pleased to pull my warm coat around my shoulders and shut out the wind. As I walked through the valley I was constantly aware of the presence of the huge convent up on the hill towering over the village like a very menacing demon.

I reached the doctors cottage all covered in ivy and tapped the brass knocker. A round woman very short and almost curved like a ball opened the door.

"I'm looking for the doctor." I announced.

"He's not here right now, who wants him?"

"My name is Alice, when will he be back?"

"He's gone to help the young Dr Dolan at the orphanage he'll probably be gone all evening. If it's not urgent come back tomorrow."

I nodded and was about to turn back.

"Where is the orphanage?"

"About half a mile up the hill take the steps is less muddy."

She closed the door and I set off down the path and up the steep steps towards my next destination, hoping with all my heart that very soon I would find some answers to my never ending questions.

Chapter 54

The orphanage seemed deserted. I had rung on the bell and knocked on the door but no one had come, so I had wondered around the building and was now peering through a window at the inhabitants inside.

A door flung open along the side and a face peered out.

"This way! You can come in through here!"

I walked in through the thin swinging door that creaked on a very rusty hinge in the wind.

"Thank you." I replied to the man that led me in.

"I've so much to do, don't know where to start. Here, take this bottle to the baby over there and then feed those five sitting in the cots, the food is in the big pot next to the stove."

"Oh" I was a little surprised at my sudden task but turned to the sounds of screaming hungry babies behind me, then continued with the job in hand. The fellow that had let me in ran around frantically giving out plates of food to some of the children.

"I'm so grateful for you coming up tonight, we weren't expecting you till tomorrow or the day after and we have been so inundated with work here. Its all been a bit much since my wife went away but she will be back tomorrow morning."

"I don't think you were expecting me, although I am quite happy to help if I can." I managed to edge in.

He turned towards me and stopped for second. In the dim light he hadn't looked at me and now he was eyeing me rather awkwardly.

"Aren't you the nurse that my wife wrote to come from Tipperary?"

"No, can't you tell from my accent?" I joked.

"Oh yes I suppose so. So why are you here?"

"I'm looking for Dr Dolan."

"I'm Dr Dolan."

"I'm looking for old Dr Dolan."

"That's my father he's lying down. He came up here, this evening to help but I sent him to bed when he started having dizzy spells, he should be all right by the morning, just needs some rest, he's been very overworked.

"Are you well?" He asked on seeing my bruised face.

"Yes quite well thank you."

"Where did that happen?"

"Up at the convent." I replied, momentarily forgetting the mother superiors words about telling tales.

"Oh" he nodded his head as if he had seen this a thousand times before.

"So" he began to ask slowly and tactfully.

"Have you just come out of that place?

I nodded silently.

"Are you looking for your baby? Did they take it away from you?"

"No, I didn't have a baby I was there by mistake…."

Before he had a chance to ask any more questions the whole dormitory let out a uniform wail for food and we all went to grab and feed whomever we could. Conversation being replaced by want and need.

An hour later there was silence in the room again and the twenty or so small bellies were comfortably full except one. The last cot on the row housed a little girl of about two years of age. She had blond curls, a round cherubic face and big blue eyes with long dark eyelashes. She sat like a patient pet waiting for her turn; because she hadn't cried as loud as the other children she had been overlooked.

"Oh poor little girl." I said, as she reached out her arms to me and I lifted her from the cot.

"Let's give you something to eat too, there's a little left in the pot.

"She's the quietest of all the children, she doesn't speak. In fact I've never actually heard a word from her." The doctor nodded .

I fed her and she took little mouthfuls off the spoon. Her eyes never left my face and I became quite endeared by this little one. The doctor watching me with her smiled and said.

"I think she likes you, don't you little Alice?"

"Alice?" I said flustered,

"*My* name is Alice!"

"Really? Well Alice meet Alice."

"Liss." Repeated the baby.

"Oh my goodness, she really must like you that's the first thing I've ever heard her say."

The child held tightly round my neck as I lifted her from the highchair and tried to put her back in her cot. She rested her head on my shoulder and instinctively I gave her a big hug.

"She's my wife's favourite too. Mrs Dolan will be back tomorrow she had to go off to Dublin for a few days to get some medicines and supplies. Quite honestly I didn't realise how hard she works till she went away. She gets up at five thirty to start cooking breakfast and doesn't finish till sometimes ten or eleven at night! Funny how you cannot appreciate someone till their not there anymore."

"Well tomorrows not far away, I'm sure she will be back soon. Anyway I am shattered. I will come back in the morning to see your father if that's all right."

I shook his hand.

"It was nice to meet you Dr Dolan."

"Alice, thank you for all your help. I couldn't have done it without you. You walked in just at the right moment."

373

"Well...." The words seemed to come out of my mouth naturally without much prior thought. "If I'm coming back in the morning would you like me to come up a little earlier and help you with the breakfasts?"

"Oh would you? I don't like to take liberties but that would be top of the world. You've seen what a zoo it can be at mealtimes!"

"Not a problem I will be here."

With that I totted off down the steps back to the inn in the village. I felt exhausted but I had a sense of purpose and felt surrounded by very good vibes that maybe tomorrow old Dr Dolan would be able to help me.

Mrs Malley woke me early in the morning as I had requested. I hurriedly got dressed and ate the toast and warm milk that she left on the tray for me. I then set off up the hill back to the orphanage. I had slept very well and felt fresh despite the early hour. When I arrived up at the orphanage, young Dr Dolan was in full flap.

"What do you mean we haven't got any more oats for breakfast? Cook this is your job you should have got this ready by now!"

"Well I've four loaves they can have bread and jam."

"Yes but that is for lunch! What shall we feed them for lunch then?"

"I doesn't know."

"Exactly! You are hopeless cook; you've only been employed here for a week and have only turned up twice. If I wasn't so busy I would fire you!"

"Mrs Dolan wouldn't be happy if you did that!"

"Mrs Dolan won't be happy when she sees how lazy you are! You were supposed to pick up supplies yesterday for the week but of course you never showed up!"

"That weren't my fault that I was drunk from the night before."

Dr Dolan threw his hands in the air. He then turned and saw me standing behind him.

"Is there anything I can do to help?" I asked, observing his dishevelled hair and flustered state.

"Ah music to my ears, see cook it is possible to be helpful and an asset and Alice doesn't even work here!"

I smiled at cook awkwardly. She in turn looked me up and down then tutted at my bruised face and went back to the kitchen.

I walked into the dormitory. Some of the children were still asleep. When little Alice saw me she stood up and reached her arms out to me. Instinctively I went over and scooped her up.

"Good morning little Alice, you've got a beautiful name."

"Liss, Liss" She repeated.

"Good morning." I repeated very slowly.

"Ning."

"Excellent! I shall teach you to speak."

"Peek" She giggled.

"Alice could you give me a hand over here?" Dr Dolan was calling me.

I put Alice down and went over to him. He was trying to cut the bread that was so fresh that it crumbled under his knife.

"Here let me." I volunteered "You have to do it really slowly"

"I can't believe that cook she's hopeless, wait till my wife gets back she'll get rid of her and do it herself in half the time. It's so hard to get good staff around these parts. Are you looking for a job? You seem to have a natural way about you with children."

"I've not really been around children much." I was trying to think how many I knew barring the Sinclair children. I suppose I had enjoyed being with Archie and we had definitely formed a bond.

"Thank you for the offer but I'm not sure how long I will be staying in these parts. I am here because I am looking for someone and that's why I need to speak to your father. The innkeeper's wife Mrs Malley thought that he would know a little about the history of the people in this village and might be able to help me.

"Well that's certainly true. Father knows everyone around these parts."

"I was hoping that you would say that. When will your father be up so that I can talk to him?"

"I told him to take it easy last night. He kindly came up here to give me a hand but after several minutes he started swooning and staggering and his pulse seemed a little weak so I sent him to bed. He's nearly seventy and I think this hectic life is catching up with him."

"I see" I said buttering the bread.

"The younger ones will have to have what is left of the oats and the older ones can eat the bread. Could you get started with the bottles for the babies?"

We worked together and methodically to get all the children fed. They were then placed on a mat whilst we stripped some of the beds of their sheets and took them to be washed.

Since no one else was available to wash them Dr Dolan gave me a large barrel and a wooden knobbly board and soap and I began washing.

"Hang them out after you've wrung them through the mangle then fold them and finish drying them on the kitchen over the stove." Shouted the Doctor as he went off on another errand.

By the time I had finished it was time to sort out lunch. The doctor had gone down to the village to get some emergency supplies of vegetables which cook had peeled and mashed and once again we started feeding the children. I made a conscious effort to feed Alice first and give her the best of what there was instead of the dry burnt bits that were usually left stuck at the bottom of the pot.

By noon we were finished and old Dr Dolan appeared.

"Hello you must be the new nurse. I've been watching you and you are doing an excellent job."

"Thank you but I'm not the new nurse I was just helping out Dr Dolan till the nurse came or till his wife came back. I've actually come here to find you. I'd like to ask you some questions about someone that I'm trying to find."

"Sounds very intriguing, but I'm sure it can wait till after lunch there's some nice fresh cheese and boiled ham in the larder."

We went through and sat down, myself and the two doctors. Half way through our meal the door opened and a woman came in dressed in travelling clothes. She took off her bonnet and shook out her long dark hair. Her face seemed young although there were faint lines around her blue eyes that smiled at me.

"Well I'm home and thank goodness for that, I couldn't wait. Dublin was mobbed; I've never seen so many people in all my life!"

"Come and sit down darling, can I make you some tea? We've lovely fresh bread."

She slumped down then addressed me.

"So how was your journey from Tipperary you must be exhausted as well?"

"Oh no darling how careless of me, this isn't the new nurse. This is Alice, she's just been helping out yesterday evening and this morning, the new nurse hasn't arrived yet.

"Where are my manners?" The doctor stammered."Let me in introduce you properly."

He nodded towards me.

"Alice this is my wife Isobel."

Chapter 55

I felt stunned, like my heart had leapt off the top of a cliff and plunged all the way to the bottom. I wondered whether anyone had noticed the colour drain from my face when the doctor had said his wife was "Isobel".

 Could Mrs Dolan be my mother? After the doctor introduced his wife it seemed that there was that possibility. However there was also the possibility that I was overreacting, there could just be two people with the same name, after all there were two Alice's.

Because I had been so perplexed I had lied in my response to Mrs Dolan about why I was here and now had to think of another strategy in which to find my answers.

We had finished lunch awkwardly especially when old Dr Dolan had asked quite kindly what it was that I had wanted so urgently from him and I had said that I had forgotten.

"Yes I have these memory lapses from time to time. Must be my age." Then realised that what I had said must be offensive to those around me as they were all older than me.

"Well if you're getting old I must be ancient!" Laughed the old doctor as he ran his hand through his still very full head of grey hair. His face was etched with lines and his brow looked like it had endured many years of troubles; his eyes peered under heavy eyelids as he looked me up and down and tried to calculate my age.

"So how old are you my dear?"

"Eighteen. Well I was in August."

Mrs Dolan stopped eating and stared at me, then recollected herself and began to eat again. She was a very attractive woman and seemed to be about the right age. Her dark hair fell over her shoulders and her eyes were a soft hazel unlike my own which were blue. She was not unlike me but then she was not dissimilar either. I knew that I had looked like my father and had been very comparable in stature and colouring to my half sister Charlotte.Mrs Dolan's accent was not too strong for someone born and bred in Ireland but I was too afraid to ask her where her origins actually were.

"Sean I'm afraid I will have to go back to bed and rest I am still feeling a little giddy but I don't like to not be at surgery this evening and let all my patients down."

"No father, don't worry." Replied the younger doctor.

"If you are complaining than it must be serious I have never known you to take to your bed voluntarily. I'll come up and take your blood pressure and listen to your heart. Just want to make sure that you really are all right."

"Don't worry dear, you go ahead and help your father out. I'm back now and need to get back to work. We'll be all right and the new nurse should be here soon." Said Mrs Dolan smiling at me.

"And of course we have our mystery helper here." She added, nodding at me.

"I never realised how hard you work, having twenty children isn't easy?"

"You can say that again! Anyway it's nice to be appreciated. How's the new cook working out?"

"She's terrible! She's only worked two days since you've been gone!"

"Oh really? Was she ill?"

"No just drunk and by her own admission. She has no shame."

"Oh dear that is a pity but you know how hard it is to come by staff, any staff."

There was a silence in the room and I felt for these people that were trying so hard to provide care and shelter for the orphans.

"I hope your nurse turns up from Tipperary."I commented.

"Well if she doesn't we'll just have to kidnap you!" Chuckled the young doctor.

"Can I make a suggestion?" I asked cautiously.

All eyes lay on me and I wondered whether it was my place at all to make any suggestions or comments, after all running the orphanage was their business and they all knew far more than me.

"Well, I know where there are some girls that would be only too pleased to come and work here and would expect no wages except some food and a bed to sleep."

Eyebrows were raised in anticipation and I wondered whether I could be audacious enough to continue.

"Well, where are they?"

"Well err, um they're up at the convent. All the girls work very hard and would much rather be here, than locked up there like slaves!"

Old Dr Dolan patted my hand.

"I don't think those girls would want to be here. Up at the convent they are looked after by the nuns, where they can get plenty of rest before their babies are born."

"But Doctor Dolan surely you don't believe that! Those girls aren't living any kind of nice comfortable life up there. The nuns are cruel to them and beat them. They have to do much harder work than they would here and much longer hours and they sleep on uncomfortable straw beds and eat gruel. If they have done so much as whisper out of turn they must sit at the penance table where they are given only stale bread and water."

"How do you know this? How can you speak of a nun in such a way?" He seemed angry and offended.

"Believe me, I am sorry, but this is all true. I was there; I experienced it all for a few days."

"So did you have a .." Began Mrs Dolan

"No no no" I interjected.

380

"I was there by mistake. I wanted to find out something and the nuns misinterpreted why I was there and treated me like all those other poor girls. I was only rescued by the village innkeeper because I had left all my belongings with him and had not returned."

"And this is all true" Asked Mrs Dolan softly.

"Yes every word of it. Those girls are very badly treated and beaten. One of the other girls told me that sometimes the girls die and are buried in a mass grave in the grounds with no records being kept about them. I agree it is disgraceful and something should be done to stop them but who would believe someone challenging a woman of God?"

"I could go up there and have a look." Said Sean Dolan. No one would question me, I'm a doctor. I could say it was in the course of my duties to check on the girls during their pregnancies."

The elder man shook his head.

"I don't like this. This is not our concern we are busy enough and we don't want to fall out with the elders of this village and their traditions that have been going for much longer than any of us!"

"But Dr Dolan if nobody ever does anything than nothing will change and then the world cannot move forward and become a better place."

As soon as the words had passed my lips I knew that I had taken that step too far. The old man did not like to be contradicted and obviously held the church in very high esteem. He threw me a disapproving look and rose from the table

"I shall go and rest now. I am feeling very excitable which I don't think is good for my heart. Good afternoon."

After he had closed the door I began apologising for having upset him.

"Alice please don't apologise. We have heard the stories but no one has ever spelt it out in black and white as you have just done. Also the fact that this is your own personal experience and not hearsay from some third hand account gives it more definition. I will go up to the convent. I shall do so tomorrow morning. Please don't reproach yourself Alice you spoke to us as any caring person would, so that we could address the situation and we will, or I will at least." Said Doctor Sean.

"It just seemed to make sense to me that you could get some help and those girls would be treated far better than they are now."

"You're a good girl Alice" Said Mrs Dolan.

"We know that you only meant well. I didn't want to say anything but is that where you got those bruises from on your face? They are fading but I'm sure they were pretty nasty a few days back."

"Yes." I flushed.

"I need to get back to the children, thank you for lunch Mrs Dolan."

"Wait Alice I'll come with you."

I waited feeling embarrassed and anxious, longing to just ask her the question that was momentarily stuck in my throat. We walked together through the house to the nursery.

"You have lovely hands Alice, Ladies hands, not work hands. So what brings you to these parts?

Well here was my opportunity to just say what I had waited all my life to say, but I couldn't, the words were jammed.

"It's a long story Mrs Dolan anyway do you and Dr Dolan have any children?"

"Oh yes" she smiled "we have lots of children about twenty at the moment, but no, we don't have any of our own, it just never happened."

"Oh I'm sorry. So where are you from, your accent isn't local?"

"Well I've lived here half my life so its half local I suppose. I wasn't born in this place, but do we belong to any place really? Or does the place belong to us?"

"Yes I suppose you're right." I thought wistfully, thinking about all the places I had called home recently.

"So Alice, you seem very brave to be travelling so far from home on your own, where are your parents?"

"I'm an orphan" I replied reluctantly.

She said nothing but put her arm around my shoulder.

"All orphans are welcome here."

"But you already have an Alice" I nodded at the cot.

"Yes we always have an Alice."

"Really?"

"Yes I name all the babies that come in and make sure there is always one called Alice."

By now I was feeling quite clammy and the space between us was charged with magnetic energy that made us both overly intrigued about each other. We stood side by side; she was about an inch shorter than me but stronger and more toughened. I wondered what she was thinking, whether her thoughts echoed my own, whether she needed to be reassured by a ghost from her past as well.

We were standing by baby Alice's cot. She reached out for Mrs Dolan instinctively then with some confusion in her eyes looked at us both and then reached out for me. I picked her up and she rested her heavy little head on my shoulder.

"Liss, Liss" she muffled into my ear.

Mrs Dolan stared in amazement as I rocked the child and stroked her hair.

"She doesn't go to anyone and she doesn't speak!"

"Yes I know your husband told me."

Again there was an awkward silence; air filled with anticipation, neither of us saying a word yet something connecting us. Something we were both too frightened to acknowledge.

"So why do you always have a child here called Alice?" She looked at me intently.

"I think you already know the answer to that question. For a brief moment in my life there was someone called Alice whom I loved so fiercely. I had to let her go and I suppose I have been trying to replace her over all these years" She looked up at me tears welling in her eyes. Her hands were trembling.

"My name is Alice Sinclair," I said, as I watched the expression on her face change.

Chapter 56

"My name is Alice Sinclair and I am looking for my mother."
The eyes into which I searched became filled with tears. She
closed her eyes and swallowed, allowing a heavy tear to spill
down her cheek. I was not sure whether I should continue
speaking or not. I decided not and instinctively put my arm
around her shoulder. We walked to a window seat and sat down
together.

"I am sorry to upset you and cause you so much pain." I began.
She shook her head and still too distraught to speak let the tears
reflect her angst. I was not sure whether this sign of emotion was
acknowledgment of my existence or true maternal response from
one that had lost their child so long ago. Finally she began to
speak as she dabbed away tears with her handkerchief.

"Alice, I don't know whether in your life you have ever
encountered loss?" She paused as the words were still thick in her
throat.

"I hope not, however there are many degrees of pain that one
can endure. One can feel physical pain when one hurts
themselves or the excruciating pain of giving birth to a child. One
can feel ache when someone dies whom they loved, I felt this
when my own mother died when I was quite young. However all
these pains do subside and fade and do not linger on the mind
constantly. But, there is a pain so deep, so inexplicable that no
one can fathom. It is the pain of almost having part of yourself
wrenched from you and leaves a hollow that can never be filled.
This is the pain when you lose a child. It is indescribable. It is an
ache that is there to remind you, when you open your eyes in the
morning and a heaviness that keeps you crying till long into the
night when you are trying to sleep. It never goes away. It never
eases. Its weight bears so heavy that there are times that you feel

suffocated by it. I have lived with this pain for so long it feels like my shadow; I have forgotten what it feels like to be free of it. They took you from me and they may as well have cut out my heart and left me to die. It is something from which I could not recover and something over which I had no control. I thought of you every day, on your birthdays, Christmas. I saw children playing and I thought of you. I wondered what you would be doing, whom you would be with, when you were happy when you were sad, who would love you and hold your hand. It pained me so much that it could not be me. My family abandoned me, treated me like a leper. My friends would not help me or believe me and I had no choice to be with you. The only choice that I had was to give you to the orphanage and workhouse for a life of uncertainty and almost certain hardship or to choose that option for myself. You know what choice I made, that was the only gift that I could make to you before I was sent away."

I was sobbing uncontrollably. This was all that I had really wanted to know, that my mother was alive and did love me, that all these years there had been someone somewhere that had been thinking about me and whom had sacrificed her own life for my welfare.

She reached out to me and I rested my head on her lap while she dabbed my tears with her already wet kerchief.

We sat in silence. She stroked my hair in a way that I had seen Lady Eleanor do with her own daughters and an action that had made me feel acutely jealous. Now here I was with my own mother being loved in the same way, finally.

So many things were flooding through my mind. I wanted to tell my mother about my whole life, I wanted her to know how sad and alone I had been but at the same time did not want her to feel that her sacrifices had not been worthwhile.

"Did you love my father?" I managed eventually.

She snorted like an angry horse.

"I don't think so! Not that brute Edward Sinclair running around with other women lying and cheating on my poor friend Eleanor."

"So why did you and he end up together?" I was almost afraid to ask.

"That wasn't the way it was at all. I was totally devoted to my dear friend Eleanor and was in fact engaged to be married myself when I warned Edward that he had better mend his ways or I would tell his wife all about the way he was behaving and humiliating her. He was furious that someone should tell him what to do or how to behave and attacked me, raped me. He said there would be more if I ever said a word. I didn't. I felt degraded and dirty and more than anything scared that he would kill me. I was very naïve and unworldly and when several months later realised that I was pregnant it all backfired on me and I was made out to be a cheating seductress that had led him astray in an attempt to steal a married man. My fiancé broke off the engagement and all my friends and family sided with Edward. I never spoke up and told the truth because I was still in awe of what he could do to me. I was sent away and ended up here. My life as I knew it ended like a slammed door."

"I am so, very sorry."

There was a word that I had longed to utter all my life that would finish that sentence, a word that had been denied to me for over eighteen years. I summoned up the courage.

"I am really sorry …..mother"

It felt strange and sobering to utter it. I felt completely happy and sad all rolled up together.

"Mother" I whispered again.

Just then the door opened and young Dr Dolan stood in the doorway.

387

My mother shook her head at him and gestured for him to go. He nodded, frowned quizzically and obediently closed the door behind him.

"I think I need to speak to my husband." She said gently.

"There are a few white lies that have just turned a little grey and need to be explained to him."

I nodded in acceptance. However hard this experience was for me it was going to be incredibly hard for her too, she would have a lot of explaining to do and I did not need to interfere with that.

"I will go then, I'll come back tomorrow if that's all well with you?"

"Yes of course we have so much to find out about each other. Perhaps when I try to fall asleep tonight they will be tears of joy?" She smiled and she kissed my cheek.

I could feel myself beaming as I walked down the steep steps back to the village. The cold air felt fresh on my face and the streaks of my tears felt dry and parched my skin. I was happy, truly, but why still did I feel so incredibly sad?

I could not understand myself. I had no explanation for the strange feeling coursing through my veins. I wanted to tell somebody, share this moment, but there was nobody. No one in the world that knew the real me, the real Alice and with whom I could shout in joy and proclaim my happiness.

The church bells were ringing for evening mass in the little church just beyond the steps. Several people were making their way through the dark wood door and into the darkness beyond. I stopped for a few seconds watching them and then followed. Not quite sure why I was.

I made my way to a pew near the back and knelt before the altar. I clenched my hands together and rested my head on my hands. My breathing was now slow and heavy.

"God?" The question hung on my lips as if I expected someone to answer.

"Do you wish to go into the confession box?" A voice sounded behind me.

I turned to the priest in his long black robes.

"No, no I don't. Thank you."

He turned and left me to my own private prayer.

I didn't pray. I didn't know how. I stayed there for ages till everyone had left the church and the solitary pair of footsteps now re approached.

"We need to close up for the evening missy; you can come back for Morning Prayer. Is something troubling you?"

I shook my head. I had spent the previous two hours thinking and needing someone to hear me, but not a stranger. I had thought that I wanted James, with his common sense approach to everything and the comfortable security that I felt when I was with him. I then went back to the forbidden place in my mind where my thoughts of Tom lived and realised that I needed his softness and emotional strength. I had in my mind the picture of Tom when he had carried Archie from the lake. That image of strength and integrity, despite his servant status. It was hopeless though to even consider Tom anymore. The Alice that he had despised when he left was a young stupid and immature Alice who had been jealous and selfish. It had only been a few months but now I felt a great deal older and wiser and more worthy of returning the true affections of one that had loved me so very earnestly.

Was there any point pondering over what could have been. I had been very foolish and irretrievably had lost my chance with Tom. He was gone and I strongly felt that I would not see him again. The reward that Lady Sinclair had given him was very substantial and he probably would have gone off and invested it in his own farm or something. Anything, but I'm sure far away from me. He must still hate me so much because if he did not he would have found me wherever in the world I was.

I could not be too despondent. I had a very fitting marriage proposal that I had still not responded to, maybe now that I had this enormous weight lifted from me I could go back and become a wife?

I got up. My knees felt stiff from having knelt for so long. I brushed off my skirt and ignored the strange looks of the priest who was not sure if I was a very fervent praying parishioner or what!

I went back to the inn. Mrs Malley was in the bar pouring ale for some locals that had stepped in on their way back from work.

"Evening lovey, there's some hot stew in the parlour help yourself."

I was starving so weaved my way through the crowd and went through to the back.

Sitting at the table was Mrs Dolan. She looked up, timid and worried.

"I'm sorry to intrude Alice."

"Don't be silly, I'm only too happy to see you. Is everything all right?"

"Yes of course. I didn't realise what a wonderful husband I had. I told him everything. He listened; understood, said it didn't make any difference to him."

I ladled myself some soup and sat beside her.

"I wanted to spend a few hours with you. I didn't know how you would be reacting, whether you would be feeling a little like I was feeling?"

"I suppose I do. I know exactly what you mean. I've just spent the evening in the church as I didn't know where else to go."

"Are you devout?"

"No, not at all. I wasn't brought up to go to church. I only started going when I lived with the Sinclair's."

"You lived with the Sinclair's?"My mother asked intrigued and horrified.

"Well how long have you got?" I joked

"The rest of my life." She answered.

We sat through the night reminiscing and catching up. We spoke till the street lights had burnt down and till the last drunk had left the inn and stumbled away singing at the top of his voice. It was only when the sun began to squint through the curtains and the cockerels started crowing that we realised, both shattered that we had better get to sleep.

"I'll go home and rest for a while, the new nurse arrived yesterday afternoon so I have a little time" confessed my mother.

"I'll come up and help soon."

We hugged and I watched her make her way up the hill back to the orphanage as I closed the door of the inn.

Chapter 57

It has been several weeks since my mother and I were reunited. I have been living up at the orphanage ever since. So much has happened. Young Dr Dolan went up to the convent to discover for himself the horrible truth of what was going on there.

"I am deeply shocked!" He declared at dinner one evening.

"I went in there even though they at first tried to refuse me entry. I demanded to be allowed to examine the girls and babies. I had to lie which seemed very unholy in a convent. I said that there was some terrible contagious illness that was carried only by pregnant girls and in fear they allowed me in."

"So what did you find?" Mother asked.

"Well the cruel tasks being inflicted on the girls amounted to little less than total humiliation! They were being fed scraps of old stale and mouldy food and the babies were kept in damp cots with limited resources of towelling and bottles! It is a complete disgrace. I shouted at the nuns and they were so astounded that anyone should come into their little sanctuary that they huddled into a corner and gazed at me with startled wide eyes. I don't think they had ever seen such an angry man before."

"Oh dear" Sighed mother.

"What shall we tell your father he won't be happy that you've been up there and caused this rift?"

"I had to do what should have been done many years ago, I'm sure father won't like it one bit but it was the right thing to do. The older generation have no qualms about turning a blind eye. I'm only sorry that I didn't do this a very long time ago."

He then turned to me.

"Alice we never would have done anything if you hadn't told us about it. It is so difficult to act on rumours but when you have hard evidence then one is able to go and sort it out. Thank you."

"No thank you." I stumbled.

"I have done many selfish things in my life and many things that I am too ashamed to even talk about. I'm pleased that we were able to save those girls and do something right and….."I hesitated slightly. "Thank you so much also for accepting me here into your family."

My mother smiled and reached out to my hand which she held for a few moments reassuringly. It had been difficult for her to explain to her husband exactly who I was but Dr Dolan had been wonderful and had accepted me straight away without any frowns of disapproval or resentment.

"Another thing Alice since you are living with us now, I think Dr Dolan is a little too formal you may call me Sean if you like."

"Thank you Sean."

"You really are an amazing girl and we are proud to have you with us. Because of you we are now fully staffed and for the first time on top of ourselves. We are renovating and building and making this place look like the proud building that it once was many years ago. The money that you have donated to us has been invaluable. We could not be in the situation that we are in without all the efforts that you have contributed to. We are forever indebted to you Alice."

"Thank you Dr…Sean, but really the money was mothers and not mine and I'm only really doing with it the good that she would have done herself."

"You give yourself very little credit my dear; many girls of your age would have found far more exciting things to spend inheritance money on!"

I shrugged it off. It was quite poignant that my grandfather's money was being used in this way after he had sent away his only daughter in disgrace.

Mother often stopped what she was doing and watched me when my sleeves were rolled up and I was scrubbing my knuckles raw at a washing board. I would look up and she would be smiling at me almost stupefied that I was actually here and part of her life at last. Inwardly I was as astounded as her that this had happened and my search had led me to a woman that I was so proud to call my mother.

Word of our wonderful establishment for girls and their babies spread; now they come down here to live, work and give birth. It has been beneficial to all concerned, so much more has been done here and the Dolan's are really able to expand and improve this place.

Old Dr Dolan felt that we were treading on the nuns toes regardless of what they had done! Sean had to put him right on that one and tried to explain to his very stubborn father that what he found up at the convent was worth any animosity. Now there is some friction between us and the convent, they probably are praying for our poor sinful souls at this very moment.

Connie was here for a while before going home. I introduced her to Mr and Mrs Malley at the inn and they instantly fell in love with her baby and have adopted him. Connie had her doubts though.

"Oh Alice they seem such nice people but do you think my baby will be all right without me?"

"Yes Connie didn't you see the way Mrs Malley took him in her arms and fed him his bottle he was so content and so happy and she was over the moon to finally be holding a very much wanted baby in her arms."

Connie began to cry.

"But I feel so bad. My child will never know his own mother. I will never know my own child."

"You will have more children. Think of all the happiness and goodness that you have done. You can go home now without the shame of an unwed mother and know that your child is not condemned to the work house."

"Yes Alice you are always so pragmatic and sensible. Please watch over him for me wont you? And write to me and let me know how he is doing."

I watched as Connie walked away to the stage coach stand to get the coach back to Rosslare and then back to England I did not envy her that journey at all.

Connie has said that she will come and visit whenever she can but I feel that won't be often.

I enjoy working with the babies. I have never been happier. I have begun singing, something that I never previously would have dreamed of doing. I sing all day. I feel like a bird, so carefree. I have written to the Sinclair's and told them that I am home and all is well. I have also written to James who has only written back once. This did bother me somewhat as he was supposed to be in love and pining for me. From the tone of his very formal letter that is just not so.

I did try to get mother to consider coming back to Somerset but she has a life and a purpose here and would never leave. I have written to Somerset and asked them to lock up the old house and dismiss all the staff since I do not see myself returning in the foreseeable future. I think that most of the staff had left any way as there had not been anyone resident for quite a long time now. Maybe one day I will move back but now this feels like home and having a mother is the most wonderful experience ever. We share so much and even out mannerisms are similar.Dr Dolan has been fascinated by us.

"So how is it that you both have mastered the exact same expression on your face when you are both angry….and happy? You even sneeze in exactly the same tone!"

Mother and I just turned and shrugged in exactly the same way which made us both collapse into giggles simultaneously. Everything that we do is so precious and I feel like I'm complete now, no missing jigsaw bits for me to try to piece together.

There is still that one regret though. I find myself thinking about Tom very frequently. I miss him terribly. I wonder whether I should go and try to find him but it would be very difficult asking James for that information. It's something that I dare not do, as I'm sure I would be rejected and hated because of it.

We have found homes for many of the children. This has been because we have started dressing them up and taking them to church and out for walks. The children are always so well behaved and polite and word has spread that there is an orphanage in Kinsale with the most lovable children and everyone seems to be coming to get one.

Little Alice has left us. She went to a family up in Dublin who I'm sure will adore her as much as we did. By the time she left us she was chatting and talking as if she had always done so. It was very sad to see her go but mother just hugged me and said that now she didn't need to rename another little girl Alice!

Mother and I spend so much time together and although we have had awkward moments as to be expected, the majority of the time we are just jubilant to have this time together. Time that we never thought would never be.

There are some things that I have not been able to bring up with mother. I told her about father's death and about Tom without whom I would probably never have found out about her existence. She was not surprised or saddened for Lady Eleanor about Edwards's death. I even mentioned that Lady Eleanor was being courted by the judge and she found that quite amusing and implied that Eleanor would be much happier. I have not mentioned the episode with Sarah. I find that I cannot. Instead I told her the story that the world knew about Sarah falling and Tom being held to trial for her manslaughter. I dare not say different. I will never say anything to anyone and sometimes when I tell myself that story enough times I really do believe it.

Spring is almost here and I have gone to pick some early daffodils from the gardens. For a moment I sit down on the bench and breathe in the sweet air of the Irish fields. There's a rustle behind me and I have the strangest feeling like I have been in this situation before but of course that cannot be so because I have never spent springtime in Kinsale.

There it is again. I get up feeling a little frightened that some beast might leap out of the bushes. Somehow it feels safe and I walk into the clearing of the woods beyond the garden. I can see a figure behind the tree. It looks familiar but still I am unsure. I step forward then stop. As the figure moves closer and I can see the straw hair and corn blue eyes that I have missed so very much.

I gasp and hold my breath afraid that this is only an apparition before me and that if I blink he will be gone.

He steps forward and I am unsure of his intention.

He is now taking longer strides as I stand transfixed to the spot, the cold sun shining on my back.

"Hello Alice."

"Hello." I reply cautiously, my heart beating excitedly.

He takes my hand and bends his head breaking the eye contact that we have maintained for the last five minutes. He kisses it and I am overwhelmed.

"Alice I came to find you, just as you came to find your mother. I cannot live without you. I have tried. I thought my new wealth would help ease my broken heart, but it has not. I have watched you and you are changed too. I have come to beg you for your forgiveness and to see if there is a place for me still in your heart? I exhale, relieved, then leap into his arms our kisses and tears mingling.

I know that I feel safe now. All troubles dissolving into what has become a past ready to be forgotten.

My life now feels complete. All those things missing in my life are now reunited. I am content, I am at peace. I take Toms hand and lead the way home.....